To my friend Jane,
Hope you enjoy my book.

John W. Long

D0861003

# RED
# BLOOD
## ON WHITE
# COTTON

## JOHN W. LONG

All rights reserved.

© 2019 by John W. Long

Print ISBN: 978-1-54397-485-0

eBook ISBN: 978-1-54397-486-7

This is a work of fiction. Names, characters, businesses, places, events, and incidents are the product of the author's imagination or are used fictitiously. Any resemblance to actual persons, living or dead, events, or locales is entirely and purely coincidental.

*This book is dedicated to my wife, JoEllen, my children, Melissa, Jason and Matthew, and my grandsons, Dylan and Jack. Thanks for being there for me the many long years it has taken to put the stories you've heard to paper.*

# CHAPTER 1

To say I was having mixed emotions would be the understatement of all time. As I watched my father's casket being lowered into the red Georgia clay, I trembled. My emotions were in tatters. My heart was in my throat one minute and in my stomach the next. I'd wondered how I would feel on this day. I had loved him, I suppose, though I had hated him through much of my life. He was an enigma, an egotistical bigot and a respected civic leader. He had been a loving husband, a good father to most of his children and a generous supporter of the community. I tried desperately to love him, though I still do not know if he had ever loved me.

The tranquility of the afternoon was suddenly shattered. Cacophonous cawing of crows and blackbirds in the pecan grove next to the cemetery made the mourners take notice. I wondered if they were clamoring to add their two cents to the passing of the patriarch of the Reynolds family. It was a brutally hot afternoon, but suddenly a cool breeze ruffled the tent beneath which we were standing. A chill slithered up my spine. An eerie feeling gripped me as if Calvin Reynolds was alive and nearby, listening to what was being said about him.

Reverend Stanfield said, "Calvin Reynolds was our brother in Christ, an outstanding citizen who did so much for this community. He was a true civic leader. He lived a long and productive life, and his generosity touched many of us. We will remember his service to the Rotary Club for many years and for his work with the Farm Bureau. He was a gentleman, a farmer of the land, a pillar of our community and someone who will be missed by all of us."

Stanfield's words rang in my ears. I wouldn't call Calvin Reynolds a pillar of the community, and I sure as hell wouldn't consider him a gentleman. Not in the way I thought of gentlemen.

I scooped up a handful of brittle red clay and let it slip through my fingers and down on to his casket. My insularity from him during the past two decades eased the pain of past confrontations. Calvin Reynolds was on his way to meet his maker, or maybe headed in the other direction. If I was a gambling man, I knew where I would put most of my chips.

I gazed at the crowd gathered around the open grave down the hill from Mount Hebron Baptist Church. I remembered a few but most were strangers. Or maybe they had just gotten too old to recognize. It was an impressive turnout. The old man still had quite a few friends, or maybe some were in attendance hoping to get the chance to piss on his grave.

As I stood in the receiving line acknowledging condolences and getting hugs from mostly strangers, I finally saw a familiar face. Susan Regan had been my high school sweetheart and my first real love—my only love. She still had beautiful skin, tanned a golden brown by the summer, shown off by her sleeveless black dress, tastefully short. Her perfect long legs still seemed to stretch to heaven. She had a dazzling smile and eyes twinkling like polished gemstones. Her ebullience bubbled like a fountain and created an aura around her. Why she had ever given me the time of day was still a mystery.

Susan and I had dated in high school and had broken up when I left for college. She was the first girl who had let me go all the way. It happened that final summer. I thought I had died and gone to heaven when we first made love. It almost changed my mind about going away.

Susan had another year of high school and it broke my heart when we went our separate ways.

"Hey Johnny, good to see you," she whispered. "I'm so sorry about your daddy. Mr. Reynolds was a good man. He always spoke whenever I saw him."

Her words eased from her lips like thick molasses pouring from a syrup boat as she gave me a lingering hug and kissed my cheek. She smelled like an acre of camellia and gardenia bushes in bloom. Her skin sparkled with tiny drops of perspiration beaded like delicate lace on her forehead in the brutal late July sun. I had carnal thoughts as I watched her walk away. She still had a perfect figure.

Susan had visited me in Atlanta a few years ago after her divorce. I had wistful thoughts of that weekend. She had always seemed so shy and pure when we dated. Sweet little Susan had learned a lot since our bumbling awkward attempts at lovemaking in high school.

I don't know why I had never asked her out again. I guess I was just too busy or maybe too dumb. I made a mental note to call her.

As the good folks of Martinsville eased away from the gravesite, I took my sister Betty Jane's arm and we headed for the exit to Pecan Hill Cemetery. I looked up the hill to where Mount Hebron Baptist Church stood, a gleaming white anchor in the community. I had attended there for years when I was a child. It seemed much smaller now. The magnolias were in full bloom and their sweet fragrance comforted me more than anyone at the funeral. I noticed a blue jay fighting with a mockingbird as we walked up the hill. They were squawking and pecking at each other as they darted in and out of the ancient oak trees draped in Spanish moss, bluish gray lichen covering their trunks. It was a reminder of how the old man and I had fought and pecked at each other our entire lives. We had been just like those birds, in constant disagreement and letting each other know it.

As we approached the exit, I noticed two men in dark suits wearing black fedoras standing under the shady arms of a large live oak tree. They stared intently at me, and then turned away and hurried off. Were they inside the church? Were they friends or foes? My father had plenty of both.

As Betty Jane and I approached our limousine, I saw the two men enter a shiny black Chevy Suburban parked at the bottom of the hill. They sped away in a cloud of red dust; it twisted and tumbled like a dirt devil. Maybe they were men who had a previous beef with my father and were just making sure he was dead.

As our driver pulled out of the cemetery parking lot, I thought of my brother, Jack. I had thought about him a lot during the past few weeks, perhaps because I knew my father was dying and he and Jack had been so close. I remembered the summer night he disappeared like it was yesterday. Jack and his girlfriend, Becky McCord, went out for a date and were never seen again.

Being in Martinsville brought back memories of Jack. They flooded into my mind like the raging muddy waters of the Flint River after spring rains. The sweet memories made me smile: hunting, swimming and fishing on the Flint with Jack and my brother Joe. Sometimes the old man would come with us and we'd camp overnight. We'd cook fish we caught on an open fire, and the omnipotent Calvin Reynolds would wow us with stories from his youth and about my grandfather. We had laughed and marveled at some of his childhood exploits. He had almost seemed human during those times. I loved those memories. I used them to block out bad memories, which seemed to bore into my soul when I thought of my father.

We drove back to Betty Jane's house where I knew we would eat and drink too much and tell stories about the old man for hours. Some stories would be funny, some would be sad, most would include my brothers. I thought fondly of them.

We entered my sister's sprawling palatial home, crowded with friends and neighbors. One of my father's best friends, John Williams, put out a withered hand for me to shake and put his arm around my shoulders.

"Mighty good to see ya, Johnny," said Mr. Williams. "We shore gonna miss yo daddy. He wuz a mighty good man. He ran our Rotary Club for years. He shamed us old farts into givin more money than we could afford to help good causes. He wuz the best president we ever had."

Mr. Williams gesticulated his wimpy arms like an octopus as he tried to emphasize the points of his tale.

"Calvin raised a ton of money for the schools and all kinda children's causes. He gave his own money too. He would always write the first check and throw it on the table. Then he'd say, 'Y'all gotta match that,' and laugh like the devil. You know when he retired he asked me to take it over. He said he wuz gettin too old to handle it."

"I appreciate you coming, Mr. Williams," I said, not caring to hear his unctuous Rotarian bullshit and not wanting to get hit by his flailing arms.

"It was great to see you again," I said as I eased away from him.

My father's sister, Aunt Eula, waddled over and hugged me so hard I almost lost my breath. She wore a flamboyant red and yellow floral design dress she had worn to the funeral. The swirls in her dress, a fire engine red, made me dizzy as I stared at them. I was sure Aunt Eula owned no black. She loved a party and always dressed in bright colors. She was probably celebrating the fact she no longer had to put up with her brother's bullshit.

"Johnny, are you still lawyering up there in Atlanta?" she wheezed, suffering from emphysema.

She had added a few more pounds since I had seen her last and had to be well over three hundred now. I caught a whiff of White Shoulders, the perfume she had worn for decades. Memories of late-night board games coursed through my mind. Everyone loved Aunt Eula. Everyone except her deceased brother. He often referred to her as a damn fool.

"I was afraid you might not come home to help bury yo daddy," she warbled. "I know y'all were not on the best of terms. But at funeral times, we must overlook the slights people gave us here on earth. You have to remember that, baby boy."

I wondered if she was thinking about the slights she had received from her brother and not those of mine. He had been wealthy; she was not. He had treated her like she was poor white trash. He had inherited a ten-thousand-acre farm, and Aunt Eula, the only other heir, ended up with a small house and only five hundred acres. How he pulled that off no one knew.

"That lung cancer don't play, Johnny," said Aunt Eula. "I told yo daddy a thousand times to leave them cigars and cigarettes alone. But he smoked like a smoke stack on that Folsom Prison train. God rest his soul!"

She wheezed a few times and placed a fat hand on a table to steady her balance.

"Lordy, how time flies! Seems like it was jest last week when we wuz all settin round y'all's house playing games. You and yo mama loved to play games: Parcheesi, Rummy, Checkers and Rook. And y'all's cook, that Emma, black as the ace of spades. She would join right in playing with you kids. Thass if yo daddy wasn't around."

She leaned back and gave a substantial belly laugh.

"Oh, I remember Aunt Eula, we had some good times, didn't we?" I patted her shoulder, and she waddled away and headed for the food table.

Lucas McDougal, one of my father's foremen, put his arm around me as he grabbed my hand.

"Johnny boy, I hardly recognized ya," he said. "Someone pointed out that wuz you, but I don't think I would a knowed ya. You wuz the size of a tadpole when I was helpin yo daddy run the farm. Now you a nice-looking gentleman. I heard you wuz a lawyer."

"That's right. How've you been?"

"I been alwright for an old geezer. I'm still a kickin but not too high."

He was as wrinkled as a prune and as weathered as an old roadside barn. He had to be in his late seventies now. He was a shadow of the burly man he had been when he managed the livestock on our farm. His suit was wrinkled like he had slept in it. He'd poured a tea-glass full of bourbon from the bar. Lucas had always liked his bourbon. I remembered quite a few times when we had found him passed out in the barn and had to drive him home. I always thought of Lucas as a scary guy. He was prone to show up where least expected and seemed to slip around the barns and equipment shelters late at night. I had never cared for him. I felt I needed to wash my hands after shaking with him. He still gave me the creeps.

"Good to see you, Mr. Luke," I said as I eased away from him and headed into the kitchen.

He yelled over his shoulder, "Take care a yo'self, boy. It wuz mighty good to see ya."

I looked over the Southern culinary spread the neighbors had provided: potato salad, several kinds of fresh beans, field peas, crowder peas, corn on the cob, macaroni and cheese, squash, fried okra, sliced cucumbers floating in vinegar, deviled eggs, coleslaw, tomatoes, watermelon rind pickles, cornbread, fresh biscuits, fried chicken, meat loaf covered in a red sauce, thick slices of roast beef in gravy, pulled pork barbecue and a huge ham.

Then there was the dessert table: several kinds of pies, a seven-layer caramel cake, brownies, banana pudding, peach cobbler, blackberry pie, a pound cake and a few mystery desserts. It was a typical Southern meal after a funeral. The food was much like I had enjoyed in my mom's kitchen.

I fixed myself a plate and poured a half glass of Wild Turkey, put in a splash of Coke and two ice cubes and settled down in a comfortable chair. It was time to hear the good people of Martinsville relate all the great things about the late Calvin Reynolds.

The legend of Calvin Reynolds grew as the late afternoon turned into night and the bourbon flowed. We were reveled with stories about Calvin the sportsman, Calvin the greatest farmer on earth, Calvin the great benefactor, "the best Rotarian ever" and Calvin the shrewdest businessman in the state.

An old friend, Hiram Mobley, recalled how Calvin had shot a ten-point buck and had given the meat to the black families that lived on our farm. He opined Calvin was a mighty kind man to give all that good venison to them black families. I wanted to tell him the only reason he did that was because there was no room in our freezer. He had already killed five deer that year, but I bit my tongue.

My father had named our farm Riverdale Plantation. It was a sprawling farm bordering the Flint River in South Georgia a few miles southeast of Martinsville. It had been in our family for generations. My father loved to extoll the virtues of land ownership and his kinship to the land.

As the evening wore on, I thought about stories I didn't hear. How about the story of Otis Brown, the head of one of the largest black families living on Riverdale? Calvin had a beef with Otis and evicted the whole family a week before Christmas. I guess not many people had heard that story. Nor did I hear anyone tell the story of the time Calvin shot and killed one of our sharecroppers for stealing gas. I guess these were stories they wanted to leave out of the legend. And they probably didn't know the Calvin that had beaten me so badly I had to miss school for days. I had bruises and whelps on my arms and legs for a week.

I realized I had to stop this negative thinking. I was being too cynical about good old Calvin. He had some virtues; I just couldn't think of any right now. And this was his night. We were celebrating his life not dragging out all the deep dark secrets of Riverdale Plantation. Celebrate we did, for several more hours.

When the crowd dwindled, I headed to my guest room, upstairs in Betty Jane's huge three-story brick home. I wondered how much it had cost. Old Cal had done well for himself over the years and had been generous to my sister; not so much to me. He had purchased this 50-tract on the edge of town and built this beautiful home for her when she got engaged to Jake Riley. He had reminded me on several occasions that I was just a "slick Atlanta lawyer," and I didn't need any help from him. That was fine with me. I had put myself through college and law school without a dime from him. I had a sense of pride from doing it all on my own. Calvin Reynolds did not have any investment in me, and I was proud of that fact.

I removed my suit and hung it in a closet. I changed into some jeans and a polo and headed back down the stairs. I hoped one more glass of Wild Turkey would put me to sleep. I also hoped to find one more helping of banana pudding or maybe some peach cobbler.

As I stood at the kitchen window filling my glass from a silver ice bucket, I saw two men outside wearing black suits and fedoras, the same ones I had seen earlier near the cemetery. They were standing at the end of the driveway. Their Suburban was parked in the street with its lights on and they were talking to a man with his back to me. From the distance I couldn't recognize them, but they seemed to be having a lively conversation. One of the men looked up and noticed me in the back-lit kitchen window. He tapped his partner on the shoulder and pointed towards their SUV. They said a few more words to the man, and then entered their vehicle and drove away. The other man headed for his vehicle, which was parked nearby. As he opened the door, the dome light came on giving me a better glimpse of him. It was Lucas McDougal.

I didn't know many of my father's friends any more. Maybe the guys in the SUV were business associates. Maybe they had business with Lucas.

Little did I know I would be seeing much more of these two characters in the coming days.

I took my drink and went to the front of the house. As I passed the library, I noticed one wall had no books but dozens of framed photos of my brother Jack. My sister had built a shrine to him. A few of the photos covered his early childhood but most were his teen years. He was tall and handsome with shaggy blonde hair and blue eyes that sparkled, perfect white teeth gleaming in every photo and a deep golden tan. It looked as though summer lived in him all year. Jack had a smile that could melt a heart like an ice cube on hot pavement. He was smart, strong, friendly and outgoing, all the things I was not. As a kid, I was frail, skinny, weak, with dozens of pimples. Once I had overheard my father say I was a mistake; he had not gotten fixed soon enough and that little squirt came along.

There were photos of Jack with my brother Joe and one of Joe in his Marine uniform. There were several with Jack and my mother. She had never been the same after Jack disappeared. Her sorrow had a profound effect on me. I was never a happy child after that. It had seemed as though a dark cloud hovered over me and Jack wasn't around to protect me anymore.

My late mother, Dorothy Jane Reynolds, had been the sweetest woman on the face of the earth. I thought of her often. She had died ten years ago. I gazed at the photos and sipped my drink. One photo warmed my heart almost as much as the bourbon. It was of me and

Jack fishing at the old millpond on our farm. Jack had his arm around me as I held a cane pole and both of us were laughing, probably at something he had said. He always had a hundred jokes or funny sayings.

I had loved Jack so much and wanted to be like him. He was a gifted athlete, and my hero. He played football, baseball, basketball and ran track. Everyone loved him, especially all the girls. He loved me and took the time to teach me things, and he protected me. God help anyone who bullied me other than my father. Jack had busted his knuckles more than a few times on my account. He had also intervened with my father a few times when I was about to get a severe beating. I remember him saying, "Now Daddy, just ease up there. Johnny is just a kid. He didn't mean no disrespect."

Sometimes he would ease up, if Jack suggested it. Other times he would tell Jack to mind his own business and then he'd make me go cut a peach limb for a switch and would whip me until I bled.

It devastated me when Jack disappeared. It changed all our lives and it broke my heart. I cried for days afterward. I kept thinking my father had just pissed him off and he would come back when he got over it. Then I thought maybe he had run off to get married because he was in love with Becky McCord and they disappeared at the same time. But my mother said there had been no fight with my father. She thought it was possible Jack and Becky had run off to get married. The two of them were so much in love.

But I never believed Jack had run off with Becky. I knew he would have called my mother; he would not have hurt her. They disappeared one hot summer night and were never seen again.

As I sipped the last of my drink, I heard Betty Jane come into the room behind me. I tried to wipe away my tears but she saw them and understood. She had stayed in Martinsville and lived with the pain. I had moved away and started a new life and had done things to help me forget. I had buried myself in my studies at college. I graduated in three years by taking extra classes and studying every summer. I immediately started law school at the University of Georgia and had graduated with honors. I was driven to succeed.

Betty Jane put her arms around me and hugged me.

"Oh, Johnny," she said. "Poor Jack, whatever happened to Jack? Do you think we'll ever know? I made this photo collage because it gives me peace to come in here sometimes and just sit and remember him, and think about all of us."

I noticed the tears running down her face as she let me go and stepped back.

"I'm going up to change," she said. "But I want us to talk when I come back. Daddy said some things right before he died that I did not understand. I know he was getting a little senile. But he made me think he may have known what happened to Jack and Becky. Let's talk. There's a photo album underneath that table you might enjoy. I put it together from a box of old photos I found when I was cleaning out Mom's things a few years ago. Take it into the den and I'll be down in a bit."

I picked up the album and went into the kitchen. I found the peach cobbler I had been craving and finished it. I poured another Wild Turkey, mixed in a thimble full of Coke and went into the den. All the mourners were gone and the funeral feast put away. The house was quiet.

My niece Kristin, Betty Jane's only child, was away at Stanford. She had forbidden Kristin to miss any of her classes and come home for the funeral. Kristin had visited with "Poppie," as she called him, a few weeks ago and had said her goodbyes.

I flipped to the first page in the album. There was a photo of Betty Jane and me when we were kids, standing in the cotton patch with burlap bags hung around our necks. The sun was rising like a red tomato in the background, and dew glistened off the white cotton. I had never seen this photo and wondered if my mother had snapped it. She owned a little camera, but my father never let her take too many photos.

"It costs too damn much money to get them things developed," he had proclaimed. But she managed to sneak around and take a few from time to time. That was back before Calvin Reynolds had become rich.

I eased back in my recliner, sipped my bourbon and was transported back to a time in my life I had tried to forget.

# CHAPTER 2

RIVERDALE PLANTATION
MARTINSVILLE, GEORGIA
SIX YEARS OLD

"Johnny, get up! It's almost six," yelled my mother from the hallway. "Your daddy wants you in the cotton field when that sun comes up. Hurry and I'll fix you a syrup biscuit to take with you. Y'all are startin in a new field across the road today. He's gone with Jack to pick up the hands. He wants you, Betty Jane and Joe to get started."

I pulled on my jeans and grabbed a long-sleeved shirt from my dresser, jammed my feet into my boots and headed to the kitchen. My mother was sticking her little finger into the side of a fat biscuit and then pouring syrup into the hole as I grabbed the milk jug out of the refrigerator, turned it up and drank the cold milk.

"Milk's almost gone," I said putting the jug back.

"I know. I'll send Emma down to milk Flossie when y'all clear the house," she said. "You be careful in the cotton patch today. It's gonna be a scorcher and rattlers will be crawling."

"I'm more worried about the damn bumble bees than the rattlers," I said.

"If I hear you say damn again, you're gonna have more problems than bees or rattlers."

"Well, Jack says it all the time and Daddy never says nothin to him."

"Jack is not too old to get his mouth washed out with soap either," she shouted as I was going out the door.

"Love ya and be careful," she yelled as I bounded down the front steps.

Jack was my fourteen-year-old brother. He was my father's golden child. He was never far from his side. They constantly laughed and joked together. Jack was given a lot of responsibility. It was as if Jack was already an adult and was a manager or a foreman on the farm. I loved Jack and wanted to be just like him. He taught me things and protected me from my father and anyone who had a beef with me.

Joe and Betty Jane were waiting beneath the peach tree in our front yard. Joe, my other brother, was twelve years old and my sister, Betty Jane, was ten. I raced to the barn to get my cotton sack. My mother had made it specially for me. It was like a huge pillowcase with a wide padded strap attached at the open end that would fit around my neck. The pads helped to keep the strap from rubbing my neck and shoulders as I picked cotton and the sack got heavier.

Joe yelled, "Better hurry, you little shit. Daddy wants us to each have twenty pounds of cotton picked by the time they get back with the hands."

We all raced across the dirt road in front of our house and into the cotton field. We each selected a row of cotton next to each other, and our long day in the field began. The cotton stalks were higher than my head and the cotton bolls were open with white fluffy cotton. I could hear the bumble bees already at work on the cotton flowers, buzzing like the saws at our neighbor Mr. Griggs' sawmill. A slight breeze was blowing from the east and I hoped that it would get cloudy and rain, but I knew that wasn't likely to happen.

The sky was a deep blue and puffy white clouds floated slowly by like giant ships on the ocean. I could smell earthy newly mown hay, and looked across the road to a field where one of the hands was mowing Bahia grass. It would dry for three days and then we would bale it and store it in the barn, another job I hated almost as much as picking cotton.

After thirty minutes in the cotton, I was drenched. The tall cotton stalks dripped with heavy dew. I stood for a minute and wiped my already wet brow as I watched two dragonflies chasing each other, their bulging eyes gleaming like mirror balls at a disco. As I picked the cotton and stuffed it in my sack, I moved slowly down the row dragging it behind me like a dragon's tail. Joe and Betty Jane were much faster than me and had moved down the row twenty yards ahead of me.

After we had been in the field for about an hour, I heard the rumble of trucks and raised up out of the cotton in time to see Jack and my father stopping their trucks about fifty yards past us at the end of the field. Jack was driving the old Ford flatbed loaded with twenty black field hands. My father drove the new Chevy two-ton truck with side boards that rose three feet above the bed of the truck. He had thirty field hands riding in the back, which included women and children. The hands jumped down from the trucks carrying their tin lunch pails with their cotton sacks wrapped around their necks. They laughed and joked with each other. They acted as though they were going to a party instead of the brutal cotton field where they would break their backs under the unforgiving August sun. I could never understand how they could seem so happy when they had so little.

The black field hands, or just "the hands" as we called them, lived on our property in rows of shotgun houses. The "black quarters," as my father called them, were located on the west side of the woods about a mile from our house. The houses were called shotgun houses because they consisted of a long hallway that started at the front door and extended to the back door. You could fire a shotgun from the front door through the house and not touch a thing before exiting the back door. Their houses were two- or three-room wooden frames with no running water. Electricity had only been installed within the past couple of years. The bathrooms were five wooden outhouses standing fifty yards behind the two rows of houses and on the edge of the woods. Two families shared each outhouse. Ten different families consisting of forty to fifty adults and children lived in the houses. They paid no rent but were expected to pay for their own electricity.

My father allowed each family to use forty acres of land to sharecrop. He would pay for the seeds and fertilizer, and they would do the work of planting, tending and harvesting the crops. When they sold these crops at local markets, they would split the profits with him. If he caught them stealing, they were evicted the next day by the sheriff and were banished forever from Riverdale.

I had learned about slavery in school and thought these poor black people were like slaves. We didn't own them, but my father controlled every aspect of their lives. I think he thought of himself as their owner. It bothered me when I saw him treat them with cruelty.

Folks in the local community raved about the generosity of Calvin Reynolds. They said he helped so many poor black people. He gave them a place to live, helped them with their crops and gave them jobs on his big farm. I realized, as I grew older, my father was not very generous. He worked those poor people until they collapsed taking care of his crops. He would beat them with a bull whip if they screwed up. He also charged them exorbitant interest rates if they borrowed money. My mom made us kids refer to them as "the hands." My father called them "the blacks."

The hands quickly stored their lunch pails under the huge oak trees at the end of the field and selected a row of cotton to pick. Some families picked cotton together with women and young children working on the same row. Most of the men preferred their own rows as they picked the cotton more quickly. In a few minutes, the field was like a giant octopus with movement in all directions. Black arms flailing as they picked the cotton. Some stooped over, others got on their knees and the children danced around the cotton stalks picking the cotton from all angles. Many sung, mostly gospel songs but some rock-and-roll. A few had beautiful voices, and I loved to hear the mixture of voices across the fields. One man was a favorite. He was a grandfather named Moses Alford. He was about seventy and had a white beard he trimmed faithfully. He had a beautiful booming baritone voice. I loved his renditions of "Swing Low Sweet Chariot," "How Great Thou Art" and "Amazing Grace."

As the hands got busy picking cotton, my father and Jack unloaded piles of burlap sheets measuring twelve foot by twelve foot. They placed two at the end of each row. As the hands loaded their sacks with cotton, they would come back up their rows and dump the cotton out on these sheets. This was to separate how much cotton was picked by each individual or family. At the end of the day, my father and Jack would tie each sheet of cotton by pulling the four corners together and tying a knot in the middle. Then they would weigh the cotton in each sheet, and they would be paid for the amount picked. The going rate was 10 cents a pound. The quick men like Elijah and Boney could pick an average of 300 pounds a day and earn $30. Most of the women could pick 200 pounds a day, and the children 50 to 100 pounds.

Betty Jane and I were expected to pick 100 pounds each and Joe was given the goal of 150 pounds. I was always short, and usually Betty Jane, Jack or Joe would give me a few pounds to keep me from getting a tongue lashing or sometimes a beating from my father when I came up short. Jack hardly ever picked cotton. He was too busy taking care of the hands, doing the weigh-ins and driving the trucks to pick up water or supplies. But when he picked for a full day, he would get over 300 pounds. He was great at picking cotton just like he was at everything else. He would usually find me near the end of the day and have a few pounds of cotton to stuff in my sack.

He would say, "Here you go sport, looks like you were chasing bumble bees instead of picking cotton again." He would laugh and dance off to joke with someone else. My father thought I was a slacker and constantly berated me for wasting time. I thought I did a good job for a six-year-old. But like everything else I did, it wasn't good enough and he let me know it.

My fingers ached from being scratched and stuck by the cotton burrs. My back ached from bending over to pick the cotton, and my knees were raw from crawling down the cotton rows. I tried to think of pleasant things as I worked to take my mind off the drudgery. I thought about fishing in the creek or the millpond or floating down the river on a rubber inner tube. Then I pretended it was wintertime, and it was as cold as a well digger's ass or a witch's tit in a brass bra, as Jack would say. I would picture icicles hanging from the barn's roof and a huge fire in the fire pit where we could stand and warm our hands. I looked down at the sweat that had saturated my shirt and had gathered around the waist of my jeans. Then I remembered where I was, and I got my mind back on picking cotton.

As we worked in the stifling cotton field, time dragged by and our progress seemed to be slower than waiting for Christmas morning. Finally, the August sun rose almost directly overhead signaling it was nearly time for lunch. I waited eagerly to hear my mom come out on the front porch and ring an iron bell hanging from the porch bannister. It signaled lunch was ready and we could all take an hour break from the grueling work. The hands would make their way to the shade of the large oak trees draped with Spanish moss at the end of the cotton field. They would sit on the ground and open their lunch pails to eat buttermilk biscuits, fried chicken livers, pork chops or sausage. They would drink tea or ice water from quart Mason jars and talk about the morning's events in the cotton field. This usually included antidotes about bumble bee stings, seeing a rattlesnake or how much cotton they thought they had picked during the morning.

Some hands would lie on the freshly picked cotton dumped on the burlap sheets at the end of the rows. Some would grab a short nap. The children would play hide-and-seek in the cotton, dig holes in the dirt, play tag or dig for doodle bugs. I wasn't allowed to play with them. I had tried that only once. My father saw me playing hide-and-seek with the black children and exploded like a cannonball hitting a pirate ship. He grabbed me by the arm, took me over to the barn and beat me with a rawhide strap.

"What the hell were you doing?" he asked. "You wanna be a black? You wanna be friends with them kids?

Next thing you know you'll be talking like 'em and stealing stuff," he yelled. "You stay away from 'em. If I catch you playing with them black kids again, you won't be able to sit for a week. Do you understand me, boy?"

I got the message.

# CHAPTER 3

My mother rang the bell and Betty Jane, Joe and I dumped our cotton sacks out on the burlap sheets lying at the end of our rows and headed across the road for lunch. We took our boots off at the front door and raced each other to the bathroom to wash up. The smells coming from the kitchen were heavenly. I could smell bacon grease mixed in with the smell of fresh vegetables and cornbread. I was so hungry I could eat a cow.

As I made my way into the dining room, my mother was carrying in a huge plate of fried pork chops, smoking and still sizzling, freshly removed from the frying pan.

Our housekeeper, Emma, a black woman in her fifties, brought in bowls of fresh purple hull peas and lima beans. They were followed with plates of tomatoes, fried okra and a huge platter of cornbread. They placed the steaming vegetables on the large oak table that had settings for eight. We were required to stand and wait for my father to make his way to the table and be seated before we could sit to eat.

After keeping us waiting for ten minutes with our mouths watering, Calvin Reynolds entered the dining room accompanied by his two foremen, Lucas McDougal and Buddy Moore, along with my brother Jack.

"Y'all can take a seat now and let's have the blessing," he said as he took his seat at the head of the table. We all bowed our heads and put our hands together in front of our chests.

"Our Father, Lord in heaven, bless this food to the nourishment of our bodies and give us the strength to carry our burdens. Lord, we pray in the name of your son, Jesus."

He started the meal by taking a pork chop and passing the plate to Jack, seated on his right.

"Better git two, boy," he said as Jack took the plate. "You gonna need some energy this afternoon, cause we gonna start baling hay. That upper pasture by the millpond road should be ready now. We cut it Friday, so it ought to be dry enough to bale. I'd like to get eight trailer loads in the barn by dark and you know we gotta knock off long enough to weigh in the cotton."

"Daddy, if we could get Elijah or Boney to help with the hay, we could get a dozen trailers in the barn today," said Jack.

"Them boys need to keep pickin cotton. I'm more worried about the cotton than the hay. If it rains, that cotton's gonna rot; the hay will dry out in a few days after it rains. You and Buddy jest keep working on the hay. If me and Lucas get done movin the cattle from the west end field, we'll come help y'all," he said. End of conversation. No one argued with Calvin Reynolds.

My mother took her seat at the other end of the table, but Emma remained standing. She would stand by to fill our iced tea or Kool-Aid glasses or bring more food if needed. After we finished, she would fix herself a plate and go sit on the back porch to have her lunch. Though I considered Emma to be almost like a member of our family, she was not allowed to eat in the house. Emma's husband, Isaac, also worked for us sometimes on the farm. He was a great mechanic who could fix anything. My father liked Isaac and let him work on all our tractors, trucks and combines.

The plates of vegetables and the cornbread were passed around, and we all eagerly gobbled up our lunch. The jovial chit-chat continued throughout lunch as everyone told a little about their morning. I usually kept quiet. I didn't think anyone was interested in hearing me tell how I had trudged up and down the rows of cotton, dodging bumble bees, or how I was behind on my goal for the day once again.

When everyone was served and had eaten what was on their plate, we could have seconds if anything was left. The rule was, you ate whatever you put on your plate. God help you if you chose something and did not like the taste. I had seen my father give some hard whippings for wasting food.

"God provided this food, and by God you'll eat it," he had wailed many times as he whacked us with a wooden spoon or a ping-pong paddle.

"Ain't no dessert today but Jell-O," my mother said as Emma placed bowls of the red and green jiggly substance in front of each of us, and then returned to the kitchen.

"Dorothy, tell Emma to get me more tea," roared my father as he handed her his largemouth glass. "You young-uns finish up now. Y'all need to get back to that cotton."

This was the pronouncement we dreaded as it signaled our wonderful break was almost over and we would be back in the field soon. We all waited for my father to slide his chair back before we could get up. We knew he was headed for the front porch where he would sit in the swing for a few minutes and smoke a cigar or roll a cigarette from his can of loose Prince Albert tobacco. My mother did not let him smoke in the house, so he never tarried long after a meal before heading to the porch.

As I was leaving, Emma squeezed something into my hand.

"Here's you a extra pork chop, sugar," she said. "I put one tween a biscuit and wrapped it in some wax paper for ya. You gonna git hungry fo y'all knock off this here evenin," she said as she hugged me.

"Thanks Emma," I said as I raced for the door.

"Here Johnny," my mother said as she handed me a quart Mason jar filled with ice water. "Y'all drink plenty of water out there. It'll be hot as blue blazes in that field."

Lucas McDougal and Buddy Moore were sitting on the wooden front steps waiting on my father to finish smoking. Lucas was chewing tobacco, and Buddy was dipping snuff. Three different men, three different vices.

Lucas was a red-faced Irishman. He was almost as large as my father at more than 250 pounds. His Brogan shoes were a size 14, and he lumbered around instead of walking. He was married and lived in a little block house in Martinsville.

Lucas oversaw our livestock. That included a thousand head of cattle, seven hundred pigs, ten horses and several chicken houses bursting at the seams with more than a thousand chickens. He was responsible for the livestock, veterinary care, our breeding program and getting all the animals ready for market.

Buddy Moore was the exact opposite of Lucas. He looked like a drawing I had seen in one of my books of a guy named Ichabod Crane. *The Legend of Sleepy Hollow*, I think the book was called. Buddy was tall and as skinny as a rail. His bones poked out everywhere and his Adam's apple came to a point that threatened to break the skin at any moment. He had sad, droopy eyes, and he found it hard to smile. Buddy always smelled like Aqua Velva shaving lotion. I never knew how he stayed fresh all day. I sometimes wondered if he kept a bottle in his pocket and splashed it on from time to time. He lived in a duplex apartment in town.

Buddy oversaw our crops. His title was "crops foreman." My father used to joke that Buddy was outstanding in his field. And then he would say, "If you don't believe me, look over yonder; there's Buddy out standing in his field."

Buddy supervised the planting of the cotton, corn, peanuts, tobacco, soybeans and watermelons. My father would designate various field hands to help him with the crops depending on the season and what needed to be planted or harvested. The hands were paid $2 an hour to do the various jobs involved with the crops, except at harvest time. Then they were paid by the pound or by the bushel.

Buddy was a quiet man. I liked him better than Lucas. He didn't scare me and wasn't creepy. Buddy liked to teach me things. He was good at explaining how things worked. He would tell me about the different fertilizers and what crops needed lime and which sprays would kill weeds, or kill you if you sniffed too much of them. Buddy was never abusive with the hands. He would show them what needed to be done and correct them if they weren't doing something right, but he was always gentle and respectful. Lucas, on the other hand, was almost as abusive as my father. He would yell and scream at the hands. He would call them dumb blacks and wasn't above hitting them if he got really mad.

# CHAPTER 4

We crossed the road and got ready for a hot afternoon in the cotton field. Most of the hands were already back at work, singing and moving quickly down the rows. I saw piles of cotton heaped up on the burlap sheets at the ends of the rows. I looked at the little pile on my sheet and winced. I probably didn't have 40 pounds yet, and half the day was gone.

"Lord, help me," I said as I looked up at the blistering sun. I walked over to a huge oak tree covered in moss as green as the lily pads in the old millpond. I picked a hiding place on the tree, stored my pork chop and biscuit in a moss-covered hole and then walked back to the field.

The cotton was shimmering under the blazing sun as I picked a new row, swung my cotton sack around my neck and got down on my knees to start the afternoon's work. I picked as fast as I could, determined to make up for my shortage. Sweat ran down my face and soon my long-sleeved shirt was soaked around the neck and on my chest. I stood up and let a cool breeze dry the sweat around my face and neck. I looked to the east and prayed rain clouds would gather, but the sky was as blue and clear as the water down at Sandy Creek. I dreamed of wading out into the creek up to my waist. I could feel the cool water rushing by me and cooling me. I dreamed for a minute, and then got back down on my knees and picked cotton like a madman.

Suddenly, I heard screaming a few rows over. It sounded like someone was dying as the shrill screams pierced the quiet afternoon. I saw

Inez Blount holding her eight-year-old daughter, Tiny, in her arms and walking quickly towards the end of her row. I thought it must have been a snake bite by the way the youngster was wailing. My father and the foremen heard the screams and ran across the road to check on her.

"What is it, Inez?" my father asked as he watched her put the girl down on a pile of cotton.

"My baby done got stung by bumble bees or some wasps or somethin!" said Inez.

I scampered over to see what was going on as the girl continued to wail. I saw she had three large welts, two on her left forearm and another on her upper left bicep.

"Ain't nothing but a bee sting," my father said as he took his can of Prince Albert from his front shirt pocket. He took a wad of the loose tobacco and put it in his mouth. He rolled it around a few times in his jaws, and then took it out and made three circular wads, each the size of a quarter.

"Lemme see, Tiny," he said as he took the girl's arm. He placed one wad on each welt and pressed them down.

"Here, hold 'em down, Inez," he said. "That tobacco will draw out the poison. In a minute she'll be okay."

The girl continued to whimper as her mom held her, pushing on the wet tobacco.

"Let 'em stay on there a few minutes, then take 'em off. She'll be alright. Y'all get back to work now. Ain't nothin' to see, just a bee sting," he said as he addressed the rest of us and put his Prince Albert can back into his shirt pocket.

I ran back over to my row, thankful for the few minutes rest from bending over the cotton stalks. I was also thankful that it had been Tiny who got stung and not me. I had been stung several times and knew it hurt like hell. I had seen my father put tobacco on stings a dozen times and knew there was some miracle in the tobacco that made the hurting go away. I picked the cotton as if I were in a race, grasping the bolls and sticking the cotton into my sack. I tried to think about floating down the Flint River, but that slowed me down. So then I thought about being in a race car and driving as fast as I could; I made good progress and was soon at the end of my row. I dumped my half-full sack on the burlap sheet and headed down another row, picking as fast as I could.

As the golden sun eased to the midway point in the sky, I thought about my pork chop and biscuit hidden in the oak tree. I was nearing the end of a new row and thought I deserved a short break. I wandered over to the tree where I had hidden it. I had placed it in a little hole in the fork of two limbs and pulled leaves and moss over it. The leaves were on the ground and the pork chop and biscuit were gone. I looked around to see if I could spot the thief, but all the hands seemed to be busy picking cotton. I took a drink of ice water and headed back to my row. I was pissed as I got down on my knees.

Out in the cotton a few rows over I heard a voice say, "That baby Reynolds boy is crazy. He thinks pork chops and biscuits grow on trees. He went to get him one and somebody done picked them all."

This was followed by shrill laughter and several snickers. I knew most of them hated me. They considered me a privileged kid who was too good to play with black children. And they were correct according to my father.

I didn't bother to try to find the thief. Laughter echoed throughout the cotton patch. I bet they wouldn't be laughing if Jack had seen who had stolen my biscuit. If this had happened to Jack, my father would have shot somebody. But I wasn't Jack. I was the major disappointment of the family. I kept my mouth shut and got back to picking cotton, determined I would get 100 pounds today.

# CHAPTER 5

The brutal August sun scorched my aching back and made me see mirages when I stood up to rest for a moment. Someone had stolen the breeze. The air was dry and still; not a leaf stirred anywhere. Even the bumble bees had decided it was too hot in the cotton and had headed for the cool shade of the nearby woods. My muscles ached and my head felt as though it would explode as I bent over once again and tried to pick a few more pounds of cotton. I kept telling myself that I would get 100 pounds. But I knew it was wishful thinking. I probably wouldn't get eighty. It was so hot! Finally, I stood up and noticed the sun making a slow descent towards the trees on the side of the field.

"Come on sun, drop out of that sky!" I yelled to no one in particular.

"You talking to the sun now, sport," I heard someone say behind me. I looked around and Jack was standing there, his smile as wide as a jack-o'-lantern.

"You got your 100 yet?" he asked.

"Probably not," I said.

"Well come on then, let's get it," Jack said as he jumped over to the adjacent row. He started picking cotton like a whirling dervish and cramming it into my sack.

He had only been at it for about fifteen minutes when I heard my father yelling, "Come on Jack, time to weigh 'em up."

Jack jumped up, shoved another handful in my sack, ran to the end of the row and climbed into the flatbed truck. He drove to the end of the cotton patch, got out and started attaching a set of scales to a wooden A-frame mounted on the back of the truck.

"Alright, y'all bring it in now!" yelled my father. "Time to weigh it up!"

The field hands stood up and slowly started making their way to the end of their rows to dump their cotton sacks onto the burlap sheets for weighing. I was so tired I could hardly drag my half-full sack to the end of the row. Betty Jane and Joe dumped their last sack of the day onto their piles and helped each other tie the four ends of the sheets together.

I slumped over on top of my cotton sheet and waited for Jack to come weigh me in. He had started on the other end of the field and would get to us last. I didn't care. *Just leave me alone and let me lay in the soft cotton.*

The tied sheets of cotton were lifted by two men and hooked onto the scales for weighing. Jack worked the scales, and my father called out the weights and recorded them in his black book.

"I'm telling all of you right now, you better not have no dirt clods or rocks in this cotton!" my father yelled.

"I took some to the gin last week and was told three of four sheets was full of dirt clods and rocks. If that happens again, I'm gonna be kicking some ass!"

"Alright Boney, you done good. 310."

"Elijah, you slippin boy. 285. You musta been sleeping out in the cotton today."

"Nattie Mae, not bad, you at 193. Jonas got 305, good job!"

"Little Nate, what happened to you, boy? You ain't got but 240. You been goofing off, ain't ya?"

And on it went with him making comments on everyone's work for the day. The hands would be paid for their labors on Friday, based on what was in the black book for the week.

My father finally got to me, Betty Jane and Joe.

"How'd you kids do today?" he asked. "It was hot as a firecracker on the Fourth of July out there today, wasn't it?"

We were too tired to respond. I just lay on the cotton dreading to hear the numbers called out.

"Alright Joe, let's see what you got," he said as Joe's sheet was hoisted to the scales.

"You got 158, Joe."

"Coulda probably got more if it wasn't so hot, Daddy."

"Well, it is what it is, and we have to deal with it. Yo name's Reynolds and we Reynolds don't make no excuses."

"Betty Jane, how much did you pick?"

"I don't know Daddy. It was mighty hot."

"Well, you close honey, 98 pounds."

Then it was my turn.

"Johnny, get yo ass off the cotton so we can weigh it. I'm guessing you got about 75 today . . . Well, well, a 105 pounds," he chortled. "Jack musta come out there and picked half of it, 'cause I know you ain't picked that much."

"Well pay Jack for half of it if you think he picked it," I said. My father stopped and stared a hole through me.

"I don't have to pay any of you a damn thing. You eat at my table every day, that ought to be enough pay. And watch yo sass mouth, boy. I ain't swatted yo ass with a peach limb lately. It's probably about time."

As my father made notes in his black book, I made some in a little book I kept in my brain. I filed it away for future use. I don't know why he despised me so much. I guess being born was reason enough for him.

Darkness had almost seized the day as I slowly made my way across the road and on to the front porch. I took my boots off and entered the house.

"Hey, honey chile," Emma said as she placed a platter of steaming rice on the dining table, her black face shining with tiny beads of perspiration.

"We got some nice ham to go wit dis rice. Go wash yo'self up now," she said as I slouched past her.

I made my way to the back porch, jumped down and grabbed the hose and washed the dirt from my hands and arms. I could hardly climb back up the porch steps I was so tired. I opened the back door and went straight into my little bedroom. I lay on the floor placing my head on an old throw pillow. I was too dirty to lay on my bed, but I was too tired to go stand under the shower.

"Come on in here and eat something, Johnny," my mother shouted from the dining room.

"Daddy and Jack went off somewhere, so it's just me, Betty Jane and Joe. Come on now, let's eat," she said.

But I was too tired. I drifted off to sleep and did not wake until Emma placed a plate of ham and rice with a couple of biscuits on my nightstand.

"Here you go, sugar pie," she said. "I'll be eatin my dinner out on the porch if you need anything else."

I finally rose and sat on the floor for a few minutes. I picked up my plate and carried it to the back porch and sat down by Emma. I listlessly ate a few bites of rice and ham. The food, normally delicious, had little taste. I could hear Emma humming as she ate her dinner. I finished a couple more bites and went into the bathroom, took a shower and then fell into my bed. I dreamed of cotton stalks and bumble bees. They both whirled around me in a silent ballet as I dozed. My wonderful sleep was suddenly shattered by yelling.

"Johnny, time to get up, sun's a rising!" yelled my mother from the hallway. "It's 5:30; you got to get moving."

Then it started all over again. Another day in the tortuous cotton field. Another day of probably coming up short. Another day of disappointing my father and getting yelled at. Another day at Riverdale Plantation.

# CHAPTER 6

MARTINSVILLE, GEORGIA
PRESENT DAY

I was still thumbing through the photo album when Betty Jane came in with a cup of coffee.

"I just made a fresh pot if you want a cup," she said as she sprawled out on the sofa.

"No, it might sober me up and I'll have to deal with reality. I'll stick with the Wild Turkey," I said.

"Now what's this about Daddy? You said he babbled some strange talk before he died?"

"Let me get my notebook; I wrote it down. I visited him every day at the hospice. Some days he was more lucid than others. But most of the time I don't think he even knew I was in the room."

She patted the sofa indicating that I needed to join her. I sat down beside her as she opened her journal.

"Here it is. I wrote it down."

"I was sitting there watching TV with him. Daddy looked at me and said, 'I got mixed up with some bad men, I'm sorry.'

I said, 'Daddy, what are you talking about?' He just stared at me and looked back at the TV. "A few minutes later, he looked at me again and said, 'I think they're the ones who took Jack.' 'Who Daddy? Who are you talking about?' I asked him. But he never said another word that whole day. "Three days before he died, I was sitting with him and he was irritable and restless. He woke up once and looked at me.

'That you Betty Jane?' he asked in a garbled voice.

'Yes, Daddy, I'm here,' I said.

"He paused for several minutes like he was thinking, then reached for my hand. He said, 'You tell Johnny to go after them guys. They up there in Atlanta. Lucas and Buddy knows 'em. I'm so sorry, baby, so sorry.'

"I don't recall him ever saying another word before he died," said Betty Jane. "You know he was shot full of morphine the last couple of weeks. I guess it was just crazy talk, but it upset me to think he may have known what happened to Jack."

I suddenly became stone cold sober. Could my father have known what happened to Jack?

"Johnny, did I tell you about his house getting broken into after he was taken to the hospice?" asked Betty Jane. "They ransacked his office and went through all his files. But they left a lot of valuable things sitting there on his desk. There was that nice gold clock the Rotary folks gave him when he retired. His coin collection was in his desk. There were shotguns and deer rifles in a case, and I found $1000 in a cigar box under his desk. It appeared as though someone was looking for something in his files. His safe was locked and didn't appear to be tampered with. Which reminds me, I need to get a locksmith to open that thing. I don't have a clue what's in there."

"Did you call the Sheriff?" I inquired. "Yes. They dusted for fingerprints. They broke the glass on those French doors leading to the back patio. I got that fixed. Deputy Moats said it was probably just kids fooling around. Kids that knew he was at the hospice. Daddy had a housekeeper come in once a week to clean and dust, so she helped me clean up. I went all over the house and nothing else seemed to be disturbed. "By the way, can you stay for a few days and help me clean out his house? There may be some things you'd like to have, like the guns or maybe some of his fishing stuff."

"Sis, I've got to get back to Atlanta. I've got a trial starting in two weeks and I really need to work on it."

"Well at least go over there with me tomorrow and let's look around. You can pick out some stuff you might want. I would like for you to take those guns."

"Okay, but I would like to head back to Atlanta tomorrow night.

Let me ask you something," I said as I sipped the smooth Wild Turkey. "Buddy Moore is dead, right?"

"Yes, Buddy's been dead a long time. He was killed in a car wreck somewhere in north Georgia years ago. You know he left when him and Daddy had a falling out about something. I never did hear what it was about. But you remember, Daddy got mad and fired him."

"So where did he go?"

"He had kin up in Blue Ridge, I think. Daddy got word he was killed in a car wreck. I asked Daddy if he was going to the funeral. He said he might go up there just to piss on his grave. He said Buddy was a thief and got what he deserved."

I finished my bourbon and headed up the stairs. I undressed and hung my jeans and polo in the closet. I wanted to get on the road back to Atlanta. The old man was dead. I had paid my respects and I wanted to be out of Martinsville as soon as I could.

I raised the window by my bed a few inches. The sultry summer breeze floated into the room like dogwood petals drifting onto the lazy flowing waters of Griggs Creek in springtime. I thought of camping and fishing trips on that creek, the boundary line separating Carl Griggs' farm from Riverdale Plantation.

The smell of the camellias blooming beneath my bedroom window filtered into the room and made me smile. My mother had loved camellias. She had planted them on both sides of our front porch. During the summer when you sat on the porch, those sweets smells would drift over you and smell so good. I lay under the cool sheets thinking about my father, my brothers Jack and Joe and our life on the farm. I tried to doze but sleep would not find me.

Suddenly, I was dive-bombed by mosquitos like Navy fighter jets providing shock and awe over Baghdad. Opening that window had been a bad idea. I got up and quickly closed it. I went into the bathroom and grabbed a can of Deep Woods Off I had seen earlier on the counter. I sprayed around my bed, hoping this would scare the little devils away. I got back into bed, pulled the sheets up around my neck and lay there staring at the ceiling. I could not sleep. I did not know why; I was dead tired.

My father's words spoken to Betty Jane haunted me: "Have Johnny go after them," "Lucas and Buddy knows them," "I'm so sorry." What the hell was that all about? Was my father delusional, or did he really know what had happened to Jack? I found it hard to believe that he really had information about what had happened to Jack and Becky after all these years. More than likely, he had dreamed something or his feeble mind had been playing tricks on him. We would never know what had happened to Jack. I closed my eyes and floated down the Flint River. Sleep finally found me just before the river emptied into the Gulf of Mexico.

# CHAPTER 7

When I woke the next morning, I smelled bacon frying and cane syrup. Betty Jane mixed a little cane syrup into her pancake batter just like Mom. It made the pancakes sweeter and gave them an even brighter golden color. I struggled out of bed and took a shower.

I slipped into my clothes and bounded down the stairs. For some reason I felt a burst of energy. I wanted to get things done and get back to Atlanta. Betty Jane was standing at the stove taking sizzling strips of bacon out of an iron skillet and placing them on a plate covered with a paper towel to drain the grease.

"I thought that bacon smell might wake you up. Got some butter-milk pancakes too. And I can scramble you some eggs if you want."

"Heavens no, sis," I said. "The bacon and pancakes will be plenty. I ate so much yesterday, I'm still as full as a tick."

"Coffee's on the stove and there's cream in that little pitcher. Recognize it?" she asked. "It was Mom's. You know I still have lots of her stuff in the attic. If you want to look through it and see if you want anything, you can do that anytime."

"Thanks, but I don't have the time."

Betty Jane placed the steaming pancakes and bacon in front of me as I sat down with my coffee. She joined me and stared pensively out at her beautifully landscaped yard.

"What are you thinking about, sis?"

"Just that I'm getting older and have never really accomplished anything. What I have was given to me. I was just Calvin Reynolds' daughter. That's my claim to fame, nothing else. I married a weasel who cheated on me, then took off with a lot of my money. And now I just feel tired and kind of useless."

"Hey, knock off that talk," I said. "You've accomplished a lot. You have the most beautiful daughter in the state of Georgia, you're the best cook in ten counties and you're the sister to a notorious lawyer. Don't go getting melancholy on me now. We have a lot to do this morning."

I finished my bacon and pancakes and carried my dishes to the dishwasher.

"Let's go see how much junk the old man had, then I'll take you out to lunch before I head back to Atlanta," I said.

We drove over to my father's house and parked in the circular drive-way. I had only been inside on a few occasions. The last was when my mom had passed away. It was an elegant brick home on fifty acres. Four huge white columns rose to the second floor and gave it the look of a real plantation house. I could see my mom's touch in the land-scaping. Magnolias graced the driveway, and rose bushes and camellias surrounded the front porch.

As we walked up to the house, I paused and thought about the last time I was here. I had received the call in my office soon after I had arrived for work. Betty Jane tearfully informed me our mother had died from a heart attack. I had raced home, packed a quick bag and headed to Martinsville.

I remembered my father's greeting as I arrived. He was sitting in a rocking chair on the front porch, staring at me as though I was a zom-bie as I approached.

"So, the prodigal son finally returns," he said as I strolled up the brick walkway. I noticed he had a drink in his hand, and wondered how many he had had for the day.

"Daddy, I'm sorry about Mom," I said as I put my bag down and tried to hug him. He pushed me away.

"Well, she was sorry too, boy. She was sorry her youngest child never would come down here to see her. Now she's dead and gone. Ain't much you can say to her now, is there? I know you stayed away because of me, but it's damn shame boy. You broke her heart."

Pangs of guilt ran up my spine because I knew he was right.

"Stop Daddy, for God's sake. Don't y'all fight," said Betty Jane as she stepped out the front door and led him back into the house. She turned and hugged me as tears streamed down her face.

I remembered entering the living room and there were so many people I could barely move. My mom had been greatly loved in the community. She had dozens of friends, and they had all come to pay their respects.

It had been two days of pure hell, being around him and his self-pity. Once we had buried my mom, I left as soon as possible. I couldn't tolerate him. My heart was broken and my guilt immeasurable. I paid my respects, cried a lot during the funeral and then returned to Atlanta and got on with my busy life. Damn him!

# CHAPTER 8

We walked up on the porch and Betty Jane unlocked the front door. The musty mildew smell of a long-deserted building assaulted my nostrils. As we entered, I was struck by vivid memories of the few times I had been here. None were pleasant. The house had been closed for several weeks and I wondered if the housekeeper still bothered to come by. The hardwood floors of the front foyer creaked as we walked in. As we neared my father's office, I immediately smelled my father's cigars. Mom never let him smoke in the house. I guess he tossed that rule when she died.

When we entered the beautifully paneled room, Betty Jane exclaimed, "Oh my God, his safe is missing! It was right there by those two filing cabinets!"

A depression in the carpet outlined where the safe had been. A couple of rips had been made in the carpet where the safe had been dragged out from the wall. A few files from his filing cabinets were strewn on the floor and his desk drawers were askew. We both looked around, but were unable to tell if anything else was missing.

"You'd better call the Sheriff," I said. She dialed the number and I went to see if I could locate where the burglar had entered the house.

I could see wheel marks leaving the office and running through the carpet towards the rear patio door. Apparently, the burglars had used a two-wheeled hand cart to move the heavy safe. I noticed glass scattered on the tile floor around the rear French doors.

"I just replaced that same glass," my sister said as she joined me at the rear door. "Sheriff's on the way and they're sending a fingerprint guy. But last time he said they were wearing gloves and all he got from the glass were fabric marks."

"I don't think it was kids this time," I said. "A bunch of kids are not going to haul off a four hundred pound safe. What did Daddy have in that safe anyway?"

"Mostly just important papers, some property deeds and the rental agreements on all the farmland he was renting out," she said. "I don't think he kept any cash in there. I came over a few times to help him with his paperwork after Mom died. He had safe deposit boxes down at the Farmers Bank. I helped him open those and I've got keys to them. He moved some papers from the safe into those boxes."

The doorbell rang and Betty Jane answered it. A young sheriff's deputy and a fingerprint technician were directed towards the office.

"They ransacked my dad's office and hauled out the safe this time," she said. "We had a break-in a couple of weeks ago here, but I couldn't tell if anything was missing. I guess they must have seen the safe and decided to come back for it. Deputy Moats came that time."

"Do you know what was in the safe?" asked the deputy, his name tag identifying him as Deputy Cielaszyk.

"No, I really don't have any idea other than some papers. I don't think he kept any cash in there. By the way, this is my brother. He's down from Atlanta for my father's funeral."

The deputy nodded as the fingerprint technician started brushing the desk with black fingerprint powder.

"Looks like they had a two-wheeled truck or cart," I said. "You can see the tracks made on the carpet heading towards the rear door where they broke the glass."

Deputy Cielaszyk followed me through the house to the rear French doors.

"They got in the same way as last time," I said pointing to the broken windowpane on the rear door.

"We'll fingerprint everything, and I'll go talk to the neighbors to see if they saw or heard anything. None too close though. Your daddy had a big lot here. Nearest neighbors are several hundred yards away. I'm assuming they probably had a truck to haul that safe off," he said as he walked out the rear door and towards the nearest house.

It took the fingerprint technician an hour to process the house. He said he picked up a few prints from the office but mostly fabric marks on the glass at the rear doors.

Deputy Cielaszyk came back to tell us none of the neighbors had seen or heard anything and that he would be turning the investigation over to the detectives. He gave us a case number and a phone number to call if we found anything else was missing. We thanked him and watched him drive away.

"I don't know Johnny. Probably someone that knew Daddy was in a hospice and just broke in to see what they could steal. Probably thought there was cash in that safe," said Betty Jane.

"That doesn't make sense. There was all kinds of stuff to steal: flat screen TVs, cameras, silver, china. But all they took was a four-hundred-pound safe. Somebody wanted what was in that safe and they probably knew what they were looking for. Let's clean up the office and check it out. Then we need to go have a look at his safe deposit boxes."

Betty Jane started on the twin filing cabinets, and I started on his desk drawers. She took a damp cloth and cleaned up most of the fingerprint powder. We both tried to put files back where we thought they belonged. I opened the top left drawer on my father's desk. It contained mostly old bills and some receipts for purchases. The bottom left drawer was deep and contained several cigar boxes. I took out the top one, placed it on the desk and opened it. It was full of photographs taken at various Rotary Club events, various Rotary pins and name tags enclosed in plastic from several years of conventions. Another cigar box contained several silver dollars and some Indian Head pennies. My father had collected coins all his life.

The third cigar box contained photos of my brother Jack. Only of Jack. They dated back to when he was five or six. There were photos of him and my father on the farm, fishing, at the cotton gin, driving tractors, camping on the Flint River, of Jack riding his favorite horse and one at a picnic. Both were smiling in all of them, happy father and son. Happy times. Some were of him in his various athletic uniforms: football, basketball and baseball. There was a photo of him and his best friend, Dylan Johnson, who was now a GBI agent. I could picture my father sitting at his desk, opening that cigar box and looking through the photos. Maybe he was wondering what ever happened to Jack. Maybe a tear ran down his cheek. But then I thought, I had never seen my father cry. When Jack went missing, did he cry then? I don't think so. I wondered how many times he had wished it was me instead of Jack.

I found a final photograph of Jack. It was a close-up of him smiling. His teeth were gleaming, his hair golden against an azure sky. I put the photo in my shirt pocket. I would keep it. It would be nice to have as I had no photos of him. He had been dead for a very long time. I thought I would put it in one of my desk drawers at the office. I would look at it from time to time and remember where I came from and how much I had lost.

The fourth and final cigar box contained several plastic cases of the type used by coin collectors to store and protect paper money. A stack of them were held together with a fat rubber band, and a faded note was taped to the top one. It was in my father's handwriting and read: "Give these to Johnny. He always liked history. They are bills that were in my great grandfather's possession when he stood with Lee as he surrendered at Appomattox."

I slid the rubber band from the stack of plastic protectors and examined them. Through the clear plastic, I could see that each contained a different denomination of Confederate bills. There were twenties, fifties, one-hundreds and the last one contained two $500 bills. I showed them to my sister.

"Cool," she said. "Keep them."

"I will," I said, surprised that my old man had thought of me and my love of history.

"Here's something," said my sister as she thumbed through manila folders in my father's filing cabinet.

"It's a file labeled, 'ABOUT MY WILL'," she said, holding it up for me to see.

I moved over close to her so I could look over her shoulder as she opened the folder. The folder contained one sheet of paper in his handwriting.

*My will is in my safe deposit box. Betty Jane has keys. There's nothing in the safe; I moved it to the bank.*

*There's a letter to Johnny. Make sure he gets it. I want him to be the executor of my estate. He's a lawyer and he will do it for free. If you use Simeon Greene like I did all my life, you won't have a penny left. Keep his grimy hands out of my affairs; he's a weasel.*

*Now Johnny, you sell my property like the will says. My house in town and the farm house at Riverdale are free and clear. I'd like to keep some land in the Reynolds' name. You are the only one left that can do that. I'm sorry about things I have done. I hope you won't hate me. I had to protect our family.*

*I love all of you. I know I didn't show it much, but I do love all of you. Your Daddy.*

I looked at my sister who was sobbing. I had mixed emotions. I'm not sure what they were.

I giggled out loud.

"What's so funny?" asked my sister.

"I was just thinking of the burglars who had dragged that heavy safe away to find it empty. Served them right."

Betty Jane laughed also. I was glad her sobbing was over.

"Well, I don't guess I'll be going back to Atlanta this afternoon," I said. "Just what I need, to be named the executor of an estate in South Georgia when I need to be at a trial in North Georgia."

"He was wanting to make sure Simeon Greene didn't charge us an arm and a leg to probate the estate."

"It's not the money, sis; it's the time," I said. "I've got a million things going on back in Atlanta. I can't be down doing probate. Let's go get that will out of the safe deposit box and see what's involved. And I want to find out about these instructions he has for me. Probably something illegal or unethical that will get me disbarred."

I took the cigar box containing the Confederate money and grabbed a photo of my mom from a bookshelf. I walked outside and put the items in the trunk of my car, got in and turned the air conditioner to full blast.

The summer sun was beating down like a fireball. I thought of the cotton patches a few miles from here where I had toiled on many days like this. I wondered what happened to all those field hands that once lived on our farm.

Betty Jane got in the car and asked, "How about Felicia's Front Porch?"

"Fine with me if you don't think Felicia will mind us sitting on her front porch," I quipped.

"It's a restaurant, silly, and a damn good one too," she said. "She's got the best fresh vegetables and her fried green tomatoes are to kill for. It'll remind you of one of mom's Sunday dinners."

"Let's do it," I said as I pulled my Mercedes out into the street.

# CHAPTER 9

Felicia's Front Porch was indeed much like my mom's Sunday dinner table. The smells coming from the tables were incredible as our hostess walked us through the restaurant to our table by a window. I was sure I smelled cornbread and sawmill gravy.

"Sure smells good," I told my sister as we were seated and handed menus. I looked around and saw platters of steaming fried chicken, catfish and barbecue on other tables. Our waitress was an older black woman who gave us a big smile and took our drink orders. She had a gold tag on her blouse telling us her name was Mamie. She was wearing a hair net, and her hair was encased in a bright red scarf twisted into a knot. Her black skin glistened with perspiration.

"Sweet tea for me," I said as Betty Jane ordered a Diet Coke.

"What's the specialty?" I asked as I browsed the menu.

"Everything Southern and good," said my sister. "All the vegetables are fresh. I love their barbecue; they make it with yellow mustard. And they always have fried green tomatoes. They put a light batter on them that I swear is Mom's cornbread recipe."

"Y'all know what ya gon have?" asked Mamie as she sat our drinks on the table.

Betty Jane ordered a vegetable plate with lima beans, cream corn, green beans and, of course, fried green tomatoes. I chose the country fried steak with green beans, collard greens and the fried green tomatoes. Mamie placed a large plate of cornbread in front of us. I grabbed two pads of butter and slathered it on the corn bread. Not quite as good as Mom's but damn close, I thought as I took a big bite.

"That was a nice memento Daddy left you, the Confederate money. Just think, from our great grandfather. Think of the history. He was with Lee when he surrendered. That's really something. I never heard that before."

"You never heard it because it's probably a lie like a lot of other stuff we were told when we were kids."

Betty Jane scowled at me. I guess she wanted me to let him rest in peace.

"Let's hurry and eat and get over to the bank."

Our lunch was served, and it was terrific. Betty Jane was correct— the fried green tomatoes were to die for. And Mamie placed a bottle of hot pepper sauce on our table for my collard greens. I tried to think of the last time I had eaten them with hot sauce. I poured a generous portion over the greens and tasted them. They were heavenly as the hot sauce gave them a nice kick. My country fried steak was crispy on the outside, fried to a golden brown, but moist and tender within. If I stayed in Martinsville, I would need a bigger car to get back to Atlanta. The food was delicious!

We were just digging into our dessert, fresh peach cobbler, when Felicia Barton, the owner, stopped by our table.

"I was so sorry to hear about y'all's daddy," she said. "I came to the service, but I couldn't come to the house last night. We were so short-handed here, I had to wait tables myself. I sent Mamie over there with some roast beef and some peach cobbler," she said.

"Thank you, Mrs. Barton," said Betty Jane. "That was really nice of you, and the roast beef was scrumptious. You remember my brother, Johnny, don't you," she said nodding towards me.

"Of course, I do," she drawled. "I used to talk with Dorothy about him. She was so proud of him going up to the University of Georgia. She used to talk about him being in the law school up there and writing the law review. Dorothy was the sweetest lady and I loved her like my own kin. I know y'all miss her. God Bless y'all!"

"Mrs. Barton, thank you for the roast beef and the cobbler; they were very good," I said.

"You're welcome, sweetie," she said. "It was the least I could do for your daddy. He was a good man. The Rotary Club did a lot of good and he ran that club for a long time. I know your daddy raised a lot of money to help poor people and kids. Well, let me get back to work," she said. "I hope y'all enjoyed your lunch and y'all come back now," she said as she sauntered off to greet other customers.

I left Mamie a nice tip, paid the check and we headed for the Farmers Bank on Broad Street.

# CHAPTER 10

I parked in the bank's parking lot under an oak tree that must have been two hundred years old. Its weathered branches reached into the sky at least 60 feet and shaded the entire parking lot. Its enormous trunk was wider than my car and decorated with a scaly gray fungus. Spanish moss draped the huge limbs and swayed in the summer breeze like a lady playing a huge harp.

We were greeted by a lovely customer service rep whose name tag told us she was Anna. She had a Southern drawl that was as smooth as cane syrup slithering off buttermilk pancakes. We told her what we needed, and she directed us towards the rear of the bank and into a quiet but musty smelling alcove that housed the safe deposit boxes.

Betty Jane and Anna took the keys and disappeared into the locked vault. They returned a few minutes later with three large safe deposit boxes, and we were directed into a small room that allowed privacy. They placed the boxes on a small table. Anna told us we could take our time and left with a whirr of skirts.

I opened the first safe deposit box and saw a large tan envelope with my name written in black marker. I placed it on the table and noted another envelope that was marked, "Last Will and Testament - Calvin LaFont Reynolds." I placed it on the table and then turned back to the first envelope. It was taped shut with threaded mailing tape. Betty Jane removed a nail file from her purse and handed it to me.

I inserted the file and ripped through the strong tape. It contained two type-written pages and a few hand-written notes in my father's handwriting. I read the pages aloud as my sister eagerly listened.

*Johnny,*

*I read about you in the Atlanta paper. I'm proud you are a lawyer. Years ago, I got mixed up with some bad people. I was trying to make some money after I lost crops 'cause of bad weather. I did some bad stuff.*

*These folks from back then may know what happened to Jack. I went after them. Told them I had evidence. They threatened to hurt our family. They burned our barn. I had to back off.*

*I hired an investigator named Horace Grimsley out of Albany. I gave him $5,000 to investigate what happened to Jack. He was a retired GBI agent. He snooped around a little, then gave me the money back. Said I needed to let sleeping dogs lie. Said it was too dangerous.*

*A week later, Grimsley was found dead. They said he killed himself, but I don't believe it. I think he stepped on some toes. I got a call telling me to stop poking around or I would be sorry. I was worried about Betty Jane and Kristin, so I dropped it. Those guys know that I'm dead now and probably think I can't do them no harm. So, I want you to take it up again. I want you to make them pay.*

*Lucas and Buddy both know things. I don't think Buddy's dead. He's hiding up in the mountains. They helped me with that bad business. They know these folks, but they may be scared to talk to you. You'll have to pay them.*

*You'll need money. There's $100,000 in these boxes and some coins. I'm making you the executor of my estate. My will spells it out. I want you to sell my house and all of Riverdale but a 1000 acres. Give the money to Betty Jane and Kristin. You keep the land. It has been in our family since back before the Civil War. My great grandfather, Luther Monroe Reynolds, had 44,000 acres at one time. Yankees and carpetbaggers took it all but*

*10,000 acres that was passed down to me. I want to keep some land in the Reynolds' name. Don't ever sell it. Pass it down to your son.*

*Finally, I've done some snooping around. I wrote down names. Play the tapes in this box; they prove what was going on. Talk to Dylan Johnson at the GBI. He was Jack's friend; he'll help. Find out what happened to Jack. I can't rest in my cold grave until you do. Take care of Betty Jane and Kristin and take care of yourself. I never told you much, but I do love you and I'm proud of what you've made of yourself. I treated you bad.*

*I'm sorry.*

*Love, Daddy*


Betty Jane saw the tears streaming down my face and wiped them away.

"What was Daddy involved in?" she asked. "Why would those people have taken Jack?"

"I have no idea, sis," I said. "And I'm not sure I want to try to find out. If this guy Grimsley was murdered, I don't think I wanna go digging around into something that occurred thirty years ago."

"Well you've got to talk to Lucas and Buddy, that is if Buddy is alive," she said.

"Well, I can talk with Lucas. He still lives here in Martinsville, right?"

"Yes, he's got a little house down at the end of Alcorn Street. Me and Mama used to get him to help plant flowers. He works around town doing odd jobs."

I removed the remaining documents from the safe deposit box, noting that a large, fat gray envelope was the last item in the box. I dumped its contents on the table. There were numerous stacks of banded bills each containing crisp $100 bills. A white index card fell out on the table. It was marked "$100,000."

A little metal box contained four micro-cassette tapes with white labels indicating the date they were made and identifying them as Tapes 1, 2, 3 and 4. There was a business card that read:

*Horace C. Grimsley*

*Licensed Private Investigator*

*918 Slappey Drive, Albany, GA 912-344-8723*

Four names were written on a post-it note: Red Slocum, Ray Slocum, Jr., Clarence Dawkins and Brady Lyle.

Two of these names were very familiar to me: Clarence Dawkins, a wealthy African American businessman from Atlanta, who was also a Georgia State legislator, and Brady Lyle, a US congressman from Atlanta. Both of whom I considered to be corrupt pond scum.

I opened another box, the heavy one, and observed it contained gold and silver coins.

I removed the coins and stacked them on the table as I counted. There were thirty-seven South African Krugerrands and forty-two Morgan silver dollars. I did a quick calculation and noted the coins were worth several thousand dollars. Another piece of paper listed several bank and savings accounts with balances totaling more than $1,000,000.

I suggested to my sister that we leave everything including the tapes in the safe deposit box for now. I needed to find a device with which to play the tapes. We took the remaining items and called the customer service rep, Anna, to help us replace the boxes. She was the epitome of a true Southern belle. If only I were ten years younger—no make that twenty years younger.

I drove Betty Jane home, telling her that I wanted to swing by Lucas McDougal's.

"Okay," she said. "But come back to the house when you're done. We have all that food left over from last night. We'll have another Southern feast."

I drove back through Martinsville trying to think of where Alcorn Street was located. I headed East and was almost out of the city limits when I saw a faded green street sign announcing "Alcorn St." I turned right and headed down the street. A small wooden house in bad need of a new coat of paint sat at the end of the shaded cul-de-sac.

# CHAPTER 11

Lucas McDougal was slouched in a faded green rocking chair on his front porch smoking a cigarette. The smoke wafted out into the yard and its strong aroma attacked me when I got out of my car. As I walked up to the front porch, I caught a glimpse of a cypress swamp fifty yards west of the house. The dank smell of rotting wood and swamp mud reminded me of the huge cypress swamps and ponds on our farm. Some good memories floated by, and some not so good hovered in the air.

"How you doing, Mr. Luke?" I asked as I climbed the steps to the front porch.

"Hey, Johnny boy, thought you'd be back in Hotlanta by now. Have a seat," he warbled as he pointed towards a rickety swing the same faded green color as his rocking chair.

It squeaked like the door on a haunted mansion as I sat, and I wondered if it would hold me.

"I had to take care of a few things of Daddy's and help Betty Jane clean some stuff out of his house. I'll be here a few days, helping her."

"Well, I know she'll appreciate ya helpin her," Lucas said, coughing between puffs of his cigarette. "It's too damn hot to even git up and spit," he said as he wiped his brow and neck with a soiled handkerchief.

"You've got your own backyard fishing hole out there in the swamp, don't you, Mr. Luke?" I asked pointing out towards the cypress swamp.

"Yeah, well, it's too damn shallow for much fishing. But they's a couple a deep holes where's you can fish if you're willing to wade some. But ya gotta watch out for water moccasins and gators."

"Well, it looks fishy, with the cypress trees and the stumps," I offered.

"Mostly catfish, but you can catch some bream and some mud fish. I caught a mud fish weighed about six pounds. They ain't much good to eat, too many bones. But they fun to catch. I caught a couple of nice catfish this morning. Gonna fry 'em up for lunch with some hushpuppies. You welcome to have a bite."

"Thanks, but I've got a lot of stuff to do."

"That wuz a nice funeral. I always respected yo daddy. I know you and yo daddy butted heads a lot. He wuz a hard man. It wuz his way or the highway. I felt sorry for you sometimes. He would beat you for jest the littlest mess-up."

"Yes sir, he sure did," I said.

Lucas puffed his cigarette and was frozen in thought for a moment.

"I used to say, 'Mr. Calvin, how come you so hard on that boy?' He would say, 'Luke, how many kids you got?' And I'd say, 'Well, none.' He would say, 'Well until you got some a yo own, don't tell me how to raise my young-uns.'"

"Yep, that sounds like Daddy," I said.

Lucas stared out at the swamp and wiped sweat off his brow. He kicked at a splinter on the wooden front porch with a dirty brown loafer. I wasn't sure he was going to speak again.

Then he said, "I know he was mighty hard on ya after Jack wuz gone. I knowed you wuz gonna be gone as soon as you got old enough. But you done good. Look at you now, you a lawyer with a fancy car."

I decided to dive in.

"Mr. Luke, I was going through some of Daddy's papers and ran across something I wanted to ask you about."

"Alright, but I ain't had much contact with yo daddy in quite a while. I did a few odd jobs for Mrs. Dorothy sometimes, but Mr. Calvin got mighty feeble and I ain't talked with him. I think the last time I saw him wuz 'bout a year ago."

"Do you remember before Jack disappeared, Daddy had a couple of real bad crop years, lost most everything?" I asked.

"Shore I remember. Them was some bad times. One year it rained ever'day for about two weeks. Then we wuz jest drying out and a hurricane came up from the Gulf and we got about ten inches mo rain. Lost ever'thang, all the cotton wuz lost, peanuts rotted in the ground, corn wuz ruined, watermelons rotted out there in the field."

"Sounds like some bad times. I guess I was too young to realize what was going on."

"Oh, it was some mighty bad times. We lost the whole crop. Yo daddy didn't make a nickel. He had to pay me and Buddy with meat from the smokehouse and a few dollars here and there from selling some cows and hogs. We wuz all hurtin."

I looked at Luke's nicotine-stained fingers and noticed they were shaking badly as he remembered those times.

He took one last drag from his cigarette and flicked it into the yard. He ruefully watched the trail of smoke as it flew through the air. He paused to reflect some more and then continued his tale.

"Then the next year, it was jest the opposite. Drought got us that year. We planted in the spring and we got no rain. We irrigated best we could but the ponds wuz drying up too. No water anywhere. That June we got a few showers and we replanted some of the crops. They started to grow pretty good, then the rain stopped. It wuz one of the hottest Julys on record. No rain and a hundred degrees ever'day. Ever'thang burnt up. We picked a few bales of cotton and got a little corn, no watermelons again and no peanuts. Yo daddy made jest enough to pay the hands and me and Buddy. He sold off most of the livestock."

"That's the time I wanted to ask you about," I said. "Daddy left me a letter. He said he had gotten mixed up with some bad people. He said you and Buddy knew about it and y'all helped him. I want to know what that was all about?"

"Oh, hell! I don't rightly know," he said. "I guess he wuz sorry he almost lost Riverdale. I know it had been in yo family for a hundred years. As far as bad people, I guess he wuz talkin bout them bankers. He borrowed a lot of money and they wuz always wantin to take the tractors or combines or wantin him to sell some of the land."

"No, I don't think he was talking about any bankers. He said you and Buddy helped him. Helped him do what?"

"Johnny, that wuz more than thirty years ago. I don't really remember much from back then."

"Daddy also said he thought them bad people had something to do with Jack disappearing. Do you know anything about that?"

"No, I don't know nothin' 'bout it. Did yo daddy say anybody's names in that letter?"

I thought it over and decided I probably shouldn't give Lucas any names. I didn't want to spook him just yet.

"No, no names. Just some bad people and that you and Buddy helped him some."

"Naw, I don't know 'bout that. He wuz gettin' mighty feeble. He done got ever'thang mixed up."

"Do you know anything about him hiring a private detective to look into Jack's disappearance?"

"Naw, ain't never heard nothing 'bout that."

"Do you remember anything else?"

Lucas McDougal took out another cigarette and lit it with a match, shaking his head like he wholeheartedly disagreed with everything I said. He inhaled deeply, coughed a couple of times and looked towards the cypress swamp. A gentle breeze blew, and I could smell the swamp clearly again. A dead animal was out there somewhere nearby. I could smell its rancid odor occasionally as the wind shifted. Lucas kept silent, smoking and looking out towards the swamp.

Finally, he said, "They's a lot of bad folks in this world. I ain't had no reason to be around none in a long time and got no plans to talk about them either. Let's jest let sleeping dogs lie, okay?"

He got up from his chair and started to walk back into his house, but I grabbed his shoulder and held him back.

"Mr. Luke, please talk to me. I can offer you some money. I'll pay you if you can just point me in the right direction. Can't you do that for me?"

He stopped and stared at me. His lips quivered and his hands trembled.

He shook his head and said, "That wuz a long time ago. Most of them folks is dead. And them that ain't, you don't want to be messing around with. I can't help you, son. Now let me jest live my last days in peace."

He pushed past me and entered his home. I was left standing on the empty porch with nothing but unanswered questions.

"Well think it over. I'll be glad to pay you," I shouted as I walked down the porch steps.

I had interviewed a lot of people in my legal career. I had dealt with a lot of liars over the years. Of one thing I was sure . . . Lucas McDougal was a damn liar.

# CHAPTER 12

I drove back to Betty Jane's house determined I would follow through with my father's wishes. If there was a possibility I could find out what happened to Jack, I would leave no stone unturned. I had made a mistake by not taking any cash with me out to Lucas' house. I had the feeling if I showed him some cold hard cash, it would change his mind. He was obviously scrapping by on Social Security in a ratty old house. If I could make his life better, maybe he would talk to me. I knew the bank would be closed by now, so I would have to get some money early tomorrow morning.

As I reached my sister's house, I decided that I would get some information from Lucas the next day. Upon entering the house, Betty Jane was in the den enjoying a cocktail.

"Great idea!" I said as I headed for the bar.

I rumbled around behind the bar and found an unopened bottle of Old Forrester. I put a few ice cubes in a glass and then decided to drink it neat. I dumped the ice, splashed a generous amount of the golden-brown liquid into my glass and flopped on a recliner.

"How'd it go with Lucas?" she asked.

"I think he knows something. In fact, I'm sure he knows something about what Daddy was mixed up in. He admitted as much. He said some bullshit about some of them people are dead and some you don't want to mess with. He said the same thing as that PI Dad hired. He said, 'We needed to let sleeping dogs lie.'"

"So you really think old Luke knows something?"

"I'm sure of it. I should've taken some cash with me. I think if I'd shown him a wad of bills, he probably would have talked to me. It looks like he's barely hanging on. Living in that tiny shack on the edge of the swamp. He chain-smokes and coughs like he's got lung cancer. I'm going to the bank in the morning and get some cash and try him again."

"Oh, by the way, you had a phone call. Susan Regan called. She wanted to know if you were still in town. She wanted to invite you to dinner."

A couple of tiny electric shock waves ran up and down my spine. The mention of Susan's name always caused them.

"I'll call her. Maybe I'll go see her tomorrow night. I'm too beat tonight. Let's dig into those leftovers from last night. Then I want a hot shower."

I carried my drink upstairs and sipped it as I turned on the water and let it get steaming hot. I put my drink on the marble sink and climbed into the shower. I let the hot water cascade down my tired body thinking about Lucas McDougal. He was the key. He knew what kind of bad business my father had gotten mixed up in. He could tell me everything I wanted to know. I just had to give him some cash. From the looks of his place, he really needed it. I would get him to tell me everything.

I dressed and went downstairs. Betty Jane had heated up another Southern feast. All the leftovers from my father's post-burial soiree were even more delicious than before. I tried most of the dishes that I had missed the previous evening. The macaroni and cheese, turnip greens and the baby back ribs were the stars of the show. I ate too much and told Betty Jane to not even think about bringing me any banana pudding, knowing I would devour it later.

We had another emotional evening. We talked about our mother a lot, and of course we cried. She was an angel and a saint. I had never heard her utter an unkind word about anyone. She could always find the bright side of any trouble. She went about with a smile on her face and joy in her heart. I probably would have gotten even more severe beatings from my father if she had not intervened. Then I thought, how could she have not known about his bad business? Maybe she had been afraid. Maybe she had to protect him. Maybe she had to protect all of us.

I asked Betty Jane if she could remember him talking about bad people or acting suspicious. She said she was clueless. She pointed out that Jack may have known something. She said she could not imagine our father doing anything without Jack knowing about it. I agreed. Jack was always my father's right arm. Jack would have had to have known what was going on. And maybe that's why Jack had disappeared.

I took that thought to bed with me. Sleep did not come easy. I tossed and turned, and when I finally got to sleep, I dreamed about high school and Susan Regan. It was a pleasant dream.

# CHAPTER 13

Lucas McDougal was on a mission. He scampered into his old Ford pickup and fired up the engine. The tires spun as he pulled out of his dirt driveway and headed to the Pick Kwick convenience store a mile from his home. He hurried inside and asked the clerk for $3 in quarters for the pay phone. The phone was an anachronism, probably the only one left in Martinsville. But since Lucas didn't own a cell phone, he had to use its service on the rare occasion when he called anyone. He had removed the number from under the floor mat of his pickup. He laid it on the metal shelf of the phone stand and dialed the number. The operator instructed him to insert eight quarters into the phone for three minutes. He did so and listened for an answer as the phone rang.

"Hello," said a gruff voice.

"This here's Luke McDougal down in Martinsville. Can you have someone call me back at this number? It's very important," he said in an excited voice.

He gave the number and hung up the phone. He waited for five minutes hoping no one else would approach to use the phone.

The phone rang and Lucas grabbed the receiver saying, "This is Lucas; who is this?"

"You called us, dirtbag. What do you want?" said an even gruffer voice.

"I've uh . . . I've uh . . . got some information about Calvin Reynolds and his boy down here in Martinsville," he said.

"Okay, what's the information?" inquired the voice.

"Well . . . uh . . . y'all told me to try to find out about Mr. Calvin's papers and what's happenin with all his stuff and to snoop around his daughter Betty Jane to see if she knowed anything. His boy, Johnny, the lawyer from Atlanta, done come to see me asking about stuff happened thirty years ago. He says he got a letter from his old man tellin him to look into his brother's death. Y'all's folks wuz down here the last few days. They told me to call if I heard anything 'bout Calvin's papers or any tapes turnin up."

"Okay, so what's turned up?" growled the voice.

"The boy said Mr. Calvin hired a private eye to look into Jack's disappearing," said Lucas excitedly. "He said he'd give me some money if I told him 'bout what wuz goin on back then. He knows Mr. Calvin wuz mixed up in some bad stuff."

"Did the boy say whether Calvin named any names or gave him any papers or tape recordings?" asked the voice.

"Naw, just said his daddy left him a letter. Y'all said you'd help me out if I kept my eyes open for ya. How 'bout y'all sendin me somethin down this way?"

"Yeah, I think we can probably do that," said the voice and the line went dead.

Lucas climbed into his pickup mumbling to himself.

"Probably never hear from them again. Probably ain't gonna send me nuthin. Don't know why they even interested in that mess anymore. That was more than thirty years ago. Mr. Calvin's dead and nobody gon say nuthin. Don't know why they gettin their panties in a wad 'bout that stuff now."

Lucas parked the pickup in his driveway and trudged up the front porch steps. Bream were swirling in the swamp in pursuit of grasshoppers or crickets who had made a fatal error. He smelled barbecue cooking somewhere down the street. He loved that smell, hickory chips on the charcoal to give it that smoky taste. Maybe he would pull out his rusty grill and cook a steak tomorrow. He was damn tired of fish and sandwiches. He deserved a steak. He should have some money soon and he would buy the biggest steak in the meat counter down at the Kroger store. He'd cook that sucker up medium rare and have a feast.

The hickory smoke wandered on to his front porch and painted his nostrils. He breathed it in and let out a sigh. Cicadas were chirping like crazy out in the swamp. A gator croaked a low mournful call. The swamp was alive with insects and all sorts of critters. Lightning bugs floated around the cypress trees flicking their yellowish glow lights like they were signaling someone.

Lucas unlocked his house and entered the musty-smelling front room. Stale grease smells assaulted him as he moved towards the kitchen. The leftover catfish from lunch were still in the frying pan on the stove. Why did he cook all three when he knew he would eat only one? The fish was beginning to stink. He emptied the pan into a plastic bag, took it out the back door where his garbage can was located and dumped the foul-smelling bag. He grabbed a beer and headed for the front porch. He wanted to sit in the swing and let the cool breeze calm his nerves. The mosquitos probably wouldn't let him have any peace. Screw the little bastards! He would swing and slap at them until they drove him inside.

As he walked out on the porch and lit a cigarette, another gator croaked in the swamp. Maybe the smoke would drive the mosquitos away for a little while. He sat down in the swing and thought for a few minutes as to whether he had done the right thing. They had told him to call if he heard anything about Calvin Reynolds' stuff, any papers or photos or tapes. They said they would take care of him. But did he do the right thing? It bothered him.

Johnny Reynolds had been a good kid. God knows his father didn't treat him right. Mr. Calvin used to beat that boy unmercifully for no reason. Especially after Jack was gone. He was a bitter man then and took it out on the boy.

Maybe he should go ahead and tell Johnny what he knew. He knew a lot. He wondered how much the boy would pay him. Would he give him enough so he could hightail it out of here, maybe go out West somewhere? He would have to get far away. They would come looking for him if he told what he knew. He would have to sleep on it. He'd already made the phone call. Maybe he could get money from both sides. Maybe he could get enough to get far away. He sailed the cigarette into the yard and went inside. He would sleep on it, make a decision in the morning. That's what he would do—just sleep on it.

# CHAPTER 14

After dinner, I settled into a lounge chair in the den and placed a call to Susan Regan. She answered on the third ring with that sexy Southern drawl that could melt the butter on your roll in two seconds flat.

"Helloooo!" she said.

"Hey, Susan, John Reynolds. Just got your message," I lied.

"Hey Johnny, I heard you were still in town and I wanted to see if you'd like to come over for dinner. I guess it's a little late now though," she said.

"Sorry, I was out running some errands and just got home and got your message."

"That's OK. I know you're probably busy taking care of stuff for your daddy. Maybe tomorrow night, if you're still going to be in town."

"That would be great! I would love it."

"Super, how about seven o'clock?" she cooed.

"I'll be there with bells on," I said.

We chatted a few more minutes, and then said goodnight.

"Get your hot date set up?" Betty Jane asked as she plopped down in the loveseat across from me.

"Yeah, I'm going for dinner tomorrow night," I said.

"Good, I always liked Susan. She's a sweet lady."

We talked until almost midnight. We laughed about some of the funny things that happened as we grew up at Riverdale. Betty Jane reminded me of the time all four of us kids got sheets of wax paper from Mom's kitchen and went out to the barn. We crawled up to the very top of the tin roof that sloped to a steep angle, waxing the tin as we climbed. Then we placed a sheet of wax paper beneath our butts and slid down the little runways created by the tin overlapping. It was a fast run and the idea was to dig your heels in just before you got to the edge of the barn to prevent you from going over the edge.

But on this day, I was barefooted. When I dug my heels in to stop, they didn't even slow me down. I zipped off the edge of the barn like a rocket and flew 20 feet in the air, landing on my bottom. Fortunately, I landed in a grassy spot. If I had landed in the clay that surrounded most of the barn, I would have broken my pelvis. I still hit very hard and could barely walk for a couple of days.

My dad was not sympathetic. When Mom wanted to keep me out of work, Dad declared, "Bullshit, he can crawl down the cotton rows." And crawl I did, and I still almost picked my required 100 pounds of cotton. My sister reminded me that for the remainder of the summer they all called me "rocket man." We laughed some more and then we cried some. We missed them all.

I told Betty Jane I wanted to be at the bank when it opened tomorrow. I was going to get some cash and see if I could get Lucas to talk to me. I then went upstairs for a hot shower. I turned the water on as hot as I could stand it and let it flow over my tired body. I stood under the shower for fifteen minutes letting the hot water soothe me. I toweled off and was in bed two minutes later. I lay there thinking about Jack and my father, and about what kind of bad business he could have been involved in.

The next morning, I skipped the sausage and pancakes, thinking that if I kept eating like I had been for the past two days, I wouldn't be able to fit into my Mercedes for the long trip home. I settled for a coffee and checked my watch to see how long it would be before the bank opened. Betty Jane said she would meet me at the bank as she had some errands to run downtown. At five before nine, I was standing outside the locked door to the Farmers Bank willing it to hurry and open. At precisely nine o'clock I saw Betty Jane approaching and Anna, from the day before, unlocking the door.

"Well, good morning, Mr. Reynolds. You're out bright and early. What can I do for you?" she asked in that velvety voice.

I told her that we needed access to the safe deposit box again. Betty Jane and Anna went through the procedures again and brought the boxes. I counted out $10,000 in cash from the gray envelope and removed the four tapes and stuffed everything into a briefcase I had brought with me. I left Betty Jane to replace the boxes, kissed her on the cheek and hurried out of the bank.

As I drove over to Lucas' house, I tried to think of how I would phrase my approach to him. Should I just walk up and offer the money for the information? Or should I play it coy and try to smooth-talk him, increasing the amount I might be willing to pay him as he inched the information out bit by bit. I still had not decided when I pulled into his driveway, noting his old Ford pickup was parked off to the side.

The cypress swamp near his house was a beehive of activity this sunny morning. Several dragonflies chased each other over the black water darting in and out like miniature helicopters. A blue heron stood on one leg and surveyed the shallow water for a fish that would make a tasty lunch. Fat bluegills swirled the water as they chased minnows in the shallows. I stepped onto the porch and knocked on the screen door. I did not receive an answer, so I opened the screen and pounded on the inner wooden door.

I called out, "Mr. Luke, it's Johnny Reynolds." Still no answer. I leaned over and peered through one of the dirty glass panes, but it was partially blocked by a faded blue curtain. I moved over to one of the front windows shielding my eyes with my hands over my forehead trying to see into the dimly lit living room. I could barely see Lucas McDougal slumped down in his recliner, apparently asleep. I knocked louder and called out, "Hey, Mr. Luke." I paused and listened to hear movement. Only silence responded. I tried the front doorknob and found it unlocked. I opened it slowly and stuck my head inside hoping I wouldn't startle Lucas. I didn't. Because Lucas McDougal was slumped deeply in his recliner, legs splayed, both arms hanging limply over the sides of the chair, a bullet hole in his left temple. Blood had run down his cheek and puddled on the left side of his shirt.

# CHAPTER 15

RIVERDALE PLANTATION
EIGHT YEARS OLD

It was late October, and I was missing another day from school. It was the seventh day I had missed, and school had only been in session for two months. My father kept all of us kids home when there was "important farm work" to be done as he referred to it. The important farm work today was harvesting corn. I much preferred working in the peanut fields as it wasn't as hard a job as harvesting the corn.

When we worked in the peanuts, I would drive a tractor pulling a trailer around the fields so the peanut combines could empty their loads. I would take the load of peanuts up to our barnyard, cover the trailer with a tarp, unhook the trailer, get an empty one and head back to the field to get another load. That was one of the easiest jobs on the farm and I loved it. But not today.

This morning we were working in the cornfield. My job was to follow the combine down the rows and pick up any ears the combine had missed. Betty Jane and I each walked between two rows grabbing the stalks and making sure no ears were left. If we found one, we ripped it away from the stalk and shoved it in a cotton sack that hung around our necks. It was dirty work, and the chafe from the corn would get down your shirt and itch like crazy as you sweated. The corn rows in this field were about three hundred yards long, and we would usually have a full sack by the time we reached the end of the row. Wooden trailers were parked at the end, and we would dump our sacks into them and head back up another two rows. This was back-breaking work and I hated it almost as much as picking cotton.

Since six o'clock this morning, I had been trudging up and down the corn rows. I thought I would pass out a few times as I became dehydrated. I couldn't believe it was still this hot in late October. A dozen black farm hands worked the rows next to us. They sang and laughed and joked as they worked.

We got to the end of a row and I told Betty Jane we needed to take a break. She wiped sweat from her brow with the back of her hand and heartily agreed we had earned a break. We both sat with our backs to a rubber tire on the corn trailers and sipped the remaining water we had in Mason jars. I watched as a doodle bug burrowed into the soft dirt, boring down to make himself a home underground. Several black crows cawed and chased each other over the field. Their feathers gleamed in the sunlight as though they had been polished with bacon fat. Crows were useless. You couldn't eat them. All they did was fly around cawing, making noise and being a pain in the ass.

A cool breeze finally came up and dried the sweat from my face and neck. I lay back and watched buzzards soaring overhead, high in the sky like fighter pilots zooming across the total blueness. I wondered if they might be hanging around to come get me if I fell in the cornfield. I was about to doze off to sleep when I heard my father's pickup screech to a halt a few feet from the trailer. A cloud of dry brown dust drifted over us as he came around the front of the truck and looked in the trailer.

"What the hell y'all been doin?" he screamed. "This trailer ain't but half full. Git your asses up and get back in that corn. You got a while before dark."

We both jumped up and trudged back into the corn.

"How's the hands doing?" he yelled as he walked down the end of the rows to inspect their trailers.

"Y'all need to hit it hard and fill up this trailer before y'all knock off!" he yelled.

Then he was gone in a whirl of dust just like he had arrived. I watched the dust trail follow his pickup as he headed somewhere else on the farm to scream at more folks.

We finished several more rows as the sun started to sink behind the pines and lightning bugs began to appear in the woods at the end of the field. Our trailer was almost full, so Betty Jane and I jumped on the Ford 8N tractor attached to the trailer of corn and pulled it back to the barnyard. We covered the corn with a tarp. I stumbled up to the back porch and washed my face, hands and arms. I could barely climb the steps. I lay down on an old sofa and fell asleep.

I barely heard Emma's voice a little later when she said, "Come on, honey chile, it's almost time for supper."

I hardly moved. I was so tired I went back to sleep.

An hour later, my mom shook my shoulder and said, "Come on, Johnny, it's time for supper. Your daddy and Jack will be here in a few minutes. It's time to eat."

I raised up from the old sofa and staggered into the house. I didn't want to eat. I just wanted to sleep. Emma's black face shined like a search light in the dim glow of the kitchen as she grabbed my arm and squeezed it.

"Come on, baby, I know you tired but you gots to eat."

I went into the dining room and leaned up against the wall waiting for my father. I could barely stand. I slipped down and sat on the floor. I started to doze.

I was awakened by him and Jack entering the house. I saw him throw his brown fedora on a hat rack in the hallway. I tried to get up but stumbled and fell back to the floor as he entered the dining room.

He took one look at me and exclaimed, "You wanna get your ass off the God damn floor, Johnny!"

I jumped up and stood behind my chair. He sat and started dishing out roast beef, green beans, small red potatoes, sliced tomatoes and slaw made from purple cabbage.

"Everybody sit," he boomed.

He said a blessing. I wondered how God looked on a man who was taking his name in vain one minute and praising him in the next. But I suppose that was none of my business. I just kept my mouth shut and ate my roast beef. I was too tired to even think about Calvin Reynolds' salvation.

"Johnny, did y'all pick up three trailers of corn today?" joked my brother Jack.

"Hell no, they didn't even get a trailer load!" boomed my father.

Jack was always joking with me and trying to protect me from my father's wrath. I loved him dearly.

"The damn blacks didn't get much corn either," my father exclaimed. "There was about fifteen of them working out there and I think they only got about four trailers full."

"Maybe the combine is doing a better job," said Jack. "Maybe it ain't leaving much corn behind."

"Naw, there's plenty of corn left behind," said my father. "Them blacks are just doing too much shucking and jiving out there instead of working. And Johnny and Betty Jane are taking a break about every ten minutes, so they ain't doing shit."

"How late is Joe going to be?" asked my mother.

"Probably another hour. Him and Lucas are moving all the cows from the river pasture over to that hundred acres over by Carl Griggs' place. I can't believe how quickly them cows eat that grass. Seems like we have to move 'em to a new pasture every week."

"I'll fix Joe a plate and stick it in the fridge," said my mother. "I got y'all a pound cake for dessert tonight."

We ate in silence after that as I tried to stay awake.

Emma served the pound cake to everyone but Betty Jane who asked to be excused so she could go take a bath.

"Hope y'all don't mind paper plates for your dessert," Emma said as she served me a huge slice of pound cake. It was as yellow as a school bus and I could see moisture glistening along the cut edge.

"I don't like damn paper plates, you know that," said my father as he handed his plate back to Emma.

"I'm sorry. I just thought it would save some washing. I'll get you a regular plate," she said.

He scowled at her as she handed him a china plate.

"Emma, we pay you to wash all them dishes. I don't like eaten nothin off no paper."

# CHAPTER 16

**W**e were just finishing our dessert when Joe came in.

"Got 'em all moved, Daddy," he said. "We had a little trouble with a couple of strays and a calf that got stuck down by the fence. So I smacked their butts to get 'em moving."

"Good job, boy. We'll probably have to move 'em again in a couple of weeks the way the cows eat that grass."

"Johnny, did you feed the horses and the cows?" asked Joe. "Cause when I pulled the jeep in the barn, the cows were all lowing like crazy and the horses' water troughs were as dry as a bone."

My heart skipped a beat as my father's eyes burned a hole in my chest.

"Oh God! I forgot," I said as I pushed my chair back. "I was tired and fell asleep on the back porch and I just forgot!" I exclaimed as I ran out the back door.

"You come see me when you're done, boy!" my father yelled from the table. "We gonna talk about your chores and taking the Lord's name in vain!"

I hurried to the barn and filled buckets with oats and took them over to the horse stalls. I was overcome with terror as I mixed up some dry feed with a little molasses to give to the cows. I knew what was coming when I returned to the house. I knew my father kept a ping pong paddle in a drawer in the dresser at the back hallway. I knew that

I would have to drop my pants and bend over while he burned my ass up with that paddle.

How could I forget my chores? My chores were always the same. I was supposed to feed and water the horses, cows, pigs and chickens before I came in the house to eat dinner. I had forgotten. I had been so tired when I fell asleep on the back-porch sofa. When I woke up, my mind was foggy and had just forgotten to take care of the animals.

I shelled four dozen ears of corn, added some water to soften it and carried the corn in buckets out to the pigs' troughs behind the barn. The stink of the pig shit and the muddy holes around the pens almost took my breath away. The pigs squealed and fought each other to get to the corn. Pigs were mean. Sometimes they would bite you if you got near their food. The big boar hog ambled over. His huge body swayed like a Conestoga wagon as he made his way to the trough. He was the king of the pig pen, a massive red hog used for breeding. He had huge tusks that stuck out four inches from his mouth. He pushed smaller hogs out of the way as he stuck his dirty nose into the trough. I stayed away from him.

As I walked back into the barn, Buddy Moore drove one of our John Deere tractors inside and parked it in an open space near the tool room. He had apparently worked late out in one of the fields.

"Hey, Johnny boy," he yelled as he climbed down from the tractor. "You a little late gettin yo chores done, ain't ya?"

"Hey Buddy," I yelled back. "I'm in trouble. I fell asleep and forgot my chores."

"Oh shit. Well, I'll help."

"If you could shell some more corn for the chickens. That's all I got to do except the watering."

"Alright then, I can do that," he said as he strode over to the corn sheller.

Buddy's thin arms looked like spindly pine tree limbs as he turned the corn sheller twice as fast as I could. He smoked a cigarette, never touching it as he placed ear after ear into the sheller, turning the handle and watching the kernels be separated from the cobs and fall into the wooden catch bin.

I filled all the animals' water troughs with fresh water and went back inside the barn to get the corn from Buddy to feed the chickens.

"Here ya go, Johnny." He handed me a five-gallon bucket full of corn. "That a enough?"

"That's plenty, Buddy," I said as I lifted the heavy buckets.

"Alright then, I'm gonna mosey on home. I'll see ya in the mornin time."

"Thanks for helping me, Buddy," I said.

I thought to myself as I sprinkled the corn around in the chicken pens. *Buddy Moore really is a good guy. He's always nice to me. Why can't my father be nice and have patience like Buddy Moore?*

As I continued to sprinkle the corn around in the chicken pens, I contemplated the beating I knew I was about to get. Maybe if I told my father I was sick and my brain had just seized up, he would feel sorry for me and wouldn't beat me. But then I thought, when had he ever felt sorry for me? Maybe I could go to Jack and explain what had happened. Jack could talk to him and maybe he wouldn't beat me. Or maybe I could offer to do extra work. But then I thought, hell, when would I ever have time to do extra work?

I thought about what I had said. I had said, "Oh, God!" Though my father took the Lord's name in vain all the time, if one of us kids did it, it was a beating offense. I knew I was about to get a hard beating.

I collected the eggs from the wooden hen house and was careful not to step in chicken shit as I crossed the chicken yard. I had a dozen eggs that I carried in my t-shirt folded over my belly to make a little cradle.

I walked up to the house, dread draped over me like the Spanish moss on the oak trees in the yard.

As I got closer, I could hear Jack talking through the open window in the dining room. Jack was acting as my guardian angel begging my father not to beat me.

"Daddy, he's only eight years old. He's going to forget stuff from time to time," he pleaded. "Why don't you just give him extra work to do tomorrow? Or make him miss a meal. That'll teach him he needs to remember the animals have to eat twice a day. He works hard most of the time. He's a good kid," Jack begged to no avail.

"Bullshit! He's lazy as hell and he doesn't take responsibility. I went to check on him late this afternoon in the corn field and he's laying up against a trailer sleeping when he was supposed to be out there picking up corn. He's got to be taught a lesson. A beating is the only thing he'll understand. I'll whup his butt and make him remember his chores. I'm tired of him goofing off. The little shit needs a peach limb on his ass."

The discussion was over, and Jack walked out the front door and down the road in front of the house. He did not want to be around to hear my screams.

I entered the back door, walked into the dining room where my father was having another piece of pound cake, from a china plate. I announced, "All the feeding is done, and I'm sorry Daddy, I was just so tired I fell asleep and forgot."

"Tired? Tired from what? You ain't done shit all day but goof off. Hell, I bet most of the corn in that trailer was picked up by your sister, a damn little girl. You are lazy and you don't take responsibility. I'm thinking about making you miss your meals for a few days to see how it feels to be real hungry like those animals were. But I think you need a good ass-whupping too!"

"Here, take this knife," he said as he removed his pocketknife from his pants pocket, unfolded it and handed it to me.

"You go out to that peach tree in the front yard and cut me a switch. I want it at least as long as my arm and as big around as this here finger," he said as he held out his index finger.

Tears streamed down my face and I was gripped with terror. I grabbed a flashlight and trudged out to the front yard. I had to climb up the peach tree to find a limb that matched his desired dimensions. I sawed the limb with his pocketknife, shinnied down the tree and headed back to the house, sobbing all the way. I looked to the sky where a million stars danced in the night sky.

"Oh God! Or Jesus, or somebody up there, please help me and make it go by quickly," I mouthed to myself.

As I entered the front door, he directed me towards the back hallway. I handed him the peach tree switch. He inspected it and nodded his approval.

"You take your pants off and bend over and grab that dresser."

I removed my pants and stood there in my underwear and t-shirt, shaking all over and sobbing mournfully.

"Take them skivvies off too, boy! I want you to feel this switch on that naked ass! That'll make you remember them poor animals."

I slipped out of my underwear and leaned over the dresser. He drew the switch back to his shoulder and hit me so hard on my butt that I nearly keeled over. He continued to swing the peach limb moving down from my butt to my thighs and calves. The bumpy growths on the peach tree limb cut into my flesh and stung like a thousand bumble bees. I cried out with each lick while he mumbled something about responsibility and laziness. Blood flowed down both my legs and felt cool on my ankles as my butt and legs burned like the fires of hell.

After what felt like an hour, it was finally over.

He finished the beating with a final swat to my back and said, "Don't you ever forget your chores again, or I will really give you something to cry about."

I picked up my pants and underwear and shuffled off to the bathroom and locked the door. I ran warm water into the tub and slowly eased down into the water. I screamed as the water oozed into my many cuts. It hurt almost as bad as the beating. I trembled, sobbed and cried as I tried to sit in the tub but could only hold myself off the enamel bottom an inch or so and let the water do its wonderous work. I was finally able to sit. I grabbed a wash rag and tried to bathe and soothe the cuts, but it stung too much to touch them. I sat in the warm water for a while and noticed it had become discolored to a rosy pink from the blood. I lay back in the tub and had almost dozed off when I heard a gentle tap on the bathroom door.

"Johnny, let me come in," my mother whispered.

"Go away," I said and turned on the hot water to warm it up again.

"Johnny, let me come in and help you," she whispered once more.

"No, you go away. You coulda stopped him, but you didn't!" I yelled. I thought I heard her sobbing as her gentle footsteps faded away.

I lay in the water until it became cold again. I slowly eased out of the tub, grabbed a towel and gently dabbed at the wounds on my butt and legs. The towel was stained red each time I touched a cut. I yelped as the cloth touched the stinging flesh. When I finally was dried off, I put on a clean pair of underwear and opened the bathroom door. Emma was leaning against the opposite wall. She had some ointment and some cloth strips in her hands.

"Come here, sugar baby, let old Emma fix you up. I be knowin how ta dress some wounds from a beatin; won't be my first time, baby."

I shuffled into my bedroom and closed the door behind me and Emma. I lay down on my stomach and Emma hovered over me.

82

"Honey, take them drawers off. You done got blood all over 'em. I done already seen yo little shiny white ass mo than a few times. Who you thank done changed yo diapers when you wuz a little baby boy? Yo momma wuz always busy cookin and runnin here and there. Old Emma took care a you and changed them diapers and fed you yo bottles and everthin else."

I covered my privates and eased out of my underwear. I couldn't believe the amount of blood that had soaked into the fabric. I thought I had blotted the blood on the bathroom towel, but my ass was apparently still bleeding.

I lay down on my stomach again and Emma began her work. She dabbed each cut with ointment and used her fingers in circular motions to rub the ointment into the wounds. It didn't hurt as much as I thought it would, but the stinging made me wince and yelp a few times. When she finished applying the ointment, she cut strips of cloth, folded them over to make extra padding and taped them horizontally across each wound.

"Alright honey chile, you almost good as new!" she exclaimed. "Git yo'self some sleep now. And you walk out thar tomorrow wit yo head held high. You dun took yo beatin and it ain't kilt ya. You do yo chores and go on 'bout yo bizness and you gonna be fine."

"Thank you, Emma," I said. "I love you, Emma."

"I love you too, child," she said with a broad smile as she closed the door.

I lay in my bed on my stomach and thought about the day's events. Yes, I had screwed up, but I did not deserve the beating I got. I thought Emma and Jack were the only ones in my family who really loved me and understood me. And poor Emma wasn't even allowed to eat inside our house. I prayed to God and to Jesus that I would heal soon and wouldn't forget my chores anymore. I prayed for my family, well most of my family. I prayed that one member of my family would burn in hell.

# CHAPTER 17

The next morning was a Saturday. No school but plenty of work in the fields. When I woke, my butt and legs were still burning. I turned over on my side and faced the wall. I hoped I could stay in bed a little while longer. A few minutes later I felt my mother sit down on the edge of my bed.

"How ya feelin, baby?" she asked. "It's about time to get up. Your daddy wants you and Betty Jane to go back to the corn field this morning. Then this afternoon, he wants you moving the peanut trailers and Betty Jane's gonna come back home to help me and Emma with some canning. Go ahead and get up."

I wasn't sure I could walk. Although my beating had been concentrated on my butt and legs, I hurt all over. I eased out of bed and stood for a minute to get my balance. I was thrilled that I would be moving peanut trailers in the afternoon but wasn't sure if I could sit on the seat of the tractor.

I fixed myself a sausage and biscuit and headed out to the barn to get the feeding and watering done. The sun was peeking over the horizon in the east. The sky was a bright blue with just a hint of pink spreading like waves rolling onto the beach. The air was crisp and cool in the early morning, and normally it would have made me feel energetic. But this morning was a different feeling. I felt very sore and very sad.

When I finished my chores, I hooked up a trailer to one of the John Deere tractors. I found an old cushion in the barn and placed it on the seat of the tractor. It helped a little, but my ass still burned. As I was pulling out of the barn, I saw Jack drive into the yard in one of our pickup trucks. I stopped the tractor and waited for him.

"Hey bud," he called out as he got out of the truck and came over to me.

"How ya feelin this morning?"

"How do you think I'm feelin? My ass hurts and my legs are still bleeding; I feel like shit."

"Hey, hey," he said as he climbed up onto the tractor, squared my shoulders and then hugged me. "I'm sorry buddy. I begged him not to beat you. He doesn't realize sometimes that you are only eight years old and you just forget things. You gotta try real hard not to piss him off."

"The fact that I'm alive pisses him off."

"Oh, that's not true! He just wants to teach you responsibility and he thinks you don't respect him."

"Well, the dumbass finally got one thing right—I don't respect him. I hate him."

I pushed Jack away and started the tractor.

"I got work to do," I said. "If I don't get the corn picked up, I'll get another beating."

I caught a glance of Jack shaking his head as he walked away. I shouldn't have sounded off to him. It wasn't his fault. He was the only friend I had.

I drove the tractor up to the house and yelled for Betty Jane to come on. She came out carrying two Mason jars filled with ice water. The ice jiggled against the glass and made musical clicking sounds as she ran down the steps. She climbed into the back of the empty trailer, and we were off to another fun-filled morning in the corn field.

The dew glistened like icicles on the weeds as I stopped the tractor at the end of the rows where we had finished yesterday. The bright morning sun was as yellow as a sunflower as it tried to rise above the pine trees in the woods nearby. About fifteen hands were already at work as we draped our sacks around our necks and trudged into the field.

"Glad y'all could make it before noon," some random voice yelled from the field. This was followed by howls and laughter amongst the workers.

"Shut yo mouth, boy!" one of the older black women yelled as she stood up and waved good morning to us.

"Least they's out here a workin," she said. "Most white folks' kids would be settin back in the house or runnin round playin. Mr. Calvin makes all a his young-uns work dees crops. He works them hard too."

*Well, thanks for that observation*, I thought to myself. Yes, old Calvin Reynolds is an equal-opportunity abuser.

It was mid-morning and the sun was again surprisingly brutal for October. My pale blue shirt turned a deep blue from the sweat it had soaked up. Betty Jane and I had been up and down about a dozen corn rows and were finding a lot of corn the combines had missed. Luckily, we had just finished a water break and had started new rows when my father pulled up in his truck. He climbed out and came over to the trailer, looked inside and then out at us. He didn't say anything but shook his head in disgust and walked over to the other trailers the hands were using and checked their progress.

"Y'all need to step it up out here!" he yelled out to the hands. "I want y'all to finish up this field today. The combines will be done with the south field this afternoon and I want y'all over there tomorrow. We gonna work all day Sunday. Got to get this corn up before the rain comes in. Y'all get movin now! Git ya thumbs outta your asses and get to work!"

*Nice pep talk, Daddy*, I thought to myself.

He was walking back towards his pickup when I heard it—the unmistakable sound of a rattlesnake. I couldn't see it, but I heard the shake of its tail like Mexican maracas as he lifted it into the air and warned us to stay away.

"Rattlesnake!" I yelled at the top of my lungs, and then jumped back from where I was standing.

I saw movement off to my left a few feet away and then I saw it. It was huge. It was a diamondback rattlesnake, coiled to strike and rattling like it was really pissed off. Its fat head moved slowly back and forth gauging where to strike. Betty Jane screamed and started running towards the end of the row. As I stood there frozen in place, the snake made a strike at me. It was about six feet in length and its strike extended its body about four feet into the air directly at my legs. It missed me by a foot, and I jumped up and tried to run but stumbled and fell.

I heard my father yelling and saw him removing a shotgun from the rack behind the seat in his truck. He ran towards me yelling for me to get out of the way. He did not have to repeat his request as I stumbled to my feet and ran as fast as I could towards the safety of the truck.

A loud *BOOM* echoed across the field.

"I got that bastard!" he yelled as he bent over and picked up the snake.

Most of the rattlesnake's head was missing but his body was still wiggling as he lifted it up to show us and the field hands who were honking and squealing like a flock of geese.

"This sucker's six feet long!" he shouted as the snake continued to wiggle. "I'm gonna take him home and skin him. This skin will make a nice belt."

He walked towards us holding the wiggling snake out to his side. Blood dripped from the fleshy pulp that was the remainder of the snake's head. He reached down and grabbed the snake's tail and pulled the rattlers up so that he could count them.

"He's got twenty rattlers; that means he's twenty years old!" he shouted.

He threw the huge snake into the back of the truck, unloaded the empty shell from the shotgun, reloaded it and hung it back in the gun rack.

"Hey, Mr. Calvin, you gonna skin that snake?" asked an older black woman named Maymie who had waddled over to the truck.

"Shore am, Maymie. Gonna go do it right now up at the barn while he's fresh."

"Rattlesnake meat make some good eatin. I'd luv to git that meat if you ain't gone do nuthin wit it."

"Come on and git in the back of the truck. You can help me skin it."

"Y'all young-uns git back to work now," yelled Maymie to her brood of kids who were staring at her from the corn field. "We gone have snake meat for dinner," she yelled as she struggled to get her ample body into the back of the pickup.

"Y'all be careful out there now!" my father yelled leaning out the window of the truck.

"He's probably got a mate out there somewhere or maybe some little ones."

He turned the truck around in the corn field, a trail of dust following it as he sped away.

"Oh great!" I said to Betty Jane. "One more thing to worry about."

"I know," she said. "I'm afraid to go back in the field."

"That snake's whole family will be gunnin for us now," I said.

We headed back down the corn rows, looking carefully before stooping to grab a corn stalk and flinching at every sound.

Sweat ran down my back, over my butt and down my legs, stinging the cuts from my beating. I suffered through it for a couple more hours, and then it was time for lunch.

Betty Jane was glad to be helping my mother with canning in the afternoon, while I was glad to be moving the peanut trailers around.

Lunch that day was a disappointment. My mother's usual fabulous lunch was not on display. It consisted of ham sandwiches and Jell-O for dessert. She and Emma were busy canning green beans, stewed tomatoes and peaches. She had no time to prepare our usual meat, bread and several vegetables.

My father was disappointed also and let my mother know it.

"Dorothy, what kinda damn lunch is this?"

Surprisingly she stood up to him. "You want to be without vegetables and peaches in the winter?"

"Naw, but I wanna good lunch on a Saturday when we're working, not a damn sandwich," he grumbled. "We got a lot a work to do. Ain't gonna get much energy from a damn sandwich."

"Then eat two or eat three sandwiches. Eat four sandwiches for all I care," she said. "Me and Emma got canning to do."

She turned on her heel and went about her canning.

Emma and I turned our heads where my father couldn't see us and giggled at each other.

I waited to see if my father would do his impression of Mount Vesuvius erupting. But he just grabbed two sandwiches, shook his head and stormed out the door. Way to go, Mom! Conflict avoided, nobody wounded . . . until next time.

# CHAPTER 18

MARTINSVILLE, GEORGIA
PRESENT TIME

I stepped over to the recliner where Lucas was slouched, reached out and touched his neck. There was no pulse. His skin was cold. His neck was cocked sideways and had turned a grayish purple. The blood had dried to a flakey garnet on his face, neck and shirt. A green blow fly lit on his forehead near the hole in his temple. I shooed it away, but it circled and returned. A foul odor permeated the living room and hung like a hot air balloon.

Lucas' eyes were open, staring at the ceiling. Not frightened, not calm, just there, cold and staring. Tiny blood tails bulged throughout. I looked in his lap and on the floor, but saw no gun. My first thought was suicide, but where was the gun? I felt along his sides and down into the recliner. No gun. I was frozen, staring at the hole in his temple. It seemed so round and neat. Not like other gunshot wounds I had seen while serving as an assistant district attorney in Atlanta. I had responded to many murder scenes, and it seemed as though the gunshots always tore the skin or made a jagged hole in the skull. This one was pristine, too neat, just a small hole and a thin trail of blood leading down Lucas' face and neck.

I looked around. There were no signs of a struggle. His living room was the same as when I saw it yesterday. It was messy: yellowed papers stacked on a ragged sofa, a table full of old magazines, beer cans sitting on the floor and a dusty table holding a small lamp. I looked on the floor behind his chair to see if a gun may have fallen under it. I was greeted by a nauseating stench rising from the floor. His bowels had collapsed and emptied. Blow flies were gathering in earnest now. I needed some air.

I walked out to the front porch, took out my cell phone and called the police.

"Sheriff's office," lilted a female voice.

"Yes, my name is John Reynolds and I think I just discovered a homicide," I said. "I'm over on Alcorn Street at Lucas McDougal's house and he's been shot."

"Oh my gosh," said the voice. "Well, you just stand by there now and I'll send a deputy. Stay on the line please and let me get some information."

I could hear her talking on the radio in the background as she dispatched a deputy to the scene.

When she came back on, she asked the exact address, got my name and address and told me not to touch anything and wait outside until the deputy arrived.

I didn't obey. I walked back into the house and looked around. Nothing seemed to be disturbed. A green blow fly settled onto Lucas' forehead. I swatted it away again and walked into the kitchen. The back door was open, and flies were swarming around the kitchen, dive-bombing a frying pan on the stove that held a couple of strips of fish in grease that had congealed. I started to close the door, but thought better of it. I probably shouldn't touch anything in the house. I knew a fingerprint team would be coming with the deputy.

I went back into the front room and looked at Lucas again.

"You just couldn't talk to me last night, could you, Lucas?" He didn't answer. I touched his arm. It was stiff and difficult to move. Rigor mortis had set in. He had been dead for several hours.

I heard a police siren and thought it wise to wait out on the front porch. As I stepped out the front door, I saw two sheriff's cars turn on to Alcorn Street with lights and sirens going full blast.

A young deputy got out of the first car, placing his hand on his holstered gun, and said, "Sir, you want to step down off the porch and come over here."

"Sure," I said.

A silver name tag on his brown shirt indicated his name was Rathburn. The other deputy was rather obese and much older. He slowly exited his vehicle and came towards us not touching his gun but sizing me up as he approached. Rathburn asked me for my ID and then asked what had happened here.

I explained that I had come over to talk with Lucas McDougal and had observed him slouched down in his recliner. I had opened the front door and stepped inside and that is when I observed a bullet hole in his left temple.

"Okay, sir, you wait out here with Deputy Milam while I go take a look," he said. "Is there anyone else inside the house?" he asked.

"No," I said.

He handed the other deputy my license.

Deputy Milam started writing down my information, and then asked, "Did you know Lucas McDougal and why were you here to see him?"

"He used to work for my dad. I've known him for years," I explained. "I came over here to talk to him about my dad who just passed away. I was here for his funeral yesterday and just wanted to chat some with Lucas. He didn't answer the door and I looked in and saw him slouched down in his chair. The front door was unlocked, so I stepped inside and called out to him. That's when I saw the gunshot wound."

Deputy Rathburn came back out said, "Guy's got a gunshot to the head. Could be suicide, but I didn't see a gun. Could be up under him though. I'm gonna get on the radio and get the crime techs rolling and call the detectives. I don't think we ought to go back in until they get here."

He sat in the front seat of his cruiser and made the calls on the vehicle's radio.

When he exited, he came back over to me and stood with his hands on his hips. Deputy Milam explained to Rathburn how I had found Lucas and why I was here to see him. He gave me back my license and asked what I did in Atlanta. I told him that I was an attorney and repeated that I had been in Martinsville for my father's funeral.

"A lawyer, huh," commented Rathburn. "Did you touch anything in there?"

"I don't think so. Maybe the front door handle. I opened the front door and went inside. Then I walked back to the kitchen and saw the back door was open, but I didn't touch anything."

"Well, you're probably gonna have to go down to the station and give 'em a set of your fingerprints. And I'm sure the detectives will want to talk to you about why you were out here to talk with a guy, then found him dead. You're a lawyer; you know the drill."

"That's fine," I said, dreading the time it would take when I had so much to do.

Twenty minutes later, two detectives arrived in a black unmarked car. One was a very large man in his forties, stretching the seams of his pale blue dress shirt as he approached. His face was red, and he was perspiring profusely. The other detective was probably in his fifties and was thin as a rail, or I should say, as thin as his tie, which was about an inch wide and had gone out of style twenty years ago. The older guy had the saddest eyes I had ever seen, and I noticed he had the nicotine-stained fingers of a heavy smoker.

Rathburn filled them in for a few minutes and then brought them over to me for introductions. The big guy was Detective Post, and the skinny one was named Harrison. They nodded and told me they would talk with me shortly.

They went inside accompanied by Rathburn. Deputy Milam stayed outside with me and made small talk about the weather and the Atlanta Braves. I got the feeling I was a suspect and he was babysitting me to make sure I didn't disappear. I sat on the hood of my car, swatted flies, gnats and mosquitoes and twiddled my thumbs while thinking of Lucas.

I was quite sure Lucas' untimely death was no coincidence. I wanted to talk with him about the bad business my father had mentioned. But now he was dead. I thought about the two men I saw talking with him at my sister's house after the funeral. They looked creepy. I also thought about the conversation I had with Lucas. He had said we needed to let sleeping dogs lie. Maybe someone was making sure sleeping dogs would keep on sleeping by putting a bullet in Lucas' head. I wondered how much of this I should tell the detectives when they interviewed me. But what did I really know? My father had been mixed up in something thirty years ago and Lucas knew about it. But what? And could it have anything to do with my brother's disappearance?

I made the decision that I wasn't going to tell them anything. I had already told them I had wanted to talk with Lucas about my dad; I was just reminiscing. I guess I could tell them about the two creepy guys driving the black Suburban. I could say I saw Lucas talking to them and they were kind of suspicious. They never came in the house that night. Maybe Lucas owed them money. I would tell them that, but nothing more.

A white panel truck pulled up behind my car. "Crime Scene" was written in green lettering on the sides of the truck. A male and a female technician wearing gray uniforms got out of the vehicle carrying suitcase-sized satchels. They both nodded to me and Deputy Milam.

"What we got, Tony?" the male asked Milam.

"Gotta white male stiff. I understand he's got a GSW to the head," said Milam.

"Self-inflicted or somebody do him?" asked the technician.

"Don't know; ain't been in there," said Milam.

The technicians entered the house, letting the front door bang shut behind them. I heard muffled talk within the house but could not understand what was being said.

A few minutes later a black station wagon from the medical examiner's office arrived. A stout older gentleman wearing a white dress shirt and khakis held up with red suspenders exited the vehicle from the passenger side. I assumed this was the ME. The driver, a young black male, exited also, and they both nodded to us and approached Deputy Milam.

"Hey, doc," said Milam. "They got one for you inside. GSW to the head, guy named Lucas McDougal."

"I know Lucas," the man said. "He used to help me with some odd jobs. Older guy, right?" he asked.

"I guess that's him," said Milam. "I didn't know him."

The ME and his assistant headed for the front door of Lucas' house. Deputy Milam continued to keep his eyes on me and made more small talk. Then we got in a contest to see who could swat the most flies, gnats and mosquitoes. I thought I was winning. He didn't seem to care as much. I guess when you lived in South Georgia, you got used to it. I was glad I didn't live here because the damn things were driving me nuts. How could you stay outside around here? I didn't remember the mosquitoes and flies being this bad when I was a child growing up here.

But I did remember the gnats. The little devils weren't much bigger than a pin head, but they would drive you nuts, buzzing around your eyes and crawling in your ears and up your nose.

I guess the bugs were bad because we were standing near the edge of a swamp. Lucas had picked a terrible place for his abode. I heard a gator croak out in the swamp. It sounded like a loud burp. A white egret stood on one leg and stabbed a fish with its missile-like beak. The bream were chasing minnows in the shallows, swirling the water and occasionally breaking the surface in their efforts to secure lunch. The swamp was alive . . . but Lucas wasn't. I started to feel bad about his death. Had I caused it? Maybe someone was watching me yesterday as I questioned him and wanted to make sure he didn't tell me anything. This was getting serious. What the hell had my dad been involved in?

After a half hour had passed, my thoughts were interrupted by the banging front door. The two detectives walked down the front steps and headed for me. Both were removing blue plastic gloves.

"Mr. Reynolds," the burly one said, "we're gonna have you come down to the sheriff's office for an interview. We need to get a statement from you. We'll probably take your prints, too, since you were all over the house in there."

"That's fine," I said. "But I didn't go all over the house and I only touched the front door."

"A little hostile, ain't ya?" asked the detective. "Rathburn said you looked around in the house and determined no one else wuz in there. He also said you wuz a lawyer from Atlanta."

"No, I'm not hostile. I just didn't go all over the house. I only looked in the kitchen and saw the back door was ajar. And I didn't touch anything. I assumed no one else was in the house because I didn't hear any noises."

"We'll git to all that down at the office," he said. "We want you to ride down there with us," he said pointing to the black unmarked vehicle.

I started in that direction but was told to hold on while one of the detectives had me lean over the hood of the car while he patted me down for weapons. Once he determined that I was not carrying any rocket-propelled grenades or other deadly weapons, I was directed to the back seat of the vehicle. The burly detective climbed into the back seat with me. I guess I was the prime suspect, and he wanted to make sure I didn't take off.

# CHAPTER 19

The ride to the sheriff's office was uneventful and awfully quiet. The detectives did not talk to me or to each other. Once we arrived at their office, I was offered coffee or a "soft drink" as the deputy called it. I declined and was placed in an interview room containing only a table and three chairs. There were no windows and I was certain the room was wired for sound and had a two-way mirror.

After thirty minutes of twiddling my thumbs and counting the ceiling tiles, the door opened and the two detectives entered the room.

"Mr. Reynolds, we want to talk with you some about how you found Mr. McDougal and what your purpose was for visiting him this morning," said Detective Post. "But before we can do that, we have to advise you of your rights and we do that with a written waiver of rights form," he said as he placed a blank form on the table and took a seat opposite me.

"I'll be glad to talk with you and tell you what I know, but I'm not signing anything and I'm not waiving any of my rights," I said.

"I guess you being a lawyer and all, you think we might be trying to trick you," he said.

"No, I'm quite sure you're not going to trick me," I replied. "But I'm not signing anything and I'm not waiving my rights. That's the advice I give my clients and it's good advice for me also. Unless you consider me a suspect and are prepared to charge me with something, there's no need for me to be advised of my rights."

"Well, it's just standard procedure and all," he said.

"Well, my standard procedure is to not sign anything and I'm quite familiar with the Miranda warnings," I said. "I'm a former assistant district attorney, so you don't have to do that with me. I'll talk to you; I have nothing to hide. In fact, I want to be as helpful as I can. Lucas was a friend of my family and I want to find out who put a bullet in his head. So, let's begin."

Detective Post sighed, turned the form over and took out a legal pad. "State your name, occupation, home address and phone number," he said.

For the next hour, I explained how Lucas had worked for my father for many years, how I was just in town for the funeral and wanted to chat with him. I had come to his house around nine this morning and found him dead. I did not mention my previous night's visit as I did not want to bring up my father's *bad business* years ago. I did tell him about seeing Lucas talking with two men outside my sister's house and they were driving a black Suburban. I described the two guys as best I could, but pointed out that it had been dark and I had not seen them well. I kept my answers short and to the point and did not speculate.

When asked, I also told them I had no idea who would want to kill Lucas and knew nothing about any of his debts or trouble he had with anyone. I got the distinct feeling they thought I was not telling them everything I knew, and they were correct. But then I didn't know enough about my father's past to know if it might be related to Lucas' death. They concluded the interview and had me give a set of my fingerprints to one of their crime-scene technicians and write a short statement about finding Lucas.

It was past two when the detectives dropped me off at my car. The Crime Scene van was gone. I was starving and called Betty Jane to fill her in and inquire about lunch. She was shocked about Lucas' death and wanted to know if it had anything to do with me going to see him yesterday. I told her that was the million-dollar question and I didn't have the answer but would be able to think better after eating.

She had lunch prepared for me when I arrived: a huge ham sandwich slathered with mustard and mayonnaise, potato salad, fresh sliced tomatoes, sweet gherkin pickles and a tall glass of iced tea. She mentioned I could have peach cobbler or banana pudding for dessert. Oh Lord, I was going to gain ten pounds from all this good food.

Between bites of my lunch, I told her about finding Lucas and my interview with the detectives. I also told her about my belief that someone didn't want me talking with Lucas or poking into things that had happened on Riverdale Plantation years ago.

My sister expressed her opinion that this was all too much: Daddy's death, having to clean out his house, sell everything, dealing with his will and now worrying about Lucas' murder. She thought she might have a nervous breakdown. I told her to hang in there; I would have a breakdown for both of us if I didn't get some answers about all this. Now bring on that banana pudding!

As I was finishing lunch, I thought of Emma Jackson, our former housekeeper.

"Sis, is Emma Jackson still alive?" I asked.

"As far as I know she is. I haven't seen her in several months. She was mighty feeble when I saw her at the grocery store a while back. I talked with her a little. I could barely understand her. She spoke in a whisper; her voice was so gravelly. She's got to be in her late eighties or maybe ninety by now."

"Does she still live in that little block house over by River Road?" I asked.

"As far as I know, unless she's moved to a nursing home somewhere."

Emma used to live with us during the week when I was growing up and would return to her little block house in town on the weekends. She was notorious for knowing what was going on at our farm and all over town. Maybe she would remember something from back then. It would be good to see her. I had last seen her at my mom's funeral. She had been very feeble then, and that was years ago. I had given her a big hug and noticed she was skin and bones, withering away with age. I had loved her and considered her a member of our family. Maybe she could provide some answers or point me in the right direction . . . if she was still alive.

# CHAPTER 20

It was almost four when I arrived at Emma Jackson's house. It was a small cement block home sitting well off the street. It looked smaller than I remembered. Huge live oak trees draped with Spanish moss guarded the home on all sides. A concrete walkway led up to the front steps. Camellias and roses grew on either side of the walkway. Their fragrant blooms reminded me of my mother's yards. Blue and pink hydrangeas lapped against the low wood on the sides of the porch. An ancient black woman with hair as white as cotton sat in the front porch swing, easing slowly back and forth. As I approached the porch, I thought she might be dozing. But when my feet touched the steps, she turned her head slowly, looked me over and then burst into a big grin.

"Lord have mercy! Dar come my baby, lil Johnny Reynolds all growed up," she said in a raspy voice.

She had a large lump almost as big as a ping pong ball below her lower lip where I was sure she had a portion of snuff. Emma always dipped snuff and carried a coffee can around with her to spit when needed. She leaned over to her left, produced a blue Maxwell House coffee can and spit into it as she struggled to raise up from the swing.

"Hey, Emma," I said, tears streaming down my face. "It's good to see you."

"Come here, honey chile, give yo old Emma a hug," she whispered, tears streaming down her face also. She struggled to stand, reached for me and fell into my arms.

I hugged her and held her close to me for a full minute, a hundred memories of sweet Emma flowing over me, of Emma being there for me and loving me. She touched my face and wiped away my tears like she had done so many times before. I helped her ease back into the swing noting she was frail as a baby bird and almost as light. Her snow-white hair was missing patches in a couple of places and her arms looked like the spiny little limbs on our peach trees back at Riverdale. The whites of her eyes weren't white but yellow now with minute red lines like state roads marked on highway maps running in all directions. Both of her eyes looked cloudy, their sparkling blue gone years ago. But her golden smile was the same, and she still had most of her teeth. Her lavender house dress clung to her frail frame and seemed two sizes too big for her.

"It's sho good to see you too, baby!" she said. "I didn't try to go to yo daddy's funeral. I been pretty sick lately and I figured Mr. Cal wouldn't want me there no way. He'd probably jump outta that casket if'n he saw old Emma standin der amongst all them white folks."

She gave a throaty laugh at the thought of that scene. I laughed too and thought of all the times Emma had stood up to him in her quiet determined way. She knew my mother would back her, and she knew all the kids loved her and got upset when he talked down to her.

"I figured you's a comin to bury yo daddy. I know y'all fought like two cats tied up in croaker sack. But I knowed you's a good boy and you'd do what was right. Thass the right thang, to come bury yo daddy and let bygones be bygones. But, Lordy, that man treated you mighty bad. I'd a liked to a kicked his white ass a few times when he wuz beatin you. And Lord, I loved yo mama. Miss Dorothy, now that wuz a good woman. She treated me like a member a yo family. I sho do miss her."

I sat down in a rickety wooden chair close to Emma's swing and thought about what I wanted to ask her. Emma loved to gossip, and she knew everything that was happening at Riverdale. Maybe she knew something about my father's troubles. We talked about old times for a while, and then I plunged ahead with what I had come to ask her.

"Emma, can I ask you about some things that happened when we were living at Riverdale?"

"Shore, baby, if'n I can remember. But my old brain done got mighty feeble now. Can't member all that done happened, but I'll try."

"Emma, about the time Jack disappeared, Daddy was having some financial trouble Do you remember anything about that? Or anything about him getting mixed up with some bad people?"

"I don't much know nothin 'bout no money problems and no bad peoples."

She moved slowly back and forth and the swing creaked.

"My Isaac got in a little trouble and yo daddy bailed him out. He drank a little too much and got picked up one night. Mr. Cal had to bail him outta the jail."

A smile widened on her face as she thought of her deceased husband.

"Isaac wuz a good man. He'd help anybody. He dun a lotta work for Mr. Cal. He could fix anythang."

"Yes, I remember."

"You know they found him up there up thar in an alley in Atlanta. Shot in the back. They said he done got robbed. I don't know even what he was a doin up thar."

Emma looked up at the sky and small rivulets of tears flowed down her face. Her hands trembled as she took her sleeve and wiped her face and eyes. She mumbled softly, something about Isaac, and then looked at me but couldn't speak. I sat down in the swing with her and put my arm around her.

"I'm sorry Emma, I shouldn't have made you think of Isaac."

"It's alright. honey chile," she said. "It is what it is. We can't go back and change what done happened back then. I jest hope the Lord had mercy on Isaac and took him upstairs and not dun sent him down below. He wuz a good man. He treated me good. Even tho I couldn't give him no young-uns, he stood by me. Thass why I luved y'all so much. I couldn't have no young-uns of my own. So I tried to take care of ya like you wuz my own."

Emma sniffled and cried some more as we sat quietly in the creaking wooden swing. I wanted to ask her more about my father and Isaac, but I didn't have the heart to press her for details. Emma regained control of her emotions and patted my knee. I gave Emma another big hug and rose from the swing. I reached in my wallet and took out three $100 bills plus a few twenties and gave them to her.

"Here Emma, here's a little something to help with groceries or to buy something you need," I said as I curled the money into her boney hands.

"Aw baby, you don have ta give me nothin," she said as she tried to push the money back to me. "I git by jest fine on my lil goverment check. An I can use my EBT card up at the IGA store."

"I know. I just want to help you a little bit," I said. "You always took care of me and I love you Emma, and I'd like to help you a little bit."

"Alwright den baby," she mumbled as she pushed the money into her bosom and started to swing again. "You know I luv ya too, baby. Come back ta see me now," she rasped.

Tears again streamed down my face as I drove away. The hard-ass, take-no-prisoners barrister had turned into a crying sponge after only two days in Martinsville. I had to pull myself together. I had to find a cassette player and find out what was on the tapes my father had left me.

After I drove away, Emma Jackson slowly made her way around her house and into her backyard. She passed between two huge live oak trees covered in green moss. She took exactly six steps past the trees and got down on her knees. She scraped away the leaves and twigs and dug into an inch of loose soil. She scraped the dirt off the lid of a five-gallon bucket buried snugly in the dirt. She pried on the lid until it popped off. She took the money from her bosom and placed it in the can on top of hundreds of other $100 bills already in the can.

Her man Isaac had always taken care of her.

# CHAPTER 21

**D**riving back to my sister's house, I remembered I was supposed to have dinner with Susan Regan at seven o'clock. I would never make it by the time I got a shower and got dressed. I called Susan and told her I would be running about thirty minutes late and sped to Betty Jane's house. After showering and changing clothes in world-record time, I kissed my sister goodbye and literally jumped into my Mercedes. When I arrived at Susan's house, I half-ran to her front door. As I was about to ring the bell, I remembered I did not bring a bottle of wine. "Well, damn!" I said loudly as Susan opened the door.

"Well, hopefully that was because you're glad to see me, but that sounded like frustration," she said laughing and reaching up to kiss my cheek.

"I'm sorry, I had meant to bring a bottle of wine and I was rushing and forgot it," I explained.

"Don't worry about it. I've got plenty of wine and whatever else you'd like," she said, her Southern accent more pronounced than I'd remembered.

She looked incredible. She was wearing a very short sleeveless sun dress with spaghetti straps. The dress had a blue floral design and swirled as she moved. Her tanned skin seemed to sparkle as she invited me to have a seat and asked if red wine was okay. I would have preferred bourbon but told her wine would be great as I settled into a plush white sofa. As I looked around Susan's living room, I could see her personality in the furnishings. Everything was airy and light with splashes of color making it feel warm and comfortable yet elegant. She handed me a glass of wine and joined me on the sofa.

"I guess you've been busy helping Betty Jane sort through your daddy's things," she commented.

"Yes, we spent some time at his house yesterday and looked in his safe deposit boxes," I said. "He made me the executor of his estate, so I guess I'll have to spend some time down here getting everything organized for probate."

"Then maybe I'll get to see you more," she said, her eyes sparkling and a mischievous smile forming on her face.

"Yes, that would be nice," I said, remembering the wonderful time we had spent together when she visited me in Atlanta.

As I tasted my wine, little chill bumps formed on my arms as I thought of what an eager lover Susan had been. I was hoping we could re-visit those times after dinner.

We chatted for a while, and then Susan finished her wine, popped up from the sofa, took my hand and guided me towards the kitchen as she said, "Come help me with the steaks. I've got a couple of ribeyes ready for the grill."

She handed me a platter holding the steaks and guided me onto her back patio where the grill was smoking. Her backyard was beautifully landscaped. Red, yellow and white gladiolas in full bloom guarded the brick patio. Azaleas, gardenias, camelias and several other verdant shrubs bordered a stone pathway leading to a white gazebo at the rear of the huge backyard. A lush Bermuda lawn covered the entire yard and was manicured like Augusta National. Several huge magnolia trees dotted the yard, and the fragrance from their large white blossoms reminded me of the dozens in our yard at Riverdale.

I raised the lid on the grill and was covered with white smoke from the charcoal fire. No gas for this girl; she preferred charcoal in the grill like I did. Susan handed me a pair of tongs and I put the ribeyes on the fire, noticing one was small and the other huge. I would never be able to eat the ribeye I was about to cook. Susan could have steak sandwiches for three days with what I would have to leave. The steaks sizzled as the flames touched the raw meat, and I closed the lid on the grill. Susan went inside, but quickly returned with the bottle of wine and re-filled both our glasses. I wasn't much of a wine connoisseur, but it was good and I enjoyed sipping it as I watched the smoke from the grill swirl around us. She put her arm around my waist and leaned into me as we stood there in front of the grill for a few minutes. I put our wine glasses on the grill's sideboard and turned towards her. I put my arms around her, pulled her towards me and kissed her gently at first and then harder as she responded to me. We embraced for a few minutes, and then I told her I was probably burning the steaks and let her go. Neither of us wanted to let go but we decided to put our passion on hold until after dinner.

The steaks were cooked perfectly if I do say so: medium rare for me and medium for her. She had prepared a terrific garden salad. She also had fresh green beans and huge baked potatoes. We ate slowly as we reminisced about our childhood and school days in Martinsville.

"How could you ever have dated me in high school?" I asked her. "I was so skinny and had big ears that stuck out like a taxicab going down the street with both doors open. And you were blonde and beautiful. You could have dated any boy you wanted in high school."

"That's not true," said Susan. "You were cute and so shy. You were kind and thoughtful and so smart. You were intense and serious. You knew what you wanted, and no one was going to stop you from getting it, especially your father. That really appealed to me. After we talked a few times and had a couple of classes together, I had this giant crush on you. But I could never get you to ask me out on a date. I dropped several hints and had to practically ask you out."

"I didn't ask you out because I knew a geek like me had no chance with you. But I loved talking with you and tried to be around you whenever I could. Then my senior year came around, and I had three classes with you. I followed you around like a puppy and finally got up the nerve to ask you out. I eased up to you while you were putting some books in your locker. Do you remember what I said?"

"Susan, would ya like to go to the picture show with me Friday night?"

"You smiled and said, 'Sure.' I almost fainted and just stood there. I couldn't think of anything else to say."

"Oh, I remember, you were so cute. We went to see a James Bond movie. I wanted you to hold hands with me, but you never did until our third date. You wanted to be the perfect gentleman, and I was dying to kiss you. In fact, I think I initiated our first kiss. We were saying good night on my front doorstep and I leaned over and kissed you on the lips. Then you stood there kissing me again and again until my mom flicked on the porch light. Seems like we progressed pretty fast after that as I recall."

"We were together every Friday and Saturday night unless my father had some farm work going on," I said. "I remember the first time we parked in the woods near our farm, getting into the back seat of that old Chevrolet of mine. I couldn't figure out how to get your bra off and you had to show me."

"But I didn't let you go much further," she said. "I wanted to but I didn't want you to think bad of me, so I made you wait a few dates, letting you go a little further each time. Then we finally made love."

"Oh, I remember," I said, blushing.

"The first time you were gentle and sweet, but didn't know what to do. But we got better as we got some practice."

"We sure did," I said.

Susan eased out of her chair, kissed me and snuggled down by me.

After another passionate kiss, Susan stood and announced, "I've got chocolate cake for dessert; we can have it now or wait if you prefer."

"Let's wait, but I'll be glad to help you clean up the kitchen."

"No, no, it won't take me five minutes to stick a few things in the dishwasher and I'll join you. I've got Wild Turkey and Old Forrester on the bar, and there's ice in the bucket beneath the bar. Go make yourself a drink and put a little Crown Royal and ginger ale in a tall glass for me."

I found the ice bucket, glasses and the liquor on the bar, and chose Wild Turkey with a little splash of ginger ale for myself and then fixed Susan's drink. I was just placing them on a coffee table in front of the sofa when Susan came out of the kitchen and headed upstairs.

"I'm gonna get comfortable," she called out.

I sipped the smooth bourbon and thought about how life with Susan every day would be. She was a sweet lady, but I had a lot on my mind and I had a hell of lot to do over the next several days. I thought about my father's letter and about my brother Jack. They had to be connected. Some of those bad people my father got mixed up with had to have been involved with Jack. I was determined to get some answers. I had to find a recorder that would play my father's tapes.

"I put some music on," said Susan as she came down the stairs. "I know you love Leonard Cohen and I have a couple of his CDs."

I could hear the up-tempo base and a tenor sax as the first notes of "Tower of Song" started to play. Susan was correct—Leonard Cohen was my favorite and I had played all of his CDs as I had driven down from Atlanta. Susan came from around the staircase and sat close to me on the sofa. She was barefooted and had changed into a flimsy short nightshirt with Japanese designs. The nightshirt had a deep-cut V-neck and her ample breasts were halfway exposed.

"Hope you don't mind me getting comfortable," she said as she reached for her drink and tucked her feet underneath her.

"Not at all," I said as I leaned back and enjoyed my drink and the view.

We enjoyed each other's company and Leonard Cohen. It was a very nice time, and I was more relaxed than I had been in days. We shared easy conversation, knowing we had plenty of time and that we would be enjoying each other upstairs soon. I told Susan a little about my father's letter. That's when it hit me!

"Holy shit!" I said as I put my drink down. "My father had a recorder in his office. It was in a bookcase behind his desk. I just remembered seeing it there as I thought about the letter. He was using it for a book end on one of the upper shelves."

"What? Why do you need a recorder?" she asked.

I explained that my father had left me some tape recordings and I had been trying to find something in which to play them.

"I need to run over there and get that recorder," I said.

"Now? Why do you have to go now? Can't it wait until morning?"

"I'm sorry Susan, I need to go get that recorder right now."

"Okay, I'll go with you. Let me go get dressed."

She appeared moments later in a t-shirt and jeans, and we headed outside to my car.

# CHAPTER 22

had to drive back to Betty Jane's house first to pick up a key to my father's house. She was watching a movie and I explained to her what I was doing.

"But what about your date with Susan?" she asked.

"Oh, she's with me," I said.

"Sounds like a real fun date, prowling around in an old house. You can't listen to the tapes until tomorrow anyway."

"I know. I just want to get that recorder tonight and see if it works."

Susan was waiting in my Mercedes. I jumped in and started to pull away. As I did, I noticed a large black Suburban pull away half a block down and across the street. It accelerated in the opposite direction and the taillights quickly disappeared. I felt I might have been followed earlier. This was getting a little weird. Someone was keeping tabs on me and possibly on Betty Jane. I had to have some answers, and I thought maybe the tapes were the key.

As I pulled into the driveway, the house was dark and looked forlorn in the hazy moonlight. Susan didn't want to stay in the car, so she accompanied me to the front door. Crickets serenaded us as we walked up the curved walkway. A whip-poor-will made its mournful cry somewhere out in the thick woods behind my father's house.

I unlocked the front door and turned on the lights. I quickly headed to my father's office and turned on his desk lamp. As I had remembered, a small recorder in a brown leather case was on the third shelf of the bookcase. I grabbed it and reached to turn off the desk lamp. Before I could, Susan screamed.

I turned and looked towards the picture window. Two figures in ski masks were staring at us. I yelled for Susan to get away from the window and reached in the desk where I had seen a gun earlier. My fingers gripped the butt of my father's Smith and Wesson .38 revolver. I pulled it out and pointed it towards the window.

Two huge forms wearing ski masks were still peering in. They raised up from the bushes, turned and ran for the street. I told Susan to stay down, and I ran for the front door. The intruders had crossed the street and were nearing a black SUV parked in the grass. One stopped, turned and drew a weapon. He fired and I saw a bright yellow flash, A bullet flew by my head and struck a white wooden column on the porch. I aimed and fired back striking the SUV with a loud ping. They jumped in the vehicle and raced away.

I walked back inside, and Susan was still crouched on the floor in the office.

"Oh my God, Johnny, what was that all about?" Susan exclaimed. "Somebody tried to kill us!"

"I think they were just trying to scare us. If they had wanted to kill us, we'd be dead."

"Well, they surely succeeded if they were trying to scare us," she cried. "Why would someone want to scare us?"

"I don't know," I said. "I think they may want something my father had. Maybe they think I have it."

"Shouldn't we call the Sheriff?" she asked.

"Yes," I said as I sat down behind the desk.

After we both had calmed down some, I dialed 911 and informed the sheriff's dispatcher there had been a shooting and gave her the address. She tried to keep me on the phone, but I hung up.

Two deputies arrived ten minutes later. I took them into the office and explained about the two guys in ski masks at the window. I told them how I had run out to the porch and showed them where a bullet had struck the column. I explained I had returned fire and had hit their vehicle.

A crime scene technician appeared twenty minutes later and recovered the slug and told me it appeared to be from a nine-millimeter weapon. The deputies searched for shell casings but found none. They put out a BOLO (be on the look-out) for the vehicle.

It was well past midnight when the deputies left. Susan and I locked up the house, and I took her home. Neither of us were in an amorous mood after what had happened. So, I said good night with a quick kiss on her doorstep and headed home.

I stopped at an all-night convenience store and bought a package of AAA batteries. I wanted to make sure I had fresh batteries for the recorder when I went to the bank to retrieve the tapes in a few hours. I then drove to my sister's house, knowing I would not sleep a wink. Someone didn't want me to find out about my father's bad business. The same someone had probably murdered Lucas McDougal and had tried to murder me.

# CHAPTER 23

RIVERDALE PLANTATION
NINE YEARS OLD

It was Joe's fifteenth birthday, and I was hoping we would be quitting early today. My mother had said she wanted to have an early dinner and a little celebration for Joe. She had baked him a yellow cake with white frosting. Joe, Betty Jane and I were all breaking our backs in the cotton field, and it was hot enough to fry an egg on a tin roof. I was guessing it was close to five from the position of the sun. I kept raising up from picking cotton to look towards the end of my row hoping Jack and my father would show up soon to weigh up the cotton.

A few minutes later I heard the *chug-chug* of the old Ford truck and I jumped up to rejoice. "Hallelujah!" I shouted as I saw the truck turn into the cotton field. The brutal day was done. We were ready to weigh up. Jack waved as he pulled the truck to the end of the cotton rows.

The three of us headed to the end of our rows to dump the cotton in our sacks on the burlap sheets assigned to each of us. I led the pack, almost running as I maneuvered through the shoulder-high cotton. I emptied my cotton sack onto my sheet and dived into the loose cotton rolling around in it and rejoicing. Another day was finished and I had not gotten stung by a bumble bee or bitten by a rattlesnake.

The field hands were all making their way to the end of their rows also, dumping their cotton in piles on their burlap sheets. The white cotton sparkled in the sunlight and it was a beautiful sight at the end of the day. I heard some loud talk down the field about fifteen yards from where I lay. Two of the field hands were arguing. The tall one was named Coleman. He was about twenty years old and had only been working for us for a few months. His black skin glistened with sweat as he dumped the cotton from his sack onto his sheet.

The other one was called Shorty. He was small, light-skinned and about thirty years old. Shorty had lived on our farm for years and was one of our most reliable workers.

"I know you dun stole som of my cotton, nigger," Shorty shouted to Coleman. "I had a lot mo than this when I last dumped. I know it wuz you dun stole it and put in on yo pile. I dun seen you down here actin like you wuz gettin water, ya damn thief."

"Who you callin a thief?" shouted Coleman as he approached Shorty. "I'll kick yo ass, you lil short-legged bastard."

"You mess with me, they gonna have to call Dixon," shouted Shorty. "And in case you don't know, thass the funeral home down here, you dumbass New Jersey nigger."

I stood up on my cotton pile to watch the fight. Shorty was small, but I knew he was strong and scrappy and would not back down from anyone. The two fighters began to circle each other, waiting for an opening to land the first punch. Suddenly Coleman lurched forward and grabbed Shorty around the neck and pulled him to the ground falling on top of him. Shorty got one arm free and started landing punches on Coleman's head and neck. The two men rolled around on the dusty ground, each landing a few punches but mostly grabbing each other and trying to use wrestling moves. I moved closer to the fight to get a better look as the field hands gathered around shouting and clapping. The older black women were cackling like our red hens in the barnyard.

"Hey, hey there!" yelled Jack as he jumped out of the truck and approached the two fighters.

"Y'all break it up, break it up now!"

Buddy Moore got out of the passenger side of the truck and ran around the front and over to where Jack was standing.

The fighters paid no attention to Jack and kept rolling on the cotton and punching each other. Then as if by magic a knife appeared in Coleman's hand. Jack and Buddy jumped back and yelled at them to stop again.

With a quick flick of his wrist, Coleman pressed a button and an eight-inch blade extended. The blade was blue and silver and it glinted in the late afternoon sunlight. Coleman shoved the blade into Shorty's stomach, pulled it out and then shoved it into his chest as they both fell onto a pile of cotton. The knife made a *pluck* sound as if it had been stuck into a grapefruit or a watermelon. Several of the women screamed and one of the men shouted, "He done stabbed Shorty!"

Coleman was like a madman, stabbing Shorty several more times before he stopped. Bright red blood covered Shorty's dirty t-shirt in an instant as Coleman pushed away from him and rose to his feet holding the bloody knife. Blood ran down Coleman's arm and dropped onto the dusty soil, making several teardrop-sized puddles as he stood over Shorty, panting from the exertion. Shorty was writhing on the cotton pile holding his stomach.

He whispered, "Oh God, help me, help me!"

Bright red blood flowed onto the cotton turning it from white to an apple-red—red blood on white cotton.

Coleman stood there holding the knife and still breathing hard, transfixed for a moment and muttering to himself, "Call me a thief, I'll cut yo ass."

He then wiped the blood from the knife on his dirty jeans, turned and started running towards the woods on the other side of the cotton field.

Jack pulled off his t-shirt as he and Buddy rushed to Shorty and got down on their knees. Jack pulled up Shorty's shirt and placed his own t-shirt over the wounds trying to stop the blood flow.

"Hang in there, Shorty. We'll get you to a doctor!" said Jack as he continued to press his shirt to the wounds.

"Get me some more cloth somebody!" Jack shouted. "I can't cover all the wounds!"

Buddy Moore ripped his shirt and handed Jack some strips of cloth.

"Let's try to tie 'em tight to stop the blood flow," said Jack. "Then y'all help me get him in the truck."

Buddy and Jack continued to work on Shorty, but blood ebbed from several wounds not covered.

"I need more cloth!" yelled Jack.

A fat black woman named Doris ripped part of her dress and gave it to Jack. He took the cloth and tried to cover a different wound, lifting Shorty to one side and trying to wrap the cloth around his waist, pulling it tight. Blood streamed from Shorty's mouth and he moaned loudly. Then he heaved a couple of times and became still. As Shorty stopped moving, an eerie silence covered the cotton field like a net. The silence was palpable. No one spoke or moved for a couple of minutes.

Finally, Jack stood up and said, "He's gone."

Some of the women shrieked and others started to moan and cry.

I heard another truck and turned to see my father pull up in his pickup truck. He saw Jack standing over Shorty's lifeless body, bare-chested with his arms outstretched and covered in blood. He jumped out of his truck and rushed to Jack.

"What the hell happened?" he shouted at Jack.

"Coleman and Shorty got in a fight and Shorty got stabbed, Daddy!" shouted Jack. "And Coleman run off headed towards the woods. He stabbed Shorty several times; I tried to stop the blood, but it was too much. Shorty's dead."

"How come y'all didn't break it up?" shouted my father as he looked around at the crowd. "Y'all act like a bunch a damn animals, a jawing and fightin. What a damn mess! Look at that cotton! Come on Jack, help me move him; he's gonna ruin the whole damn sheet of cotton," he said as he bent over and grabbed Shorty's feet.

Jack grabbed him by the shoulders, and they lifted him off the cotton and laid him on the dusty ground. Blood continued to run down both his sides and puddle in the dust. The blood changed in color from bright red to almost black as it touched the gray dirt. I could not believe how much blood had flowed from his body. A foul smell like iron ore mixed with stale meat emanated from Shorty. I moved away, hoping I would not throw up.

Buddy Moore stood there shaking his head. Both his hands and arms were covered with blood.

I could not stop staring at Shorty and the bloody cotton . . . red blood on white cotton. The contrast was disturbing, and I started to feel a movement in my stomach. Then the smell of the blood hit me again. It wafted into my nostrils. That did it. The sight of the blood and the smell combined to turn my stomach over, and I ran for the cotton patch. Fortunately, I made it into the tall stalks before I started to retch. I spread my entire lunch over a few of the cotton stalks. I wiped my mouth on my shirt and quickly looked around to see if anyone was laughing at me. But most of the hands had moved far away from Shorty's body and were congregating in small groups and murmuring quietly.

I heard my father tell Jack to stand by with Shorty while he went to the house to call the sheriff. He instructed Jack to get everything ready so when he returned they could start weighing up the cotton. He told him to keep the hands here as the sheriff might want to talk with some of them.

I wanted to go stand by Jack and talk with him, but I did not want to get too close to Shorty's body, afraid I might throw up again. So I went over to Joe who was sitting on his cotton pile.

"Hell, it happened so fast, I couldn't a done anything to stop it," Joe said to me.

"I know; nobody could. You think they'll find Coleman?"

"Yeah, Sheriff will bring dogs. They'll track him down in them woods," Joe answered. "Nice birthday, huh? I thought we was gettin off early. Should be eatin dinner and then ice cream and cake. But we just sittin out here in the cotton field waiting on the sheriff. Some damn birthday."

I took one last look at Shorty, and then moved closer to Joe.

"Happy birthday to me!" he sang.

He stared at me and shook his head. I wandered out into the cotton and sat down. I tried to get far enough away so no one could hear me crying. I felt sad. Poor Shorty! Poor Joe! Why did God let such bad things happen? I looked up into a sky starting to darken like ink stains on white notebook paper. Was God up there somewhere? If he was, why didn't he do something? I shook my head and cried some more.

# CHAPTER 24

My father returned from the house and announced, "Sheriff will be here in a little bit."

He picked up a burlap sheet and placed it over Shorty's body.

"Alright, let's get this cotton weighed up. Joe, you stand by here until the sheriff comes. Don't let nobody come around Shorty."

We continued our daily routine as if nothing had happened. My father and Jack moved down the line of cotton sheets at the end of the rows, weighing them, my father marking down in his little black book how much cotton each person had picked as Jack operated the scales.

Just as they were finishing the weigh ups, I saw a green and white sheriff's car pull into the field. Sheriff Carpenter got out, hitching up his gun belt over his abundant stomach as another sheriff's deputy exited from the passenger side of the vehicle. The sheriff was a huge man, well over six feet and probably close to three hundred pounds. His boots had been brown at one time, but were covered with so much dust they looked gray. He removed a handkerchief that had been well used and wiped the sweat from his brow and neck as he walked over to where Shorty's body lay covered. His white Stetson was sweat-stained and cocked sideways on his head. My father and Jack drove up in their truck causing a huge cloud of dust to engulf everyone standing nearby.

"Hey Jim," my father said as he walked over to the sheriff and shook his hand.

"Hey Calvin, what we got here?" he asked as he stooped over Shorty's body.

"We got a dead one, done got stabbed; they was a fightin. Names Shorty Johnson, been with me for years, lives here on my place with his grandmama. I think you probably got a sheet on him. I came down and bailed him out once a few years back. He was drunk and fighting in town and y'all threw him in the pokey for a few days. He was a cocky little devil; he'd fight a buzz saw."

"And who done it?" asked the sheriff as he looked over the blood-soaked clothing clinging to Shorty's body. He looked over the field hands standing around as if the suspect would raise his hand.

"One of my hands named Coleman Mabry. Come down here from New Jersey a few months back. Livin with some of his cousins down the road from the Griggs' place. I gave him a job pickin cotton but he wasn't worth a damn. Always a shuckin and jivin, trying to start some shit. I shoulda done run him off. They said he ran down in them woods over yonder."

"Guess we got plenty a witnesses," said the sheriff.

"Yep, 'bout thirty, including all three a my boys here."

"Well, I done called Dixon to come on out and pick him up. If y'all don't mind standin by til they git here, me and Bobby gonna ride over to where this Coleman was stayin and see if he mighta gone that way. What's them people's names over there? His cousins?"

"They're Mabrys and Bennetts. They stay in them two houses 'bout a mile past Griggs' place down the road on the left. They're all related, but be careful—there's a bunch of 'em and they mean as snakes. Two or three of them boys done been to prison."

"Thanks Calvin, we'll watch ourselves," said the sheriff as he got back into his car. He rolled his window down and called out, "Calvin, tell the folks from Dixon to take the body to the coroner's office. That this here is a murder."

"I'll tell 'em," he said as he waved goodbye.

"Jack and Joe, y'all take two trucks and carry all the hands home. Me and Johnny gonna stay here until the funeral home people come. Johnny, when they get Shorty loaded up, I want you to pull all that cotton that's got blood on it out of the sheet there from his pile. Try to save as much of the cotton as you can. If it's just got a little blood on, shove it down in the middle of the pile, but if it is soaked through, throw it away."

"Yes, sir," I said, thinking that I was surely going to be sick again.

The folks from Dixon's funeral home arrived a few minutes later, and two attendants loaded Shorty's body on a gurney. As they lifted him up, a large amount of blood ran down the leg of his jeans and drained onto the cotton and the dusty ground. I could feel my stomach churning, and sweat beaded on my face and arms. *Hurry*, I thought, *I can't hold it much longer.* They finally zipped him up in a body bag and loaded the gurney in the hearse and closed the back door. I turned away and held my hand over my mouth hoping my father wouldn't see me. But he did, and he laughed as the hearse drove away.

"What's the matter with you, boy?" he shouted. "Ain't nothin but a little blood. You're a weak-kneed little sissy. Am I gonna have to git yo sister out here to clean this cotton? Now git yo ass over here and git this cotton cleaned up! You better not be throwin up on it either!"

# CHAPTER 25

Thank God he headed for the house so I could walk out into the cotton patch and throw up without him seeing me. I heaved until there was nothing in my stomach, and then I dry heaved some more. I sat down in the cotton patch and rubbed my throbbing head. I cried a little but didn't know if it was for myself or for Shorty. It was starting to get dark and I saw stars twinkling in the blue and crimson sky. Shorty wouldn't be seeing any stars again or anything else. And if I didn't get moving and get that cotton cleaned, I might not see anything again either.

It took me twenty minutes to remove all the blood-soaked cotton and throw it in a ditch at the end of the field. I had Shorty's blood on my hands and arms. I tied the burlap sheet with the clean cotton inside and drug it across the road and to the barn where we kept cotton until it could be taken to the local gin. I washed my hands and arms, and then I washed them again. I could still smell Shorty's blood on me.

I had just fed all the animals and was starting to put fresh water in their troughs when I heard the barn door open. My mother entered and walked over to me.

"We're waiting on you to eat birthday cake. Everybody else is done. I'm gonna let you eat your dessert first tonight and then you can eat your dinner."

"Momma, I don't think I can eat anything," I said. "My stomach's still rolling over after seeing all that blood and then havin to clean it up. And I can't stop thinking about Shorty. He was always good to me. Jokin with me and callin me little bit. And now he's gone forever. I just keep seein all that blood."

"I know baby, it's terrible, seein something like that at your age," she said as she gave me a hug. "Let me help you finish so you can at least come eat cake and we're gonna celebrate Joe's birthday."

"I'm almost done," I said. "I've just got to run some water for the pigs."

I turned on the hose and we stood there and watched the water run into two huge troughs. The sky was painted with stars now, and a three-quarter moon gave off enough glow to turn the sky from almost black to a lighter blue. I stared up at the heavens and wondered when Shorty might be headed up that way or if maybe he was going in the other direction. But he was a good guy, or at least he always treated me good. I think he went to church, the black church down by the Flint River. I didn't know much about any of the black hands who worked for us. My father wouldn't allow us to associate with them. But I hoped Shorty was headed up and not down.

My mother put her arm around me as we walked up to the house and to Joe's birthday party. *Happy birthday Joe*, I thought. *Sorry you had to see a murder on your birthday.*

When we went in the back door, my mother turned left and went into the kitchen to get the cake. I turned to the right to go into my room to change my dirty clothes. As I was putting on fresh pants and a shirt, my father entered my room.

"Did you get all that cotton cleaned up?" he asked.

"Yes sir, I got all the bloody cotton out," I said.

"How much wuz ya able to salvage?" he asked.

"There was probably 150 pounds left. I couldn't lift it; I had to drag it across the road and into the barn."

"Hell, there shoulda been more than 200 pounds left. You probably threw most of it into the ditch so you wouldn't have to carry it to the barn. You are totally worthless! Hurry up so we can give Joe his present and eat cake. We been waitin on yo ass for thirty minutes."

I entered the dining room still feeling like I could not eat a thing. Everyone was gathered around the table, and there was a long-wrapped package lying across the table in front of Joe. My mother and Emma entered carrying a caramel cake (Joe's favorite) along with dishes and ice cream. Betty Jane produced a single candle and stuck it in the center of the cake.

"Sorry but you are not worth fifteen candles, Joey boy," she said as she lit it.

We all sang "Happy Birthday" and Joe was able to blow out the single candle. We congratulated him on being able to do that all by himself and kidded him with various jokes and catcalls.

"Okay son, open your present," commanded my father. "It's a good one. I bought it myself."

Joe tore the wrapping paper from the elongated package and found a heavy cloth covering the mystery object. He unwrapped the cloth and removed a Remington Model 1200 twelve-gauge shotgun.

"Now you can get rid of that old 410 and maybe you can hit some quail with this one," said my father.

Quail and dove hunting was a big thing in our family, and the men were expected to be good shots. Jack had been working with me teaching me how to shoot, and I hoped to get a shotgun for Christmas. Jack was an excellent shot like my father, and they spent many afternoons hunting.

"Thanks, Dad, I love it!" said Joe.

"I'll teach you how to shoot it," said Jack. "That way maybe you'll be able to outshoot your sister one day."

"Ha, ha, very funny," said Joe. "I can already outshoot the both of you. I can a hit a gnat's ass sitting on a gatepost at a hundred yards. You guys couldn't even hit the gatepost."

Betty Jane was a pretty good shot. My father had taught her and Joe how to shoot. I kept thinking that maybe when I got a little older, he would take the time to teach me. But that probably wasn't going to happen. Besides, I would rather Jack teach me anyway. He had more patience and wouldn't scream at me or make fun of me when I missed.

My father was an incredible marksman. He'd won all kinds of shooting trophies and was known all over the county as one of the best. Jack had told me when they were quail hunting, he could identify the male birds as they took flight on the covey rise and would shoot only the males, thus leaving more females alive to lay and hatch eggs, which would increase the bird population.

We finished the birthday celebration for Joe and went to bed. I only ate a small piece of birthday cake. My stomach was still rolling around.

We learned the next day when the Sheriff called that he would not need any of us to make statements about Shorty's stabbing. There would be no trial. Coleman Mabry had been caught. They had tracked him with bloodhounds and caught him in some woods over by the Griggs' farm. He had tried to resist arrest and had been shot and killed. I guess he must have pulled that switch blade on the deputies and they had shot him . . . thirteen times.

I made a big mistake the next day. I asked my father if any of us were going to Shorty's funeral. He slapped me in the face and knocked me down. I think he thought I was being a smartass. I wasn't. I was just thinking out loud about paying my respects to someone who had always respected me. I rubbed my stinging face and stared at my father. Neither of us had to speak. We said what we were feeling with the looks we gave each other.

# CHAPTER 26

MARTINSVILLE, GEORGIA
PRESENT DAY

It was five o'clock. I couldn't sleep. I wanted the bank to be open. I got out of bed and wandered downstairs. I made a pot of coffee and settled in the den with some photo albums.

Leafing through them I had to admit we had more good times than bad: hunting, fishing, camping, joking with one another and just running all over our huge farm. My father had been a tyrant, but he had also done a lot for us. He had been fiercely proud of his family and had fought to protect the farm from going under when times were bad. He had probably done some bad things. But he did them for us, and to keep the farm in our family name.

As an attorney, I had defended a lot of people who were guilty as hell. Some of them had done bad things to protect and provide for their families. Were those mitigating circumstances? I had sure argued like hell that they were in a lot of courtrooms and I had been quite successful. What bad things had my father done?

Betty Jane had heard me rumbling around or the coffee maker signaling the brew was ready. She came into the den wearing a robe and a look of concern on her face.

"What happened?" she asked. "I thought surely you'd be spending the night at Susan's."

I told her what had happened and that I thought the men were after the tapes.

"Obviously someone doesn't want us to know about what was going on thirty years ago," I said. "We need to get to the bank and play the tapes. They should tell us what going on. The tapes are the key and we can play them as soon as the bank opens."

"Don't you think we should get the sheriff involved?" she asked.

"No way!" I said. "This was our father. They may try to keep us out of it. And they may not follow up on it like we would. I know people in Atlanta with the GBI and FBI. If we need to notify them, we will. But I want to play the tapes and see what happened. This could even have something to do with Jack's disappearance."

"Don't you think Daddy would have gone to the Sheriff back then if these people were involved with Jack?" she asked.

"Maybe, but maybe not. Daddy said they threatened to hurt us. Maybe he couldn't go to the sheriff. He was protecting us. But now he wants us to do this. He wants us to get justice for Jack if they were involved. And that's what we will do, just as soon as that damn bank opens."

"Well, it's not open yet, so sit down and I'll fix you some breakfast. Then I have to go get dressed so I can go to the bank with you."

"Just another cup of coffee for me and I'll run upstairs and get a shower. I'm skipping breakfast; I've eaten so much since I've been down here, I've probably gained ten pounds. I had forgotten how good this country food tasted. It sure as hell beats a quick energy bar or a half sandwich during court recesses which is what I usually do."

# CHAPTER 27

I showered and dressed, but it was still only six o'clock. I decided to ride out to our farm and look around. I told Betty Jane to meet me at the bank at nine. Most of the land was rented to some of our neighbors, and according to Betty Jane one of them with a big family was living in our old house.

As I pulled into the circular dirt driveway at Riverdale, I saw an older man driving an ancient Ford tractor across the barnyard. The tractor made a *putt-putt* noise as he geared it down waiting for my approach. Blue diesel smoke poured from the tractor's smokestack and escaped over the top of the weathered, once-red barn. The tin roof had rusted in several places, and the sunlight striking it made it look dirty and worn. I drove across the yard in his direction, and he stopped the tractor and waved to me. He looked familiar, but I could not recall a name. I got out of my car and approached him as he remained seated on the tractor.

"Good morning," I said. "You're out mighty early."

"Early bird catches the worm. Got a lot to do today, got hay on the ground, getting ready to go fluff it up some so we can bale it later this morning."

"Well, I won't hold you up. I just wanted to look around some. I'm John Reynolds. I guess me and my sister, Betty Jane, are gonna be your new landlords since my dad passed this week."

He extended a wrinkled hand covered with liver spots.

"I'm Matthew Lonergan. Sorry to hear about your daddy. He was a good man. A fair man, made me and my brother a fair deal on renting this place. We're farmin it together and me and my five young-uns are living in the main house. I went to the funeral. I seen you there but didn't get a chance to give you my condolences. They was such a crowd there and all."

"Thank you, I appreciate that," I said. "You mind if I look around some at the barn and around the fields and woods, maybe drive down to the old millpond? I won't bother your family up at the house, just doing a little reminiscing."

"Shore, help yo'self," he said. "You own this place now; you can do what you want. The rent's paid up. I guess Betty Jane told ya we got five hundred acres of corn, two hundred soybeans, two hundred peanuts and then all the hay fields. Another fella's rentin all the cotton and tobacco. That would be too much for us to fool with. I just pay rent on the house here monthly and I kind of take care of fixing things if they break. That's the deal I had with yo daddy."

"Well, whatever you worked out with Daddy will work for us," I said.

"I got to get to work," he said as he started the tractor. "Pleasure a meetin ya."

He drove out towards the east field behind the barn. The smell of diesel brought back memories of all the tractors and farm equipment I operated as a small boy. I looked up towards the main house. It could use a fresh coat of paint as the gray wood was showing through in several places. That was my responsibility now. I would tell Betty Jane to get a painter out here and touch it up some.

I walked into the faded red barn and looked around. The smell of hay and cow manure was strong. It smelled the same as I remembered. I thought of all the hours I had spent in this barn, shoveling manure, putting fresh hay in the stalls and shelling corn for the pigs. My horse was a brown and white Appaloosa mare. I had got her for Christmas on my sixth birthday. My father had told me she was an Appaloosa, and I had thought that was her name. I looked up at the hay loft packed tightly with bales of hay. It smelled rancid and mildewed.

I could hear my father's voice ringing out across the barnyard.

"Johnny, be careful about any hay with mildew on it! It'll make the cows sick. Throw that in the back of the wagon and we'll burn it. Git yo ass movin boy!"

Giant spider webs draped the walls of the barn like garland on our Christmas trees. This had been a grand place for playing hide-and-seek. Jack could find me right away, but would pretend he didn't see me scrunched down in the hay. He would walk all around the barn pretending to look for me, and then finally he would swoop down in the hay and grab me and tickle me until I cried. Then we'd both flop down in the hay laughing and rolling around. I laughed at the memory. Then a tear rolled down my cheek.

"Damn it, Jack, what happened to you?" I said out loud. "I'm gonna find out, I promise you, I'm gonna find out."

I walked out of the barn and away from those pleasant memories and ran into some unpleasant memories. Up the hill about twenty yards from the barn, two giant peach trees surrounded a dilapidated wind-mill. They had been small and easy to climb in my youth. The wind-mill had provided water from an open well. I had pumped thousands of buckets of water from that well and carried it down to the barn to fill the water troughs for the horses, cows and pigs. But the peach trees had not been my friends. On dozens of occasions I had been forced to climb them and cut a small limb that my father would fashion into a switch. He would beat me on my legs and butt. I looked at the two trees and shuddered. How could they have grown so big? I surely had cut off most of their limbs. A chill ran down my spine, and I turned around sharply and headed for my car.

I drove around the circular dirt driveway and headed back out to the paved road. It had been dirt when I was a child. I remembered the red clay dust swirling around our yard and house whenever a vehicle passed. It had painted everything with a dirty reddish glaze. I turned right and drove down the road for almost a mile until I spotted a dirt road leading into the forest on my left. Weeds and small brambles scratched the sides of my car as I entered the forest road. We had kept this road mowed when I was a child. Now you could barely tell where the road led. I drove on for another hundred yards and came into a grassy opening. An earthen dam fronted the millpond so that you could barely see the water from where I stopped. I got out of my car and walked up the steep grassy knoll until I was standing on top of the dam.

The old millpond stretched out in front of me. Hundreds of cypress trees draped with Spanish moss stood like toy nutcracker soldiers throughout the pond. Giant verdant lily pads covered most of the surface of the water. A bullfrog croaked and leaped into the water a couple of feet below where I was standing and startled me. I stood there frozen in time looking out on the pond and remembering all the good times we had here fishing and camping and just running around in the woods above the pond. I could hear Jack and Joe's voices shouting out in the sticky summer afternoon.

I shook my head as I looked at the old boat house. The wood was rotten and the roof had caved in. The whole structure had toppled into the water. Our farm had been left unattended as if no one gave a damn anymore. I think my father had started to not give a damn the day Jack disappeared. I walked up the overgrown trail into the woods on the east side of the pond. I remembered some of our good fishing spots. I looked for the grassy open area where we had camped several times. But the entire area was so overgrown I could not find it.

I walked all the way around the millpond getting my pant legs wet with dew as I moved through the grass and underbrush. When I arrived back at my car, I looked at my watch. It was past eight. I headed back to town driving past fields of green corn, soybeans and stalks of cotton glistening white in the summer heat. A green and yellow John Deere cotton picker moved down the rows of cotton. *Lord, why didn't we have machines to pick that cotton when I was a kid?* I thought to myself as I drove.

# CHAPTER 28

I arrived at the bank at ten minutes before nine and sat in my car waiting for Betty Jane. She pulled into the bank parking lot at exactly nine o'clock. We entered the bank together and headed for the desk of the lovely Anna.

"I bet y'all want to git in yo daddy's boxes again," she said.

"Yes please," said Betty Jane as we were led to the rear vault. "And if you don't mind, could we have a private office for an hour or so? We've got a lot of things to go through."

"No problem," said Anna. "We're here to please." And I swear she winked at me as she took the keys from Betty Jane.

We located the four tapes and I set the recorder on the table.

"Since we don't know how long they are, why don't we just play Number 1 here and then we can take the others back to your house and play them there," I said.

"Sounds good," she said.

I put the tape labeled "Number 1" into the recorder and pressed Play. The machine whirred a few seconds, and then my father's voice introduced the tape. A chill ran down my spine as I heard his voice. It was as though Calvin Reynolds was still with us or talking to us from his grave. I noticed tears running down Betty Jane's face, and I reached over and held her hand.

"This here is Calvin Reynolds and I am the owner of Riverdale Plantation. I'm making this recording to tell about some things going on here on my place. And over the next couple of weeks I'm gonna record the voices of the men who got me mixed up in some nasty business. I'm making this tape to leave for the law in case something happens to me. I'm gonna tell everything that happened and identify all of them by name. I want the law to arrest them all."I want to start by saying I'm sorry I ever got mixed up with these characters. I got in a financial jam after losing my crops for two years and being in debt. One of my hands, Isaac Jackson, introduced me to some redneck Atlanta boys. They come down here to talk to Isaac. I took one look at them and I told him hell no, stay away from them boys, they was bad news. So Isaac—"

The tape broke. It whirred for a few seconds, and I reached over and turned it off. I could see brown flakes where the tape was disintegrating.

"This tape is more than thirty years old," I said. "It's very fragile; it's coming apart. I don't think we should try to play the others. I'll take them back to Atlanta with me. I've got some friends at the FBI and GBI. We'll see if their technicians can do anything with them."

"What do you think Daddy got mixed up in?" asked Betty Jane. "He says he got mixed up with some bad people and apparently Isaac was talking with them too."

"I don't know," I said. "You heard him say that he told Isaac not to get mixed up with them."

"Well, maybe Isaac did get mixed up with them and that's why he got killed," said Betty Jane. "And maybe Daddy knew something about it."

"Maybe," I said. "But I don't believe Daddy would get mixed up in something illegal. But we'll know more when we can hear the rest of these tapes."

"Hey, you remember the notes Daddy made?" asked Betty Jane. "We looked at them yesterday in the safe deposit box. Do you think the Brady Lyle that Daddy listed in those notes could be the same guy who's a Georgia congressman?"

"I don't know. It might be. He is a sleaze ball."

"It's got to be someone with the same name. It couldn't be that congressman, could it?"

"I don't know," I said.

I put all four tapes in my coat pocket. I put everything else back in the safe deposit boxes and notified the lovely Anna that we were ready to leave.

We drove to Betty Jane's house and had a quick lunch of roast beef sandwiches, potato salad, baked beans and cole slaw left over from the funeral feast. I put the four cassette tapes into a large plastic sandwich bag and placed them in my briefcase.

I was debating whether to head back to Atlanta or to call Susan Regan and try once again to have a romantic evening with no interruptions. The debate with myself did not last long, and the Susan Regan option won hands down. I was just dialing Susan's number when the front door to Betty Jane's home was thrown open and two men wearing black ski masks burst into the living room. One held a sawed-off shotgun and the other a Sig Sauer nine-millimeter automatic. Both were pointed at my head.

# CHAPTER 29

RIVERDALE PLANTATION
NINE YEARS OLD

It was going to be a good day. I was so excited! It was a humid Saturday and all my morning chores were done. We had loaded up three big trucks with loose cotton, each of them was pulling a trailer loaded with more loose cotton and we were going into Martinsville to Ryland's Cotton Gin. We would wait in line at the gin until it was our turn and then pull the trucks and trailers forward under the huge vacuum pipe. An employee from the gin would climb into the rear of the trucks and trailers and vacuum the loose cotton out and into the gin. There it would be cleaned, processed and compressed into large bales of cotton that would weigh approximately five hundred pounds. My father would be paid for the cotton based on the weight of the bales. This was big money time, and he was usually in a good mood.

This process would take a couple of hours and my brothers and I were allowed to roam around the town, go into the general store that sold candy and then over to the hot dog stand down the street from the gin. I was looking forward to buying a Baby Ruth candy bar and maybe a couple of hot dogs that I would slather in mustard and ketchup. I got a Coca Cola over crushed ice from the fountain in the drug store. It was so cold when I drank it, it made my teeth hurt. Grumpy old Mr. Humphrey, the owner, actually smiled at me. I could only recall him doing that once before. That was the time when I entered his business with a broken arm. He gave me a big smile that day as if to say, "You got what you deserved kid. Hope it hurts like hell!" He was not a friendly guy.

My brothers were also in a great mood. They joked with me and ran around acting like kids my age. Jack purchased a double-meat hamburger from the hot dog stand. He got everything that you could possibly put on it: mustard, ketchup, onions, pickles, lettuce, tomato, relish and even a splat of barbecue sauce. He always joked, "The best place to get a hamburger in Martinsville is the hot dog stand." Joe got one hot dog and one hamburger. He could never decide which he liked best. But the main thing he liked was being away from the farm for a few hours and all the back-breaking work we did in the fields each day. We were so happy to be free for at least half a day, we screamed with delight.

We ate our burgers and dogs, and then made a quick stop back by the cotton gin to check on the progress of the ginning of our cotton. My father said it would take at least another hour, so we headed up the street to the city park for an intense fight with pinecones. The park had dozens of pine trees and the grass was littered with pinecones. Jack was as strong as an ox and he could heave a pinecone at you at 30 miles an hour. He nailed me a few times in the back and legs but was always careful not to hit me in the head. Joe, on the other hand, liked to aim at my head and took delight in beaning me and drawing blood. But I was fast and managed to avoid him for the most part on that delightful sunny day.

After an hour-long pinecone fight, we were exhausted. We took our boots off and dangled our feet in the water of the small pond in the park. A couple of geese wandered by and honked at us to let us know we were invading their territory. A group of Monarch butterflies drifted by whirling and dancing on the stiff breeze, and it felt good on our warm skin. We splashed water on each other to cool off, and then headed back to the cotton gin.

My father was in the business office securing checks for the bales of cotton he had sold. He showed them to Jack.

"Pretty damn good day!" he said. "We got 21 bales out of them loads and four of 'em weighed over 450 pounds. Let's load up and head for the barn!" he shouted, slapping Jack on the back.

I rode in the truck with Jack, and he sang Beatle songs all the way home. I joked that he was no Paul McCartney, but he did sound pretty good. He rustled my hair and tried to twist one of my ears, but I dodged him. I just stared at him for a minute while he laughed. I would have given anything to be like him, to be handsome and strong, to be loved by everyone and to be able to do anything. I loved Jack. Why couldn't everyone treat me like he did?

When we arrived home, I gave my mother some coconut patties I had bought in town. They were her favorite. I had also bought some jawbreakers I gave to Betty Jane.

My mother said she had a surprise for us. She went out on the back porch and came back in a few minutes carrying the cutest Boxer puppy I had ever seen.

"Mr. Griggs' Boxer had five puppies and he wanted you kids to have one," she said putting the puppy down on the floor. "It's six weeks old and it's a boy puppy. Y'all will have to come up with a name for it."

I grabbed the puppy and held it near my face. It licked me several times. He was short-haired, a medium brown and had perfectly round black eyes that gleamed like chunks of coal. He had dark brown coloring around his eyes making him look like he was wearing a bandit's mask. His pointy ears flapped down on his head but perked straight up when I scratched behind them. His front legs were white from the knees down as if he were wearing socks or had been standing in the snow. He also had a patch of white hair on his chest.

Joe said, "Let's name him Bandit; he looks like a bandit."

"No way," I said. "He's a sweet dog. he's not a bandit."

Betty Jane chimed in, "Let's name him Socks. He looks like he has on a pair of white tube socks."

She crowded me trying to pry him out of my arms, but I would not let go.

A few other names were thrown out: Buddy, Herman, Brownie and Bobo. But I informed everyone this would be my puppy and I would take care of it. I immediately chose the name "Master." He would grow to be big and strong and would be the Master of the Universe, I informed everyone, or at least the Master of Riverdale Plantation.

So, Master it was, and I now had my very own dog. The others might not agree, but I knew this would be my dog. He would sleep in my room until he got bigger. I don't think I had ever been happier. I took Master into the living room and put him on the floor. I lay down on my back and let him crawl all over me.

I heard the front screen door slam, and my father entered the front foyer. I looked over at him to see what his take was on the new puppy. He was actually smiling. I almost fainted. He seemed to be enjoying the puppy's antics as he stood and watched. I had never seen him enjoy much of anything. I was happy but a little scared. If my dad was smiling, it might be a sign hell was about to freeze over.

I played with Master for a little while and then remembered I had evening chores to do. I brought him with me to the barn and introduced him to the horses, pigs, cows and chickens. They all liked him except for the chickens. He wanted to chase them around, and they wanted to peck at him. I could see this might be a problem, so I watched him closely and protected him when they got too rowdy. I was shelling ears of corn to put in the pigs' trough when my father came into the barn.

"Boy, you did a piss poor job this morning of cleaning out them stalls for the milk cows. Look at all that shit in there! You grab a shovel and get all that shit out of there and put new hay down. Nobody wants to be standing in shit to milk the cows."

His joy watching the new puppy was over. Operations back to normal. He hated me. I wanted to scream, "That's brand-new shit, Daddy! I left them spotless this morning. Cows do new shit every day!"

But I just bit my tongue and grabbed the shovel. Master sat just outside the cow stalls and watched me shovel shit.

When I finished my chores, Master and I rushed up to the house to see what we were having for dinner. We usually had a good dinner on Saturday night. Emma grabbed me as I entered the back door.

"Wash yo'self up now, Johnny!" she said. "I dun fixed a water bowl and some food scraps fer that new little puppy too. Supper gon be on dat table in a lil bit."

"Great! What are we having?" I asked.

"We gon have us a fish fry tonite, honey chile," she said clapping her hands together. "Old Emma dun fried up some breams, a couple a bass fish and some catfish. Me and my man Isaac dun caught 'em down at the millpond. Got some hush puppies, some french-fried potatoes and I dun made up my purple cabbage cole slaw."

I was starved and rushed to wash my hands and face. I entered our dining room and found myself to be the first at the table. I stood like a toy soldier behind my chair and waited for my family to come take their places.

Emma and my mother placed steaming platters of fish, hush puppies and fries on the table. We all waited, and when my father was seated, we took our places. I drank most of my Kool-Aide in one gulp and smiled at Emma who knew to re-fill it for me. My father chose a fish or two for everyone's plate, and then announced we could serve ourselves from the other platters as they were passed around.

Master played at my feet under the table. I sneaked him little pieces of fish and fries when no one was looking.

Emma asked my father if it would be okay if she went out to the back porch to eat with her husband Isaac, who had come over for the fish fry. I guess it was only fitting since he had caught and cleaned the fish.

"Suit yo'self, Emma, but come back when I call you if we need more fish or drinks," he called out. "In fact, you come back in here and check on us in a few minutes. The way these young-uns are eatin I know we gonna need more."

"Yassir, shore will now," Emma said as she winked at me.

I felt bad for Emma. My father treated her like a slave and constantly ranted or yelled at her. But she seemed so happy. She took him with a grain of salt and always smiled or sang when she was around us. God forbid if my father ever knew it, but I really loved her!

My father's good mood continued through dinner, which was somewhat unusual. He bragged about the good price he had received for the cotton and the fact that the weight was more that he thought it would be.

"We need to hit it hard in the cotton patch next week," he said. "We need to get all that early-planted cotton done and sold while the price is up a little. Everybody's gonna start floodin the gin with their cotton, then that price is gonna fall. Jack you go over to Simon's and Vernell's and tell them to see if they can get some of their family that live over in Salem to come pick cotton for us next week. We need all the help we can get. You and Joe stop cuttin hay next week and git in the cotton patch too. Every little bit will help."

"You want me to go tonight, Daddy?" asked Jack. "'Cause I was about to go pick up Becky and go to the drive-in movie."

"Yes, go tonight, 'cause I want them talkin to their kin in the morning at church," he said. "It won't take you but a few minutes to run over there, then you can go get Becky."

"Emma said she had some strawberry shortcake," said Jack. "I was gonna have a little of that and then go."

"Tell Emma to fix you one to go or wait and eat it when you get home."

Emma came back into the dining room and said, "I'll fix ya one to go, Jack."

"He don't need no shortcake," said Joe. "He's gonna be gettin some sugar from Becky at the drive-in. Plus it'll leave more for us."

"I'll make you eat some sugar," said Jack as he picked up a hushpuppy and threw it at Joe.

"Boys, boys," said my mother. "Don't be wasting food."

"Besides, you could've hurt yo brother," said my father. "Some of them hushpuppies are hard as rocks. Who the hell cooked them things, was that you Emma?"

"Some of dem stayed in the grease a little too long," said Emma. "I'm sorry 'bout that Mr. Cal."

"Just get me some of that shortcake. I want to eat dessert and go watch television."

Everyone finished their dessert including Jack who wolfed his down and took off. My mother and father went into the living room to watch television, while Joe, Betty Jane and I played with Master and then played board games at the dining table, our normal Saturday night activity.

# CHAPTER 30

We all went to bed around eleven. I fixed a box with a blanket in it for Master at the foot of my bed. He whimpered and cried, and I couldn't sleep. I put him in my bed and tried to get him to lay down, but he wanted to play. I listened to some music on my radio and then read a book to try to get sleepy. I think I drifted off to sleep around one, only to be awakened by heavy footsteps and whispering outside my door a short time later.

I raised up in my bed and heard my father's voice whispering something about getting the gun. I heard the screen door open on the back porch and soft footsteps. I pulled the curtain aside on my window and looked out, but could see nothing. The night was black. Ominous dark clouds were covering the moon and stars. I could see the dark clouds racing across the sky. I shivered and pulled the blankets around my shoulders.

I heard a rifle shot and a yelp out near the barn. This was followed by yelling and another shot. I jumped out of bed and ran to the back porch. My mother was standing near the back door, and she pushed me back towards my room. Master jumped up at my legs and I reached down and picked him up.

"I think I hit one of 'em. The other one ran off towards the woods!" yelled my father. "They wuz stealing gas outta the big tank by the barn. Woke me up when I heard the lock bang against the tank. They musta cut the lock off. Give me that big flashlight, Momma; lemme go see."

I saw him pick up his revolver from the top of the washing machine and stick it down the front of his pants and sling the rifle onto his shoulder. Jack had a shotgun and he followed my father down towards the barn. My mother and I walked out onto the back porch and watched as flashlight beams played across the ground as they walked towards the barn. Master whimpered in my arms, so I held him tight and stroked his head. We were soon joined by Betty Jane and Joe. We could see the light from the flashlight shining on a body lying down by the gas tank.

"I was sleepin and got woke up by some banging on the tank," my father was saying to Jack. "Look down here. See them bolt cutters. They cut the big lock off the tank. The lock fell and clanged on the tank and that's what woke me up. I grabbed my rifle and slipped out on the porch. I could just make out two of 'em, filling up five-gallon cans. Look here, they had two cans."

Two red five-gallon gasoline cans were overturned, one spilling gasoline into the dusty soil. I could smell the pungent odor of the gasoline.

"Daddy, he's still breathin," said Jack. "Should we call an ambulance?"

"Let's call the sheriff. If he wants to call an ambulance, let him call 'em. I don't care if he dies. He was out here tryin to steal my gas.

Joe, run back to the house and tell yo mama to call the sheriff. Tell 'em I dun shot one out here, stealin from me."

My mother heard the instructions and stepped back inside to call the Sheriff. I eased down from the back porch and slowly approached the area of the gas tank, holding Master close to me. The grass was wet with dew and was cold to my bare feet. Mosquitos dive-bombed my head and shoulders, and lightning bugs flittered in the peach and magnolia trees dotting the yard.

As I came closer, I heard a gurgling noise and saw a black man who appeared to be in his early twenties lying on the ground, twisting and turning, holding his stomach. Blood seeped out between his fingers and made splatters in the dusty soil. Then it made rivulets as it seeped into the damp grass. I shivered, I think more from seeing the man lying there in agony than from the chilly damp night air. My father just stood there shining his flashlight in the man's grimaced face. He moaned a couple of times and then became silent. My father got down on one knee and leaned over close to the man.

"He's gone. A 243 Winchester don't play. Look there, Jack. Look at that hole it made in his belly. Y'all recognize him?"

"I've seen him around some," said Jack. "I think he's one of them cousins been stayin down at the Portevents. I think I've seen him ridin around with Molely Portevent."

"Yeah, I think you're right," said my father. "One of them New Jersey blacks down here for the summer. Up to no good. Always tryin to steal something. Well, he won't be stealing nothin else now, will he? He's deader than a doornail! We can go ahead and call Dixon!"

"Daddy, you want me to run over to the quarters and tell the Portevents 'bout what happened?" asked Jack.

"Naw, we'll let the sheriff do that. Joe, go in the barn and get a tarp and throw it over him. I'm gonna go see if Mama will put on a pot a coffee and get me a piece of that strawberry shortcake. Jack, you and Joe hang out here until the Sheriff comes."

I stared at the body lying in our barnyard. He wasn't much older than Jack. His eyes remained open staring up at the heavens, his arms splayed out from his sides like a jet plane's wings. A few minutes ago, he had been a living and breathing soul. And now he was not breathing and his body was getting cold. It had happened so quickly. A cold chill ran up my spine. I shivered. I looked at Jack, and he looked back at me and shook his head.

Master and I headed back into the house. My father had just killed a man. I wondered what that felt like. I guess it didn't bother him much.

Not enough to interfere with him drinking coffee and eating strawberry shortcake. My mother was very quiet. She told me to go back to bed, but I knew there would be no more sleep for me tonight.

I lay in my bed and hugged Master up to my chest. He squirmed and licked my face. I already loved him so much. He was a living, breathing thing that just wanted to be loved. Didn't we all? I was sad. Maybe he could cheer me up. I could not get over the fact that my father had just killed a man. Not even a man, not much more than a boy. He had killed him for trying to steal gas. I felt numb. I wanted to cry. I thought about how life was really cheap and really short for some people.

I thought about Shorty. He had been a happy-go-lucky, good guy. His life had been short too. I wondered if he was in heaven. I wondered if there was a heaven.

It was almost an hour before a sheriff's deputy showed up. My father invited him in and asked if he wanted a cup of coffee. He said ought to go look at the body first and find out what happened. My father took him to the back porch and showed him where he was standing when he had seen two black males stealing gas. He explained the black boy might be a relative of some folks that worked for us named Portevent. The deputy took a notebook from his shirt pocket and made a few notes.

"Well, I don't see any problem," said the deputy. "You was within your rights shootin him. He was on your property illegally and he was tryin to steal from you. I got the coroner coming. We'll let him take a look and then Dixon can haul him off. "Mr. Reynolds, I probably ought to take that Winchester to the office just to be proper and legal and all. I'm sure the Sheriff will let you have it back in a few days. Let me put this rifle in my car, and then I'll take that coffee."

And that was it. The investigation had taken all of ten minutes. A man was dead. But no gas had been stolen. That was a good thing, I guess. We could all go back to bed now. The homestead had been protected, and everything was wonderful again on Riverdale Plantation.

Except I couldn't sleep for three days. Every time I closed my eyes, I kept seeing the young black man's eyes wide open staring up into the heavens. I kept seeing the bloody hole in his belly and smelling the foul odor of his blood mixed with perspiration and cow manure from the barn nearby. I wanted to gag. But more than anything, I just felt sad and alone. I kept Master close to me and cried. I cried for a man I did not know and I cried for a man who was my father and was the cruelest man I ever knew.

# CHAPTER 31

MARTINSVILLE, GEORGIA
PRESENT DAY

**B**etty Jane screamed as one of the men grabbed her arm and pulled her off the sofa. I was frozen in time and could do nothing but sit and watch as the intruder with the shotgun pushed it towards my face. Betty Jane started to cry and the man holding her arm shook it and told her to shut up.

"I think ya got something we want!" the other one snarled. "Now let me have all those tapes and we won't have to spill any blood. Cause there's nothin I'd enjoy more than bustin a cap on a lawyer. Yo daddy was messin with the wrong people. He called up threatnin our boss. Said he was gonna give them tapes to the GBI."

I slowly opened my briefcase and removed the four tapes. He took them from me and stuffed two in a shirt pocket and the other two in a side pocket of his wrinkled khakis. I was sure these were the same guys who took a shot at me last night.

They confirmed it when one said, "That was a warning shot last night. You keep pokin your nose in our business, the next one won't miss."

The robber started to back out towards the front door holding the shotgun in one hand still pointed in my direction, and then stopped.

"Now listen to me," he growled. "There's some folks in high places gettin pissed off. Yo daddy's dead and gone. You wanna drag up what's done happened thirty years ago, everybody's gonna know yo daddy was a criminal. You got no evidence, you can't prove nothin, so jest drop it. No more snoopin around, or somebody's gonna get hurt. You understand me, asshole?"

I nodded and said, "Sure."

The intruder holding Betty Jane's arm shoved her down on the sofa and backed towards the front door also.

"You best wait until we're long gone before you go callin the law," he shouted. "Or we gonna come back and we will spill some blood next time."

The front door slammed and I could see them running towards a black SUV parked in the trees across the street. I dialed 911, told the operator we had just been robbed and gave a description of the vehicle and the two men. I then went to the sofa where Betty Jane was sobbing uncontrollably.

"You okay?" I asked as I sat down by her and hugged her.

She nodded but continued to sob.

"I thought they were gonna kill us. Thank God they just took the tapes."

I hugged her and tried to comfort her but she wouldn't stop shivering.

Fifteen minutes had passed when two sheriff's cruisers screeched to a halt in the driveway. Two deputies hurried to the front door as I opened it.

"What's going on?" asked a tall lanky deputy whose name tag identified him as Deputy Harrison.

"We gotta call about a robbery!"

"Two thugs wearing ski masks just burst into the house and took some items belonging to us," I said. "I gave your 911 operator a description of them and the vehicle they were driving. They've been gone about fifteen minutes. Hopefully she put out a BOLO on them."

"Yeah, we heard it go out on the radio on our way here, but there's a hundred black SUVs around here," said the deputy. "But maybe we'll get lucky. We'll tell the highway patrol too. Maybe they'll spot 'em. Can you tell us anything else about the vehicle? Any damage, bumper stickers, anything that might stand out?"

"I think it was a Suburban and it had dark tinted windows. It may have a bullet hole in it on the left side. Because the same two guys took a shot at me last night and I fired back at them."

I explained the events of last night, and the deputies looked at me as though they didn't believe me.

"How about the robbers? You told the dispatcher they were wearing ski masks."

"Yes, they both had on black ski masks with eye holes trimmed with a white stitching. One had a sawed-off double-barreled shotgun. It was sawed down to about eighteen inches and the stock was wrapped with black electrical tape. The guy with the shotgun had on a black long-sleeved shirt and khaki pants, black shoes and wearing black gloves. He was about six foot four, 250 pounds. The other one had a black automatic pistol. I think it was probably a Sig Sauer because it looked just like the one I own. That guy was wearing a khaki long-sleeved shirt and dark pants, black shoes and black gloves. He was about six foot, stocky and 200 pounds."

"Well if they were both wearin gloves, there ain't no need to call out a tech to dust for prints," the deputy said.

"I guess not. They parked their SUV across the street in those pine trees. You might be able to get molds of their tire tracks. It's kind of damp over there."

"I'll go take a look," said the other deputy.

"What were they after? You said they took some stuff belonging to your father?" asked Deputy Harrison.

"They took some tapes my father had left for me in his safe deposit box," I said. "He died a few days ago and he left me some letters and those tapes. He made them a long time ago. I'm not sure what was on them, but apparently these guys knew."

"Well if it happened a long time ago, what the hell do they care about it?" he asked. "Statute of limitations has probably tolled by now. Probably couldn't get them in trouble anymore."

"These guys might be too dumb to know that," I said. "I think they were just trying to make sure that any evidence was destroyed."

"Don't sound like enough of a reason to do a home invasion," he said. "And how did they know yo daddy had made those tapes?"

It was too confusing to explain. I just told them I didn't know. I felt it had been a mistake to call the Sheriff. They weren't gonna find these guys and didn't seem too interested in what had occurred. But at least I thought it might make Betty Jane feel better, knowing the sheriff was looking for these guys.

"Look, my sister lives here alone and I'm about to head back to Atlanta," I said. "Could you guys swing by and check on her and maybe patrol around here some for the next few days?"

"Sure, we can do that," said Deputy Harrison. "I'll talk to the Sheriff and I think he'll agree to let us keep an eye on her for a few days. But I doubt them guys are coming back. They got what they wanted and they're probably long gone now."

The other deputy returned and informed us the vehicle had been parked on grass and pine straw. There were no impressions, so no chance of getting a mold of their tire tracks.

I thanked the deputies for their quick response as they were leaving.

"You're not going back to Atlanta tonight, are you Johnny?" Betty Jane asked.

"Thinking about it," I said. "I've really got to get back. I've got a big civil trial starting in a week and I need to prepare. Plus, I'd like to talk to a guy I know at the GBI. Maybe he could get their cold case squad to look at Jack's disappearance based on what's happened here."

"Please just stay tonight. With all this stuff that's been happening, I don't want to be alone. I was planning on doing some barbecue chicken on the grill tonight. We could invite Susan Regan over and just have a nice time. Please just stay tonight and you can get on the road early tomorrow morning."

At the mention of Susan Regan's name my ears perked up. Our previous evening had been interrupted by me being an idiot and wanting to rush over to my father's house to retrieve his tape player. Maybe we could pick up where we left off, if we could convince my sister to go to bed early.

"Okay, sis, I'll spend the night. You had me at barbecue chicken," I said.

"Yeah, right, I had you at the mention of Susan Regan," she laughed. "Shall I tell her to bring her pajamas?" she asked, laughing and giving me a sly grin.

"I'm not sure, but I don't think she sleeps in pajamas," I said, laughing and giving her a sly grin in return.

# CHAPTER 32

**S**usan Regan arrived just after six looking like she had stepped out of a colorful ad for women's summer clothing. She wore short and extremely tight white shorts with a royal blue sleeveless blouse and brown Italian sandals. Gold bracelets bounced on both arms, and a dainty gold chain with a small medallion ventured into her blouse and rested comfortably in her cleavage. Sparkling gold earrings with tiny diamonds adorned her ears and sparkled in the late afternoon sun like a thousand stars in a Texas sky.

"Hey Johnny, I'm so glad you haven't left for Atlanta,'" she said as she kissed my cheek and gave me a hug. Her perfume was like a field of lilacs, and it stayed with me as she pulled away and entered the house. She was carrying a bottle of wine and a small plant in a robin egg blue vase. She presented both to Betty Jane and gave her a hug.

We opened the wine and all shared a glass as we made small talk in my sister's den. I told Betty Jane not to mention anything about our encounter in the early afternoon. I did not want to scare Susan and let her know that evil was still following me around.

"When are you heading back?" she asked.

"Early tomorrow morning," I said. "I really have to get back and prepare for an upcoming trial. If I'm out of the office for more than a day or two all hell breaks loose. My law partner has been carrying the load on trial prep for the past week. So, I really have to get back and get busy on this case."

"Well then, we'd better make the most of your remaining time," she said as she smiled and winked at me.

I immediately looked at Betty Jane for a reaction, but she only smiled and said she needed to get the chicken ready for the grill.

We had another glass of wine and moved our conversation to my sister's back patio where the grill was smoking; the aroma of smoldering mesquite chips on charcoal filled the air. A mockingbird lit on the limb of a dogwood and chirped loudly to let us know she had a nest nearby. A gentle breeze floated across the patio, which chilled Susan so that she snuggled with me and I put my arm her.

"Oh, and by the way, Betty Jane asked me to stay over tonight," said Susan. "She said we might have a cocktail or two and I probably shouldn't drive home. What do you think about that?"

"I think my big sister has my best interest at heart."

"I asked her if she had a spare bedroom for me. She assured me she had an extra room for me."

"Yeah, right, I'll find whatever room you're in later on," I said. "Since we were rudely interrupted last night."

I put my arm around her and held her close and thought all was right with the world. Then I thought, all was right with the world except I had buried my father, found a guy who had been murdered, had been shot at, robbed and threatened all in the course of three days. Otherwise, everything was right with the world.

I grilled the chicken as my sister prepared the side dishes for our dinner. I basted it with barbecue sauce, turning it over every four minutes. Susan caught me sampling a small piece and threatened to tell on me. When the outer skin was starting to blacken and the barbecue sauce had thoroughly coated the chicken, I notified Betty Jane we were at minus three minutes and counting. She brought me a large china platter, and Susan acted as my sous chef holding the platter while I used a pair of tongs to carefully extract the smoking chicken from the grill.

Betty Jane had outdone herself on preparing side dishes. We sat in her formal dining room at one end of a huge oak table that would have seated half a platoon of soldiers as she scurried back and forth to the kitchen bringing in the remainder of our meal. She and Susan brought in bowls of corn on the cob slathered in rich butter, lima beans, fried okra, potato salad, purple hull peas, fresh sliced tomatoes and her famous cornbread sticks that were just like the ones my mom used to make: slightly toasted, crispy and oozing flavor. The chicken was cooked perfectly if I do say so. It was tender and juicy with just the right amount of barbecue sauce baked on and blackened. And the mesquite chips had enhanced the taste, working perfectly with the charcoal to add an extra smoky taste.

Another meal to die for! Everything was so good, I found myself going back for seconds on a couple of items. I had just finished and pushed back from the table when Betty Jane announced we could have coffee and key lime pie in the den. I almost collapsed and told her no way. She advised me that I would change my mind, and she was right.

We kept our conversation light as we sipped coffee and nibbled on exquisite key lime pie. Then we sipped good bourbon as we talked mostly about high school, gossiped about the lives of some of our classmates and told stories about funny things that happened out at Riverdale. There was no mention of my father, Jack or Joe. We consciously avoided anything that might bring sadness. Susan was an excellent conversationalist. She brought up things that had happened in high school that I had not thought about in years. We laughed until we cried and then laughed some more. It was a nice evening.

Around ten, Betty Jane yawned a couple of times and then announced it was her bedtime. I knew this wasn't true as she was a night owl who never went to bed before midnight. But it was nice of her to get out of our way and let us have some alone time.

She had hardly made it to the top of the stairs when Susan leaned over and kissed me. I held her tightly; she felt so good against my chest. I could hear her heart thumping restlessly and she shivered when I touched her bare shoulder.

We kissed for a few more minutes, and then headed up to my bedroom. Susan did not have a difficult time convincing me to forego my pajamas for the night. And apparently, she had forgotten to bring hers. She stepped out of her black bikini panties and stood completely naked before me. Her perfect body looked as good as it had in high school. Her tanned legs glistened in the streaks of moonlight that peeked through the thin curtains in my room. She kissed me hungrily and reminded me that we had some catching up to do from last night. I gathered her in my arms and we fell back into my bed. We made love quickly the first time and then more slowly an hour later. Susan was a wonderful lover who had endless energy. It was quite a night, a night I needed after the drama of the past three days.

I awoke to the sound of the shower running. A few minutes later Susan stepped out of the bathroom wrapped in a fluffy towel, with another wrapped like a turban around her hair. She looked beautiful with no make-up. Her skin gleamed in the early morning sunlight. Little beads of water dimpled her arms.

"Well good morning, hotshot!" she said as she came over to the bed and kissed me. "That was some quality love-making for an old guy."

"Old guy my ass!" I said. "I think you are in the same age range, lady. Besides, you're only as old as you feel, and after last night, I feel about eighteen."

"I do too," she said. "I feel great! But I've got to get moving. I have a dental appointment and I know you want to get on the road to Atlanta."

"True," I said as I kissed her again and jumped in the shower. Fifteen minutes later we were dressed and headed downstairs.

Betty Jane had another feast laid out in the breakfast nook off her huge kitchen. She must have heard us stirring upstairs and had timed everything perfectly. She was just placing a platter of sizzling scrambled eggs on the table that already held plates of link sausage, bacon, biscuits and a steamy bowl of grits into which she plopped two large globs of butter. She was determined to not let me escape to Atlanta without gaining two or three more pounds.

My sister winked and asked if we had slept okay. We both said "Great" simultaneously and smiled at each other. The conversation was light as we hurriedly ate so we could get on with our day. We finished, and I said a quick goodbye to Susan, accompanied by a hug and a kiss and a promise we would see each other soon either here or in Atlanta. I then ran upstairs to pack.

As I came down with my bag, Betty Jane handed me a bag containing left-over chicken and some containers of peas, beans, potato salad and other goodies.

"I also filled a Yeti tumbler with iced tea. You won't even have to stop unless you need gas. Or you can pull over at a rest stop and have a picnic."

*God, thank you for creating the creatures known as "Southern women,"* I thought as I loaded my bags and my goodies into the car. They are indeed precious, my sister and Susan Regan being two of the most precious. I gave Betty Jane a kiss and hug, and then hopped into my Mercedes. I told her I would be back soon to handle the probate and waved goodbye as I pulled out of her driveway. I was determined to make it to Atlanta in less than five hours.

# CHAPTER 33

RIVERDALE PLANTATION
TEN YEARS OLD

The rains came in torrents. There was a lot of talk about Noah and the Ark. It swirled in sideways and pelted us from different angles. The droplets hurled by tropical winds felt like grains of sands stinging my legs and arms as I ran back and forth from the house to the barn to do my chores. It was the middle of August and all our crops were at critical stages. The early-planted cotton was just starting to make the fields look like rows of blooming gardenias with their bright white bolls bursting forth with a bumper crop. The peanut vines were as green as the lily pads in our mill-pond, with thousands of peanuts sprouting beneath the ground. The corn, tobacco and watermelons had looked fabulous before the rains came. Now there was almost a foot of water standing in the rows of our most important cash crops.

My father was in a foul mood as he sat on the front porch and smoked his hand-rolled Prince Albert cigarettes one after the other, throwing the butts into the muddy water swirling around in the yard. Buddy Moore and Lucas McDougal sat on the porch with us and watched it rain. Lucas cussed and Buddy chain-smoked and shook his head. There was no work to do other than feed our animals and try to keep the water from flowing into the barn. None of the hands had worked in the fields for almost two weeks. Everyone was depressed, even Jack who always had a smile on his face.

"Look at that damn rain," said Lucas McDougal. "It's been rainin like a cow peeing on a flat rock for two weeks now. Lord, make this damn rain stop."

We all shared his sentiment. We probably couldn't express it quite as colorfully as Lucas, but we shared it.

The rains had been the result of two hurricanes. The first was a slow mover, which came up into the Gulf of Mexico and made landfall just south of Tallahassee, and then it pushed up towards Martinsville dumping 15 inches of rain on us over three days as it staggered slowly north. The second one was six days later. It came across from the Atlantic, making landfall just below Jacksonville and then it blew into South Georgia spawning tornados and dumping an additional twelve inches of rain on us. We could do nothing but watch it rain and listen to my father cuss.

"Another day or two of this and we're gonna lose everything," my father proclaimed. "Damn watermelons gonna rot on the vines. They wuz about big enough to start cuttin'. Hell, if it stops tonight, we're still gonna lose half of everything. Water will stand in the fields for a week. It ain't got nowhere to go. Damn fields are already saturated. Peanuts gonna rot on them vines, shore as hell."

My mother tried to console him by coming out on the porch handing him a glass of iced tea and then standing behind him, rubbing his neck and shoulders and proclaiming that God would provide a way to get us through this.

"Hell, he's the one done sent all this damn rain," he said. "He must be pissed at me for something."

"Now Calvin, don't talk that way about God," she said. "He's not mad at you. It's just Mother Nature and she's gonna have her way."

As I sat on the porch and hugged Master, I thought of why God might be pissed. How about the killing of a poor black kid for just stealing gas? That might have given Our Holy Father a case of the ass. Or how about beating your youngest son half to death with a belt or a peach limb for no good reason? I doubt Our God Almighty was too thrilled about that one either, I thought to myself. Or how about kicking a poor black family out of their house a few days before Christmas? That might have caused the Heavenly Father to get a little pissed. But as usual, I kept my mouth shut. I knew better than to offer my opinion about anything.

Emma secretly offered her assessment of the situation when she whispered in my ear.

"Mr. Calvin dun brought dat bad luck. Dun tole him befo, don't ever thro a hat on de bed. I dun seen him do dat a dozen times. Bad luck ta thro a hat on de bed. Das whuss bringin all dis bad luck. Don't ever thro ya hat on de bed, baby, das bad luck."

Emma was full of old wives' tales and funny sayings. But maybe she knew more than all of us. I remember she had told me to always hold my breath if I passed a cemetery. She said the spirits hanging around won't be able to get in your body. I had laughed at her, but then I always held my breath as we were leaving church passing Pecan Hill Cemetery.

The rains did not stop. They came for another week. The hurricane rains were replaced by an active tropical depression that swirled around in the Gulf, and then stalled and pushed out bands of rain. The watermelons, peanuts, corn, cotton and tobacco all rotted in the fields. The crops were a total loss. No cotton was ginned, no tobacco cooked and sold, no corn or peanuts harvested. My father sold absolutely nothing. There was no money to pay Lucas McDougal and Buddy Moore. We had to pay them in meat from the smokehouse and vegetables my mother had canned. Both were forced to look for part-time work in town doing handyman chores just to get by. All our hands were out of work also. Some moved away, and others went to stay temporarily with relatives in Atlanta or Florida.

To say my father was depressed would be a huge understatement. He ranted and raved and blamed God for his misfortune. I got severe beatings for such things as blowing a bubble and popping it too loud in the house, dropping a cup and breaking it and for not being respectful. I took my beatings, kept my mouth shut and was consoled by my mother, Jack and Emma and, of course, Master. But my hate was growing. I had finally realized I could do nothing to please him. I just stopped trying and became a morose and sullen child.

After weeks of begging and pleading, my father finally convinced the banks to give him more time to pay back the loans for fertilizer, seed, equipment and diesel. He had been on the verge of having to sell trucks, tractors, combines and possibly some of our land. But he knew the bankers from the Rotary Club and they restructured the loans with the warning, "He'd better have a great crop next year."

Christmas that year was a sad time. Santa's sleigh must have broken down and some of our presents fallen out, because it was slim pickings under the tree. I think my only gift was a sling shot. I'm pretty sure an elf named Jack had carved it for me. But we had plenty to eat from the farm animals we raised and the canning my mother and Emma had done. They kept us well fed, and we had happy mealtimes occasionally.

I was embarrassed that my school clothes were the ones I had worn the previous year. My jeans had patches in quite a few places. I was kidded about wearing "high water britches" because I had grown taller and my pants were way too short. I had got into a few fights because I couldn't take the kidding. But all that ended abruptly when Jack heard about it and came to the school playground. He announced that any-one who wanted to keep all their teeth probably should not be kidding his brother. That was it. No more kidding. Boys in my class avoided me. They apparently were fond of their teeth. God, I loved Jack. I would have given anything to be like him.

It was spring before we knew it. Dogwoods were blooming along the fence line, and the peach trees in our yards went from ugly spiny switch material to verdant green giants. My mother's daffodils and roses produced so many blooms she had cut flowers on the dining table for weeks. The smell of fresh flowers in our house made me smile. My mother loved flowers, and I loved to see her happy. It was a glorious planting season, and we put millions of seeds into the ground, knowing we had to make up for the awful times we had suffered the previous year.

As May slipped into June, a thousand acres of green corn stalks waved in the early summer breeze. The peanut and cotton fields were so green my father kept saying, "Them fields are the color of money." We seemed to get a good soaking rain at least once a week. This was perfect for the growing season, and everything flourished.

Then the rain stopped. And when I say stopped, I mean stopped. From the first week of June until late July, we did not get one drop of rain. The summer temperatures soared and the crops were parched. The soil in the fields was dry and cracked. We went from floods one year to the worst drought in decades the next. Dust whirled and twirled all around our house. Everything was covered in red clay dust. All the cars, trucks, tractors and combines wore a vail of red dust. My father was able to salvage a few hundred small watermelons to be sold at the farmers' market. We harvested a few bales of cotton and a few trailer loads of corn. The tobacco was a total loss, as were the fields of peanuts and soybeans.

My father was forced to sell some of our trucks, tractors and combines. I overheard him telling my mother that he was talking with Mr. Griggs about buying some of our land. We went into fall just scraping by, and I was dreading another austere Christmas. Then my father pulled off a miracle somehow. By Thanksgiving, he had some money. I don't know if he borrowed it from the bankers or maybe he robbed a bank. But we had money again and we had a great Christmas. Presents flowed like the Flint River, and my father actually smiled a lot. Even Master had a half dozen Christmas presents. I knew something was up. Something was going on, but I did not know what. I asked Jack, and he told me that our father was a genius. He had made the banks restructure our loans. I knew better. I had read a book about a genius named Albert Einstein, and though their mustaches looked similar, I knew my father was no Albert Einstein.

One strange thing happened during this time. My father came to dinner one night and told us there had been an accident on the Flint River at the southeast corner of our property, which was mostly thick forest and swamp. He said a barge transporting dangerous chemicals had gotten loose, slammed into the bank at high speed and ruptured. The chemicals had spilled on the bank and had run onto our property. The swamp and the area around it were filled with toxic chemicals. Buddy and Lucas had erected a gate and put up some barb wire to make sure no one got into that area. He told us all to stay the hell away from that area. He said the EPA was coming to clean some of it up but it might be dangerous for months. Buddy told us if we got too close to those chemicals we would be glowing in the dark. He told Jack to go tell all the hands not to be hunting or walking around down in that area by the river unless they wanted to be glowing like lanterns.

We all stayed away. Buddy had previously warned me about certain chemicals that we sprayed on our crops to kill bugs and weeds. He said some of that stuff could kill you if you got it on your hands. I made sure I avoided that area like the plague.

# CHAPTER 34

ATLANTA, GEORGIA
PRESENT DAY

Traffic was heavy as I approached Atlanta. I called my office to see who was in residence. I learned from my secretary, Melissa, that my law partner, Jason Lang, was in court and the other eight attorneys of Reynolds and Lang were out and about somewhere. I informed her I was coming to the office and planned to work late into the night. She asked if I needed her to stay and assist me, but I told her to go home and get some rest as we might burn the midnight oil during the next few days. I was several days behind and needed to catch up with my preparation for a major trial that would start in two weeks.

It took another ninety minutes to creep through Atlanta traffic and make it to my office on the twenty-seventh floor of the Bank of America Tower on Peachtree Street. I parked in the underground garage and took the elevator up to my office. Two of my attorneys and two paralegals were hunched over boxes of files in our conference room. They all stood as I entered and offered condolences for my father's death. I thanked them and informed them that I would be camped out in my office for the next few hours getting caught up.

I opened my mail, and made a few notes to return phone calls the next day. Then I got to work on my upcoming trial. I was suing an insurance company concerning a fatal auto accident. The defendant was a commercial truck driver who had lost control of his vehicle, jumped a low median and slammed into the vehicle driven by the husband of my client, killing him instantly. The truck driver was employed by a large nationally known company. Lab tests revealed he had traces of methamphetamine in his system. The company carried a $2 million limited liability policy with a $3 million umbrella. The insurance company had refused to admit his liability and had offered a meager settlement of $1 million. My client's husband, Philip Banyon, had been a thirty-five-year-old father of a ten-year-old daughter. A substantial settlement was needed to replace years of lost income, and I was hell bent and determined I was going to get it for them. The trial was set to start in two weeks.

For the next two hours I pored over an actuarial report I had received from an expert witness I had hired. He estimated Banyon, an IT manager, would have earned more than $4 million during his remaining working years. I memorized some facts and figures and made a list of a dozen questions I would ask my expert to solidify his report. Then I worked for a couple more hours on other issues I anticipated might come up. I had been in negotiations with the insurance company's attorneys for weeks and I was demanding the full policy limit of $5 million. They had indicated they were ready to roll the dice as to how much a jury would award. They were betting it would be much less than I was demanding. I was ready to take them to the mat. I was betting a jury of good Southern folks would do the right thing and take care of my client's family for the rest of their lives. I just had to make sure I had all the ammunition I would need to convince them.

I looked at my watch, saw it was after midnight and decided I would call it a night. I lived thirty miles north of the city at Sugarloaf Country Club. It took me almost an hour to navigate the maze of downtown Atlanta red lights and street closures. Atlanta" aging sewer system was falling apart causing endless sinkholes, water main breaks and flooded streets. This caused a nightmare for Atlanta drivers.

On Piedmont Avenue I stopped at a red light and noticed a night-club on my left. It was called "ATL Gentlemen's Club." It had a full parking lot, and the place appeared to be hopping with loud music pouring from an open door where a bouncer stood at a tiny lectern to check IDs and collect the cover charge. I noticed the place because I knew it was owned by Clarence Dawkins, the state legislator and busi-nessman my father had listed in the notes he left for me. I made a men-tal note to check into Dawkins' background. I had heard some rumors about him in the past, indicating he was corrupt and his vote was for sale. I needed to know if he was connected to Congressman Brady Lyle and why my father had listed their names.

I had made up my mind on the ride from Martinsville that I would pursue every lead my father had left for me. I would find out what kind of business he had been mixed up in and why some people wanted his tapes destroyed bad enough to kill. My father had been told to let sleeping dogs lie. I wasn't going to do that. People had lied to me, shot at me, robbed me and killed an old acquaintance. I was not about to let sleeping dogs lie. I was pissed off, and I and was going after them.

# CHAPTER 35

My intention had been to get up early, beat the mad rush down Interstate 85 to Atlanta and be in my office by seven o'clock. Since I had slept restlessly, I had assaulted my alarm clock when it buzzed, and then turned over and gone back to sleep. Now it was six thirty and I was faced with sitting in traffic for two hours to get downtown. I made the command decision to work from home until at least mid-morning and then try to make it downtown in an hour. I called Melissa to let her know I would be in around ten.

I was troubled about losing the tapes my father had made. Apparently, he had evidence about some criminality that had occurred more than thirty years ago. But even if I had the tapes, alone they probably would not have been enough evidence to prove a crime. Even if I could prove the crime, the statute of limitations would probably have tolled. Unless one of the crimes was the murder of my brother, Jack, and his girlfriend. There was no statute of limitations on murder.

These thoughts whirled around in my mind as I ate breakfast and sipped coffee. I called Melissa again and asked her to get me Dylan Johnson's number at the Georgia Bureau of Investigation. I stayed on the phone until she returned with the number. Dylan was an old family friend. He had grown up in Martinsville and had played high school football with Jack. He had attended the University of Georgia and joined the GBI after college. He was now the assistant director of the GBI. I had worked several cases with when I had been an assistant district attorney, my first job after law school.

Dylan's secretary put me on hold, and then came back and told me he was in a meeting but would return my call. I left my number, cleaned up my breakfast dishes and grabbed a quick shower. I had just finished knotting my tie when Dylan called.

"Hey Johnny, sorry to hear about your dad. I was planning on going down to Martinsville for the funeral but I got tied up on a case and couldn't make it. My guys busted a big meth lab up near Dawsonville and the director requested my presence up there to do a press conference. You know how that BS goes."

"No problem, Dylan, and thanks for the condolences. I appreciate it."

"Yeah, your daddy was a big deal in Martinsville. I guess y'all had the biggest farm around those parts; it must have been about twenty thousand acres. You had about a dozen tractors and combines. I did a lotta hunting and fishing with Jack. I loved Jack like a brother. We had some mighty good times. I remember you were about knee high. Then years later I walked into court one day and you are a district attorney. I couldn't believe it! Little Johnny Reynolds all grown up and got him a law degree."

"Yeah, you and Jack were like two peas in a pod," I said. "You stayed out at our place about as much as you were at your own. I remember y'all playing football, baseball and basketball together. You two were the stars in Martinsville."

"Yeah, Jack coulda played at Georgia like me if your daddy woulda let him go up there. But Mr. Calvin wanted him to stay and run the farm. He was my best friend, then he was just gone. Presto! Like he just disappeared into thin air. He was just gone and never heard from again. I couldn't believe it. Still don't. Everybody said he ran off with Becky, but I never believed that. He loved your momma too much. I believe he met with foul play somehow. I just shake my head every time I think about it."

"I know, I don't believe he ran off. I believe he was kidnapped or murdered. And that's what I wanted to talk with you about, Dylan. My dad left me a letter and some notes. He wanted me to follow up on some things about Jack for him. Do you have some time to meet with me to discuss it?"

"Yeah, but not today. I'm busier than a one-legged man in an ass-kicking contest today. I got meetings out the ying yang today and tomorrow. I could meet you Friday. Why don't we get together for lunch? How about the Capital Club about one thirty after it clears out some?"

"That works for me. Listen, I'm gonna want to talk with you about any dirt you might have on two of our friendly legislators and maybe some background about what they were up to years ago."

"Oh hell, you wanna get me in trouble, don't you," he laughed. "Anything I tell you would have to be unofficial and I'm not sure what I could say. And I can't talk about any ongoing investigations. You know that, right?"

"I know," I said. "I don't want to get you in any trouble. I just need to know whatever you can tell me about Clarence Dawkins or Congressman Brady Lyle and two guys named Ray and Red Slocum. Just background stuff, where they made their money and if they've ever been in trouble."

"Oh man, you're asking a lot," he said. "Two politicians and two career criminals. There's lots of rumors about them guys. I guess I owe it to Jack and your family; they were always mighty good to me. I'll dig around a little bit. One of my guys was putting together some stuff on Dawkins a while back. Not enough to take to a prosecutor. But seems like he has his hands in a lot of pots. And he has his hand out a lot too, always seeking campaign money. You know he owns a bunch of strip clubs mostly down on the southside. And Lyle made his money in the construction business, supposedly. But there's lots of rumors about him being shady too. Anyway, I'll see what I can come up with and I'll see you Friday."

"Thanks, Dylan, I really do appreciate it," I said and hung up.

I worked on a couple of case files I had brought home with me for another hour as I waited for traffic to clear, and then headed to the office.

# CHAPTER 36

Traffic had cleared somewhat as I headed down Interstate 85 and wound my way through downtown Atlanta to my office building. The office of Reynolds and Lang was a beehive of activity. Several clients were seated in our lobby. I didn't recognize any as I walked by. My secretary Melissa said, "Good morning," and handed me a dozen phone messages as I walked past her desk.

"Let me know when you're ready to talk about a few things. Go over your calendar for the week and sign some checks for me," she said.

My law partner, Jason Lang, walked out of his office, patted my shoulder and said, "Sorry to hear about your dad. I would have come to the funeral but I had that status conference with Judge O'Malley on the Byron case and about a million other things going on."

"Thanks Jay. I didn't expect you to come."

"Did you see the flowers the office sent?" he asked. "Carol and I sent some also."

"Yes, I saw all of them and they were very nice," I lied.

I hadn't looked at any of the flowers. There must have been more than a hundred arrangements. Betty Jane had pulled all the cards from the flowers and would take care of writing the Thank-You notes. I was never good with that kind of stuff.

Jason was not only my law partner; he was also my best friend. He had met Carol Brinkley when they were both undergrads at the

University of Georgia. They had gotten married after graduation, and somehow their marriage had survived while they attended law school at Georgia State University. Carol was an attorney for Coca Cola, but she still had not been able to uncover their secret formula for making Atlanta's most famous beverage. We had given her that mission when she took the job, but so far, no luck.

Jason and I had met when we were both assistant district attorneys in Fulton County. He was a tiger and could prosecute the hell out of criminal cases. We had put our time in fighting in the trenches in the Atlanta courts mainly to gain experience. Then we had both moved on to separate private firms to make our fortunes. I had asked him to be my law partner seven years ago when I had decided to drop out of the major firm where I was toiling away ninety hours a week. I felt that Jason could bring his tenacity to the personal-injury business, and I had been correct. We had made a good team and had been expanding our firm. We had become close friends and I trusted him explicitly. Though still a small firm, we had all the business we could handle and had a sterling reputation. We didn't do mass media advertising like some of the large firms. We had an ad in the yellow pages, were on Google and had a terrific web site. That was it along with word of mouth for us. We weren't getting rich, but we weren't working ninety hours a week anymore either.

I unlocked my office, threw the phone messages on my desk and headed for my personal Keurig. Jason followed me in to get me caught up on what was going on in the firm. He closed my office door and sprawled into a leather chair near my desk.

"You wanna cup?" I asked.

"No, I've already had my two-cup limit for the day."

"Then fire away and tell me what's been going on."

"Well, it looks like the new kid is about to get a good settlement in the Rhodes case."

"The new kid" was Scott Echols, our newest attorney. He was not really new anymore as he had been with us almost a year. But we still called him "the new kid." He was a great hire: young, eager, aggressive and full of piss and vinegar. He had been working on a personal-injury case involving a tractor-trailer slamming into the back of a car parked on the shoulder of Interstate 20. Our client, Charles Rhodes, had been near the front passenger side of his vehicle changing a tire when the semi hit his vehicle. He had been thrown into the air and down an embankment. He had sprained his neck, broken his right shoulder and fractured a couple of ribs. Though he had no permanent injuries, he had missed two months of work and had endured much pain and suffering. The truck driver admitted to the state patrol that he had fallen asleep and lost control of his vehicle. It was a slam dunk case; we were just arguing about how much the pain and suffering was worth.

"What's the offer?" I asked.

"They've offered $600,000 plus medical expenses which were over $100,000. I think that would tickle the hell out of our client. The new kid is hanging tough at a million, which is their policy limit, but thinks they'll meet us halfway at $800,000. I'm sitting in with him this afternoon. I'm sure we'll settle today; they aren't going to trial. So, if you need him to be second chair on your Banyon case, I think he'll be free. He's already read a lot of your trial prep. You could let him handle some of your background witnesses."

"Sounds good. What else?"

"K.T. is sailing along on her nursing home case. We've added a few more clients on that one, so I asked Rusty to help her out with it."

"K.T. will do a good job. Glad you gave her some help. What's she got, a dozen clients now?"

"Fifteen, with the new ones added. We've had a couple of new auto accident cases come in and a MARTA accident.

"The folks in the lobby are all waiting to give depositions in the railroad accident case that Melanie is handling. Oh, and I picked up a probate case, a friend of the family. Looks like about a $5 million estate. It should be relatively simple. No residence to sell, he lived in a nursing home. It's mostly stocks and bonds, and the guy had $400,000 in a checking account. Only two heirs, a son and daughter. I think that's about it."

"Well, I picked up a new probate case also," I said. "My father's. He made me Executor of his estate. So, I guess I'll have to go down to Martinsville a few times to settle it. It's just me, my sister and my niece, so hopefully it will be fairly simple."

"Okay, I'll let you get caught up."

I didn't tell Jason about what had happened while I was in Martinsville. I don't know why. I guess it just still seemed surreal. I couldn't believe I had been shot at, robbed and had found a dead man. I also didn't tell Jason I was meeting with the assistant director of the GBI. Nor that I was about to investigate a US congressman. I wasn't planning to let sleeping dogs lie.

# CHAPTER 37

RIVERDALE PLANTATION
TEN YEARS OLD

I was awakened by my mother's screams. People were running through the house.

"The barn's on fire!" she screamed. "Help, y'all, the barn's on fire! Call the Fire Department!"

I jumped out of bed and ran to the back porch. I saw my father, Jack and Joe running towards the barn. Bright red and orange flames were leaping from the front window of the barn. Black and gray smoke rose into the mimosa trees on the northwest corner of the barn. I could smell it and feel the heat from the fire. My dog, Master, ran towards the barn, barking at the fire. I jumped off the back porch and ran after him to keep him away.

"Joe, get the water hose!" screamed Jack as he and my father ran into the burning barn.

A couple of minutes later I saw Jack riding my horse, Appaloosa, out of the barn. He hopped down from her back, slapped her on her rear to make her run and then ran back in to get other horses. My father came out pulling two horses by ropes as Joe started hosing down the main part of the fire. My father ran back into the barn as Jack came out again chasing and yelling at two of our milk cows. I stood frozen, watching the fire, not knowing what to do. My father came out of the barn driving one of our John Deere tractors pulling a large trailer. He parked the tractor under the peach trees and ran back into the barn.

A moment later he came out carrying two saddles. "I got the back doors open!" he yelled. I looked towards the rear of the barn and saw our new colt and two milk cows running out from the huge double doors that had been slung open.

"Don't just stand there, boy!" he screamed at me. "Git some water buckets from the back porch and throw water on the fire!"

Master and I raced to the back porch, where I filled two wooden buckets from the water spigot and ran towards the burning barn. Jack saw me and grabbed the buckets and threw them on the fire. His face was covered in black soot and his formerly white t-shirt was a dark gray and was ripped in two places. His right arm was covered in blood. He had cut it somehow but didn't take the time to care for it. I could feel the intense heat from the fire as I took the empty buckets and ran back to the porch. I saw Jack race back into the barn. I knew he was trying to shoo the remaining cows and horses out the rear door.

Joe was fighting a losing battle with the water hose. The single weak stream was doing little to douse the fire that had burned through the front doors and was rushing up into the hayloft. The flames were jumping into the mimosa trees, setting them on fire. I watched the colorful pink flowers on the trees turn to black and start to burn. I had climbed those trees a hundred times and then jumped from them onto the roof of the barn. They were completely engulfed in flames now and would be gone soon.

I heard a loud cracking sound and saw the front portion of the barn's roof collapse and fall onto the burning doors, blocking the exit and sending thousands of red embers into the night sky. Jack and my father were in the barn. I dropped the buckets and ran towards the burning doors.

"Jack, get out!" I screamed. "Run out the back door. The roof is falling!" I yelled. But the fire was roaring and crackling and I knew he couldn't hear me. Master barked and jumped towards the flames wanting to fight the fire with us. The flames singed my eyebrows and the front part of my hair. The heat was so intense I had to fall back. I grabbed Master and pulled him back. I was so hot I thought I might be on fire. I dropped to the grass and rolled over several times. I ran back away from the leaping flames and ran around to the rear doors of the barn. Jack and my father were outside in the pig pen adjacent to the barn. They were knocking down the wooden fencing and shooing the pigs into the adjoining pasture.

"Johnny, help get these pigs outta here!" yelled Jack.

Master and I jumped the fence and got into the pen with the squealing pigs. I waved my arms and yelled. A mixture of stinking mud and pig shit flew into the air and landed on my head and arms as the frightened pigs scurried away. A couple of the larger ones ran right over me, their sharp hooves cutting the tops of my feet. When all the pigs were out of the pen, we went back to the front of the barn to help fetch more buckets of water to throw on the fire. Master was at my side continuing to bark and whimper as if to tell me it was a lost cause.

I heard sirens in the distance and saw red flashing lights coming down the hill about a half mile away from our house. The fire truck arrived a few minutes later and screeched to a halt. The firemen quickly connected their hoses to the tank aboard the truck and applied huge streams of water onto the flaming barn. The fire hissed, and massive streams of white smoke billowed into the sky. We all stood back and watched as the firemen did their best to salvage our barn. But it was a lost cause. The remaining roof collapsed into the main floor as hay continued to burn.

The fire crackled and sizzled. I heard breaking glass. Probably exploding quart jars of teat balm for the milk cows or jars of salve

I rubbed on the horses' ankles when they had cuts and scrapes. The intense heat from the fire kept us well back. The firemen finally took control. No flames were visible in the fire, just white swirling smoke, sparks and ashes that drifted up into the night sky like Chinese lanterns. Embers escaped into the night and died quickly as they reached cooler air.

Our beautiful red barn was a smoldering mess. The barn where I had played hide-and-seek in the hay, where my beloved horse Appaloosa lived and where I had toiled for hours doing my chores was now gone. It was sad. I stood there looking at the corpse of our beloved barn and I cried. My mother put her arms around my shoulders as we stood there. She squeezed me and assured me it was going to be alright. Master nuzzled my legs and whimpered as if to echo my mother's words.

At least we had saved all the animals and the tractors. The main victim besides the barn was a John Deere corn combine that had been parked on the north side of the barn near where the fire appeared to have started. It was a total loss. The large rubber tires still flamed a little as the firemen sprayed water to douse it.

The fire continued to pop and hiss like a steam engine as the water touched the remaining flames. The smell of the smoldering rubber mixed with hay and cow manure was so strong it burned my nostrils. My eyes were still watering from the smoke and my throat felt like the Sahara Desert. I couldn't stop sobbing. All of us were covered with soot. Jack joked that we all looked like West Virginia coal miners.

"What the hell are you cryin about?" asked my father as he walked over to us. "We got all the animals out and we saved that tractor while you wuz standin there with yo thumb up your ass."

"Calvin, hush!" said my mother. "We all did what we could. Johnny was totin water with the rest of us."

"Bullshit!" he yelled. "He ain't done nothin but stand there and look. He might as well got some marshmallows and been standin around roasting 'em. That boy ain't worth a shit for nothing."

I was sobbing uncontrollably, partly from thinking about how close we came to losing Appaloosa, and partly because of my father berating me.

Emma walked up behind me and rubbed my shoulders as I stood there sniffling and sobbing.

"Jest be thankful ain't nobody got hurt," she said. "Ain't nothin but a old barn."

I looked down at my bare feet covered in soot, blood and barnyard dust. My face and arms were scorched from getting too close to the fire. I hung my head and pretended I was a thousand miles away. I wanted to crawl beneath the dirt and hide I was so embarrassed. I couldn't stop sobbing. My horse had almost been burned to death and our barn was gone. The barn where I had hidden from him. The barn where I had lain in the hay and recovered after so many beatings.

"Sorry about your barn, Mr. Calvin," said one of the firemen walking up to my father. "We got here as fast as we could, but it was almost gone. That fire burned mighty hot. Listen, I smelled a lot of gas fumes. Did you have gasoline stored in that barn?"

"Ain't been no gas in that barn," he said. "We don't use much gas, mostly diesel. Only gas we got is in that small tank over there by them pecan trees."

"Well, there's definitely a strong gasoline odor and I'm sure that's where the fire started," said the fireman. "You got anyone you been having trouble with? Cause I'm thinking that fire was set with gasoline."

"There's always some kinda trouble with some of the blacks that work for me," he said. "They're always a pissin and moanin 'bout something. A lot of 'em get pissed at me about this and that."

"Well, let us know if you come up with any suspects," said the fireman.

"We got us an arson investigator now. I'll send him out here in the morning. Y'all keep an eye on the barn overnight. Make sure nothing don't flame back up."

"Thanks. I appreciate y'all trying to save it."

My mother said she and Emma would fix us some breakfast while we all washed up. Master and I walked out to the pasture where Appaloosa was grazing. I wanted to check her out and make sure no flaming embers had landed on her and burned her back. Master nuzzled at her legs. They were friends but a little jealous of each other. Both wanted all my attention. I rubbed her face and neck and ran my hand over her back. It turned black with soot so I decided to bring her up to the house and hose her down. As I opened the gate to the pasture and led her out, I saw my father get into his pickup and drive away quickly. I wondered if he was going over to where the hands lived to accuse some of them of burning our barn. I hoped he wasn't going to kill another one. Scared and sad, I gave my horse a good bath and then got one myself.

# CHAPTER 38

The next few weeks were a buzz saw of activity. We salvaged as much as we could from the barn. My father brought several of the hands in from the fields to help clear the debris. Buddy Moore supervised them and had all the salvageable materials covered with tarps. The non-salvageable items were burned or hauled off to the woods. All the animals had to stay in various pastures or open pens with wooden fences that we had quickly constructed. The milk cows were a problem. We had no place to put them except out in open pastures. There they would graze on bitter weeds, which made their milk taste sour. We couldn't drink it or cook with it. My mother tried to make some butter from it, but the yellow creamy butter had a sour taste.

"This crap tastes like saturated horse piss," cried Joe one night at dinner as he ate some of the tainted butter on a biscuit.

"You're gonna get the saturated horse piss beatin outta you boy if I hear any more cuss words at my dinner table!" yelled my father.

My mother quickly threw the butter out. Conflict avoided. Operations back to normal. I loved my mother, the peacemaker.

My regular chores took a couple of hours longer than usual now. I had to go out to the corn fields and pull ears of corn, stuff them in my cotton sack, lug them to the back porch and shell them with the hand-cranked corn sheller. I poured the corn into iron pots and filled them with water so the corn would soak to make the kernels soft so the pigs could eat them. I carried the water-soaked corn from the previous couple of days down to the pig pens and poured it into the troughs for several hundred pigs. My arms ached from lugging the heavy buckets of corn from the porch down to the pig pens.

All our hay had burned in the fire. Our new baled hay had to be stored under tarps out in the pasture. For my final chore of the day, I had to hook a trailer up to a tractor, drive down in the pasture and load bales of hay. Then I had to take it to the cows who were in pastures all over the farm. This was done as the stars were coming out and the moon was rising over the large hill down by the small pond.

My father yelled at me several times to "get off my ass and get them cows fed." I wanted to scream that the pigs, chickens and horses had to eat too; somebody had to eat after dark. I was usually in the cotton fields, corn fields, tobacco fields or hay fields working until sunset. But I kept my mouth shut and my head down. I had learned that a severe beating was only a word away. I had already gotten so many beatings this summer that I was ashamed to wear shorts or get into my bathing suit. The welts and scars on my bottom and legs were numerous. I wore long jeans, kept my mouth shut and did my work in silence. But the hate was mounting. I thought about running away . . .

The arson investigator from the Martinsville Fire Department confirmed our barn had been intentionally destroyed. He told us the fire had been set near the front northwest stall by gasoline. He asked about suspects, and my father told him there were fifty blacks living on our farm that had all had a beef with him from time to time. The investigator interviewed a few but an arrest was never made.

Something was going on. Emma's husband Isaac seemed to be hanging around a lot but wasn't doing much work. He would occasionally work on some of our trucks or combines if they needed fixing. But there wasn't much work for him, yet he was always around. He and my father seemed to whisper a lot and would stop talking and walk away if I came around. Isaac had just purchased a new Cadillac and seemed to be washing or polishing it all the time. He and my father were gone a lot at night. I wondered where they were going but didn't dare ask. I asked Jack about it and he just shrugged his shoulders and said that they had a lot of stuff going on.

Our new barn was completed just after school started that year. I sure was glad. We could keep corn and hay in the barn now and I didn't have to lug it from the fields. It was a nice barn. It was bigger than the old one. It had twelve stalls for the horses and milk cows. But I worried it would be more work keeping all the horse and cow shit shoveled out and putting new hay in them.

Appaloosa had a nice big stall. I sawed a flat piece of wood I found in a scrap pile and made a name tag for her stall. Jack helped me take a soldering iron and burn the letters into the wood. I nailed it to the top board on the gate to her stall and stood back and admired it. It looked great! I was so proud. I bragged to everyone that I had made it myself. Jack just winked at me whenever I said that, knowing he had done most of the work.

We were back in the money! I guess the crops we sold that year brought top dollar. My father bought a brand-new pickup truck, and he bought Jack a Pontiac GTO. It was royal blue with a white vinyl top. The interior was red leather trimmed in white. Jack bought floor mats that had the Georgia Bulldog logos on them. It had a stick shift and a four-speed transmission. Jack kidded that it had "four on the floor," referring to the gear shift. He would take me riding and it would fly. He got it up to over a hundred on the paved road leading into Martinsville. On the dirt roads it would raise a dust cloud that looked like a tornado as he sped towards Riverdale Plantation. I enjoyed riding in that car with Jack. I loved him so much. Little did I know my time with him was coming to an end.

# CHAPTER 39

I was busy with case prep for my upcoming trial and getting caught up on all the other cases in the office. It was Friday before I knew it, and my luncheon meeting with Dylan Johnson from the GBI was upon me. I jumped on the MARTA (Metropolitan Atlanta Rapid Transit Association) train at the Art Center Station and headed for the Five Points Station from where it was an easy walk to the Capitol Club. The CC, as it was affectionately known by Atlanta's movers and shakers, occupied the top floor of the Landmark Tower, a block from the State Capitol Building. I exited the train and raced towards the stairs that would dump me out at the exit onto Peachtree Street near Underground Atlanta. The smell of urine in the stairwell almost choked me. Atlanta had a huge homeless problem and those unfortunate souls usually slept in the stairwells of the MARTA stations. I squeezed my nose with my index finger and thumb and managed to make it out of the station without any further gagging.

Bright sunshine and a light humid breeze greeted me as I crossed Peachtree. The leaves rustled in the huge oak trees across the street in Woodruff Park. The ancient oaks were magnificent specimens, most over a hundred years old. It was a shame that so many were being removed to make way for one more building in downtown Atlanta.

I entered the Landmark Tower, and pressed the elevator button for the penthouse floor. As I exited, I showed my membership card to the attendant and was guided to an alcove table at the rear of the club. Dylan Johnson was already seated enjoying a blooming Vidalia onion and a beer. He was also slathering rich butter on a huge brown roll.

"Sorry about the lousy table," he said. "I thought we might need some privacy and this little nook should provide it." He grabbed my hand and shook it with his huge meaty paws. Pain shot up to my shoulder from his hammer lock grip. Dylan was still all muscle.

"This is fine with me."

I sat down removing my coat and hanging it on the back of my chair while ordering a Michelob Light.

Dylan was a huge man, over six foot six and weighing around 290 pounds. He wasn't fat at all and looked as if he was ready to go ten rounds with Mike Tyson. He had sandy blonde hair that he wore parted in a little boy's haircut. His ruddy face and arms were covered with freckles. His deep green eyes darted around as if he was expecting an attack from all sides. I think it was just a nervous tic, but it made me uneasy and I decided to move closer to him and keep my voice down. Dylan had been a defensive tackle at the University of Georgia and he appeared as though he was ready to suit up and play again tomorrow.

The Capitol Club was an exclusive Atlanta restaurant and private club. The food and service were renowned. Dark paneled walls were covered with paintings of Atlanta sports stars: Greg Maddox, Tom Glavine and John Smoltz from the Braves, Tommy Nobis and Claude Humphrey from the Falcons and Dominque Wilkins from the Hawks, to name a few. The carpet was dark green and felt as though it must have had two inches of padding beneath the beautiful pile. Real Tiffany lamps gave off green and amber glows to various parts of the rooms.

A faint odor of cigar smoke was present but not overwhelming. Smoking was confined to a special room at the rear of the club. Drinks were mixed behind a dark mahogany bar. The bar and adjacent tables were occupied by several patrons I recognized. A few were some of Atlanta's leading citizens, and others were low-life pond scum. They were all united by the fact they each had acquired abundant assets in their lifetimes allowing them membership in the Capitol Club, some legally and several by illegal means. Though they did not co-mingle, all was forgiven within the walls of the club.

It was rare for a public servant to be a member, but I knew Dylan had acquired the necessary assets from the passing of his father, the largest pecan grower in the state of Georgia. He had also married well. His wife, JoEllen, had been a University of Georgia cheerleader and the daughter of an Atlanta insurance magnate. Their home on West Paces Ferry was a show place where I had been invited to parties a few times. They traveled extensively, and their home was filled with antique and exotic decorations from around the world.

I had asked Dylan once why he had gone into law enforcement when he could have been an insurance executive after his marriage to JoEllen. He had laughed and told me that he had always wanted to be an FBI or a GBI agent. He joked that he had applied to the FBI but they had found out his parents were married and therefore it disqualified him from being an agent.

"Let's order some groceries, then we can talk," said Dylan in his South Georgia accent.

"Sounds good to me," I said.

Dylan ordered a T-bone steak, rare, with a salad and loaded baked potato. I thought about what I had eaten while down in Martinsville, so I decided on a salad with grilled chicken and low-fat Italian dressing.

"Damn Johnny, are you dieting or something?" he asked. "You ain't got no fat on you, man. You need to carry a rock in your pocket to keep your ass from blowin away."

"Dylan, you know how it is in South Georgia," I said. "I ate so much when I was down there, I couldn't hardly fit in my car to get home."

"I know how good them fresh vegetables taste," he said. "And you probably had some ribs and fried chicken. Damn, I'm gittin hungry thinking about it. Hope that T-Bone comes soon."

"To start with, what can you tell me about Clarence Dawkins and Brady Lyle?" I asked.

"I got to be careful. I know some stuff that I can't tell you. Stuff that's in our intelligence files. You understand, don't you? Some things came from confidential informants and some things might relate to current investigations."

"I understand," I said. "But can you just give me some background on Dawkins and Lyle and the Slocums? Daddy mentioned them all in some notes he left for me and he seemed to think they may have had something to do with Jack's disappearance."

"Wow, that would be something!" Dylan exclaimed. "You're talking more than thirty years ago. I never knew of any of them guys ever being around Martinsville."

Our food arrived. The chicken on my salad had been marinated in some type of sweet pungent sauce and then blackened on a grill. It was tender, juicy and delicious. Dylan's T-Bone arrived on a sizzling metal plate, the hot grease adding a slight char to the huge steak. It was cooked to perfection, rare and a little bloody. His baked potato was covered with cheese, sour cream, bacon bits, chives and slathered in rich creamy butter. Dylan added ample amounts of salt and pepper and stated we should eat now and talk later.

# CHAPTER 40

**D**ylan finished the final bite of his dessert, a mammoth slice of Black Forest cake covered with several scoops of butter pecan ice cream. I had declined dessert but enjoyed watching him savor his. If eating were an Olympic sport, Dylan would win a medal.

He reached around behind his chair and lifted a brown leather briefcase, opened it and removed three manila folders. He opened one and removed several sheets of official-looking documents. I noted some of the pages were yellowed and appeared very old.

"Now, I don't want you to write any of this down," he said. "This is all background stuff, just to give you an idea of how Dawkins and Lyle got started years ago. I'll make some comments about them and you better forget you heard it from me. Some of this stuff is from some mighty old files and from talking with the guy that trained me as a rookie agent. He's been retired a long time. His name is Josh Tilden. He remembered a lot about all these guys.

"Okay, here we go. Red Slocum and his son Ray were some real badasses back in the day. Congressman Brady Lyle worked with them years ago. Red has passed away but Ray, Jr., is still around and runs a criminal empire that is all over the state and is into everything. I'll explain how they all fit together in a moment."

"Okay, fair enough."

"Red Slocum was a two-bit small-time thief who grew up on the streets of Atlanta. He was your typical dirtbag, into a little bit of everything. He was arrested for robbery, burglary, car theft, aggravated assault and a few other things. He did hitches in the state prison three or four times. He was nicknamed Red because of his hair. Ray, Jr., his son, grew up to be just like his daddy. A punk, in other words. They were able to pool together enough money from their illegal activities to buy a big nightclub down on the southside. It was a cesspool where all types of criminals hung out, and Josh Tilden remembers at least seven homicides occurring there. He said they were dealing drugs, selling moonshine and running hookers out of the place from the day it opened."

"Sounds like a nice place," I said sarcastically.

"Apparently crimes pays," said Dylan. "Because within a few years they had expanded their business and owned six other clubs around the city. Then they opened clubs in Macon, Columbus, Augusta and Savannah. According to Tilden, they were getting into a little of everything: gambling, drugs, stolen cars and pawn shops that were just places to fence stolen goods. Tilden says the GBI had several investigations involving them but could never get enough evidence to put them away. He suspected they had some city cops on their payroll and got tipped off before they were raided. But GBI couldn't prove anything."

"What about Calvin Dawkins and Brady Lyle?" I asked. "How did they fit in with the Slocums?"

"Hang on, partner, I'm getting there," said Dylan. "Dawkins was just a little street urchin who grew up in Forest Park and hung around Slocums' clubs. He went from sweeping and cleaning the places to being one of their bouncers and gofers. Then, he ended up managing one of the clubs. He worked for the Slocums for years. When he started making some money, he started buying up houses in Forest Park and Riverdale. When they expanded the airport, Dawkins cashed in and sold his houses for quite a wad, which helped him buy a couple of clubs of his own. But he was still involved with the Slocums and all their criminal enterprises. The money he made helped launch his career in politics. He started as a county commissioner. He remained tight with the Slocums, and they always backed him and helped get him elected to the state legislature. He's been there for more than twenty years and believe me, we have tried and tried to take him down, because he's as crooked as a snake."

"And Brady Lyle, was he involved with the Slocums also?" I asked.

"According to Tilden, Lyle was good friends with Ray, Jr., when they were in high school. Lyle worked in the clubs on weekends and during summers. He was a punk and was involved in some of their criminal stuff. Mostly keeping hookers in line. He also got to be good friends with Calvin Dawkins."Lyle's parents were killed in a car wreck. He got a large insurance settlement from the accident. He hooked back up with Ray Jr., and they invested in a club together. They made a little money. But then Ray, Jr., got arrested for drugs, and when he went to prison, the club folded, so Brady went back to work for Red Slocum."Red started legitimizing his businesses. He started buying restaurants, car washes, taxi cabs, bail bond offices, real estate and construction businesses. Ray, Jr., got out of prison and was pissed that his dad was trying to go legit. He started over with the clubs, the gambling, the hookers and the drugs. He's still involved in all those rackets and is a constant thorn in our side. Red retired but remained a silent partner in some of the businesses with Ray, Jr. He also funded Lyle in opening a construction business.

"With Red's money Lyle was able to expand from erecting small buildings to the road construction business. There were rumors of bribes and bid rigging, but nothing stuck. He got rich on airport contracts that he got with the help of Dawkins. In a few years, Lyle became one of the largest road building contractors in the state and a million-aire overnight."

"And I guess the rest is history," I said. "He later got into politics, was elected to the state legislature and then got elected to Congress a few years ago."

"Yes, and guess who is the largest backer and vote-getter for Lyle today?" asked Dylan.

"I'm guessing Calvin Dawkins."

"You're guessing right.

Dawkins controls most of the black vote on the southside, and he makes sure his voters support Lyle. His district is 80 percent black so he can deliver the votes Lyle needs. And Lyle takes care of Dawkins and his minions, according to our sources."

"Ray, Jr., and Brady Lyle aren't bosom buddies anymore, huh," I said.

"Au contraire," said Dylan. "We've got good intel they are as close as ever; they just have to do it on the QT. We have learned that Ray funnels some large campaign contributions to Lyle through Dawkins, and they are silent partners together in several businesses, some shady and some legit. Dawkins owns a bunch of topless clubs. He also owns several restaurants, a few used car lots and a couple of strip malls down on the southside. We believe Ray Slocum provides Dawkins with stolen cars for his car lots and runs a couple of chop shops to make the cars look legit."

"Do you have any investigations going on that might result in any of these assholes going away for a while?" I asked.

"Johnny, you know I can't talk about any active investigations," said Dylan. "I'll just say, stay tuned, watch your six o'clock news and maybe you'll hear something in a few weeks."

"Okay, I'll stay tuned, and thanks for the information, Dylan," I said getting up from the table. "It helps me understand how all these guys are connected."

"So, why was your pop looking at these jokers? What was his connection to them?"

I did not want to tell Dylan Johnson that my father had possibly been mixed up with these guys years ago. I was too embarrassed, but I had to tell him something. I was going to have to tell him my father may have been a criminal.

"How about give me a lift back to my office and I'll tell you what I know," I said as I paid the check.

# CHAPTER 41

As Dylan pulled out into traffic, he looked at me and asked, "Okay now, what's your interest in these four dirtbags?"

"Dylan, I really don't know anything about them, but let me start from the beginning and tell you why I'm asking about them."

"Okay, fire away."

"As you know, I went down to Martinsville for my father's funeral. My father left me a letter. He told me about hiring a PI to look into Jack's disappearance. He had hired a former GBI agent named Horace Grimsley down in Albany."

"Oh hell, I know Horace," said Dylan. "He was a damn good agent. He was with the GBI for twenty or thirty years. He got depressed or something when he retired and he ate his gun a while back. Albany Police did the investigation. We looked it over because he was an agent and all. But there was nothing to show it was anything but a suicide."

"Well, my father had hired him a few weeks before his suicide. He paid him $5000 to investigate Jack's disappearance. Grimsley did some digging and then gave him the money back. He said it was too dangerous to go digging into old stuff. He said some of these folks were in high positions now and that he should let sleeping dogs lie. A few days later Grimsley was dead. Soon after, my father started getting threatening phone calls telling him to drop his meddling or his daughter and granddaughter would be hurt; so he did."

"Damn man, maybe we ought to take another look at Grimsley's suicide."

"Well, let me tell you about a couple of other things that happened while I was down there. You remember Lucas McDougal who worked for us at Riverdale?"

"Yeah, I remember him," said Dylan. "He was a crabby old bastard. Always crabbing at Jack and complaining about something. Jack used to make fun of him and talk like him behind his back."

"Well, I went to see Lucas to talk with him," I said. "I thought he might know something about what happened to Jack. I talked with him and he kind of hemmed and hawed and I thought he might be hiding something. I told him to sleep on it and I would come see him again the next day. So, when I went back to see him the next morning, I found him dead with a bullet hole in his head. This wasn't a suicide. No gun was found. Somebody just shot him in the head."

"Yeah, the sheriff down there called the GBI to come assist them with a murder investigation," said Dylan.

"Okay, hang on, I got a couple of more things to tell you," I said. "My father left me four little tapes in his safe deposit box. He said he had secretly recorded some conversations with some folks about some bad stuff they were doing. I got a recorder and tried to play the tapes but they were very old and they started to break apart and the film on the tape ribbons started to flake off. I stopped trying to play them and was going to bring them up here to you to see if your lab techs could preserve them and then play the tapes."

"So, let me have them."

"That's the next thing I was going to tell you. I got robbed! Two masked men burst into Betty Jane's house and took the tapes from me. They had on ski masks and one was holding a sawed-off shotgun and the other a nine-millimeter Sig. They took the tapes and sped away in a black SUV."

"Holy crap man!" exclaimed Dylan. "Did you call the sheriff?"

"Yeah, they came out and took a report and put out an APB for their car, but they never stopped anyone. I don't know what my father's connection was to these guys. I guess he could have been mixed up with them at one time, but I just don't know how or why he knew these guys. I was hoping Lucas could shed some light on it but then he was murdered before I could talk with him again."

"And that's all they took were the tapes?" asked Dylan. "And you don't know what was on the tapes?"

"My father said in the note he left me he had gotten evidence on these guys for doing some bad stuff, that he had secretly taped them admitting stuff. He had written those four names down: Lyle, Dawkins, Red and Ray Slocum. I'm thinking the tapes must have been conversations with those four guys."

Dylan had pulled his car to the curb in front of my building. He put a blue light on the dashboard and sat there shaking his head.

"Obviously, it was important to someone for those tapes to never be played," I said. "They were bold enough to come into my sister's house in broad daylight and rob us to get the tapes."

"Alright Johnny, I'll tell you what I'll do," said Dylan. "I'll have our Albany office look at Grimsley's suicide. Maybe they missed something. Maybe it was a murder. We owe that to Horace to make sure. And then, I'll contact our agent that is working with Martinsville's sheriff and tell him to go over Lucas McDougal's murder with a fine-tooth comb. In the meantime, you stay out of this until you let me see if I can develop something. Also, you didn't hear this from me, but there is a real good chance old Calvin Dawkins might be about to take a fall. If that happens, we can squeeze him and see what he might know about any of this stuff. I know he is still very tight with Ray, Jr., and our good congressman. But you let us handle it."

"Sure," I said. "I don't have the time anyway. I've got a big trial starting in a week and I'm gonna be busy. But I would really appreciate it if you could look into this."

"I'll do my best. Great to see you and thanks for lunch."

He pulled the big SUV into traffic, and I headed up to my office.

# CHAPTER 42

I sat down at my desk and thumbed through my messages. Nothing was urgent. Melissa buzzed me a moment later to tell me I had a call.

"John, Bob Miller here," a stentorian voice boomed. "Wanted to go over a couple of things with you."

"Okay, Bob, you wanna get together?" I asked.

"We can talk on the phone. John, we need to settle this thing," said Miller, referring to the Banyon case. "We do not want any more bad publicity. And you know a two-week trial of this sort is going to be in the *Journal-Constitution* every day. It pulls at the heartstrings. Little girl lost her father, terrible accident and all that. I represent a company trying to do the right thing."

I was astounded. Miller was just repeating all the points I had made to him at our last settlement meeting. He had vehemently disagreed with these points earlier. I guess maybe they had had a "Come to Jesus" meeting and had decided to fold.

"What are you saying Bob?" I asked. "Are you telling me you are agreeing to the five million which was what we had asked for all along?"

"Not exactly, but close," said Miller.

"What's the figure, Bob?"

"Well, first let me say again, Judge Croft urged us to settle this thing. He told us to try to reach an agreement."

"What's the figure, Bob?"

"We're offering $4 million and that's our final offer."

"We're still a million apart, Bob," I said and hung up the phone.

 He called back ten minutes later.

"Now John, don't be rude and hang up the phone. I'm trying to make you a very good offer," said Miller.

"Bob, Mrs. Banyon and I feel we need an adequate settlement to replace the loss of income and loss of spousal consortium. Plus, we need to provide for the future education of their little girl. We need $5 million, which is your policy limit. Our position is that a jury of fair-minded citizens after hearing all the facts in this case would feel obligated to award the max. The Banyon family is entitled to that amount and I'm ready to go to trial."

"You drive a hard bargain, John Reynolds. But we are ready to do the right thing. We'll settle with you for $5 million. Okay if we get together Monday to do the paperwork?"

"That will be fine, Bob," I said as I made a fist pump.

I wanted to call Stacey Banyon and tell her the good news, but decided to wait until all the papers had been signed. I was ecstatic. I packed up and left the office. I was ready for the weekend.

The weekend was the best I had had in a long time. I played golf with a couple of friends and relaxed in my pool and hot tub. I was renewed and ready to go out and fight the world on Monday morning. The horrible traffic didn't even bother me as I drove downtown singing along with Leonard Cohen. Old Leonard was complaining about being held in the "Tower of Song." I was thinking about Susan Regan. I needed to call her today and let her know I had been thinking about her.

I pulled my Mercedes into the underground garage and headed upstairs for another day of combat in the legal trenches. I couldn't get Leonard out of my head and was singing the "Tower of Song" on the elevator:

*"Well my friends are gone and my hair is gray,*

*I ache in the places where I used to play,*

*And I'm crazy for love, but I'm not coming on,*

*I'm just paying my rent, every day in the tower of song"*

I started getting some scornful stares from my elevator mates. I couldn't understand people who didn't like jazz. I was sure my voice was not the irritating factor. I could ape Leonard Cohen all day. *Bitchy people, get a life*, I thought as I exited the elevator.

I entered the lounge area of my office, saw a man seated in a leather chair near the door and dropped my briefcase like a lead balloon. I couldn't move; I was as frozen over as a January pond in Minnesota as I stared at the dead man.

Buddy Moore gave a slight wave to me and said, "How ya doing, Johnny?"

# CHAPTER 43

RIVERDALE PLANTATION
ELEVEN YEARS OLD

Jack had graduated from high school, and it had been an exciting year. The previous fall Jack's high school football team had played in the State Championship. They had gotten beat in a hard-fought game. Jack had done his part. He had completed twelve of fifteen passes and had run for two touchdowns. But a fumble on the kickoff by one of his team's return men had given the other team a cheap touchdown late in the fourth quarter. This had sealed their fate, and they lost by two points. Jack had been heartbroken for a few days, but quickly returned to his normal good-natured self.

Vince Dooley, the head football coach at the University of Georgia, had attended the game and talked with Jack afterwards. He invited Jack to come to Athens for a visit and to discuss the possibility of a scholarship. Jack was on cloud nine but my father was not. They argued about it. He wanted Jack to stay at Riverdale and saw no need for him to attend college.

"College is for people who want to learn a skill so they can get a job later in life," he had argued. "You already have a job. You can stay here and manage this plantation with me and make a good salary. Heck, you can make some big money when the crops are good. You can make a lot more than at some nine-to-five job as a pencil pusher. You don't need no college and you're gonna get your neck wrung trying to play football."

But Jack had dreamed of attending the University of Georgia and he wanted to play football.

"Just let me go up there and try it; let me see what I can do," Jack begged. "If it doesn't work out, then I'll come back home and help you run this farm."

"You're gonna get hurt up there," said my father. "Look at who's on that team. It's mostly black boys and they're mean as hell. I'll bet you there ain't ten white boys on that team. You go up there they gonna be tryin to hurt a white boy. They gonna be gunning for you. They gonna try to kick your ass."

The argument was at a stalemate. Jack went to Athens for his visit and was offered a scholarship. My father hit the ceiling and threatened to take Jack's car away. He told him he would get no financial support. The university would pay for tuition and his room and board but he would still need extra money, and my father wasn't going to give him a dime. Jack was in an uproar. He didn't know what to tell the university. He was worried that he could not survive without a little help from home.

After a week of moping around like a sad sack, he turned down the scholarship. He got a promise from Coach Dooley: if he changed his mind he could come to Georgia at any time and walk on, but he would have to earn a scholarship. He had given up what he wanted to do and the opportunity of a lifetime to please the omnipotent Calvin Reynolds. I told him he was crazy and he agreed he probably was, but my father's hold on him was too strong.

We were still in the money. Christmas had been great. We had new trucks, tractors and combines. Even Betty Jane had a car, and she hadn't even gotten her license, just a learner's permit. My father joked that he had bought her a used car so she wouldn't bang up his truck learning to drive.

The old man seemed to be a little more tolerant of me. I hadn't gotten a beating in several months. I didn't know if it was because our relationship was better or if it was because I had learned everything that pissed him off and was an expert at avoiding those things at all cost.

The crops were looking good. The rain had been perfect and the June sun was turning everything a bright green. I was happy to be out of school for the summer, but a little sad that I would be stuck in a cotton, corn, peanut, watermelon or tobacco field most of the time. I had just finished my morning chores when Buddy Moore approached me.

"Your daddy says you can help me today," he said. "We gotta go clean up limbs in the pecan grove. Lots of limbs done broke when that storm come through here last week. We gotta get 'em all up and burn 'em. Then I can start mowing the grove. Gotta keep them weeds and grass down. With all the rain we been havin, it's a growin up like crazy."

"Great!" I said. "I'd thought I was going with the hands to pull weeds out of the peanuts."

Weed pulling was a back-breaking job, and I hated it almost as much as picking cotton. So I was thrilled to learn I'd be working with Buddy. He was really a nice guy and took the time to teach me things. He was patient and didn't mind taking lots of water breaks. He never yelled at me, and he loved to tell stories about when he was a kid growing up in the North Georgia mountains.

"Go get the little John Deere and hook it up to a cotton trailer and I'll meet you down by the barn," said Buddy. "Fill up a five-gallon can with gas from the tank over there and get a chainsaw or two. We'll need the gas to get them limbs a burnin. I'm going up to the house. Yo momma fixed us some ham and biscuits and a gallon jug of iced tea to take with us. We probably gonna be in the grove most of the day."

I yelled for Master to come with me and headed for the barn where the little John Deere tractor was parked. When I started the tractor, a huge plume of grayish blue diesel smoke escaped from the front exhaust pipe and filled the rafters of the barn. It smelled awful, but disappeared in a few seconds. I had grabbed two chainsaws and attached them to the right side of the tractor with bungee cords. The John Deere made a *tut-tut-tut* sound as I drove it out of the barn and headed to the gas tank.

As I filled a five-gallon can with gas, I thought of the young black boy who had been shot at this very spot a few years ago. I wondered if he was in heaven now or if trying to steal gas from Calvin Reynolds was a sin that would get you sent straight to hell. It still made me sad to think about it. He was so young and his life ended so quickly. I wondered if Calvin Reynolds would be sent straight to hell for killing that boy. My thoughts were interrupted by Master jumping up on me and barking. I think he was telling me to hurry up, he was ready to go. I topped off the can, put it on the tractor, secured it with a bungee cord and headed over to where we kept our empty trailers.

The trailers were parked under several giant oak trees about fifty yards from the barn. A stiff breeze ruffled the leaves of the trees and a few acorns fell like dive-bombers into the trailers. The giant oaks were probably more than a hundred years old. They were beautifully draped in Spanish moss. Their huge trunks looked like boulders, covered with green moss and lichen. I hooked the tractor up to one of the big trailers and drove to the house to pick up Buddy.

"I may eat me one of them biscuits now," said Buddy as he jumped off our back porch carrying a large brown paper sack along with a gallon jug of tea. "They smellin mighty good and I ain't had no breakfast yet. You want one, Johnny boy?"

"No thanks, Buddy," I said. "I'm still full of Sugar Smacks from breakfast. Emma gave me an extra bowl when Momma wasn't lookin, so I'm pretty full."

"Good old Emma," he said. "She looks after ya, don't she boy? That old black woman knows she can cook up some groceries. She gave me a bunch of cookies in this here bag with the biscuits. Said she made two big old trays of 'em last night for y'all's dessert today. Come on boy, I know you can eat a cookie."

He reached into the bag and handed me one along with the jug of tea and crawled up on the tractor and sat on the left fender, unwrapped a ham and biscuit from wax paper and took a huge bite. He put the paper sack into a toolbox mounted behind the tractor seat. I put the tea between my feet. With my cookie in one hand and the steering wheel in the other, I headed for the pecan grove, eating, laughing and talking with Buddy.

The grove was about a mile from our house. It encompassed more than two hundred acres and probably had a thousand trees. I yelled for Master to come on as I raced down the dirt road fronting our house. Master barked and raced after us. He usually accompanied me to whichever field I was working in that day. He would usually find a shady spot to take a nap while I worked. The tractor wheels churned up the red clay dust from the road and we looked like a red tornado racing down the road as I put the tractor's throttle to full speed.

# CHAPTER 44

The morning dew glistened like sparklers on the Fourth of July on the grass and weeds in the pecan grove. I turned the tractor into the barely visible dirt road entrance to the grove, which required me to cross a drainage culvert. The tractor bumped and Buddy grabbed my left shoulder to hang on.

"Easy there, Johnny boy," he said. "You turned that tractor in here like you was at the Daytona 500. You gonna throw my little skinny ass off this here tractor."

I laughed. The way Buddy said some things just cracked me up. Sometimes I wished he was my father. I pulled the tractor in between two massive pecan trees that had broken limbs hanging down. Buddy and I jumped down from the tractor and started our work.

Buddy pulled the cord on one of the chainsaws, and it buzzed like a machine gun. He began trimming smaller branches off the huge broken limb, and I started loading them into the back of the trailer. Master ran around and barked until he got accustomed to the noise of the chainsaw and decided to lay down and take a nap.

We drove up and down the rows of trees, pulling down broken limbs, cutting them and storing them in the trailer. After an hour we had a trailer-full, so we drove down to an open space near the Flint River and unloaded the trailer. We made a huge pile, and Buddy soaked the limbs with gasoline and started a fire. The fire popped and crackled like firecrackers, and fiery embers sailed into the sky as the leaves caught fire and took flight.

Buddy stood by chain-smoking cigarettes and punching at the fire with a shovel. Master and I walked down to the river and watched the swift brown water rush by. Little black water bugs zig-zagged in the still waters of the brown sandy shallows. A blue heron stood on one leg and leaned his narrow top-knotted head close to the water seeking a fish. His dark blue feathers shown purple in the morning sunlight. He darted his crooked head down into the water but came up empty. He took a few careful steps and continued his quest for lunch. His neck so thin and curved it looked like a horseshoe. I could smell fish and noticed bream beds in the clear water near a large sand bar. The small circular craters of the beds made the sandbar look like the surface of Mars. The bream swirled the water and splashed, chasing other fish from their beds. I made a mental note to catch some grasshoppers and come back to this spot on Saturday afternoon if we didn't have work to do. Bream fishing ought to be good if they were bedding. I'd tell Jack; he loved to fish as much as I did.

When the fire had burned down, Buddy yelled and said we needed to get back to the pecan grove and get another load of limbs. I liked working with Buddy. He made the work fun, or maybe it was the fact that he liked to take a lot of breaks.

"We'll get another load and come back down here and fire it up again," said Buddy. "Should be about time for lunch by then. We'll get that fire a going and then set up under them willow trees over there and eat our ham and biscuits. I got enough to even give old Master one."

I drove the tractor back into the pecan grove, and we started loading broken limbs into the trailer. Buddy and I made a good team. He wielded the chainsaw, and I loaded the limbs into the trailer.

The sun climbed into the clear blue sky and was getting close to being directly over us, meaning it was near noon. The summer humidity was high, and the temperature had rapidly climbed. Buddy and I were soaked in sweat, as evidenced by our dark sticky shirts.

"Gettin mighty hot out here. Let's go burn this load of limbs and take a lunch break."

"Sounds good to me!" I shouted as I loaded a large limb into the trailer.

"Grab them two little limbs up there at the next tree," shouted Buddy pointing to a large pecan tree about ten yards ahead of where the tractor and trailer was parked. "They don't need to be sawed; jest pull 'em down. That'll finish off this load. I'll gas up the chainsaw so we'll be ready to go after the break."

I made my way through the tall weeds and underbrush towards the tree where Buddy had pointed. Two small limbs were covered in dead leaves and hanging down from the tree but still attached. Master followed at my heels, his sloppy red tongue hanging out as he panted from the heat.

I reached the limb and was jerking on it trying to pull it down when I saw Master bark and jump at something under the hanging limb. He barked and growled and jumped up and down. I let go of the limb and took a couple of steps towards him.

"What's the matter, boy?" I said looking in the tall weeds growing around the limb.

Master was going crazy. He jumped and barked leaping sideways and then jumping at something under the pecan limb.

Then I saw it. A huge rattlesnake barely visible in the tall weeds was coiled and ready to strike. I heard his rattlers shaking like dead corn stalks rustling in the wind. Then he struck at Master. Its fat head missed Master by inches as the snake extended its strike by more than half of its body. I could see the distinctive diamonds on its back and the pale-yellow underbelly when it struck at Master. The snake coiled again and trailed Master's movements with its darting head, its forked tongue darting rapidly in and out.

"No, Master, get back, get back!" I yelled.

But Master would not obey. He leaped on the snake, his large paws pouncing on the snake's body, barking and growling.

"Buddy, help!" I yelled. "Rattlesnake, rattlesnake!"

Buddy grabbed a shovel and ran towards us.

"Get back, Master!" I yelled my voice breaking up as I screamed.

Master jumped towards the snake again just as the coiled snake struck. Its fangs hit Master squarely on the top of his head over his left eye. Master yelped and spun in a circle and ran off into the tall weeds.

Buddy arrived with his shovel and pushed me back farther away from the snake. With one swift swing of the shovel he hit it in the head. He pushed the shovel down hard on the snake's head and severed it. The remainder of the snake's body continued to wiggle and coil as Buddy stepped back. The snake was huge, more than six feet long and as big around as a Coke can. Its rattlers continued to shake.

I ran to Master and put my arms around him. He had blood running down his head and two fang marks just over his left eye. The fangs had torn his skin, and he was bleeding badly from both cuts. The cuts were beginning to swell and his left eye was completely shut. I hugged him and he whimpered making little squeals as he shook and fell to the ground.

"Buddy, Master got bit!" I yelled. "We gotta get him to the vet!"

Buddy ran over and looked at Master lying on the ground. He shook his head and ran towards the tractor.

"Come on Johnny!" he yelled. "Let's unhook the trailer and you drive the tractor. I'll sit on the fender and hold Master in my arms."

I quickly unhooked the tractor from the trailer and I climbed into the driver's seat. Buddy gathered Master into his arms and climbed on to the tractor's left fender. We drove as fast as the tractor would go and arrived at our barnyard in less than fifteen minutes.

My father was just getting out of his truck when he saw us racing into the yard.

"It's Master, Mr. Calvin!" Buddy yelled. "Done got bit by a rattle-snake. You want me to put him in yo truck, take him to the vet?"

Master shook and whimpered as Buddy eased him down onto the ground. The area around the snake bites had swollen to the size of a baseball. Master" pink tongue lay to the left side of his mouth, and he panted weakly.

"He'll never make it to the vet. Snake bite on the head like that" gonna be fatal."

"It was a big 'un, Mr. Calvin," said Buddy. "That rattler was six feet long, 'bout twenty rattlers."

"Daddy, we gotta try," I yelled. "Please can we get him to the vet? Please, please."

"Hush, boy, ain't no way he's gonna make it," he said.

My father sat down on the ground by Master and rubbed his neck. Master blinked his one good eye a couple of times and gave a final pant. He then lay his head down on the grass and his breathing stopped. Master was gone. I cuddled him in my arms and squeezed and hugged him. I could not stop crying. My best friend was gone. Bitten by a damn snake but probably saving my life in the process. My father left me alone. I sat there holding Master and sobbing quietly. After a while I felt my mother's hand on my shoulder, rubbing and then pulling me.

"Come on baby," she said. "Let's go in the house and get you washed up. I'll get you some cold tea and a bite to eat."

I saw Buddy walking out of the barn carrying a cotton sheet. He put it on the ground and rolled Master onto it. Then he picked him up and carried him into the barn putting him on some soft hay.

We buried Master later that afternoon. Buddy had dug a grave for him. I found some pretty rocks down by the river to mark his grave. Jack found a nice piece of wood and made a sign. He burned the words into the wood with a soldering iron: "MASTER, a real good dog."

# CHAPTER 45

**B**uddy Moore looked like a dead man. He looked as though he had walked off the set of a zombie movie. He had always been thin, but now he was emaciated. His narrow jaws were sunken and his Adams apple stuck out like an arrow. His eyes were recessed back into his head. Dark circles surrounded them. Wrinkles creased his face and forehead like cracked clay on a dried riverbed. His tiny neck stuck out of his blue work shirt like it was on a stem. He was almost bald with just a few small tufts of white hair on his tiny head.

I probably would not have recognized him except for his piercing blue eyes. They were the same. Clear and beautiful, they appeared to be pleading with me. He pushed himself up from the plush chair with difficulty and took a step towards me. I was still frozen in place, but then thawed enough to reach out to him. I started to shake his hand, but changed my mind and hugged him. I could feel the bones in his shoulders sticking out against my chest, and I was afraid I might break him if I squeezed too hard. I held him in a hug for several seconds unaware that tears were streaming down my face. I finally let him go and looked down at his wrinkled hands. They were tiny and nicotine-stained. Buddy looked to be a hundred years old. But I knew he was a lot younger than my father, so he had to be in his sixties.

"You gotta little time to talk?" Buddy whispered in a raspy voice.

"Sure I do, Buddy," I said. "Come on in my office. Can I get you something? You want some coffee or a bottle of water?"

"I could use a cup of java," he whispered. "Black, please."

Melissa hopped up and headed for the coffee maker. She knew to fix me a cup also. I took Buddy's elbow and escorted him. He shuffled his feet and made slow progress. It appeared every step caused him pain. He grimaced a few times and finally made it into my inner sanctum.

I was still in shock. I pulled a leather chair up close to my desk and pointed for Buddy to have a seat.

"Buddy, I thought you were dead."

"Well, thass what I wanted everbody to think. I wuz runnin from some bad folks and I had to get away. Hid up in the mountains for a while and then headed to California. Stayed out there for quite a while. Would slip back to see my folks ever now and then. Wuz workin on a farm that growed lettuce. You know I can grow anything."

"Oh, I know. You could always grow anything at Riverdale. Daddy used to say, 'Old Buddy could throw seeds down in the dessert and up would spring an oasis.'"

"Guess I wuz just born with a green thumb. I always loved growin thangs. Loved the smell of the soil, loved to plant seeds and see all kinds of thangs growin. Green shoots poppin outta the ground like prairie dogs."

Buddy coughed a couple of times and took a soiled handkerchief from his shirt pocket and wiped his mouth. It appeared the conversation had taken all his strength. He looked down at the floor and then studied the backs of his tiny hands splotched with liver spots.

Melissa brought our coffees. Buddy tasted his and gave a nod of approval. I put mine down on my desk where it would get cold. I had a million questions for Buddy. I just hoped he was up to it.

"How's your folks?" I asked.

"Daddy died last year and my momma died three months ago."

"Sorry to hear that, Buddy," I said.

"Well, they wuz old, both well up in their eighties. Both had bad hearts."

"How about you, Buddy? How's your health?"

"I got cancer, Johnny," he rasped. "It's lung cancer. Fifty years of smokin done finally caught up with me. Been gettin chemo but it's a lost cause. Told 'em to stop. I can't take it no more."

"Aw Buddy, I'm so sorry," I said.

"It's okay, Johnny. I done had a good life. Ya know I wuz in the Navy, got to travel all over the world. Then working for y'all and livin on Riverdale, that was a pure joy. I loved all you kids, especially you; you wuz my favorite. I worked for some nice people out in California. They treated me good, paid me good. Also, I met a pretty little Senorita out there. Lived together for a few years. Then she had to go back to Mexico to take care of her parents. But it was good. I've had a good life."

I smiled but couldn't speak. Something had crawled up into my throat and blocked it. I also couldn't see because of the tears streaming down my face.

"Aw, come on now Johnny," said Buddy. "Don't go gettin all sad on me. Everbody gonna die someday."

"Buddy, I love you," I said. "You were always like a father to me. You taught me things and were always so patient. You protected me."

"I love ya too, boy," he said. "Been missing you all these years. Checked up on you a few times. Heard you wuz a lawyer. Proud of that. You had a good heart, loved animals and you cared about everyone, and worked yo little ass off."

I couldn't speak. I cried openly now. Buddy cried too.

"Buddy, you've got to keep taking the chemo. It can add some time to your life."

"Naw, ain't gonna do it Johnny," he warbled. "I'm 'bout ready to go. Ain't no life being sick and pukin all day. I'd rather be at peace. Sit out by the lake, look at them mountains where I was born. No more chemo."

Buddy sat quietly for a few moments and so did I. I wanted to get up and hug him but was afraid I might break a bone in his chest. So, we finished our coffee and I let him rest for a few minutes.

Buddy spoke first. "I heard Mr. Calvin died."

"Yes, a couple of weeks ago. I went down to Martinsville for the funeral."

""Yo daddy wuz a good man," Buddy whispered. "He wuz a hard man. He always treated me good up until we had a fallin out and I had to move on. I know he didn't treat you good. He was awful hard on you. I hated that."

He crossed his scarecrow legs and looked directly at me for a full minute without speaking.

"I got some stuff to tell you, Johnny. Might be stuff you don't wanna hear. I'll let you decide. I'm pretty sure I know what happened to Jack."

I was shocked. Chill bumps covered my arms. I didn't say anything for a moment.

"I don't know for sure, but I know yo daddy got himself in a jam with a bunch a no-good scum suckers. They wuz mean as swamp gators. And yo daddy really pissed 'em off."

Buddy stared at the back of his hands for a full minute and didn't move.

"Johnny, I need to take a leak and I need a smoke. Then I'll tell ya all I know."

# CHAPTER 46

Ten miles south of downtown Atlanta another meeting was taking place. Clarence Dawkins and Ray Slocum, Jr., were meeting in the upstairs office at CD's Top Hat Club, a strip joint owned by Dawkins near Jonesboro.

"Clarence, I got a big load a meth coming down from Dawsonville tonight," said Slocum. "I'm gonna have Tiny and Manny hanging out in here for security purposes 'bout midnight. With that much meth ya can't have too much fire power. And you be sure Tyrell ain't runnin his mouth 'bout this meth."

"No problem, Ray," said Dawkins.

"You know you gonna have to sit on 'bout half this load for a few days," said Slocum. "My boys from Savannah and Augusta can't get up here til the weekend. So, you gonna have to babysit it for a few days."

"Ray, you know I don't like that," said Dawkins. "The police might be sniffing round here. They'd love to bust my ass. I wish we could stow this shit somewhere else. I don't like it in my places that much."

"I thought you done paid off the police around here," said Slocum.

"Hell, I can't pay 'em all off. You never know when some new ones might be stopping by here."

"Well, you gonna have to keep it here. I ain't got no place else to put it right now. I got a hell of a deal on it for buying twice what we normally git and they're fronting half of it to me. We gonna make some big money on this load, baby!"

Slocum slapped Dawkins on the shoulder as they headed down the stairs and out into the club. Slocum grabbed a beer from a cooler behind the bar.

"We do a few more deals like this one, partner, and I'm goin on vacation the rest of the year."

Dawkins shook his head and grabbed a beer for himself. He did not like the fact that Slocum wanted to do larger and larger loads. Larger loads meant getting too many people involved to move the meth. And it took longer to move, meaning they had to keep it stored somewhere, usually at one of his clubs or storage units. He felt uneasy. He had been trying to ease out of the drug business. The GBI and DEA were cracking down on meth. He just wanted to run his clubs, collect a few bribes from contractors and run his stolen car ring. That was enough to keep him in the lifestyle he had become accustomed to for the past twenty years.

"I'm 'bout to head out, Clarence," said Slocum as he grabbed another beer for the road. "The Dawsonville boys should be here shortly after midnight. They gonna ask for Tyrell and will tell him how they want to unload it. I done paid for it. A couple of my boys will be outside scouting things out. They'll make sure no G-men or robbing crews are hanging around. Them Dawsonville boys will have plenty of firepower. Get Tyrell and his crews workin. Let's get this stuff movin tonight."

"No problem, Ray," said Dawkins. "We know the drill."

# CHAPTER 47

Tyrell Knight, aka Tyrell Hardeman, aka Demetrius Tyrell, real name Anthony Jackson, was a four-time loser who had yet to serve any prison time. So far in his criminal career he had escaped by the hair on his chinny chin chin. Originally busted for crack cocaine in Charleston, South Carolina, he was back to dealing crack the next day. He'd received probation for the crack charge. Arrested for marijuana and heroin a year later, he pulled ninety days in the county jail. Busted twice more two years later for heroin and methamphetamine, he was looking at prison time. Fortunately for Tyrell, the DEA was more interested in his supplier than seeing Tyrell go to prison. He ratted out his source of purchase in exchange for his charges being dropped.

Tyrell then moved to Atlanta and got a job as a bartender in a club owned by Clarence Dawkins. It did not take long for Dawkins to recognize the young man's potential. He began selling heroin and meth from behind the bar in a couple of Dawkins' clubs. Dawkins took a personal interest in him and moved him up to bigger and better things. Tyrell had the personality to assist Dawkins in his political campaigns and to move within social circles where he could sell drugs. Within two years he became one of Dawkins' most trusted employees. He moved large amounts of heroin, meth and cocaine for Dawkins who trusted him explicitly.

Life was good for Tyrell until he sold a half kilo of cocaine to a beautiful young lady he had met at one of the clubs. She turned out to be an undercover DEA agent. Tyrell's identity was discovered when his fingerprints were sent to the FBI. Tyrell was finally headed to prison.

Then the DEA approached him about providing information about his employer, The Honorable Clarence Dawkins, Georgia State Representative. It took Tyrell all of five minutes to decide, and he had been providing information on Dawkins and activities at the clubs for the past three months.

Assistant GBI Director Dylan Johnson had been coordinating with DEA Special Agent-in-Charge of the Atlanta office, Gary McKinnon, on the Dawkins investigation for those three months. They had exchanged intelligence concerning Dawkins activities and were evaluating the information Tyrell provided. He had informed them Dawkins would be receiving a large shipment of meth within the next few days, and the lawmen had decided it was time to conclude the investigation and put Dawkins in jail. Tyrell who had always refused to wear a wire had agreed to call them when the meth was unloaded at the bar. A joint DEA/GBI Operations Plan had been developed, and agents were on stand-by to execute the plan.

Tyrell arrived at the club at ten o'clock accompanied by two members of his posse: Quintavios Ammons and Marquis Mobley. The club was packed. Rock music exploded like rocket-propelled grenades from 60-inch speakers in the four corners of the club. Three topless dancers occupied the three small stages adjacent to the huge oak bar that extended for 50 feet down the center of the club.

Clarence Dawkins wasn't at the club much. He let his managers manage and he stayed away unless he had to be there. He was a state legislator and felt his image would be tarnished by hanging out too much at his clubs though he owned five of them.

Dawkins treated Tyrell like a son. He was smart, had a great personality and could move more meth and heroin than anyone in his organization. Slocum didn't trust him; thought he was too slick. But

Calvin loved him and relied on him. Tyrell handled everything once the drugs arrived. He would unload, store and move the drugs out to his street dealers in a timely manner. Dawkins tried not to be in the club when drugs arrived. He was ready to leave as soon as Tyrell came up to his office for final instructions.

Dawkins told Tyrell that Tiny Marlowe and Manny Acevedo, two of Slocum's hoods, would be hanging around the club somewhere. They gave him the creeps. They were both rough guys. They handled a lot of the collections for Slocum and were known to bust some knees if people were late paying. They had been down in South Georgia lately trying to clear up some problems.

He thought about what they might be doing in South Georgia. He had bad memories from down there thirty years ago. He had been a young pup trying to make an impression on Slocum's father, Red Slocum, one of the biggest crooks in the state of Georgia. He had been a worker bee and a gofer. But it had paid off a few years later when Red took a liking to him and made him a manager at one of his clubs. Now he owned more clubs than Red ever had. He owned other businesses and real estate all over the southside. He didn't need Slocum anymore, and he was afraid of the drug business. He wanted out. As soon as they made a good score on this deal and he got his cut, he would inform Slocum he was calling it quits.

Tyrell knocked on the door to the office. Stacks of paper were piled up all over the desk almost hiding Dawkins from view. Tyrell just wanted to get tonight's deal done and he would run like hell. He planned to go to the Bahamas. He hated the thought of what he was about to do to his mentor. But survival was an instinct, and he planned to survive.

"Hey Tyrell, we got a big night going on," said Dawkins. "Lemme give ya the lowdown on whaas about to jump off."

"Is this the big load a meth you been expectin?" asked Tyrell.

"Yep, an it's gonna be a big one," said Dawkins. "Ray dun arranged a really big load. Gonna be comin down with some boys from Dawsonville. Two hundred pounds of meth. Them boys should be here just after midnight and they gonna ask for you.

Y'all can unload at that rear storage room door. We gonna have to keep it in the liquor storage room until we can move it. I want you to pack it in some empty liquor boxes. Take out what you gonna move over the next coupla days. You got yo boys to help ya, right?"

"Yeah, I got two of my boys, but damn Clarence, that's a lotta meth to move," said Tyrell. "Probably take me a few weeks to move all that."

"You ain't gettin it all," said Dawkins. "Ray's got his boys from Savannah and Augusta comin up this weekend to get half of it. But you gonna have to put the other half somewhere. I can't store it here at the club, too dangerous."

"I'll put in a couple a gym bags and move it over to my place. It'll be alright there. I gotta alarm system and a door camera."

"Sounds like a plan," said Dawkins as a knock on the door announced two of Dawkins' least favorite people, Tiny and Manny.

"You guys doin okay?" asked Dawkins.

"Just enjoying the beer and the sights down below," said Tiny. His black shirt was a size too small and his ample gut was about to burst the bottom two buttons. He wore a black fedora and a huge gold chain that was visible around his fat neck. Manny was taller and not quite as fat. He looked like a pro wrestler. He sported a black turtleneck and a gray fedora with a black band. He appeared as though his nose had been broken several times. It was badly mangled.

Both guys were ugly as sin. Dawkins had always wanted to ask Manny, "Is that your nose or are you eating a sweet potato?"

"Ray said you guys were gonna be checking around outside, right?" is what Dawkins really asked.

**224**

"Yeah, we headin out there now," said Tiny. "You got Tyrell's cell number. Y'all see anything suspicious, you call him right away."

"Yeah, we got it and we know what to do," said Tiny as he and Manny headed for the door.

"Them boys are a coupla peckerwoods. I don't like 'em around here. But they's Ray's muscle. They do all the rough stuff for him. You just listen for them callin. If they see any police or robbin crews, you boys scatter. I'm 'bout to head out. You got any problem, you call me."

Dawkins wanted to be as far away from the club as possible when the drugs arrived. He was nervous about this deal. It was too much meth.

# CHAPTER 48

Tyrell entered a bathroom at the rear of the club, sat on a commode in one of the stalls and typed out a text message for Gary McKinnon at the DEA:

*200 lbs meth at Top Hat after 12*

*2 Slocum goons watching outside in black Surburban*

*Will text when meth here*

The DEA and GBI agents went into full operational mode. Units were staged in surrounding neighborhoods a mile away from the club. Six undercover agents—two black, two Hispanic and two in full biker regalia—entered the club at intervals. No Atlanta police were asked to join, as Tyrell had informed them several were on Dawkins' payroll. Dylan Johnson and Gary McKinnon took up a position in the parking lot of a chicken restaurant a mile away from the club.

Inside the club, Tyrell sat at the bar with his posse and had another beer, which he sipped slowly. He checked his watch and saw that it was a few minutes past midnight. He was nervous. He wanted this deal over, and he was ready to split. He knew when the agents raided the club, he would be arrested. It was part of his cover. Hopefully, he wouldn't have to sit in jail too long before they sprung him. He had no intention of testifying against Dawkins or Slocum at a trial. He didn't want to end up dead. He planned to be in the Bahamas or maybe Mexico a few hours after he was released.

Ten minutes later, two white males sporting ponytails entered the club. The shorter one looked like death warmed over. His skin was so pale he could have passed for a zombie. He wore dirty jeans torn in several places and a red plaid long-sleeved shirt. His baseball cap was courtesy of Red Man chewing tobacco. He was missing several teeth and hissed as he asked for a Coors. The taller one wore a green John Deere baseball cap, dirty jeans and a navy-blue T-shirt. His ponytail hung to the middle of his back. He may have had some Indian blood evidenced by his dark features and smooth skin. He ordered no drink but showed an interest in the dancers entwined on the poles on the stages around him.

Tyrell looked the two guys over and decided they had to be the boys from Dawsonville. *In fact*, he thought to himself, *if you looked up meth dealers in the dictionary, these two goons' pictures would surely appear.* But he sat and waited for them to make the first move.

When the short one was almost finished with his beer, he asked the bartender where he could find Tyrell. The bartender pointed across the bar, and the two guys eased off their bar stools and headed over to him.

"You Tyrell?" asked the short goon, the obvious leader.

"Yep, thass me," said Tyrell.

"I'm Darrell. This here is Jimbo. We gotta a little something fer ya."

"Let's go up to the office," Tyrell said as he motioned for Quintavious and Marquis to follow him. They were packing the fire power. If these rednecks tried anything, they would handle it.

Tyrell unlocked the door, and the five of them entered the office. He invited the Dawsonville men to take the two chairs in front of the desk and motioned for his guys to stand behind them.

Tyrell sat down at Dawkins' desk and asked, "How we gonna do this?"

"You got a back door we can pull close to in our van? We in a white van, says 'Barber Plumbing' on the side."

"Yeah, pull around to the northeast corner," said Tyrell. "The door with the light over it, that leads right into the back storeroom."

Tyrell directed Quintavios and Marquis down to the storeroom, and the boys from Dawsonville left to move their van.

Tyrell closed the office door and typed a text message to Gary McKinnon:

*Unloading meth now from Barber Plumbing van at rear of club*

McKinnon alerted all DEA and GBI units to move in. The raid on the club was underway.

# CHAPTER 49

RIVERDALE PLANTATION
ELEVEN YEARS OLD

It was a late Friday afternoon in August, and we were finishing up the last trailer of watermelons for the day. Jack was anxious. He had a hot date. He was taking his girlfriend Becky McCord to the movies. He had been so busy working on our farm that he had not seen her in a week. I kidded him about "being in love" and he chased me. He kept looking at his watch as he neatly stacked the watermelons in a wooden trailer. It was my job to drive the John Deere tractor down the rows in the watermelon patch and stop at piles of melons we had cut and stacked earlier. Two of the hands, Boney and Nesbitt, threw the melons up to Jack who stacked them in wheat straw to keep them from getting bruised. A tractor trailer from a grocery store in Atlanta would arrive tomorrow, and we would transfer the melons from our wooden trailers into their truck.

A whirlwind of dust told us my father was speeding into the field in his new pickup truck. He stopped near us, jumped out of the truck and came over to the trailer to peek inside.

"Jack, y'all got enough melons to finish out this trailer?" he asked. "We gotta have ten full trailers to load up that semi that's comin in here tomorrow."

"We got plenty cut to load out this one," said Jack. "Got some nice melons in this field. These here Charleston Grays are some big melons. It don't take many to fill up a trailer."

"Good job! Y'all finish up here."

Jack motioned for me to pull up to the next pile. He told Boney and Nesbitt to hurry; he wanted to be done in an hour. The two field hands threw the heavy watermelons up to Jack as fast as they could.

When we finished loading the last pile, the trailer was brimming with the lizard-green melons. Jack yelled for Boney and Nesbitt to jump on the trailer and then told me to haul ass for the barn. The sun was just setting in the west as we left the watermelon patch. Orange swirls of clouds mixed with purple and blue hues, they covered the western sky. I loved to watch the sunsets. They were more beautiful than any painting I had ever seen.

As soon as we parked next to the other trailers loaded with watermelons, Jack jumped down and ran towards the house.

"I'll see ya in the morning, sport," he yelled over his shoulder as he ran.

I knew he was headed for a shower and would probably not be joining us for dinner.

Boney unhooked the trailer from the John Deere, and I pulled it into the barn. I began my chores. I hurried as I loaded hay from the barn on to a flat-bed trailer. I hooked it to the John Deere and headed for the pastures to feed the cows. When that was done, I fed the pigs and the chickens from buckets of corn I had filled earlier. I then fed the horses and gave all the animals fresh water.

I was just finishing when I heard my mother yell, "Johnny, you 'bout done out there? We're putting supper on the table. Come on in and wash up."

I ran for the back porch and washed my hands, arms and face at the outside spigot. I dried off on my pants and shirt and headed in for the dinner table. I was starved.

My mother and Emma didn't disappoint. Friday nights in the summer usually meant a fish fry, and I could smell the fish and hushpuppies cooking. I entered the dining room and saw my father, Joe and Betty Jane already seated. My father was laughing and talking with them. That was unusual; he wasn't normally a jovial fellow.

"Them watermelons we sold to the Winn Dixie last week was the most we ever got from a truckload," he was saying as I sat down. "We got $3000 for that one load and we got another semi coming in here tomorrow. They love them Charleston Grays and them Cannonballs. I wish I had planted more a them instead of all them damn little Honey Dews."

Joe piped in to let us know he was hungry enough to eat a cow. Betty Jane told him that was too bad since we weren't having steak tonight. My father laughed and told Joe she'd gotten him on that one.

I was concerned. My father was being funny, nice and talking with everyone. That didn't happen much in our family. I was afraid there was a dark storm cloud forming somewhere.

My mother and Emma brought in steaming platters of catfish, French fries and hushpuppies. Emma went back in the kitchen and returned with a huge bowl of coleslaw.

"Y'all eat up on dem fish now, ya hear," she said. "Den we got us a huckleberry pie wit sum ice cream. Emma done been down dare in the huckleberry patch and got us some nice berries."

"Sounds good, Emma," said my father, who then said a blessing for our food.

"Johnny, did you get all yo chores done?" he asked.

"Yes, sir, I finished up before I came in," I said.

"I want you gettin up early in the morning and get all yo chores done. Then I got a special job for you tomorrow. I'm gonna have you putting labels on them watermelons when we load 'em up on that semi from Winn Dixie. They want 'em on all the melons we ship up there. It'll be an easy job, like having the day off tomorrow. And if we get 'em all done and get that truck outta here by noon, we can go fishin.'"

I was shocked. Here it was right in the middle of the harvest season and Calvin Reynolds was talking about going fishing on a Saturday. Something wasn't right.

Something was different. I knew I hadn't gotten a beating in several months when earlier I used to get them at least once a week. Maybe he was just mellowing as he grew older. I would still keep my mouth shut and my head down. I knew he could explode at the drop of a hat.

"I guess Jack ain't gonna be joining us tonight," he said.

"No, he hopped in the shower and then grabbed a couple of ham and biscuits on the way out," said my mother. "Him and Becky are going to see some new movie tonight. He was in a hurry to git gone."

"Dat boy done got the love jones," said Emma laughing. "He cain't be away from dat Becky fur long. Y'all need anymo tea or anythang else afore I git me a little sumthin to eat?"

"We're good here, Emma," said my mother. "Go ahead and get ya some fish. I'll serve that pie when they get ready."

Emma grabbed two pieces of catfish off the platter along with some hushpuppies, slapped them on a paper plate and headed out to the back porch to eat her dinner. I would have preferred to take my plate and go join her, but I knew better than that.

Emma came back twice to check on us. She knew my father would yell if his glass was empty for too long. She also ended up serving us the huckleberry pie. She gave me an extra-large piece and a huge dollop of homemade vanilla ice cream. She winked at me as she as she gave me the pie and squeezed my shoulder. She often told me she needed to "fatten me up," that I was as "skinny as a rail."

# CHAPTER 50

Jack Reynolds was in love. He had been dating Becky McCord for over a year now, and they had talked about getting married. Jack loved her and was sure she loved him. But he worried about their future. He wanted to go to the University of Georgia to play football. He would give it everything he had to try to make the team. His best friend, Dylan Johnson, had gotten a full scholarship to Georgia. Maybe they could be roommates.

Calvin Reynolds was the problem. He wanted Jack to be a farmer. He did not want to disappoint his father and had agreed to put off his dreams for a year. He needed to save money. He had more than $3000 in a savings account, but that wouldn't last long at Georgia. He needed to save more money, get stronger, get faster and get tougher. Then he would call Vince Dooley and tell him, "I'm comin up there. Y'all better get ready."

But what about Becky? He loved her. Would she follow him? Would she stand by him while he was playing football? Her parents wanted her to go Emory University in Atlanta. That's where her mother had gone. Atlanta was only 60 miles from Athens. Could their love survive driving back and forth every weekend? She could come to Athens to watch him play. These thoughts filled Jack's mind as he drove to pick her up. He had a big surprise for her tonight after the movie.

Jack had planned it all out. He had scouted a new place for them to park after the movie. The police had run them out of their last parking spot down by the lake in Martinsville. He had come up with the perfect parking spot for tonight. No one would bother them.

Jack thought of Becky as he drove. She was beautiful. Her smile would light up a room when she walked in. Her golden blonde hair hung past her shoulders, and she sometimes wore it in a French braid. Other times she let it hang partially over her right eye, making her look like a sexy movie star. She had a strong athletic body, tanned to a golden brown from spending time by her parents' pool. She was like a Goddess.

He had solved a problem for them tonight. They wouldn't be cramped in the backseat of his car this time. They had dreamed about making love in a real bed. How wonderful that would be, to stretch out and take their time, and not have to worry about someone driving up on them. That time he had told Becky's parents they would go to the Steak Burger Drive-In after the movie, where they would get a bite to eat and sit around and talk to all their friends. In actuality, they rushed to park somewhere and make love.

This time Jack had picked a spot out on Riverdale Plantation that would be perfect. He had scouted out a dirt trail that ran back in the woods for about a half mile not far from the river. It was near where his father had put up a gate to keep everyone away where a barge had spilled chemicals. Jack thought the chemicals must have dissipated by now. Not that they would get too close to that area.

He had chosen a little road that was only a pig trail that went off the dirt road about two hundred yards before the warning gate. It was wide enough to drive his car back into a group of huge oak trees where there was a little clearing. A perfect spot for making love.

And they would not be in his back seat tonight. Jack had taken care of that also. He had gone to the barn earlier that day and grabbed a brand-new burlap cotton sheet. He had placed it in the trunk of his car and filled it with soft white cotton from a trailer sitting in the barn waiting to go to the cotton gin. He picked through the cotton to make sure there were no leaves or burrs. He would get Becky to help him lift it from his trunk and spread it out under the oak trees. They would have a bed softer than any feather bed in any hotel in town. It would be perfect for making love. Becky would be thrilled. They would finally have a bed. He was excited as he thought about it. He had thought of everything. He had mosquito spray and a couple of soft pillows from the patio furniture in the backyard. He turned into Becky's driveway and had a huge smile on his face as he walked up the brick walkway and rang her doorbell.

# CHAPTER 51

It had been a good night. Everyone enjoyed the fish fry, and my father was in a good mood. Betty Jane, Joe and I played board games while our parents watched television. There was no more huckleberry pie, but Emma served us homemade vanilla ice cream. I ate it too fast and announced I was getting a brain freeze. Joe remarked that was impossible because I didn't have any brain to freeze.

Emma said her husband Isaac was outside waiting to pick her up. She gave me a big hug and squeezed me into her chest. My father scowled. He didn't like Emma getting too affectionate with us. But he didn't say anything.

We all went to bed around eleven. I wasn't sleepy and lay in my bed staring at the ceiling for a while. I could hear a hoot owl down in the woods below the pasture. His mournful *who- who* sounded spooky to me. I finally drifted off to sleep and was dreaming about fishing. Then I heard a bell ringing. No, it was our phone.

I heard my mother bump her knee on something in the dark and then answer the phone. It was Becky McCord's mother. Becky had not come home, and it was past two. Her curfew was at midnight and Jack had never been late getting her home.

"Oh my gosh, Louise!" said my mother. "I didn't realize Jack wasn't home yet."

She put the phone down and went to Jack's room. His bed was undisturbed. She then looked out near the barn where he parked his car and saw it wasn't there. I heard my father getting out of bed.

"What the hell is going on?" he asked.

"It's Louise McCord," she said. "Becky ain't home yet and Jack's car ain't out there."

She turned back to the phone and spoke again with Mrs. McCord.

"Louise, I don't know what's going on. You know it ain't like Jack to be late. They may have fallen asleep somewhere. I just don't know what to tell you."

"Well, we were thinking about calling the sheriff," said Mrs. McCord.

"Oh no, don't do that. There's got to be an explanation," said my mother. "Maybe Jack's car broke down or they had a flat tire or something."

"I know Jack's a good boy," said Mrs. McCord. "We love Jack and know he would not disrespect us. We were just thinking they may be in a wreck, God forbid."

"Well, I'll have Calvin drive around some and look for them. Why don't y'all do the same thing?"

"Okay, we'll do that, but let's call each other back in an hour and see if we know anymore."

My mother hung up and got dressed to go with my father. They told us to go back to bed, but that wasn't going to happen. There was no more sleep for any of us that night. Joe said he thought Jack and Becky might have run off and got married. He noted that Jack had been really upset with our father about not getting to go to the University of Georgia. Joe said he had been real mopey all summer.

I thought Jack had gotten over it. He was sad for a while but then he was the same old Jack, laughing and joking, taking me places and always up for a good time. I couldn't see him running off with Becky. He wouldn't do that. It would have upset my mother and the McCords.

Emma cooked pancakes and sausage and tried to force us to eat, but we were all too worried. I nibbled on a sausage and biscuit but could not finish it. Betty Jane started to sob uncontrollably. Emma hugged her and assured her Jack would be okay.

The search went on until dawn. No sighting of Jack and Becky was made anywhere. They got the sheriff's office involved around five, but they weren't very interested. They said Jack and Becky probably had eloped. They put out a lookout for Jack's car but they were not too alarmed. They advised they wouldn't even take a missing-persons report until they had been gone at least twenty-four hours.

The McCords came to our house. That was painful to watch. Mrs. McCord and my mother cried a lot. The fathers stood around kicking at the dirt and discussing whether Jack and Becky may have run off and gotten married. My father demanded the sheriff come take a report. A deputy showed up but my father ran him off. He yelled at him and said he wanted the sheriff to come out personally.

He called Buddy and Lucas and told them what was going on. He told them to go all over the farm and see if Jack's car was stuck somewhere. He told them to check along the Flint River and to go back in the woods where that barge had spilled chemicals and check around that area. He pointed out that Buddy knew all about poisons and to be careful; that area was still contaminated.

The semi from Winn Dixie pulled into our yard at eight. Joe and I, along with several of the hands, started loading watermelons on the truck. I jumped into my job of labeling them, but I couldn't get my mind off Jack. I had a feeling something bad had happened. I convinced myself that a wreck had occurred. Jack had run off the road somewhere and he and Becky were trapped in the car. They were alive, just trapped. I told Joe when we were done loading the melons, me and him should ride the roads and look in ditches and ravines until we found them. He agreed, and I noted the tears running down his face.

We had just finished the melons when the sheriff and a couple of deputies drove up. The sheriff went into our house and the deputies leaned up against their cars. I was afraid I would hear yelling and see the sheriff come flying out backwards, but thankfully that didn't happen.

What did happen was the sheriff took the complaint very seriously. Calvin Reynolds was a big campaign donor and a leading citizen. He needed to be responsive even though he was convinced the kids had run away to get married. He notified the state patrol and surrounding law enforcement agencies. He had his deputies on duty start riding the roads slowly checking ditches, ponds and out-of-the-way places for Jack's car. He came back twice that day to assure us they were doing everything they could to locate Jack.

My father and Joe drove down to the houses where all the hands lived. He went around to each family to ask if anyone had seen Jack's car and told them he wanted all of them to look around and let him know if they spotted it.

Buddy and Lucas came back to the house and reported they had covered every square inch of our farm and had ridden the roads surrounding it looking for Jack's car with no luck.

Emma fixed crispy fried pork chops for dinner. She served them with lima beans, fried okra, fresh corn on the cob, cornbread and watermelon rind pickles. We all sat around the table and picked at our food. No one ate much.

My father ate half a pork chop, pushed his chair back and stormed out of the house. I saw him head down to the barn and heard him banging on something. My mother and Betty Jane started another crying fit, so Joe and I got up and headed down to the small pond near the lower pasture. The stars were out and it was a beautiful evening. I heard a whip-poor-will off in the woods somewhere. It sounded like "Chip the widow's white oak, chip the widow's white oak." The mournful cry made me even sadder, if that was possible. We sat on the wooden dock and dangled our feet in the water. We didn't say much. Everything had been said. We hoped they had eloped. Neither of us believed they had. Something bad had happened, and we were just waiting around to get the news.

"He was really pissed at Daddy 'bout not be able to go to Georgia," said Joe. "Their relationship has changed a lot. They aren't close like they was before. Jack was steaming inside. He was totally pissed. He told me he wasn't staying here much longer. He said Daddy was unreasonable and mean."

"He was planning on staying another year and saving some money so he could pay his way at Georgia," I said. "He was lifting weights down in the barn and running. He was staying in shape and he told me he was gonna play football up there."

"Well, I couldn't blame him if he did run off," said Joe. "I ain't staying here much longer. I'm tired a workin my ass off all the time and getting yelled at. Getting up before day and workin into the night. Hell, he treats us worse than he does the hands. I'm joining the Marines. I done talked to a recruiter and I'm takin a test to see about gettin in."

"You can't go in the Marines," I said. "You're only seventeen."

"Well, they think I'm eighteen," he said. "I told 'em I wuz and they don't know no different. If I pass that test, I'm signing them papers and I'm gone. Now you better not tell them. If you do, I'll kick your ass. I'm serious."

I just stared at Joe for a minute. What was that saying about not being the sharpest knife in the drawer? Joe was the dullest knife in the drawer. He needed to finish school and forget about the Marines. I decided I would to tell my mother what he was planning. She would put a stop to that nonsense.

We headed back to the house and went to bed, but none of us could sleep. I heard my mother roaming around in the house and then sitting out on the back porch sobbing. I heard my father go sit with her. They both mumbled something about Jack, but I couldn't make out what they were saying. No one knew what to do. Jack was gone and our family was coming apart.

On Sunday afternoon the preacher came over and sat with my mother for an hour or so. She was weeping uncontrollably when he left. Word had gotten out all over Martinsville. Jack Reynolds and Becky McCord were missing. The last official sighting of them was at the movie theatre on Friday night. They were seen by some of their friends leaving the movie around ten. No one had seen them since.

# CHAPTER 52

ATLANTA, GEORGIA
PRESENT DAY

After Buddy had visited the men's room and had two more smokes, he walked back into my office and ambled towards the same chair. It appeared he might break some of his fragile bones as he lowered himself. His withered face sprouted a few gray spiky whiskers around his chin. He looked around my office and nodded slightly as if to say, "The boy's done alright." He sat for more than a minute looking at me without speaking. Finally, he leaned forward, coughed and began. He stopped and continued to stare at me. He grunted as though he had something caught in his throat, and then struggled on.

"Johnny, this is mighty hard on me. I don't know fer shore what happened to Jack, but I got an idea. Lemme go back and start at the beginning. I'm probably gonna be dead in a few days, so it don't matter. I ain't been able to say nothing because of my folks. I didn't want them gettin hurt."

He leaned back in the chair and grunted as if he were in severe pain. Tears streamed down his face. He took out his soiled handkerchief and wiped them away.

"Okay Buddy, just take your time."

"I'm hurtin, Johnny. This here cancer is eatin my ass up. And what I'm 'bout to tell ya is hurtin more than the cancer. I'm pretty shore I know what happened to Jack."

"I understand, Buddy. You were looking out for your folks; nobody can blame you for doing that. Just tell me what you know. Who do you think took Jack and Becky?"

"Do you member when yo daddy lost them two big crops one right afta another? You mighta been too young to know what wuz goin on."

"Yes, I remember. We had kind of a bleak Christmas."

"Well, thass what started it all. Yo daddy almost lost Riverdale. He borrowed a buncha money. He was sellin equipment and tryin to keep his head above the water. Hell, me and Lucas wuz workin for almost nothin. Yo momma wuz givin us canned beans, tomatoes, peaches and some meat when y'all killed a hog or a cow."

"Yeah, I remember. Those were rough times."

"Well, ya remember Isaac, Emma's husband? Isaac was a moonshiner. He made the best moonshine in the state a Georgia. Black folks would come from all over to buy Isaac's shine." Lucas coughed a few times and looked at his fingers for a few minutes like he had just discovered them.

"Some folks from Atlanta got wind of Isaac's shine and went down there to talk to him. They wanted him to make some fer them to sell up in them black clubs in Atlanta. Well, he didn't have nothin but a lil ol still out backa his house. But they wuz wantin him to build a big still. They told him they would back him and get him all the corn and sugar and everything he needed to make shine.

"Johnny, you hav ta understand. Yo daddy wuz about to lose everything. He wuz desperate. He thought it would be alright to let Isaac make a little shine out on Riverdale and he could get a cut outta it. I ain't sayin it's right. But he thought he could make the bank payments and get some money to farm with."

"So, you're telling me he became a moonshiner?" I asked staring down at my hands. "Calvin Reynolds, the president of the Rotary Club, the well-respected gentleman farmer was a moonshiner?"

"Well, he wuz for a while, until he got back on his feet. I'm sorry, Johnny. I knowed this wuz gonna hurt ya, but I thought you oughtta know the truth."

"Please don't tell me Jack was into this too," I begged.

"Naw, naw, Jack didn't know nuthin 'bout it. But lemme finish and I'll tell ya what I think mighta happened ta Jack."

"Okay, go ahead, Buddy."

Buddy wheezed and leaned far to his right. I thought he might fall out of the chair, but he slowly eased back upright. He paused for a minute, looked out the window and then continued.

"Isaac built the biggest moonshine still I ever see'd right down there near the Flint River. Thass so they could use the water out of the river. It wuz back in some thick woods. Yo daddy come up wit the idea to tell y'all there wuz a barge run aground and spilled chemicals. He had me and Lucas put up a gate and some signs so's nobody could get down that dirt road that run back there. Had us put a big padlock on that gate. All the loadin up of the shine took place after midnight, so's ain't none a y'all would be around. Guys come down from Atlanta once a week in a big truck on Thursday night to load up all Isaac had made."

"Buddy, I can't believe they had that going on right under our noses. We were all over that area hunting and fishing; surely we would have seen something. I remember the story about the barge spilling the chemicals but I thought they cleaned it up in a few months. I remember going fishing down in that area."

"Naw, Mr. Cal made shore y'all went north a where that still wuz. Them Atlanta boys always come on Thursday night to get that shine in the clubs fer the weekend. I oughtta know, 'cause me and Lucas done the loading ever Thursday night."

"So, you and Lucas knew all about the moonshine and y'all actually helped with it?"

"Yeah, we did, Johnny. We needed money as bad as yo daddy did. We suffered when them crops wuz lost too. We ain't made no money. Mr. Calvin wuz giving us plenty of groceries but we ain't had no money. So, he started paying us to help Isaac. We'd deliver sugar and firewood and load the shine on trucks comin in."

"So how long did this go on, Buddy?"

"Little mo than two years, I reckon."

"So why did ya stop?"

"Well, afta 'bout a year or two, Mr. Calvin got in a fight with them guys from Atlanta. They started growing marijuana in that field along the edge of the woods. They had plants growing in the corn too, and Mr. Cal got mad and wanted no part a that. He told 'em to stop and he threatened to bust up the still. But they wuz some hard-ass guys and they kept going. "He kept arguin with 'em and they finally brought the big boss from Atlanta down. A guy named Red Slocum. He was a tough guy, redneck mafia guy. They argued back and forth, and Mr. Cal told 'em to pack up; they wuz not using his land no more. That night they burned y'all's barn down. 'Member that?"

"Yes, I remember when the barn burned down."

"Well, that was them, sending him a message. They told him they would burn the house down next. So, he backed off and let 'em keep on a going. They kept at it 'bout another year I reckon. But then Jack disappeared and then old Isaac got killed up there in Atlanta."

"Yes, I remember when Isaac was killed," I said. "That was a few days after Jack disappeared. It tore the heart outta Emma. She cried for days."

"Yeah, Emma didn't know much 'bout what wuz goin on. I think she kept her eyes closed and didn't wanna think about what wuz happening. She knew Isaac sold a little shine, but thass 'bout all she knowed."

"So Isaac gets killed up in Atlanta and they had to shut the still down—is that what happened?" I asked.

"Yep, thass what happened, 'cause he wuz the only one that could make that good shine. Nobody else had ever done it. Didn't know how to do it like Isaac did. And yo daddy wuz still giving 'em hell. He wanted 'em off his property. He made some tape recordings of 'em talkin and threatened to give 'em to the GBI. So, it seems like ever'thang all came together at once. Mr. Calvin threatened to go to the police, Jack come up missing and a few days later Isaac got killed. So, they had to shut the whole nasty business down."

"Buddy, you said the big boss was a guy named Red Slocum; do you remember who the others were?"

"Shore, like I tole you, I worked with 'em, every Thursday night. Red Slocum had a son named Ray. He usually had one or two flunkies with him. There wuz a young black buck name Clarence Dawkins and a lil white pissant name Brady Lyle. He wuz a real smart ass, always a jokin and actin like he was hot shit. They wuz all 'bout twenty."

"Buddy, did you know Clarence Dawkins is now a state legislator and Brady Lyle is a US congressman?" I asked.

"Naw man, that ain't possible. Them peckerwoods wuz as dumb as a stump. They couldn't pour piss outta a boot. Ain't no way they coulda ever amounted to a hill a beans."

I smiled at Buddy's colorful language. It was hard for me to believe these two guys had been moonshiners and drug dealers in an earlier life, but then I remembered what Dylan Johnson from the GBI had said about them; they were both as crooked as a snake.

"Johnny, lemme tell ya about what happened one Friday night. Ya see, like I said, they always come on Thursday night to get the shine in all the clubs fer the weekend. But one time something done happened. They wuz late. They said they would be there Friday instead. It wuz the same night Jack disappeared. And they wuz actin strange when me and Lucas got there to load up. They'd been a cuttin some the marijuana and loadin it up and then Ray he said—"

Buddy moaned and made a grimace as he changed positions in his chair. His hands were shaking really bad.

"Buddy, are you okay? Can ya hang in there a few more minutes?" I asked.

I had to hear more about what might have happened to Jack. But now I knew why my father had made the recordings and I knew why certain people wanted to make sure they never saw the light of day. I needed to call Dylan Johnson at the GBI. I needed to get Buddy over to him and have him make a sworn statement. And I needed a court reporter to take it all down. I wasn't sure Buddy could tell the story again.

Buddy moaned loudly, leaned forward and fell from the chair. He struck the floor hard and slumped sideways like a pile of rumpled clothes. Blood ran from his mouth and nose and soaked into the carpet. I screamed for Melissa to call for an ambulance.

# CHAPTER 53

Ten DEA and GBI units that had been stationed within a mile of CD's Top Hat Club screamed into the parking lot. Gary McKinnon from the DEA directed two agents towards a black Chevy Suburban parked under an oak tree at the outer edge of the south parking lot.

"ID the occupants and hold 'em!" he yelled as he headed into the club.

The other agents surrounded the club with guns drawn. Two cars blocked in the Barber Plumbing Van and screamed for the guys unloading white bags to drop them and put their hands over their heads. The undercover agents inside the club identified themselves, drew their weapons and directed everyone inside to line up at the bar with their hands over their heads. The dancers slid down from their poles, and joined their customers with their hands over their heads. Two of the agents blocked the hallway to the storage room to prevent anyone from escaping into the club. The maps of the layout of the club drawn by Tyrell Knight proved useful in blocking all points of egress.

Tyrell was coming down the stairs when the ruckus started. He was shoved up against a wall and told to put his hands over his head. He was not excited about having a Sig Sauer automatic stuck in his ear. But he had to go along with the program. He assumed his two posse members were in the storeroom going through the same process. A Beretta pistol was removed from his rear waistband by one of the agents who roughly handcuffed him and told him he was being arrested for carrying a concealed firearm and read him his rights. He was shoved to the floor and told not to move.

The agents who entered the rear door to the liquor storeroom caught the drug dealers at the exact right moment. The meth was half unloaded and the liquor boxes in the storeroom had not been covered leaving the meth in plain sight.

"Drop the bags and raise your hands!" screamed the agents pointing their weapons at Darrell and Jimbo.

They looked at each other and thought about running, but they were not in the mountains above Dawsonville where they could run and hide. They were in the mean streets of Atlanta and had just gotten busted. Someone had ratted them out. And when they found that someone, he would be dead.

Darrell and Jimbo were in handcuffs within sixty seconds of the agents' arrival and were placed on the ground outside the back door. The agents also cuffed Marquis and Quintavios who had just gotten into the storeroom and started to pack the meth in the empty liquor boxes.

Five bad guys were in custody and no shots were fired. This was a successful operation and Gary McKinnon and Dylan Johnson beamed at each other. The only fly in the ointment was the fact that The Honorable Clarence Dawkins wasn't in the club. But they were confident they would have him in handcuffs shortly. They had an arrest warrant with his name on it in their briefcase. Tyrell Knight had provided enough testimony under oath against Dawkins in the past few weeks. All they had to do was pick him up.

They also had a search warrant for the entire club. It turned up a half kilo of cocaine, several ounces of meth from the dancers' dressing room, seven dime bags of heroin and nine bags of marijuana. As for searches of the customers in the club, six had outstanding arrest warrants, three others had concealed weapons, four were felons in the possession of a firearm and various ones had drugs or illegal pills. A total of nineteen people from the club were arrested on various felony charges—a good haul for a Thursday night.

Tiny Marlowe and Manny Acevedo had spotted the agents moving in to raid the club. Tiny had tried to pull out of the parking lot as Manny tried to call Tyrell, but got no answer. Two agents approached the car with guns drawn and forced them onto the ground. Tiny was arrested for an outstanding burglary warrant and Manny for a concealed weapon.

The raid on the club was winding down. It was time to find some of the other players.

"Let's go see if we can find Dawkins," said Dylan Johnson.

"Sounds good," said McKinnon. "I'll grab a couple of agents. Why don't you do the same and we'll head over to his house."

Clarence Dawkins was in bed when the agents arrived. He came to the door barefooted wearing gold silk pajamas, his wiry hair pointed in several directions. His fat gut hung over the top of his pajama pants and pulled his shirt tight. The agents identified themselves and told him they had a warrant for his arrest. They also informed him his club had just been searched and would probably be seized because of the drugs found there. He shook his head and wiped the sleep from his eyes. He asked to call his attorney, but was denied that privilege until he was booked.

"I hope y'all know who ya messin with," said Dawkins. "I'm a state legislator. You ain't got no right to come bargin in here. I don't know nothing 'bout no drugs. I'm a businessman. Hell, I own businesses all over this city."

"We are quite aware of who you are Mr. Dawkins," said Johnson. "In fact, we have been quite aware of your activities for some time now."

Dawkins breathed hard and decided to be quiet. Sweat dripped off his fat face. He was allowed to change clothes, and was then handcuffed and taken out to one of the agent's vehicles.

On the way to the jail he pleaded his case some more. He said he only owned the club and had no responsibility if drugs were being sold there. Then he decided to remain silent.

*Damn that Ray Slocum*, Dawkins thought to himself as he rode in the back of the agent's car. He should have never let Ray talk him into storing meth at his club. He was a businessman. Look at all the good he was doing for the people of his district. Maybe the judge would take that into account. He shook his head and tears rolled down his face. The good life might be over.

Tyrell Knight wasn't happy. He had ridden down to the Atlanta jail in the back of a GBI van with his legs shackled to the floor and his hands cuffed behind him along with Marquis and Quintavios. They wanted to talk, but he shushed them and said the police had these vans wired for sound. He kept shaking his head and pretending they were all in dire straits.

# CHAPTER 54

**B**uddy Moore was rushed to Grady Memorial Hospital. The paramedics who treated him said his blood pressure was eighty over fifty, hardly any pressure at all. They said he was extremely dehydrated, and they started an IV to get some liquids into his body. They worked on him for a few minutes, and then carried him out on a stretcher. He looked up a me at couple of times but made no effort to talk. I feared I would not see Buddy again. He had been on the verge of giving me what I so desperately wanted to know about Jack. He had also confirmed my worst fears about my father—he had been a criminal. And the money he had made to save Riverdale had come from moonshine and marijuana. The President of the Martinsville Rotary Club and one of its leading citizens had been a drug dealer and a bootlegger. I was the son of bootlegger. I guess we were all so afraid of him, we never questioned anything he said or did.

Did Jack know about any of this? Buddy said no, but Jack was extremely smart. I can't see my father doing anything without Jack knowing about it. What about my mother? She would have known about some of this stuff. She would have seen the money. Wouldn't she have questioned where it came from? These questions haunted me as I went to the parking garage to get my car and drive over to Grady. I parked in a No Parking space because the $25 ticket was worth it to park anywhere in the asphalt jungle that was downtown Atlanta.

I inquired about Buddy at the Emergency Room Admitting Desk and got no information. I took the opportunity to dial Dylan Johnson at the GBI to bring him up to speed. I was told he was not available, so I left my number and grabbed a magazine. I needed to get Buddy over to his office and have a court reporter record his information. But like Dylan had said, that was thirty years ago. The statute of limitations had tolled on those crimes by now. I had no proof or evidence, just Buddy's word about what had happened. That was probably worthless now. But maybe we could embarrass the hell out of Clarence Dawkins and Brady Lyle. I was sure they had done everything they could to suppress their pasts before they had run for office.

An hour after my arrival I was told Buddy had been moved upstairs to the ICU. I headed up to the fifth floor and inquired at the desk about his condition. After waiting for twenty minutes, a nurse approached me and told me Mr. Moore was seriously ill and could not be disturbed. I played the lawyer card and told her Mr. Moore was my client and I had to see him on urgent legal matters. When she said this was impossible, I requested to speak with his attending physician. I was told she would get a message to the doctor.

Forty-five minutes later Dr. Emile Ashanti approached me.

"Mr. Reynolds, I understand you are the legal representative for Mr. Edward Moore," he said.

Edward Moore? Hell, I don't think I ever knew Buddy's first name.

I stammered, "Y-Yes sir, I'm Mr. Moore's attorney and I need to speak to him on some urgent legal matters."

"Well, Mr. Moore is extremely ill," he said. "If you are his attorney, you must know he suffers from stage four lung cancer. I'm afraid Mr. Moore only has a short time to live."

I had suspected as much but it still hit me like a sledgehammer.

"I know that doctor, and I was hoping to have a few minutes with him concerning urgent legal matters we must cover," I lied.

"I'm sorry. He's sedated at the moment and probably will not wake up for several hours, if he wakes up again. You should summon his next of kin."

"Yes, of course, I'll do that," I said.

Dr. Ashanti disappeared. I grabbed my cell phone and found a quiet corner of the waiting room. I called my secretary Melissa and told her to get a court reporter down to Grady as soon as possible. I also told her to grab a video camera from our office and meet me in the ICU waiting room. I had to get whatever else Buddy knew about Jack's death into a sworn record, and I wanted a video recording of it also. We were in a race for time, and I was hoping Buddy could hold on a little longer.

# CHAPTER 55

RIVERDALE PLANTATION
TWELVE YEARS OLD

Jack had been gone for almost a year. Life at Riverdale Plantation had continued, if you could call our existence a life. We were all miserable. Life without Jack was almost unbearable. Especially for me. My brother, my best friend, my protector, the shining light in my miserable life was gone. We tried to tell ourselves that burying our sorrows with hard work would help ease the pain. But nothing eased the pain. My father made sure we all stayed busy. He worked us like slaves in the fields from sunup until sundown every day. I was so tired at night, many times I would just collapse on my bed without eating dinner or taking a bath.

He moped around and tried to stay busy. He walked fast like he had a purpose everywhere he went. But we knew he didn't. He was lost. He couldn't concentrate. He would start a job and never finish. He was constantly driving away in his truck, and he would be gone for hours. I smelled alcohol on his breath more than a few times. He had never been a big drinker. I guess he was trying to drown his sorrow. I wished I could find something to help me drown mine.

Joe, Buddy and Lucas ran the farm. They kept all the hands busy. They took care of the livestock and kept the harvest moving along. I admired Buddy more and more. He was fair and tried to make everyone's life easier. But he had a sadness about him. He was hurting like the rest of us.

Lucas on the other hand was a jerk. I did not like him. He was always complaining, and he always had something smart to say. He was hard on the hands. He would call them lazy and criticized everything they did. He was a heavy drinker and more than once I saw him too drunk to drive. Riverdale Plantation was in limbo. Its heart and soul were missing.

Joe worked all the time and didn't say much. The trauma of Jack's disappearance had changed him. He talked more about joining the Marines.

My mother stayed in bed most of the time. Emma did most of the cooking and cleaning. But she was grieving too. Emma had mourned her husband Isaac for a couple of weeks, and then seemed to pick up the pieces and get on with her life. I asked why we didn't go to Isaac's funeral and got a beating for being a smart ass. Emma had always been a part of our family; I guess Isaac wasn't.

When I wasn't in the fields or doing some other meaningless chore, I found solace in burying myself in books and my studies at school. I became the smartest person in my class. I did it for Jack. He was always smart in school, so I made up my mind to be just like him in as many ways as I could. I read everything I could get my hands on. I soaked up knowledge like my brain was a sponge. I stayed up very late at night reading and studying. I was driven. I was doing it for Jack. I thought he was probably up in heaven now and I wanted him to look down on me and smile.

"You're doing a great job, sport." I could hear him laughing and saying that. He had always called me sport.

My sister Betty Jane tried to cheer everyone up. She tried to get my mother to get out of bed to go shopping or to church. But she just didn't seem to have the energy to do anything. Betty Jane served her most of her meals in bed. She and Emma hovered over her as if she were an invalid. If I wasn't working in the fields or doing my chores, I sometimes lay in bed with her and she hugged me. I think she was trying to hold on to the ones she had left. It made me very sad. I became a morose child. My only joy came from riding my horse Appaloosa fast across the pasture and down by the lake. Then of course, I had my books and my love of reading. I could escape through books, and I loved them.

I asked if I could get another dog but my father said we had enough damn animals to feed.

A few months later, my brother Joe gave us a shock. We thought he had also disappeared. He told us he was spending the night with a friend of his, Brian Smith. But the next day Brian came by the house to talk with Joe and informed us he hadn't seen Joe in a week.

Luckily, Joe called to tell us he was at Paris Island, South Carolina. He had joined the Marines and was starting his basic training. Joe had escaped. He had broken out of Riverdale Plantation just like he always said he was going to do.

My mother stayed in bed sobbing for two whole days over the loss of Joe to the Marines. She said she had now lost two of her three sons. My father just kept saying, "Damn him, damn that boy."

I was happy for Joe. He was doing what he wanted to do. He had escaped from underneath my father's thumb, and the Marines would probably be good for him. *Good for you, Joe.*

We had money, not that it made us any happier. Our crops had been very good, I guess. The cotton, peanuts, tobacco, watermelons and corn had all done well. Lucas and Buddy got bonuses. We had new cars, trucks, tractors and combines. We had built a super-duper new barn. Betty Jane and I went on a shopping spree for school clothes. I had never had so many new pairs of jeans and shirts.

We tried to get my mother to do some shopping also, but she would not leave the house. She was convinced Jack had just gone away for a while and he would be coming back. She would be waiting for him when he returned. I worried about her mental state. I didn't think Jack was coming back. Something bad had happened to Jack and Becky, something evil. I could feel it in my bones. I was terribly sad but I had accepted it. I wished my mother would just do the same.

Emma was the one who saved my mother's life. I'm convinced of it. One day Emma made her get out of bed. She fixed her a fine breakfast of eggs, grits, bacon and toast with fresh blackberry jelly and sat down with her and made her eat it along with strong black coffee. Then she got her involved in canning green beans, tomatoes and peaches. They also baked three batches of cookies. My favorites: chocolate chip, oatmeal raisin and lemon snaps.

In no time at all, my mother was showing signs of getting back to her old self. She was still sad and she still had times for sitting silently and sobbing. But she was doing things and taking an interest in her daughter and son at home and writing letters to her son who was away. That became her routine every day. Emma didn't let her deviate. And Emma was always there with her at all times. She loved my mother and was not going to let her while her time away in bed and spend hours crying for her missing son.

Emma told her, "I be missin my man, Isaac, too, but life dun gotta go on."

And they were going on together. They hugged a lot and Emma constantly came up with things for them to do.

I loved Emma for saving my mother. Betty Jane and I had tried to do it and had failed. She wouldn't listen to us, but she listened to Emma.

"You jest hav ta pick yo'self up off dat floor and ya go on with yo life."

Great words to live by, Emma. Later in life, I would remember Emma's words. Whenever I got knocked down, including several times by my father, I picked myself up "off dat floor" and carried on with my life.

# CHAPTER 56

The Honorable Clarence Dawkins, Georgia state representative, businessman, club owner, restauranteur, landlord, real estate mogul and now out-on-bond drug dealer, sat in a conference room at GBI Headquarters with his attorney Simon Berger. Also present were Special Agent Charles Stevens of the DEA, Special Agent Chuck Crowley of the GBI and Assistant Director Dylan Johnson of the GBI and Special Agent-in-Charge Gary McKinnon of the DEA. Special Agents Crowley and Stevens had been the case agents for a six-month joint undercover operation into methamphetamine and cocaine sales from adult entertainment clubs across Atlanta. Johnson and McKinnon were sitting in because the subject was a public official. The FBI had been notified as required in public corruption cases and were waiting to take their crack at Dawkins for suspected bribes involving state construction contracts they had been investigating for months.

Assistant Director Johnson led the interview.

"Mr. Dawkins, you have acknowledged your constitutional rights in the written form you just signed and your attorney is present with you, correct?"

"Thass right," mumbled Dawkins.

"We have all identified ourselves to you and you understand we work for either the GBI or DEA and as such are sworn law enforcement agents, correct?"

"Thass right."

"You have been charged with several felony counts involving the sale and possession of narcotic drugs. It is our intention to charge you with several additional counts relating to a narcotic drug operation we have been investigating for more than six months involving your businesses and certain businesses owned by others. We have witness testimony, video surveillance evidence, wiretap evidence from your home and business phones and a mountain of other evidence we will present to a grand jury here in Atlanta within the next few days.

Do you understand that?"

"I don't much know 'bout dat," spat Dawkins.

"I can assure you we have ample evidence to send you to prison for a very long time."

"Don't know 'bout dat!"

"Well, we do, and we are going to do just that. However, as I told your attorney moments ago, you can have a major impact on just how much time you do in prison and where you do that time. But this is your one opportunity to affect those two things. Once we walk out of this room, all bets are off. If you fail to cooperate with us, we will hit you with so many charges, you will never take another breath of air except from behind prison walls."

"Sounds lika threat to me," said Dawkins.

"No, it's not a threat—it's a promise. I will not lie to you. I am a man of my word. If I tell you trains give milk, you can get a bucket and go to the train station, 'cause the milk train is a comin."

"Most police I knows is nothin but liars," said Dawkins.

"Well, maybe the ones you have on your payroll are liars. Those are some more charges we're considering. We know which police you have paid off, and they are going down too."

Dawkins pushed back from the table and wiped his sweaty face with both of his hands. His meaty paws were shaking and his breathing was heavy. He looked at his attorney who was staring straight ahead.

Johnson began again.

"We have been conducting an undercover operation into activities at your clubs and certain other businesses for the past several months. We will be happy to show you and your attorney some of that evidence in the form of video surveillance tapes and recorded conversations. We are also aware of your long-time association with Raymond Slocum and several of his associates."

"I don't know him."

"Stop, Clarence, stop right there," said Johnson. "If you want any consideration from us, you'll have to tell us the complete truth, you'll have to cooperate with us and you'll have to provide us with some information and possibly some testimony. We just seized more than two hundred pounds of methamphetamine from your club, and we know it was a joint deal you had going with Slocum. So, stop lying."

Dawkins put his face down in his hands.

"Lemme talk wit my lawyer, den we'll see," said Dawkins.

"You're goin to prison. No way we can stop that. But we can help you with how much time you get and where you serve it."

The interview was concluded with a plea from Simon Berger to give them a couple of days to discuss things, and Berger wanted to see all the evidence.

"Time is of the essence," said Johnson. "We'll give you twenty-four hours. We have other arrests to make. And by the way, Clarence, you know most of the people we will be arresting today and tomorrow and we have a lot of independent evidence on each of them. So, make up your mind in a hurry."

# CHAPTER 57

GRADY HOSPITAL
ATLANTA, GEORGIA

I slept for a short while overnight in a chair in the waiting room outside the Grady Hospital ICU. Buddy Moore had not regained consciousness. I did not want to be a pest, but I was going to start bugging them again shortly. I took the elevator down to the coffee shop. My secretary was supposed to arrive soon with a court reporter. I sipped my coffee and called Dylan Johnson at the GBI again. This was the third message I had left for him, but still no call back.

When I arrived back at the ICU, I went straight to the nurses' station to plead my case for seeing Buddy Moore. The head nurse told me Dr. Ashanti would be making his rounds shortly and he would determine if I could see Mr. Moore. I was just taking my well-used seat when Melissa arrived with the court reporter. I recognized Rebecca Ellmand from several previous court cases. She was a top-notch court reporter and I was happy she was here. I explained the situation and informed her we were waiting on the doctor's approval to take a sworn statement from a seriously ill patient.

Another thirty minutes passed before Dr. Ashanti found me in the waiting room.

"Mr. Reynolds, your client is doing a little better this morning, so I'm going to let you see him. But I want your visit kept short," said

Ashanti. "No more than thirty minutes this morning. Then if he is up to it, I'll let you see him again this afternoon. Is that understood?"

"Yes, doctor, I will keep it short."

"You must understand, he is very weak and he has a morphine drip to ease his pain. He may not be totally coherent."

"Understood," I said as I ushered Rebecca and Melissa towards Buddy's room. Melissa cranked up the video camera and started recording. Rebecca prepared her reporting machine.

Buddy was flat on his back with a tube up his nose and an IV attached to his left arm. He had a sheet up to his chest and appeared to be asleep. Though I didn't think it was possible, he looked worse than he did in my office. His eyes were more sunken in, and his face appeared to have a few more wrinkles. His tuft of white hair was standing straight up and he had a white residue dried on the right side of his mouth. Machines beeped in the background and I thought he had gone back to sleep. The room smelled of antiseptics and Lysol. The ammonia coming from the bathroom burned my nose and I hoped the ladies would be okay.

"Buddy, it's me, Johnny Reynolds," I said as I touched the sheet where I could see the outline of his bony arm.

He opened his eyes halfway and a little smile crinkled his mouth.

"I was wonderin if I'd ever see ya again," he said in a voice little more than a whisper.

I motioned for Rebecca to start transcribing. I spoke into a microphone and laid the predicate for the sworn statement, identifying the participants and stating the date, time and location. Melissa operated the video camera.

Rebecca had Buddy raise his right hand and she gave him the sworn oath. Buddy swore to tell the truth.

He coughed and said, "Ain't got much time left in this world, Johnny. This here cancer is 'bout to kick my ass."

"You hang in there, Buddy. You've got some more good days left. These doctors are gonna take care of you. They'll have you walking outta here in a few days."

"Ain't gonna be no mo walkin, Johnny. I know I ain't getting outta this here bed. But thass awright; I'm 'bout ready ta go."

"Don't talk like that, Buddy. You're tough; you can fight this thing. Buddy, they are only giving us thirty minutes, so I need you to quickly outline what you told me yesterday. Cover the moonshining and marijuana and what you know about what happened to Jack. You need to name the people involved and put it in a time sequence as best as you remember. Can you do that? It's very important if we are going to get justice for Jack."

"I'll try," he said and sat up in the bed exposing his skinny arms and heaving chest. Liver spots dotted the backs of his hands and arms. But his beautiful blue eyes were clear, and he understood the purpose. He wanted justice for Jack like I did. He was going to give it his best.

For the next forty minutes, Buddy covered the same things he had told me in my office. Only this time he provided more detail and was sure about the time frames. He also threw in the fact that him and Lucas had both made more than a $100,000 in less than two years just being helpers in the operation. He looked at me and wasn't sure what to say about my father. I told him to tell everything he knew. He was dead and I wasn't worried too much about his reputation. That's when he dropped the bombshell about my father and what he had seen on the fateful night Jack and Becky had disappeared.

# CHAPTER 58

**W**e had finished the interview with Buddy Moore, and I was still reeling as I walked out of Grady Memorial Hospital. The hospital staff had been very generous and had given us a total of forty-five minutes with Buddy. I wanted to return after lunch. I still wanted to fill in a few more details but I had a good idea of what went on the night Jack disappeared and I had shocking information about my father.

I was thinking about running home for a shower and a nap. I was still wearing the same Joseph A. Bank suit I had worn to office the previous day and it had about a dozen extra wrinkles today. I told Melissa I would drop her at the office and I was heading home for a shower and a couple of hours of sleep since I had had practically none in the chair at Grady.

She had just gotten out of the car when my phone rang. It was Dylan Johnson.

"What's up Johnny? I see ya called a few times?"

"Hey Dylan, I thought you were mad at me or you were off on one of your exotic trips.

I left you three messages. I've got some hot scoop for you."

"Sorry man, I've been busy, and I've got some hot scoop for you too."

"Can we get together?" I asked.

"Can you come over to my office? I got so much going on I can't leave right now."

"Forty-five minutes?"

"Yeah, that'll work. See ya then."

I wasn't going to get a shower or a change of clothes after all. I needed to fill Dylan in on what Buddy Moore had told me. I was embarrassed about what I would have to reveal about my father, but I was sure he could use the information to sweat Clarence Dawkins, Ray Slocum and our Brady Lyle. I headed for his office on Panthersville Road.

Dylan was on the phone when I was escorted up to his office on the fourth floor of the GBI building. I waited outside in a plush baroque chair. I guessed that Dylan's wife, JoEllen, had decorated his office; it was tasteful and had expensive furniture. I noticed a photo of Sanford Stadium and photos of various other scenes around the University of Georgia campus. This brought back conflicting emotions as I perused the photographs from the place where I had toiled for six years to get my undergrad and law degree. I had worked three jobs most of the time to pay my tuition and living expenses. Thank heavens for the scholarship money I had received. Except for a few dollars my mom had pilfered, there was no money coming from home. Calvin Reynolds had been pissed when I refused to stay at Riverdale to help with the farm. He had refused to part with a dime for my college education. But that was okay. I had done it without him or anyone else to help me. I was fine with that.

The door to Dylan's office sprang open, and he walked out and grabbed my hand in both of his beefy mitts.

"Come on in, counselor," he said. "You want coffee, tea, coke, anything?"

"No, I just want a few minutes to tell you what I have learned about our friends Dawkins, Slocum and our good congressman, Brady Lyle."

"Okay, you go first, then I got something to tell you about them myself."

I sat down in front of Dylan's massive red cherry desk and told him the whole story of how Buddy Moore had risen from the dead and had appeared in my office. I recounted the things I'd learned about Dawkins, Lyle and Slocum, and what Buddy had seen and heard the night Jack disappeared. I also told him about the shocker he had revealed about my father. He nodded as I covered the details.

"Johnny, that's great about Buddy Moore," he said. "But you realize the statute of limitations has tolled on all of that stuff."

"Oh, I know that Dylan, but there's no statute of limitations on murder. If we can prove these guys had something to do with what happened to Jack and Becky, we can charge them. And Buddy provided quite a bit of circumstantial evidence in his statement."

"Let me tell you the hot scoop I have for you. Dawkins is in jail, and my agents are out looking for Slocum; we have a warrant for his arrest. We raided Dawkins' club and seized more than two hundred pounds of meth."

"That's great. Is Dawkins talking or did he lawyer up?"

"Oh, he lawyered up immediately, but I think he may work with us some. We've got more than a dozen charges on him. We've had an undercover operation going on with the DEA for more than six months. I can't say much more because we still have an investigation going, but I think Clarence will be ready to talk with us very soon. He's looking at spending the rest of his years in jail if he doesn't. And the FBI has several bribery cases on him also. So old Clarence is hurting. We will offer him a deal to cooperate and to testify against Slocum and several others."

"That's great. When are you going to interview him again?"

"We gave him twenty-four hours."

"Based on the information Buddy provided, do you think you can make him talk about happened to Jack?"

"We'll give it try, Johnny. That's all we can do. That was some very interesting info you got from Buddy Moore. We'll hit Dawkins with it and see what he says."

"And don't forget about our good Congressman, Brady Lyle," I said. "He was mixed up to his neck in the bootlegging, growing marijuana and selling it when he was a young buck. I doubt he would want people to know he ran with the Slocums back then. I'm sure he doesn't want that to come out."

"I'll see what we can do, and I'll let you know."

"Thanks Dylan. Just remember, we owe it to Jack," I said as I was leaving.

# CHAPTER 59

I drove like a bat out of hell to get home and get a shower. I needed sleep, but I knew that wasn't going to happen today. I had to get back to the hospital and talk to Buddy. I wanted him to fill in as many details as he could.

The steaming hot water felt heavenly as it splashed my tired aching body. I shampooed my hair and then did it again to get the dust and hospital smell out of it. I was still in shock over what Buddy Moore had revealed about the Friday night Jack had disappeared. I was saddened about my father's role in the criminal enterprise on Riverdale Plantation right under our noses.

How could Jack not have known what was going on? Did he know and was he a part of it like my father, Buddy and Lucas? No way, that wasn't possible. Jack had morals and integrity. There was no way he would have been involved. But if I learned that Jack was involved, it would devastate me.

Buddy had said the bootlegging had gone on for about two years. How in the world had they kept it quiet for that long? My father's business associates had burned our barn and almost killed our animals. Nice folks to be in business with, Dad. Was he crazy? Had he lost his mind? And what about the sheriff? Did he know about it? Had he been paid off? These questions were driving me crazy as I dressed and got ready to go and see Buddy again.

Buddy had a good idea of what had happened to Jack and Becky. He had seen and heard a lot. He had never mentioned any of it when we were looking for Jack. Had my father told him to keep quiet? While my mother was crying and losing her mind, apparently my father knew a lot. What kind of monster could do something like that? The same type that could beat a six-year-old child unmercifully with a peach limb?

Buddy's revelations made me understand certain things now. I thought back to those years and understood why we had new cars, tractors and combines. I just thought we had good crop years. Now I understood. It was moonshine and drug money. It was ironic. My father had been generous and had done a lot of good in the community through the Rotary Club. What a riot! The Martinsville Rotary Club had funded good deeds with drug money. No wonder they let Calvin Reynolds be the president for so many years. I laughed, and then I wanted to cry. What a screwed-up mess!

I drove back to Grady Memorial Hospital. Dr. Ashanti had indicated if Buddy was feeling okay, I would be able to talk with him some more this afternoon. It was past four, so he should be awake and available to visit with me for a few minutes. I elected not to bring the court reporter back for this visit. I had a notebook and a tape recorder. I would tape this session and make a few notes. I just wanted Buddy to fill in some details.

I went up to the ICU floor. I didn't recognize any of the nurses and realized a shift change had taken place. A beautiful Filipino nurse asked if she could help me. I went into my speech about being Mr. Edward Moore's legal representative when she stopped me by raising her delicate hand.

"I'm very sorry, sir," she said. "I'm afraid Mr. Moore passed away this afternoon."

I stood there in shock. No, it couldn't be true. Not yet, Buddy, I had more questions. But Buddy Moore . . . Mr. Edward Moore had died at 2:15 P.M.

Buddy Moore who had befriended me as a child was gone. Buddy who had been a gentle soul, a lover of the land, crops, animals and me, had not been able to beat lung cancer.

Tears cascaded down my face. I walked over to the ICU waiting room and sat down. I put my face in my hands and cried. I would never get any more answers from Buddy. But he had given me a lot. Now it was up to Dylan Johnson to get the rest.

When I finally composed myself, I walked back to the ICU desk and got the name for the coroner and the location as to where Buddy would be taken. I assumed no autopsy was necessary. Buddy had no other relatives. I gave the nurse my business card and told her to inform the coroner I would take responsibility for burial. I wanted to take Buddy back to his home. He often told me stories about hunting and fishing in the North Georgia mountains when he was a boy. I wanted him to go home to those mountains. It was the least I could do for a good man. Buddy Moore had given me the information that would lead to solving the mystery of what had happened to my beloved brother Jack, and I couldn't thank him enough for that.

# CHAPTER 60

RIVERDALE PLANTATION
THIRTEEN YEARS OLD

Things had returned to almost normal at Riverdale Plantation. Emma and Betty Jane made sure my mother stayed busy. She was better. Not good, but much better. Sometimes her grief overwhelmed her and she had to take to bed for a few days. But she managed to get up and get going again after she had cried herself out.

It had helped her tremendously when Joe had come home from the Marine Corps on leave. He had gained a few pounds of muscle and looked very handsome in his dress uniform. My father gave him the cold shoulder, but Joe didn't care. He knew he had escaped the clutches of Riverdale, and he was happy. He told me that being a Marine wasn't nearly as hard as working the cotton and tobacco fields. He strongly suggested that I give it a try when I got old enough. I didn't think so. I was going to the University of Georgia. I didn't have any athletic ability, so I wouldn't be playing football like Jack. But I did have some smarts and I would fill the legacy where Jack never had a chance.

Dinner the night Joe got home was memorable. There was some good news and some bad news. The good news was the dinner. My mother and Emma went all out. It was as if they thought the Marine Corps had not been feeding Joe.

They brought in a huge platter of sizzling steak. It was followed by a platter of fat thick crispy home fries, bowls of fried okra, purple cabbage coleslaw, fresh sliced tomatoes, corn on the cob, a basket of hot buttered rolls and a peach cobbler with homemade vanilla ice cream for dessert.

Emma ran back in the kitchen and yelled, "I gots sum ketchup and sum steak sauce a comin now and I gots mo rolls warmin in da oven!"

Joe ate like the Marines had not been feeding him. My father even commented on his huge appetite. We had a good time. Joe had developed a personality in the Marines. He had never had much to say around the dinner table. But this night was different. Joe told stories about his training, laughed at some of the funny things that had happened to him and his fellow trainees and wanted to know everything that was happening at Riverdale.

After Joe had eaten about half a cow and two bowls of peach cobbler covered with rich ice cream, he got around to the bad news. His unit, the First Battalion, Eighth Marines was deploying to Lebanon. He couldn't talk about it much. He just said President Reagan had ordered the Marines to be part of a peace-keeping force and he would be heading to Lebanon in five days.

My mother burst into tears and left the table. Joe followed her and told her he would be fine. I could hear them whispering from her bedroom. Joe was telling her he was a Marine now and he was trained. There would be a thousand more going and he would be safe.

I wasn't so sure. I read the newspapers and watched the news every day. I knew Lebanon was not a safe place. There was a bloody civil war going on over there and lots of folks were getting killed. A militant group called Hezbollah was taking names and kicking asses. I was worried. I told him to keep his rifle up and his head down. Joe was the only brother I had left in this world. I couldn't even think about losing him.

Joe returned as my father threw in his two cents' worth: "Ain't nothing but a damn fool would go off and be fighting for them folks. They ain't Americans. They ain't nothing but a bunch a rag-heads. Ain't got no business goin off over there. You a damn fool for going in the Marines in the first place."

I almost spoke up. I wanted to scream, "He's not a damn fool; he's your son! And he's a man, a Marine. He's doing what Marines do; he's protecting people that can't protect themselves. That's what Americans do. You're the damn fool!"

But I kept my mouth shut. I was a coward. I was afraid of my father. I had gotten too many beatings and been slapped in the face too many times. I just sat there like a weasel while my father ranted.

Finally, I got up and went to my mother's bedroom. She was crying quietly and mumbling something about Jack. I couldn't take it. I left and went down to the barn. I gave Appaloosa some oats with honey and a couple of sugar cubes. She nuzzled my neck and neighed at me.

"I know, Appaloosa," I said. "The whole world has gone crazy. Everybody but you and me. We got it figured out, don't we girl?"

I went back up to the house and went to bed. But I couldn't sleep. I saw a dark cloud hovering. I thought about Jack. Then I thought about Joe. I prayed he would be safe, but the world was a crazy place and I was mighty worried.

# CHAPTER 61

Joe went to church at Mount Hebron Baptist with us the next morning. My father didn't go. He hadn't been since Jack disappeared. He was at war with God and he seemed to take His name in vain more and more. I guess he blamed God for everything. I had been a little mad at Him myself for a while. I kept asking Him why he let something like this happen to a good guy like Jack. He never did answer me, so I quit asking and after a while I got over it. I didn't blame Him anymore, but I wasn't listening too closely to what the preacher said every Sunday. I guess I was a skeptic.

Joe wore his Marine dress uniform to church. He looked like a recruiting poster for the Marine Corps. He was strikingly handsome. He walked with his back so straight. I think he had grown a couple of inches taller and had put on some weight in the right places. My mother was so proud of him. After the service, he stood around outside the church greeting friends and neighbors. A couple of girls who hadn't given him a second look in high school sauntered over to him and tried to catch his eye. Joe laughed and enjoyed the attention.

We had a Sunday lunch that came close to beating our steak dinner the night before. While we had all been at church, Emma had been cooking up a storm. We walked in, and she immediately started serving us. She brought platters of hot crispy fried chicken. That was followed by bowls of field peas, green beans, turnip greens, cream corn, small red potatoes, corn bread and the rolls left over from last night.

She said dessert would be a surprise. But I had already peeked in the kitchen and spotted a pound cake she would top off with strawberries and whipped cream.

Joe tried to set a world record for stuffing himself. He ate five pieces of chicken plus second helpings of most of the vegetables. He told us stories about the Marine training regimen. He had spent a lot of time crawling around in the swamps at Paris Island and had met up with some critters like snakes, alligators, leeches and ticks.

My father scowled. He didn't care to hear much about the Marines and reiterated his stance that Joe had made a mistake going into the Marines.

That afternoon, Joe and I went fishing down at the millpond. We caught a couple of nice bass and some bream and catfish. Joe laughed and joked with me. He reminded me of Jack. We had a great time. We lost track of time and were late for dinner. I did my chores in the dark.

As I was finishing, Joe came out to the barn and sat on the fence and talked with me. When I was done, he told me he was going into town to see some of his friends. I joked that I had seen him eyeballing those girls at church and I knew which friends he was seeing. He laughed and slapped me on the shoulder.

It was the last time I ever saw my brother Joe, alive.

# CHAPTER 62

When I woke the next morning, Joe was gone. I had no idea he was leaving so early. He had gotten up early and my mother had driven him to the bus station. He caught a Greyhound bus to Atlanta, and then boarded a plane for California where he was stationed with the Marines.

My father had not seen him either. I knew Joe had planned it that way. He didn't want to hear any more of my father's bitching about the Marine Corps. He told my mother to tell everyone goodbye for him and he would see us in about a year.

Three months passed, and we had only received one letter from Joe. He said it was hot and dusty in Lebanon. I knew he couldn't talk much about what he was doing over there. He said he was fine. The Marines were staying in a nice barracks, and he said the food was pretty good for Marine chow. They were doing important work. Lebanon had been torn apart because of the civil war. He had seen a lot of homeless people and a lot of destruction. He wished everyone a happy Halloween, Thanksgiving and a merry Christmas in case he didn't have a chance to write again. Mail service was not good from Lebanon.

My mother cried each time she re-read Joe's letter. I hugged her and told her Joe would be fine. He was a Marine and he could take care of himself. I didn't believe my words. I was worried about him. He was in a foreign land, and there was a lot of shooting going on over there. I saw stories about it on CNN. I hoped he would keep his head down. I prayed for him each night. I told God I would be a better person, would watch my swearing and I would do my chores and keep my mouth shut if He would please look after Joe. I felt pretty good about it. I had made a pact with God and I was holding up my end, except when my father really pissed me off. Then my swearing was pretty bad. But God had to understand, didn't He?

It was the week before Halloween, and we were just finishing our cotton harvest. I had been forced to stay out of school two days to pick cotton. I was looking forward to the next day. We were taking the cotton picked that week to the cotton gin in Martinsville. I would have to drive one of the trucks pulling a trailer load of cotton to the gin. It would be an easy day, and I would get to wander around Martinsville while we waited on the cotton to be ginned.

I completed my regular chores, washed up and came into the house looking forward to a Friday night fish fry. Emma announced it would be another thirty minutes before dinner was ready, so I went into the living room and plopped down in a recliner. Not my father's recliner. I would never be that bold. My father was off on the farm somewhere.

I turned on the television and flipped through a few channels. I caught the tail end of the local news and then flipped it over to CNN. A reporter was standing near the smoking remains of what appeared to be an apartment building. He was saying something about a truck bomb and many injured Americans. I turned up the volume, slid out of the recliner and got closer to the television. The reporter stopped my heart with his next words.

"The bombing occurred an hour ago in Beirut, Lebanon. We are being told two trucks loaded with explosives drove into the compound and parked near the barracks where they detonated a massive load of some type of explosives. An entire building was destroyed. We have confirmed with US forces, the building was housing American troops and we believe there are a number of casualties."

I turned the television off and went into the room where my mother and Betty Jane were sewing. I wondered if my face was white. I didn't know what to say. I just said hello and turned around and left the room. I didn't want them to know what I had heard. They would be horrified. I walked through the kitchen and told Emma to call me when dinner was ready. I walked out to the barn and crawled up onto the gate of Appaloosa's stall. She was drinking from her water trough. She looked up and came over to me and nuzzled my leg hanging over the gate.

I wanted to throw up. My heart rate was accelerated, and my face felt damp. I was about to burst into tears when I stopped myself. Joe was probably fine. He knew how to take care of himself. He probably wasn't even in the building. That was just where he slept. He was probably out doing Marine stuff. I prayed to God he was okay. I walked around in the barn and then out the back door into the pasture. The sun had set, and stars were beginning to peek out from the clouds overhead. I looked up and wondered if God was up there looking down on me. I prayed again and felt somewhat better.

I heard the back door of our house bang and Emma called out, "Johnny, come on ta supper now."

I didn't want to go in the house. I knew I could not act normal. I called out to Emma and told her I had to finish my chores, to go ahead without me.

"But hits gonna git cold."

I heard the door slam again and knew Emma had gone back inside. I knew I couldn't stay in the barn all night. Maybe I could wait for my father to come home. He would turn the news on and then he could tell the family about what happened in Lebanon. I couldn't look at my mother and see her fall apart again. Then I thought of a plan. I walked about halfway to the house and called out for Emma. A couple of minutes later she came out on the back porch.

"Whatcha need, baby? You needs ta come on in here and eat."

"Emma, somethins wrong with Appaloosa's foot," I lied. "I'm gonna be out here in the barn rubbing some salve on it. Tell Betty Jane to come out here when she's done eating."

I turned quickly and walked back to the barn. I would tell Betty Jane when she came out. I'd let her decide if we should tell our mother.

"I'll tell her," said Emma as she walked back into the house.

I went into the barn, found some foot balm and went over to Appaloosa's stall. I rubbed a little of the salve on her left hind foot, and then sat down on a nearby bale of hay. I leaned back and thought of Joe. I prayed again that he was safe. Then I thought that was selfish, so I prayed that all the Marines were safe.

Just as I suspected, my father got home a few minutes before eight. Ten minutes later, I could hear my mother's wails from the barn. As much as I didn't want to, I walked up to the house and asked what was going on.

My mother, Betty Jane and Emma were all around the television and were softly sobbing. My father watched the screen intently but the reporters weren't giving out much information.

"We don't even know if he was at that place," said my father. "Thass a big damn country; he could be anywhere over there."

"But he's a Marine, and that's where he was supposed to be," said my mother. "They said Beirut on the television. That's where his letter came from, Beirut, Lebanon."

"You don't know that. He could be anywhere over there," he said.

We watched television for a while, but we didn't get much information. My father went out to the front porch and lit up a Prince Albert and sat in the swing. I could hear it squeaking as he rocked back and forth. Betty Jane went to her room and played some music. Finally, my mother got up and went into her bedroom. I could hear her sobbing so

I went in and lay down with her. I hugged her and told her Joe would be okay and we prayed together.

I went to bed a little after midnight. I lay in my bed staring at the ceiling and thinking about Joe. I thought about Jack also. I prayed again for both of my brothers. I was pretty sure one of them was dead. I sure hoped they both weren't dead. Sometime around two or three I drifted off to sleep. I woke up on my own around five. I got up, got a shower, got dressed and walked into the kitchen.

My father, mother and Emma were sitting at the small kitchen table drinking coffee. I could tell my mother had been crying, and she looked like she had not slept a wink. My father had a sour scowl on his face, but what else was new. No one mentioned the bombing in Lebanon. I sure as hell wasn't going to bring it up.

"Whatcha doin up so early, honey chile?" asked Emma. "You be wantin breakfast? I can scramble ya up some eggs and fry up some bacon, baby. An I dun got biscuits in dat oven."

"I think I just want some orange juice and maybe a biscuit," I said.

My father pushed his chair back and got up from the table. He leaned over and patted my mother on her shoulder.

"Johnny, grab you a biscuit and then go git yo chores done," he said. "We gotta get that cotton to the gin in a little while. I want you to drive the old Rag Shag truck pulling two trailers. I got Lucas and Buddy coming at seven and I'll pull two trailers behind my pickup. This is gonna be the last good cotton we gonna git this year. I'll have the hands out there scrappin in the fields next week, but I doubt they'll get more than a few bales. Been a good year though. We done sold more than a 1000 bales. Good year for cotton."

I looked over at Emma, but she showed no expression. I felt sorry for her. She had a heart of gold and worked her fingers to the bone, never complaining. She was always happy, singing and doing her work.

I wondered when she grieved. Her husband had been murdered and she had no other family but us. I wondered about God again. He shined his light on some people, and others He seemed to kick in the butt.

"God help me to understand how you pick and choose," I silently whispered to myself.

# CHAPTER 63

Saturday had been a good day, except for me thinking about Joe. We had spent all of it at the cotton gin. Most farmers from around the area were finishing up their cotton crops and the gin was crowded. By the time we got there we had more than a dozen trailers ahead of us. I was allowed to walk around town. Buddy and Lucas stayed with our trailers and pulled them up in line as they snaked their way towards the gin.

I don't know where my father went. He just disappeared for a while. No sweat off my butt. I was glad he was gone. He wouldn't be around to yell at me. I headed off to find something to eat and to do a little shopping in town.

I ran into a couple of my friends, and we hung out together eating hot dogs and sitting on benches at the park by the huge lake. They asked about Joe and wanted to know if he was over in Lebanon. One of them volunteered that more than two hundred Marines had been killed in that bombing over there. They offered their wishes for Joe's safety.

A little past three, I sauntered over to the gin and saw they had finally started to work on our trailers. Buddy and Lucas had not seen my father but thought he had probably gone to get something to eat. He came driving up in his pickup just as the gin was finishing our last trailer. He went into the office to collect the checks and came out beaming.

"Thass the best price per pound we got all year," he said. "Cotton's getting a little scarce here at the end of the year and the price is goin up. Let's go to the house, boys," he said.

We all jumped in our trucks and headed home. I wanted to catch the news on CNN, but I was afraid to watch it.

We watched it anyway. All of us were huddled around the television set. We learned two trucks carrying tons of explosives had plowed into the Marines barracks. More than two hundred Marines were thought to have been killed or were missing. The militant group, Hezbollah, was claiming responsibility.

My mother grabbed some tissues and left for her bedroom. Betty Jane went with her. I did not want to watch any more about the bombing, so I went to my room and grabbed a book. I tried to read, but couldn't keep my mind on the novel. I got up and went out on the front porch. My father was sitting in the swing, rocking back and forth and smoking his hand-rolled Prince Albert.

"When you think we'll hear something about Joe?" I asked.

"Don't know," he said. "From the looks of that building on the TV, they might not be able to find some of them boys for weeks. I hope he can call us or get a message to us somehow. If he don't yo momma's gonna be a basket case."

I thought to myself, *He almost seems human at times like these.* I thought back to when Jack went missing. He was a basket case for weeks. He swore and moped around. He screamed at me and gave me beatings like it was my fault. I wondered if he would be like that if Joe didn't come back. I didn't want to think about it. I said goodnight and walked out to the barn to see Appaloosa. I talked with her a while. She didn't have much to say, but I knew she was feeling my pain. I rubbed her neck and nuzzled her. She nuzzled me back and told me she understood my pain without saying a word.

We went to church the next morning. I was surprised. I figured my mother would be still be too upset. I didn't think she would want to be around her friends. But she wanted our preacher to pray for Joe and for all the Marines over in Lebanon. The preacher did. And when he mentioned Joe's name, she sobbed uncontrollably. Betty Jane and I held her hands.

Our usual happy Sunday lunch was different this day. We all ate and talked quietly. No one wanted to mention Joe or the bombing in Lebanon. It was as if by avoiding talking about it we could make it go away. The tension was palpable and hung in the air like a dark rain cloud.

I was walking out to the barn to take Appaloosa for a ride when I saw a car pull into our driveway. It was an olive-green sedan, and I knew it was the Marines. I ran back to the house and followed my father to the front door as he let the two Marine Corps officers in and told them to have a seat in the living room. We sat down across from them. My mother leaned over, put her face in her hands and started to cry.

"Mr. and Mrs. Reynolds, I'm Captain Kenneth Caldwell and this is Lieutenant Leland Armstrong. We are from the United States Marine Corps Depot, in Albany, Georgia. I am very sorry to have to inform you that your son, Lance Corporal Joseph Stanley Reynolds, was killed in action while serving his country in Beirut, Lebanon. He was one of 220 Marines whose lives were lost in the bombing of the Marine Corps barracks last Thursday. The Commandant of the Marine Corps extends his deepest condolences and wants you to know the entire Marine Corps family is here to help you any way we can."

"You can't bring him back!" screamed my mother. "He didn't need to be there. He was just a boy!"

She wiped her brow and then put her face in her hands again and leaned over on my father who put his arm around her and patted her on her shoulder. She had already cried so much waiting to hear, there wasn't much left. She sobbed quietly as the Marine officers sat by and waited for her to recover.

"We are sincerely sorry for your loss," said Captain Caldwell. "Your son was an outstanding Marine and was part of the Marine family. He was serving his country with honor as part of a peace-keeping force in Lebanon. We would like to give you some information concerning his return to the United States and advise you of some options for his military burial if that is your choice."

Tears streamed down my face as I held Betty Jane's hand. Emma slipped up behind me and put her arm around me and grabbed my other hand. She had heard and was crying also.

"Your son was killed in action and is therefore eligible for burial at Arlington National Cemetery if that is your desire," said Captain Caldwell. "We can provide you with the name and a phone number of a liaison person who can make those arrangements for you. We do not know at this time when Lance Corporal Reynolds' body will arrive back in the United States, but you will be contacted should you desire to make the trip to Andrews Air Force Base, near Washington, D.C., for the ceremony of his return. It is our understanding that President Reagan will attend the ceremony and may wish to speak with you at that time."

"Thank you, Captain Caldwell, Lieutenant Armstrong," said my father as he shook hands with them. They turned and headed for the front door. My mother stared at me for a full minute. I couldn't move. I was still in shock though I knew this moment was coming. Betty Jane let out a wail and turned to go to her bedroom. Emma followed her. My mother came over and hugged me. I was the only son she had left, and I think she was telling me that she would hold on to me forever. My father walked the officers out, and I could hear them mumbling about arrangements and burial options and travel arrangements. But it all went over my head. I held on to my mother as she quietly sobbed. Jack was gone and now Joe. How much more sorrow could one family take?

# CHAPTER 64

Ray Slocum, Jr., was in a pickle. He was waiting on a phone call to let him know the drug delivery had been completed. He had smoked a dozen cigarettes and checked his watch every fifteen minutes. No phone call was bad news. Something must have happened. He didn't trust those rednecks from Dawsonville. He shouldn't have paid them so much up front. Though he had dealt with them several times before, this was a big load. Two hundred pounds of meth was a huge investment. It was a target for a rip-off. If those rednecks had ripped him off, somebody was going to die.

He paced the floor, smoked some more and made his fourth phone call. He ought to get high. He had some coke in the bottom drawer of his desk. But he needed to stay sharp just in case he was needed somewhere. His guys from Augusta and Savannah were coming to Atlanta. They should be bringing him $200,000. They would pick up some of the meth and distribute it in their areas. His network was expanding. He had a lot of good people working for him. Several he had met in prison. Trust was the big factor in selecting his dealers. He didn't trust anyone who he had not known for a while.

He and Clarence had been together for more than thirty years. He remembered when Clarence swept the floors in his father's clubs. Now they were both millionaires. Their history went back to their days of hauling moonshine from a South Georgia still. They shared dark secrets. Secrets that could get them the death penalty.

He lit a joint and sat behind his desk and propped his feet up. He started thinking about Clarence Dawkins again. Clarence was a little too trusting. He had people working for him he had known less than a year. Slocum didn't approve of some of them. Clarence was talking about getting out of the drug business. He was worried about getting caught. He wanted to go legit. But Clarence was as crooked as a snake. He could never go legit. He liked the money too much.

He decided he would give it thirty more minutes and then drive over to Clarence's club or at least drive by it. Something was wrong—he could feel it. This was confirmed when one of the dancers he dated from the club called and told him of the raid. He tried to call Tiny and Manny again, but the calls had gone unanswered. This could only mean one thing. He was next. He panicked. He didn't plan on being around when the police showed up at his headquarters.

He ran to his wall safe, quickly twisted the dial, took out $50,000 and his Beretta and put them into a gym bag. He sprinted for the rear door to his Cadillac Escalade. He jumped inside, backed out of his parking space and ran straight into a convoy of six cars loaded with state and federal agents. He slid the gym bag under the seat and put his hands on the dashboard.

The DEA and GBI agents removed Slocum from the vehicle, searched him and informed him he was under arrest for trafficking narcotics and a host of other charges. They also informed him they had search warrants for his business and his cars, and other agents were searching his home in Lawrenceville, a few miles away. Slocum was placed in the rear seat of one of the agents' cars. Two agents climbed in, and he was whisked off to jail in Atlanta. Slocum knew the drill from previous arrests and said nothing other than requesting to call his attorney.

Tiny Marlowe and Manny Acevedo were also in a pickle. Though they screamed they were just two innocent guys headed into a dance club for a little fun, the GBI knew better. Both had extensive criminal records and outstanding warrants for their arrest. Tiny had been a collector for the mob in New Jersey and had an outstanding warrant for aggravated assault. Manny was originally from Miami and had met Marlowe when they were in prison together. They had delivered drugs to an undercover agent at a club in Savannah. The Bobbsey Twins, as Dylan Johnson liked to call them, were headed back to prison for a long time.

The search warrants on Slocum's office and home produced three illegal automatic weapons, seven handguns, a half kilo of cocaine, ten pounds of marijuana, some brown heroin, various illegal prescription drugs and $973,000 in cash in a floor safe in his garage. The agents also found two stolen cars and a stolen motorcycle in the garage.

During the next twenty-four hours, fifteen employees of Slocum's syndicate were taken into custody for various felony charges. In the past six months the DEA/GBI Task Force had made more than two dozen controlled drug buys from Slocum's employees in Atlanta, Savannah and Augusta. They had used undercover operatives, wiretaps, body wires and various other investigative techniques to obtain evidence against Slocum. The sheer number of crimes committed by Slocum's organization provided substantial evidence of racketeering and of an organized criminal enterprise. Slocum was headed back to prison for a long time.

This information along with video-taped confessions from several perpetrators was provided to Clarence Dawkins and his attorney. The agents also showed Dawkins taped confessions from a number of people who had paid bribes to Dawkins for construction and MARTA transportation contracts. Dawkins and his attorney had reviewed all this material during the past twenty-four hours. He was feeling ill watching people he knew turn on him and Slocum.

Dawkins was headed to prison for a long time also. He was not a young man. But all was not lost. The agents had a deal for him. They wanted to know what he could tell them about Congressman Brady Lyle: some illegal campaign contributions, some money laundering through Lyle's construction companies and bribery on highway construction contracts. Finally, they wanted to know what he and Lyle might know about a certain moonshining and marijuana operation more than thirty years ago and the murder of Jack Reynolds and Becky McCord.

# CHAPTER 65

ATLANTA, GEORGIA

I sat behind my desk trying to think of all the things Buddy had said in the last interview. I asked my secretary to hook up the DVD player to the television in my office and to put Buddy's interview tape on for me. I wanted to hear him tell it again.

The machine clicked, and there was Buddy lying in his hospital bed a few hours before his death. His skin was grayer than I remembered. He looked like a tiny bird; his limbs so frail they might break off at any moment. He had only a few hours to live, and he was trying desperately to tell me everything he knew that might help solve the mystery of my brother Jack. We both knew he was on his deathbed.

Buddy coughed a couple of times and whispered, "I'm ready, Johnny."

I heard my voice speaking the predicate for the tape: date, time, place and who was present. I asked Buddy to briefly recap the events he had told me the day before in my office about his knowledge of a bootlegging operation on Riverdale Plantation more than thirty years ago. He spoke in whispers and gasps. I turned the volume up so I could hear better. I watched again as Buddy recounted his tale. I hit fast forward and got to the part I considered most important.

"They got the idea to start growin marijuana in little small patches in the corn and oak trees down by the river. Me and Lucas wuz told to look after it during the week. Make sure it got plenty a water and fertilizer. Yo daddy didn't like that. He wuz pissed. He didn't want no

294

part of no marijuana. But they kept on anyhow and tole him they'd be givin him a nice cut when they sold it. Ray's daddy, Red Slocum, came down and met with Mr. Calvin and worked outta deal. They gave him and Isaac a cut of what wuz sold: liquor and marijuana. They brang 'em a whole paper sack full a money every week. "The money was flowin in and Mr. Cal wuz gettin a nice cut since it wuz his land and all. Them guys wuz a sellin marijuana at the colleges in Atlanta and over in Athens. Them college kids had money and wuz a buyin it up. They wuz a plantin bigger and bigger patches of it near the river. An me and Lucas wuz cuttin it and packaging it up. We wuz workin more down there than on the farm."

Buddy had a coughing fit. He finally got control and resumed his tale.

"After a while, Mr. Cal caught them boys cheating him. So him and Isaac started selling shine and some pot on da side. Isaac would haul shine and pot up to Albany and Columbus and sell it to folks he knowed. Afore too long Mr. Cal done made enough to pay off all his bank loans and buy new cars and trucks and combines. Then he started putting da cash in his safe deposit box in town and then in five-gallon buckets and burying it all over the farm. After a coupla years, he had piled up more than a million dollars."

I stopped the tape and replayed the previous two or three minutes. I heard Buddy recount the financial details again. I wanted to make sure I heard it correctly. He said my father had made more than a million dollars and had buried some of it in five-gallon buckets around our farm. I couldn't believe it. I was flabbergasted. Over a million dollars! I remembered when we seemed to have money again but I thought it was from good crops. It was good crop alright—good marijuana crops. How the hell had he ever pulled that off? But now I knew where all the money came from in his later life. I guess he would just go dig up a five-gallon bucket when he needed money. He sure as hell never dug up one to pay for my college or law school. But I wasn't sorry. I was glad. At least my education wasn't tainted by drug and bootleg liquor money.

I thought back to his funeral and Reverend Stanfield's words: "His generosity touched many of us." His money made from growing marijuana and selling bootleg moonshine allowed him to be generous. "A pillar of the community." I laughed out loud.

# CHAPTER 66

Dylan Johnson was at the DEA office with Gary McKinnon. They were discussing the upcoming interview of Clarence Dawkins.

"I got a call from his attorney," said McKinnon. "They're beggin for a few more days to think over the plea agreement and Berger wants to see everything in writing from the US Attorney. The FBI is bugging me to interview Dawkins on the bribery cases they have on him. This whole thing is turning in to a circular firing squad. I'm gonna shortstop it and get it finished. I told Berger they could have until tomorrow at nine o'clock. They will have one chance to accept the plea deal, or all bets are off. If they don't take it, we'll hit him with every charge in the book and he will never see sunshine as a free man again. I also told Berger we are in the process of seizing all of Dawkins' clubs, businesses and rental properties. We have proof they were bought with drug money. If they cooperate, we'll think about letting him keep a few so he won't be a pauper when he gets out of prison. Hell, the cases are made on him. We just need his testimony against Slocum and Brady Lyle."

"Sounds good to me," said Johnson. "But what are we gonna do about the FBI?"

"I'm gonna tell them they can have him after we're done with him tomorrow. The US Attorney knows about the bribery charges. He can roll everything into one package. Dawkins is not gonna get any more time by them adding on a few more counts. We have to have his testimony against Slocum and that slime ball Congressman Lyle. The FBI just wants to clear their cases, and they'll be tickled to help take down a congressman."

"True, but you better call them and let them know what's going down. You know how they get their panties in a wad if you don't include them in public corruption cases."

"I know," said McKinnon. "I'll call their SAC and give him a full briefing on what we are doing."

"How do you want to do this tomorrow?" asked Johnson.

"Well, we got a lot of players involved. You've got all the background on the stuff from thirty years ago."

"You want me to take the lead?" asked Johnson.

"Why don't we meet with Berger first, say around eight," said McKinnon. "We'll have the US Attorney there and let him hash out the agreement with Berger and give him the range for prison time for Dawkins. Tell him about letting him keep a few pieces of property. But Berger has got to understand that we want Dawkins to testify against Lyle and Slocum, and he's got to tell us what he knows about the two murders. Some of those guys could have been involved in that and Dawkins knows about it. If he doesn't agree, then we hit him with every single charge we can come up with and we take all of his property."

"Sounds like a plan," said Johnson.

He headed back to his office, but then changed his mind and drove downtown. He called the Law Offices of Reynolds and Lang. He had decided he needed to watch the video John Reynolds had made with Buddy Moore. He might pick up a few things that would be helpful when he was interviewing Dawkins the next day. John had said Moore provided some information about Jack Reynolds' disappearance.

Melissa, John Reynolds' secretary, informed him John was in and would be expecting him. As he drove towards the midtown office tower, Johnson thought back to all the times he had spent with Jack Reynolds when he was growing up in Martinsville. Jack had been a great friend and teammate. He'd spent many hours hunting and fishing with Jack. They had a lot of fun times together. He had loved Jack Reynolds like a brother. He'd been shocked and devastated when Jack disappeared. He remembered spending hours searching the woods and lakes around Riverdale Plantation for Jack and Becky. Not a trace was ever found. If Slocum, Dawkins and Lyle had something to do with their disappearance, he owed it to Jack to prosecute them and to see that they spent the rest of their lives in prison. It was a mystery that had bothered him all his life. He had spent hours trying to come up with a reason for Jack disappearing. He had always felt something bad had happened to him and Becky. He was excited as he felt he might be about to find out after all these years.

He parked in the underground garage and hurried towards the elevator. A thirty-year mystery was about to be solved, he hoped.

# CHAPTER 67

Joe wasn't buried in Arlington National Cemetery. My mother thought it was too far away. She wanted him brought home, to Mount Hebron Baptist Church and to Pecan Hill Cemetery. She wanted to be able to visit him. The Marine Corps complied. They brought Joe home on a cold November afternoon, a couple of weeks after we learned of his death. They gave him a full military funeral with honors.

There was an American flag draped over the casket. Six Marine Corps pallbearers brought the casket into the church. They were in full dress uniform, white gloves and all. They were snappy and called out a lot of commands as they moved Joe around. They were as grim as an old man with a toothache. They wouldn't let us open the casket. I knew it was only pieces of Joe in there. He had been blown up. The bombs had killed 220 Marines. Most were blown up like Joe. I had heard all about it on CNN. People were giving President Reagan hell for sending our Marines over there. But I wasn't mad at him. I liked what he was doing for the country. He sent soldiers where they were needed in the world. I just wished Joe hadn't been needed there. I had no more brothers. Nobody left but me and Betty Jane. A veil of sadness cloaked me.

The preacher talked about service to one's country and making the supreme sacrifice, a lot of flowery words about dedication, duty and serving his fellow men. It was a nice speech, but I didn't think it meant much to my mother. Joe was dead and gone. Just like Jack. She only had one son left now. And according to her husband, that one was a fool and totally useless. My mother cried; everyone cried. Everyone except my father. He sat there with a scowl on his face and continued his war with God. I think God was winning, because I never saw a man who was so unhappy.

After the service we all walked out to Pecan Hill Cemetery down the hill from the church. My father had bought a plot big enough to bury the whole family. Joe was the first entry of the Reynolds family. I wondered if Jack would ever be buried there. I wondered if I would. My father would probably want me to be buried around back somewhere.

The preacher said some more words at the gravesite and then the Marine Corps pallbearers lifted the flag off the casket and folded it neatly. They made triangles as their white gloves snapped the flag in perfect folds. They handed it to my mother and said something to her, but I couldn't hear what they said. Joe's casket was lowered into the hole. We all got to throw some red clay on top of it and that was it. The service was over. Joe was properly buried, and another piece of the family's heart and soul was buried with him.

When we got back to the house, half the town of Martinsville was there. It was chilly, and the wind was blowing hard in from the north. There wasn't enough room in the house for everyone, so some of the men fixed a plate of food and stood around inside our barn. I was afraid Appaloosa would get nervous. She wasn't crazy about too many people besides me. I grabbed a piece of roast beef and a biscuit and went back to the barn. I got in the stall with Appaloosa and brushed her while the men stood around and talked. I was a little worried about all of them smoking around all the hay, so I watched closely for embers. I had already seen one barn burned to the ground.

After a couple of hours people started to drift off, and before too long it was just us and Emma. She fixed me a plate of food, and I sat at our dining table by myself and ate. As I was finishing, Emma came in carrying a huge slice of red velvet cake.

"Here's ya go, baby," she warbled. "I knows you be lovin sum a dat velvet cake."

She had a cup of coffee and sat down with me as I ate. I was worried because she wasn't allowed to sit at our table.

"It's okay, baby. Mr. Cal dun drove off in his truck."

"Where's Mom and Betty Jane?" I asked.

"Betty Jane dun put ya Momma ta bed and she's a sittin in thar a readin to her."

"I think I'm gonna go read too when I finish this cake," I said.

"How wuz Mister Joe's funeral, baby?" she asked.

I told her about it as I ate my cake. I told her what the preacher said and how the Marines looked and about his casket being draped in a flag. Then I told her how they had folded the flag and had given it to my mother.

"I sho wish I couda been thar at dat funeral. Dat woulda been something ta see. An I woulda like to a said goodbye to Mister Joe. He wuz a sweet boy, dat one. He wuz like you, a sweet boy."

"I wish you could have been there too, Emma."

"But Lord, yo daddy woulda had him a hissy fit if I sho'd up. He'd still be a yellin and cussin old Emma. But I luvs all you's chillin."

I stood up and hugged Emma. I started to cry. Not for Joe—I had cried enough for him today. I cried for Emma. A tremendous new sadness came over me. I wanted to scream or cry or lash out. This profound sadness coursed through me. This was a screwed-up world. Good people were hurt and bad people just seemed to be doing fine.

"I'm going to bed now, Emma," I said.

"Okay den, baby," she whispered. "Old Emma gots to wash all deez dishes. Go on ta bed, Johnny baby. I'll see ya in the mornin.'"

I went to bed, but I couldnt read and I couldnt sleep. I lay in my bed thinking of Joe and Jack, and then I thought of Emma. Thinking of the three of them made me overwhelmingly sad.

The next day I became even sadder. Buddy got fired. I never understood why. He had come into the barn to find me and tell me goodbye. I hugged him and asked what was going on. He said he had gotten into an argument with my father and had been told to leave; he was fired. I asked what the argument was about, and he told me it didn't matter. Not to worry about it.

Buddy told me he was heading back up to North Georgia, to the mountains where his mother and father lived. They said he always had a job waiting for him up there. He said he would miss me and was so sorry about Joe. I hadn't seen him at the funeral. He didn't think my father would want him there, so he stayed away. They had not gotten along lately, and it was time for him to go.

"You're a good boy, Johnny," said Buddy. "And you're smart as a whip. Ain't nobody got to carry yo water. You gonna do alright in life. 'Cause you are smart and you care about animals and people. Don't ya let nobody tell you no different. You is one a the good ones."

I gave him a big hug and noticed the tears flowing down his face. Mine was covered with them also. Buddy walked out of the barn, stopped and turned around. He came back, reached into his pocket and brought out his buck knife. He gave it to me, and then turned and got into his truck and waved goodbye. I was shocked, because Buddy loved that knife and he had paid a lot for it. He drove out of the barnyard in a hurry. Red dust rose into the air, and he was gone.

I continued doing my chores, crying all the time. My father walked into the barn and leered at me.

"What the hell you cryin 'bout, boy?" he yelled.

"Nothin!" I yelled back.

"Buddy Moore is a no-good son of a bitch!" he screamed. "He got to be a smartass. He thought he could go around tellin me what to do. He thought he wuz runnin this farm. He got too big for his britches and I fired his ass. So quit ya cryin and git on with ya chores!"

"That's a damn lie and you know it!" I screamed back. "Buddy Moore was a good man. He never hurt a soul and he wasn't a smartass!"

He turned and I could see his face grow beet red. He raced towards me and grabbed my shirt collar. He pulled hard and lifted me off the ground, tearing my shirt as he threw me to the ground. I held up my hands to block the boot I knew was coming. But he just stood there shaking. He lifted me up by my shirt collar and slapped me hard in the face.

"Don't you ever cuss me, boy!" he screamed. "I'll beat the crap outta you if I ever hear you cuss me again! Git ya chores done and then you come meet me on the back porch. You bring that leather strap hanging over there cause ya gonna git an ass beatin. You don't talk to yo father that way. Whass between Buddy an me ain't none a yo damn business."

I finished my chores not thinking about the beating I was about to get. I thought of Buddy Moore. I thought of all he had taught me and of all the fun we had together. About how he made work fun. I thought of what a kind man he had been, of how he loved animals and growing things. I don't think I ever knew a kinder or gentler soul. Then I thought about Joe, and then about Jack. I sat on a bale of hay and cried until I could cry no more. I had lost all three of them. I would never see any of them again. I tried to cry some more but no tears would come.

I didn't care about the beating I was about to get. He couldn't hurt me anymore than I was already hurting. I thought about leaving.

Maybe I should just disappear like Jack. But then I remembered one of Buddy's favorite sayings.

"When the going gets tough, the tough gets a going."

I made up my mind then and there—I would learn to be tough. It changed my life. I became tough as nails over the next few years. Nothing would ever stop me from doing what I wanted to do.

I got one of the worst beatings of my life that night. My father hit me so many times with the leather strap that my legs were bloody. He took his frustrations of losing Jack, Joe and now Buddy out on me. My mother came out on the porch to make him stop. He shooed her back inside threatening to hit her with the leather strap. Then he continued to hit me.

It hurt; it felt as though a thousand fire ants were stinging my legs. I screamed when he first hit me. But then I thought about learning to be tough, and I didn't scream again. I bit my lip and gritted my teeth as the blows stung my legs. After that night I became tough. I started to become a man. I worked hard at it. He would never hurt me again. I wouldn't give him the satisfaction. I was much smarter than him. I figured out ways to stay out of his way. I did all my work in an exemplary fashion. I had to—I was working for Jack, Joe and Buddy.

# CHAPTER 68

**M**elissa informed me Dylan Johnson had arrived, and I greeted him in the lobby of my office. She fixed us both a cup of coffee, and we sat in comfortable chairs in front of my desk. I re-wound the video I had just been watching of Buddy Moore.

"Dylan, this video embarrasses the hell out of me, but you need to see it," I said. "I'm not very proud of what Buddy Moore revealed about my father. Apparently, he made most of his money from selling bootleg liquor and marijuana."

"What!" exclaimed Dylan. "No way, not Mr. Calvin. He was one of the leaders of the community back then. I always had a lot of respect for him. And I know there isn't any way Jack was involved in that."

"No, I don't think Jack knew about," I said.

"But he might have found out about it and that's what got him killed."

"Play the tape. I've got to see this!"

When the video was re-wound, I started it and watched it again with Dylan. He made several exclamations as Buddy recounted how the operation began with Isaac and my father building the still with the help of him and Lucas. Dylan shook his head several times and said he couldn't believe it. When Buddy got to the part about my father burying five-gallon buckets of cash around Riverdale, it was too much for him. I paused the tape for a minute.

"Johnny, I can't believe this," he said. "Not your daddy, not Mr. Calvin. Hell, I was out at your farm dozens of times with Jack. We were all over that place hunting and fishing. I don't see how they could have kept it hidden."

"Well, if you remember, Dylan, Riverdale was a huge place, more than ten thousand acres. Do you remember Jack ever saying something about a barge wrecking on the Flint River and chemicals spilling on our land?"

"Yeah, I do remember that. They put up a gate and nobody could go down there. The EPA was cleaning it up. But that didn't last for two years, did it?"

"Yes it did. Do you remember you and Jack going down to that area again? Y'all were told to go north if you were going to fish on the river. We were told we would be glowing in the dark if we got any of those chemicals on us. I remember Buddy telling me those chemicals would have gotten in the soil and there was no way to get them out. It would take years to clear up."

Dylan looked at me and shook his head again. I knew he was having a hard time believing Buddy. Just like I did at first. But I needed him to see the rest of the video. He hadn't got to the good part yet. The part that should help him when he interviewed Clarence Dawkins.

I started the video again, and Dylan heard Buddy identify everyone who was involved and to note Slocum, Dawkins and Lyle were all about twenty years old back then. That was correct because they were all around fifty now.

Buddy continued.

"So now about Jack," he whispered his voice changing to a low guttural growl. He coughed and sat up straighter in the bed.

"It wuz a Friday night," he said. "I remember it well 'cause it wasn't their regular night. They always come to git the liquor and the pot on

Thursday night. That way they could have it in them clubs fer the week-end. But this here night they come on a Friday. Something happened. I think a truck broke down. But anyway, me and Lucas done cut down some pot and had it wrapped up in some burlap sheets. They come down to the field in a box truck and we started loadin it up. They wuz pissed and said it weren't enough. They said they had to cut some more. They told me and Lucas to go back up to the still and help Isaac load up the shine in another box truck they brought down. So thass what we did. We give 'em some more burlap sheets and Slocum, Dawkins and Brady Lyle headed out to the pot patch to cut down some mo and package it up."Me, Lucas and Isaac loaded up the shine on the other box truck. 'Bout a hour passed and we wuz done and we wuz sittin there smokin and talkin when we heard the other truck comin up to where we wuz a sittin."

Buddy wheezed and lay back in his bed. I had been worried he couldn't finish. He closed his eyes and rested for a moment. He opened them, but did not sit up. He lay there and then turned his head and looked out the window. It appeared he was thinking of something far away. He turned back and looked at me, and I could see tears streaming down his face.

Buddy continued. "Ray Slocum got outta the truck and asked Isaac how many gallons a shine wuz on the other box truck and Isaac told him it wuz a little over a hundred gallons. I was close to Ray and I saw some blood on his shirt. It wuz below his right pocket and on his right sleeve. It wuz a good bit a blood. Ray told Clarence to drive the truck to Savannah, unload fifty of them gallon jugs and then come to Atlanta with the rest. Clarence come around to git in the truck and he had blood on his shirt too. Brady Lyle wuz a standin there and he wuz jest a shakin his head and a lookin down. I couldn't see his face until later, but I'll get to that."

Buddy coughed and drank some more water and then continued.

"Isaac asked Ray, 'How you cut yo'self?' Ray look down at his shirt and said, 'I cut myself while cuttin the marijuana.'

"They usually have big machetes to cut the marijuana down. Isaac looked at Clarence and asked if he cut himself too."

Buddy coughed violently and drank some water. He paused for a few seconds and then cried out loud. The tears were flowing freely now. Buddy's cries became sobs. He sobbed for a couple of minutes. I could be seen in the video patting his shoulder. Buddy finally looked up and continued.

"I wuz near the back of the truck where they had loaded up the pot. I saw a pile a cotton in the back a the truck in a croker sheet and the cotton had blood on it too. It stood out. Red blood on white cotton. I know what I saw. But I didn't say no mo cuz I was too scared. Them wuz some rough boys. I looked over at Clarence.

"Clarence looked like he had done seen a ghost. He was shakin and wuz real nervous. He said he didn't wanna go by himself to Savannah and asked 'bout Brady riding with him. Ray said he needed to go by himself. Ray put his arm around Clarence and told him it would be alright; not to worry 'bout nothing. But I'm tellin you, that Clarence he wuz upset. He look like he wuz 'bout to pass out."

Buddy paused and breathed heavily. He looked around the room like he didn't know where he was. He then looked at me and raised up in his bed and continued.

"Now 'bout Brady Lyle. I walked over to the back of the truck and I saw Brady in the light fer the first time and he had three big scratches on his face. They looked like they wuz deep. He grabbed a handful of that cotton and held it up to his face. He was blottin that blood that be on his face from them scratches. Then I saw him get up close to Clarence and he whispered something. I couldn't hear. Clarence shook his head a few times and started walking towards Ray. Ray shouted at him real loud. He said, 'Get yo ass in the truck and head to Savannah, now. Everything is gonna be alright.'

"Clarence turned and walked towards the truck. He wuz a shakin like he had the palsy or something. He got in the truck and left. Then Ray and Brady got in their truck and drove off. They ain't said another word.

"The next day, we learned Jack and Becky wuz missing. Soon as I heard, I went to Mr. Calvin and told him 'bout seein the blood on them boys. I told him 'bout seein the blood on the cotton in the back of the truck. He jest shook his head and said that didn't have nothin to do with Jack. "I told Mr. Calvin he oughtta talk with Red Slocum, the big boss. Something done happened, and I thought them rednecks knew something 'bout it. I told him how that Dawkins boy was acting. He wuz all shook up and he had blood on him too. Yo daddy jest blew me off. But I knew they wuz connected. It tore me up. I argued with yo daddy, but he screamed at me and told me to mind my own business, that Jack had done run off to get married."

Buddy coughed and drank more water. He looked at me and shook his head. Then in his raspy voice, he finished his last words.

"Me and Isaac talked 'bout it. Isaac was mighty upset. He said he wasn't making no mo liquor for them peckerwoods. He didn't care 'bout no mo money. Said he had enough money to last him. A few days later, him and Mr. Calvin went down there with baseball bats and broke up both stills. They threw all the tanks and bottles and pipes in the river. Then Isaac told me he wuz goin up to Atlanta and he wuz gonna find out 'bout Jack. And ya know he wuz found dead up there in an alley. That scared me and Lucas. We thought they might come after us. Afraid they might think we busted up the still. So, we kinda laid low. "Me and Mr. Calvin didn't get along after that. He fussed at me, and I fussed right back at him. You 'member when he fired me. I moved on, and well, you know the rest. I went up in the mountains. I got word them guys was lookin fer me, so I disappeared jest like Jack had done. I felt in my bones, them stupid rednecks done killed that boy. I jest knew it, but I couldn't prove nothin, and Mr. Calvin didn't wanna hear nothin 'bout that. So thass it, thass all I know."

Buddy leaned back in his bed and closed his eyes. The video stopped abruptly.

"Well, what do you think?" I asked Dylan.

"It's good circumstantial evidence, but without an eyewitness and the recovery of their bodies we would never make a murder case against any of them. And you know, if they did it, they probably dumped the bodies in the river. All we can do is hit Clarence with it when we interview him."

"When's that gonna happen?" I asked.

"Hopefully, tomorrow morning. We told his attorney the clock is ticking. We will have the US Attorney over there for all the drug charges, and we'll let him know we want to talk with Clarence about this and we might be able to connect a congressman to an old murder case. I think he will be very interested in seeing this video. I'm glad you got a sworn statement and used a court reporter. "Okay Johnny, I'm gonna head out," said Dylan as he rose from his chair. "I'll let you know how it goes tomorrow with Clarence. We'll probably be with him for quite a few hours."

I escorted him out, and returned to my office to make a few phone calls.

I called Betty Jane. I had not talked with her in a few days and wanted to give her some details about what was going on. I wanted to tell her about Buddy Moore. I wasn't ready to tell her all of the details. I preferred to do that in person, but I wanted to let her know he had been alive and I was with him right up until his death. She had always loved

Buddy, and she needed to know about him. She was shocked Buddy had been alive and then saddened to hear about his cancer.

I also called Susan Regan. I just wanted to hear her voice. Somewhere in the back of my mind I knew I was developing some feelings again for Susan. Or maybe I had never really gotten over her from high school. I just knew I loved hearing that sweet honeysuckle voice. She did not disappoint. She said she had been thinking about me and was going to call soon if she hadn't heard from me. We talked for thirty minutes and promised to get together soon.

I was beat. I had not slept much, so I decided to take off a little early, beat the mad rush through Atlanta traffic and head for home. I wanted to sit in my hot tub, sip a stiff Old Forrester or maybe a Wild Turkey and think about getting back to the practice of law. I would leave it up to Dylan Johnson to solve the disappearance of my brother. He was a good man, and I felt he could break Dawkins if anyone could.

# CHAPTER 69

RIVERDALE PLANTATION
FIFTEEN YEARS OLD

L ife at Riverdale Plantation never returned to normal after my brothers and Buddy Moore were gone. I had more work to do than ever before. But I welcomed it. It kept me busy, and I hardly had time to think or grieve. And the hard work and my resolve were making me tough.

My father continued to be a jerk. He yelled at me and screamed at the hands. No one could do anything right. I apologized for being an imbecile and kept on with my work. My joy was in the little pleasures that come with living on a ten-thousand-acre farm. I took Appaloosa on long rides. When I wasn't working, I was reading, fishing or hunting. I had friends over, and we camped out on the Flint River and fished all night. Life was reasonably good, but the tension in the air was palpable. I always knew I was a whisker away from getting a beating or having all my privileges taken away.

I loved school. I studied hard and soaked up knowledge like a sponge. The harder the lessons, the more of a challenge they were, and I loved a challenge. I think living under my father's rule had prepared me for how to handle challenges. I won a lot of awards. My mother swooned; my father scowled.

I secretly took up the fight to make Emma's life better. She had done so much for our family, I felt we owed it to her. She was getting older and her workload was difficult, so I helped when I had time. I tried to slip her a little extra cash, but she usually refused.

My mother was living in another world, a world without Jack and Joe. She had lost all energy to do anything around the house. She stayed in bed a lot, which worried us all. Betty Jane and I wanted to scream at her: "Hey, you've got two kids left! Enjoy them, spend time with them, love them."

But she just didn't seem to have the will to do much with us. I understood. Sometimes the overwhelming grief hit me so hard I felt I couldn't go on. Then Buddy Moore's words would find me.

"When the going gets tough, the tough gets a going." I was becoming tough; I just had to get going. And I usually did.

My father decided we only needed Emma three days a week. So, she stayed at her house in town more than she stayed with us. I sneaked food to her and put a few dollars in the paper sack. She no longer had a husband to provide for her and she was dirt poor. I stopped by to see her if I was in town. We had some fun. We played checkers and chess. She was good. Not as good as me, but she tried hard. I let her win most of the time and she would laugh and slap her knee. Her favorite expression was: "Baby, you ain't seen dat move a comin, did ya now?"

The day I almost got killed was a brisk, balmy day in late November. A cold wind blew in from the north, and the fact I had bulky clothes on probably saved my life. I had stayed home from school to help clear a patch of new ground we planned to turn into a field for truck crops: eggplant, collard greens and cabbage. The area was about fifty acres. It had been thinly wooded, and my father decided it could be easily cleared and turned into open land for growing vegetable crops. It was near the river, and the soil was rich and black. We had cut most of the trees down during the summer. Now it was time to get the stumps and roots out. Some of the stumps had been burned, but several were stubborn and would not burn in the damp loamy soil.

I was told to get a shovel and dig around the base of the few remaining stumps. When I had cleared a trench and most of the dirt away from the base, I was to get the big John Deere tractor, tie a chain around the stumps and pull them out using the tractor's traction and horsepower.

The first two were a breeze. My father nodded his approval as I hooked the chain around them, attached the chain to the hitch of the John Deere and pulled them slowly out of the ground. I triumphantly pulled the huge stumps over to a fire pit we had dug. I splashed them with gasoline and lit the fire. It whooshed as the gasoline caught fire and the stumps started to burn.

The third stump was huge. It was the remnant of a live oak tree. I had dug away as much soil as I could with a shovel and had a deep trench around the tree. I attached the chain around the stump and hopped on the John Deere. I increased the throttle and let out on the clutch. The tractor jumped and jostled, but the stump did not budge. I increased the throttle, popped the clutch and made the stump squirm a little. Now we were making progress. Just a little more power and I could break it loose. I gave the tractor more throttle and popped the clutch really hard. The stump did not move. Instead the front end of the tractor lifted off the ground and climbed slowly into the air. This had happened a few times before. I just needed to ride it out, and it would break the stump loose or bang back down onto the ground.

But the stump did not move, and the front end of the tractor rapidly climbed into the air until I lost control. It had raised into the air until it was completely vertical, and then it eased past vertical and flipped over backwards. The tractor's massive engine and front end were hurtling directly towards me. I jumped to my left. The weight of the front end of the tractor hurtling backwards made the high rear wheels spin sideways. The left rear wheel hit me in the back. I was thrown high up into the air and landed with a huge thump, face down in the muddy soil. I was knocked unconscious.

My father and a couple of the hands had been watching and rushed to me. They lifted me and laid me on my back. My nose was bleeding profusely and I had a sizable gash in my scalp over my right ear where I had landed on a protruding root. They tried to stop the blood flow with greasy rags but were unsuccessful. My father carried me to his pickup, and I was rushed to the small hospital in Martinsville.

When I woke, I was being placed on a stretcher and hauled into the emergency room. I heard a doctor standing over me shouting something about starting an IV and getting more blood as I had apparently lost a lot. I felt him poking and prodding me, and I screamed when he touched my broken ribs. I say ribs, plural, because I had four broken ones. The tractor tire had hit me with such force it really did a number on the right side of my rib cage. As I began to regain consciousness, I remembered what had happened. I had raced the throttle too hard and had popped the clutch on the John Deere in a reckless manner. This had caused the tractor to completely flip over. A beating would be coming. They must have given me some painkillers, because I don't remember much after that.

The next day my mother, sister, Emma and, believe it or not, my father sat in my hospital room. I was one sore cookie and could barely move. I didn't want to turn my head to look at my father because I had destroyed a $10,000 piece of machinery, and I was scared.

But what's that saying about the Lord working in mysterious ways? It was a miracle. My father came up to my bed and patted my shoulder and told me he was glad I was okay. He told me it was a miracle I wasn't killed. He said the tractor completely flipped over and it could have landed on me and crushed me to death. He told me not to worry about the tractor; it was insured.

My mother hugged me. It was painful, but I didn't stop her. Betty Jane hugged me and told me I was an idiot. Emma hugged me and called me her baby. And Lord, for the first time I can recall, my father hugged me and told me to get well soon. I cried tears of joy and thought I was dreaming. But it was all real.

I stayed in the hospital for three days. I was up and moving around some, but the doctor wanted to keep an eye on me for a few days. I had a concussion and he wanted to be sure I didn't have brain damage. Betty Jane assured him I had no brain so no possibility of damage. Thanks, sis.

When I got home, I went to the barn to see Appaloosa. I took my mother's advice and didn't ride her. But I wanted to brush her and let her know I was okay. I gave her an apple and some oats with a dab of honey. She neighed and nudged me and said she missed me. I told her about my accident and about my father saying it was okay and giving me a hug. She shook her head as if to tell me she didn't believe me. You can't fool a good horse. I couldn't blame her for not believing me. I wasn't sure it was real either.

# CHAPTER 70

**C**larence Dawkins and his attorney were facing a dilemma. The Feds and the GBI were squeezing them like a vice. They wanted an answer today. Attorney Berger had viewed enough evidence to know Dawkins was up the creek without a paddle. He was going to prison for a long time, and he was about to lose everything he owned. The drug seizure laws would take all his real estate, his clubs, his car dealerships and even his residence. All the Feds had to do was to link any part of those assets to ill-gotten gains from drug proceeds used to purchase them and he was toast. He could fight the Feds in court, but he would eventually lose. Berger saw no way out except to cooperate and try to get the best deal possible for his client.

Dylan Johnson and Gary McKinnon watched from the other side of a glass partition in an interview room as Assistant US Attorney, Leland Tanner, and the case agents interviewed Dawkins. Tanner advised he had drafted a twenty-four-count indictment he would be presenting to a federal grand jury in a few days. If Dawkins was convicted on all counts, he could get ten years on each for a total prison sentence of 240 years.

Dawkins put his face in his hands and roughly rubbed it. Simon Berger told him to remain calm and listen to what the attorney had to say.

Tanner stated, "Mr. Dawkins, agents from DEA and GBI have been conducting an undercover drug investigation for the past six months. They have numerous video tapes, taped phone conversations and witness statements as evidence of your direct participation in a large-scale drug operation in a conspiracy with one Ray Slocum, Jr., and various others whose names will be included in the indictment."

Dawkins looked up at Tanner, perspiration dotting his forehead like tiny bubbles in a champagne glass. He rubbed his massive hands together and slumped back in his chair.

"Now, Mr. Dawkins, let me be clear," said Tanner. "It is very unlikely you would be sentenced to 240 years. I doubt you will get more than 100 years. How old are you? Around 50? Well then, you should be out by the time you are 150 years old. In other words, you'll die in prison."

"Naw, man, that can't happen," said Dawkins shaking his head.

"Now, Mr. Dawkins, the good news is that we need your cooperation. You are in a unique position. You were not the head of the organization responsible for saturating our community with deadly drugs and dozens of deaths. The head of that organization is Ray Slocum, Jr. We want Mr. Slocum to get about 240 years in prison. And we want to dismantle his entire organization. You are in a position to be able to help us do that. Are you beginning to get a picture of what we want from you, Mr. Dawkins?"

"I jest don't wanna be no rat," said Dawkins. "Slocum's got a lotta mojo. He could have me knifed in prison. I jest don't wanna havta look over my shoulder all the time."

"Well, unfortunately, you don't have a choice," said Tanner his voice rising. "You can cooperate with us, or you'll be gone for a long time.

To make it simple, you can be a government witness or you can be a government defendant. And don't think of yourself as a rat. Think of yourself as a government consultant. You've been a legislator, for God's sake. Now you'll be a government consultant to the DEA and GBI. How does that sound, Mr. Dawkins?"

"I don't like it one bit," said Dawkins.

"You don't have to like it. This is the real world and everything is not candy and ice cream. It's death and sorrow and despair and depression and hopelessness. Because of you and Ray Slocum, Jr., and the poison you have peddled for years."

"That ain't much me; thass more 'bout Ray. He the drug man. I jest run my clubs and sell some cars."

"Bullshit, stop lying!" screamed Tanner. "You either start telling us the truth or I'll end this interview right now and you can go to hell. And believe me, I'll put you in a prison that is pure hell."

Dawkins rubbed his face and looked at Berger who nodded to him.

"If I cooperate, how much time I'm gone git?" asked Dawkins.

"In my experience, cooperating witnesses who provide substantial assistance receive very favorable treatment from the court. I can also advise you, if you do not cooperate, then I will do everything in my power to see you die in prison, that you never take a breath or stand in the sunshine again as a free man. And we will take everything you own under the federal seizure laws. Is that clear?"

"Yep," mumbled Dawkins.

# CHAPTER 71

RIVERDALE PLANTATION
SIXTEEN YEARS OLD

It was the summer before I started eleventh grade. My father was still a hardass, but he left me alone for the most part. I didn't know if he was just indifferent or maybe he had worn his arm off beating me with a limb or a leather strap. He reminded me that I wasn't too old to whip, but then he didn't whip me anymore. I think maybe he had just decided to tolerate all my failures and just let them go.

I guess the crops were all good lately. We seemed to have more money than we ever had before. He bought more new trucks, tractors and combines. He bought new cars for my mother and Betty Jane, who was going to college in Atlanta. I got brave one day and talked with him about buying me a car. He laughed at me and told me he was afraid I might wreck it like I did the tractor. He told me I could drive one of the old trucks.

I was pissed. I thought I had earned it and more. I had worked like a dog all my life on this farm. I had jumped in after Jack and Joe and Buddy were gone and done a lot of their jobs. I made up my mind to save my money and buy my own damn car. And I did it. It took a year of scrimping and saving, but I did it.

He enjoyed telling me I would never amount to anything and I was an idiot and a dumbass. But mostly he chose to ignore me. I wanted him to know a few things. If I was dumb, why was I the smartest person in my class? Why had the school guidance counselor told me I could take college courses and get a jump on going to the university? Why was I chosen for all AP classes? Why was I tutoring four students in math and chemistry? And why was I having to request books from libraries in other counties because I had read most of them in the Martinsville library? I knew I wasn't dumb. It was just a name for him to call me when he was pissed off, which was most of the time. I knew I was smart. I was smart enough to realize he was still grieving and taking his grief out on me.

My mother wasn't doing well. Her heart was still aching. She sat alone staring off in the distance like she was waiting for Jack or Joe to come walking down the road. Losing both of them had almost killed her. She still wept a lot and often held on to me. I was all she had left in the male category, and she wasn't letting me go.

Emma, God bless her! She was a godsend. She did most of the housework, all the food preparation, all the canning and took care of me and Betty Jane like we were her own.

The only thing my mother enjoyed was reading. She had always liked to read. She checked out books from the library a dozen at a time and tried to read at least five or six a week. One of my favorite things was discussing books we both had read. We would talk for hours about different characters and their motivations and about authors we liked and the ones we did not like. She could forget her grief for a while when she read. So, I encouraged her.

I fell in love for the first time that year. Only it was love from afar. A girl named Susan Regan had been in some of my classes, and it was love at first sight. She was a year younger than me. I never had the courage to actually talk to her, but I admired her and dreamed about her. She was beautiful. She had blonde hair and blue eyes, and she had the smoothest skin I had ever seen. She had a captivating smile like a flower bursting forth in springtime. She had a low husky voice that gave me chill bumps when I heard her talking in the hallway. She was always tanned, but I didn't think she got it from working in the fields like I did. I only caught glimpses of her at her locker or from across the room, but I was in love with her. It would take another year for me to actually talk to her and ask her out on a date.

I was given a lot of responsibility for getting things done on the farm. I oversaw picking up the hands and getting them to the right fields and making sure they were working. I kept all the journals to track the hours they worked and how much they were paid for picking cotton, harvesting tobacco, peanuts, corns, soybeans and all the other crops. It was tedious work, but I loved it, because I was the manager and the paymaster. I laughed and joked with them a lot and got to know the different families. It was a tough balancing act. My father wanted me to know them enough to keep track of their work and to know who the workers were and which ones were the slackers. But he did not want me to associate with them, and joking with them was out of the question. I did a pretty good job of managing them so they didn't hate me, but I knew I wasn't Jack and I knew I wasn't respected. I was referred to as "Baby Reynolds," and that was okay with me. I had been called a lot worse.

# CHAPTER 72

DEA HEADQUARTERS
ATLANTA, GEORGIA
PRESENT DAY

Clarence Dawkins had finally decided to come to Jesus. He had wrangled with his attorney and himself and saw no way out. He had to cooperate. The Feds had also agreed to charge him in the federal system and get him sentenced to serve time in a federal institution, which would be much nicer than a state institution.

The Feds agreed not to seize his personal residence and to let him keep one of his clubs and make his cooperation known to the sentencing judge. According to his attorney, that was the best deal he was going to get. He decided to take it and was ready to spill his guts . . . as most criminals referred to it.

Assistant US Attorney Leland Tanner listened as the case agents from DEA and GBI led the questioning. The session was video-recorded.

DEA Agent Stevens: "Mr. Dawkins, can you tell us when you first met Ray Slocum, Jr?"

Dawkins: "Well, I met his daddy first. His daddy wuz named Red Slocum and he ran a bunch a clubs 'round Atlanta. I started workin for him when I wuz seventeen years old at his club in Forest Park."

Stevens: "And what did you do for Slocum?"

Dawkins: "At first, I jest swept up an took out da trash. Den I had mo responsible jobs like runnin errands and stockin liquor. Afta 'bout a year, I did some bar tendin and haulin liquor 'tween his other clubs. Sometimes I'd take liquor down to his clubs in Savannah and Augusta."

Stevens: "Was this legal liquor or moonshine?"

Dawkins: "Both. Sometimes we had shine and then we had regular liquor too."

Stevens: "What about drugs? Were there any drugs in the clubs and did they belong to Mr. Slocum?"

Dawkins: "Yeah, they wuz drugs. There wuz pills, marijuana, heroin and cocaine. We'd have it behind da bar and certain customers could buy it."

Stevens: "And when did you meet Ray Slocum, Jr.?"

Dawkins: "Back then, he wuz there, workin in da clubs and a goin ta college. He wuz doin mostly the same as me, errands and stuff. He wuz his daddy's flunky. He sold some drugs too."

Stevens: "How about a guy named Brady Lyle?"

Dawkins: "Yep, he wuz there. He wuz friends with Ray, Jr. He worked in the club some and he helped us haul liquor. He sold drugs and he liked to use 'em too. He was a pothead. Smoked 'bout as much as he sold."

Stevens: "Now, Mr. Dawkins, is that Brady Lyle you knew back then, is he the same person you know now as United States Congressman Brady Lyle??

Dawkins: "Yep, one and da same. I knowed him all my life. I hauled shine, sold drugs, smoked some drugs with him and paid 'em bribes and laundered money with him. He's the same as he wuz back then. A money grabbin sucker that'll stab ya in the back if ya ain't lookin close."

Tanner and the two agents looked at each other. They had heard a myriad of rumors about Lyle. Now they needed dates, times and places.

If they could get substantiating evidence of some recent crimes, they could put cuffs on a United States Congressman.

Stevens: "Mr. Dawkins, we want some background on how you started in this business and who you worked with back. Can you help us with that?"

Dawkins: "Yep. If I'm gonna jump off da deep end, I might as well tell ya all of it. I knows 'bout stuff on all of 'em. On Red, Ray, Jr. and on that lyin Brady Lyle. Congressman my ass. He dun sold me down the river a few times. I'm the one what got him elected. He wanted me to deliver the black vote for him. I dun it two times. He ain't dun nothin fer me. Lyin sack a shit. I give him a $100,000 and I ain't got nothin back fer it. I give em a $50,000 bribe fer a contract what turned out to be nothin. He's a liar and a crook. I hope ya lock his ass up."

And for the next four hours Clarence Dawkins bore his soul to the agents. He provided names, dates, times, places and corroborating details of the Slocum criminal enterprises and on Congressman Brady Lyle. They took a break and brought in a late lunch. They walked around and stretched, smoked a few cigarettes and then they went back at it. Finally, Dawkins was ready to talk about what had happened on a Friday night more than thirty years ago in the woods near a moonshine still in South Georgia. A night that saw two young lives snuffed out forever.

# CHAPTER 73

I was on pins and needles waiting to hear back from Dylan Johnson at the GBI. I had waited all day and had not heard a word from him. Their interview with Clarence Dawkins was supposed to start at nine o'clock this morning. It was approaching four, and I thought surely they had to have finished by now.

I fixed myself a cup of coffee and propped my feet up on my desk. I was too nervous to work on any of my cases. I had tried to concentrate and work on a personal injury case. But I could not keep my mind on my work. My thoughts bounced around like a pin ball machine. One minute I was working on the industrial accident case I was getting ready for trial, and then I would bounce to the interview Dylan was conducting. I had called his office once. Maybe it was time to call him again. Maybe he had forgotten to call me. Maybe Clarence Dawkins had not told them anything about Jack. Maybe he had changed his mind and refused to cooperate.

All these things flooded my mind, and I couldn't work anymore. I finished my coffee, threw the dregs into the sink and grabbed my coat. I would take a walk around the block, and then come back and call Dylan again.

After I walked around the block a few times, I walked back to my office hoping I would have a message from him. But there was no such luck. I tried to work some more, but it was no use. I couldn't concentrate.

I decided to head home. Maybe I could get a jump on traffic. I packed my briefcase and was walking out when my secretary stopped me.

"John, I've got Dylan Johnson from the GBI on line one for you," she said.

I raced back to my desk and grabbed the phone.

"Hey Dylan, did you interview Dawkins?" I asked gasping for breath, I was so excited.

"Yeah, we just finished. It's been an all-day affair. He's been telling us a lot of stuff about Ray Slocum and his daddy Red Slocum. He laid out the whole drug operation and has got records of payments. He knows where they were buying drugs and told us about some people who worked for them selling drugs. We're getting warrants for several other individuals. He told us a lot of good stuff about Congressman Brady Lyle. About how he got mixed up with him in the first place and all about bribes he has paid him."

"Did he say anything about Jack?"

"Yes he did, Johnny. We need to get together to talk about that. We'll be taking Dawkins down to Martinsville on Friday. We've got to line up some equipment, get a medical examiner and the local sheriff's office onboard. Then we've got to make arrangements to transport him down there."

"Does he know if Jack was murdered, Dylan? I've got to know," I said. The hairs on the back of my neck were standing up. I had waited thirty years to find out what had happened and now I was so close.

"I think Dawkins can tell us what happened that night. We don't have all the details yet. That's why we want to take him down there. We want him to walk us through it and show us exactly what occurred."

I almost dropped the phone. I was shaking. Beads of perspiration popped out on my forehead. I couldn't say anything. Something rolled around in my stomach and my throat was like the Sahara Desert.

"Johnny, you still there?"

"Yeah, I'm here. I'm just trying to cope with all this."

"I'll call you back tomorrow after we've made all the arrangements," said Dylan.

"Sounds good."

"Tomorrow, then."

The phone went dead. I stood there holding the phone and shaking. Was Dawkins about to tell us Jack and Becky had been murdered? I had always thought that had been their fate. I grabbed the desk and settled into my chair. I sat there for an hour wondering just what happened. Was I about to find out?

# CHAPTER 74

RIVERDALE PLANTATION
MARTINSVILLE, GEORGIA
EIGHTEEN YEARS OLD

I had finished high school, taking mostly gifted courses and several college courses at the local junior college. I had my University of Georgia acceptance letter in hand and had two academic scholarships lined up. I should have won another one given by the Rotary Club, but a certain president of that organization felt it would be inappropriate to award it to his son. He felt it may have shown favoritism, and he certainly didn't want to be accused of that. Sue Ellen Briarley walked away with that check for $2500. It was supposed to go to the student with the highest grade-point average, the valedictorian, which was me. But he screwed me again.

My goal was to work during the summer and save as much money as I could. The old man had let me know I wasn't getting a cent from him. He was totally against me going to college. He tried to make me feel bad by saying he really needed me. My two brothers were dead, and now he had no family to help him run his plantation. I pointed out he had approximately fifty black field hands to do the work. He just had to pay and supervise them. He ranted and raved and tried to make my life miserable the last few weeks. He came up with extra jobs and kept me in the fields working until after dark nearly every night. I took it all in stride and worked and smiled and worked and smiled. I would be away soon pursuing my dreams. I was tough; I could take it. Bring it on, big man!

He wasn't aware I had a secret weapon on my side. My mother had saved some money, and she would send me some when she could. She had already given me $500. I planned to get a couple of jobs in Athens and had applied for a work study position with the university's Internal Audit Division. I wasn't worried. I knew I could do whatever I needed to do to make it through school. I had already talked with the financial aid folks and knew I could always get a student loan if things got too tough.

It was Saturday night, and I was pushing my mother and Emma to get dinner ready a little early as I had a hot date with my girlfriend Susan Regan. We had been dating for almost a year now, and I was in love. It was breaking my heart because Susan had another year of high school. Leaving her and going to college 250 miles away was weighing heavily on me.

Emma brought in a sizzling platter of crispy pork chops and placed them on the table.

"Got yo favorite, baby doll," she said as I leaned against the dining room wall.

"I knows you be liking some of dees crispy poke chops, don't cha, baby?"

"You know I do," I said.

She had a special recipe for the pork chops. She coated them in a mixture of crushed saltines and breadcrumbs, put on lots of black pepper, basted them in butter and fried them in a special oil. They were crispy as could be and were delicious. I normally ate at least three.

We were waiting on my father to get there. The smell of the pork chops was heavenly. Emma went back in the kitchen to bring other dishes.

My mother and Betty Jane came in carrying bowls of vegetables. Betty Jane had fresh purple hull peas and tomatoes, and my mother had lima beans and cream corn. They were followed by Emma carrying a plate of cornbread.

Emma winked at me and said, "Got banana pudding fer dessert, baby."

I heard my father come up the back steps and go into the bathroom to wash up.

"Why we eatin so early tonight, Mama?" he asked as he came into the dining room drying his hands on his jeans.

"Johnny's got a hot date," she said. "Him and Susan are going to the movie and it starts at seven."

"Well, that's too damn bad," he said. "He ain't goin nowhere but to the tobacco barn. I got barns full a tobacco cooking and he's gonna havta watch it for me. I gotta go to town to bail out one of the hands got arrested this afternoon. T-Bird got in a fight and got throwed in the pokey. We're cropping tobacco tomorrow and he's the best one I got."

"Are you shitting me?" I said before I thought.

"Watch your mouth, boy!" he yelled. "I hear another cuss word outta yo mouth, you ain't gonna be able to eat no pork chops. You ain't too big to whip. You might think ya are, but ya ain't."

"Calvin y'all aren't gonna crop tobacco on Sunday, are you?" asked my mother.

"Got to. We got another field that's ready. We got to get out there and crop it. I want Johnny and T-Bird on one tractor, Miley and Sam on the other. We gonna start at six o'clock and go all day. I think we can get that southwest field done and git that tobacco in the barn by sunset."

Cropping tobacco was the job I hated most. A tractor pulled a tobacco-cropping platform through the field. Two hands were seated in low-slung chairs side by side. The tractor pulled the platform slowly along between four rows of tobacco. Each cropper was responsible for two rows, and his chair slid along between them. The hands pulled off (cropped) the lower tobacco leaves that were ripe. The tobacco leaves were handed up to a stringer standing above the chairs on a metal platform. The stringer grabbed the leaves, wrapped three or four leaves together and entwined a string around them. They were attached to a stick approximately four feet in length. The stringer controlled the stick and held it on a metal brace. When the stick was full of tobacco leaves the stringer would hand it off to another worker who would hang the stick on a metal rack. The process was repeated over and over until the cropping platform was full. Then the tractor pulled the platform to the end of the row, and the sticks were off-loaded to trucks to be hauled to a tobacco barn for cooking.

At the barn, the sticks would be unloaded and hung on racks. Gas flues on the lower tiers of the barn were lit, and the tobacco was cooked until most of the moisture was cooked out of the leaves. The dry leaves would then be loaded into burlap sheets and taken to the tobacco market for sale.

"Where you gonna cook it?" my mother asked. "Your two barns are full already. They won't be done tomorrow, will they?"

"I already talked to Tom Griggs. He ain't got no tobacco ready to go in his barns. So, I'm gonna use his for the next coupla days."

"I just don't like y'all working on Sunday," she said shaking her head in disgust.

"Got no choice," he said as he wolfed down a pork chop.

"Do I really have to go watch the tobacco tonight?" I asked.

"Yes, you do. I want you to watch both barns. You know how to adjust the temperature if you need to. I don't want that tobacco burnt now. You watch it real close."

I got up from the table, pushed my chair back and threw my napkin down in my chair. I had eaten half a pork chop, but I wasn't hungry anymore. I had to call Susan and cancel our date. This was the third time this had happened this month. Always at the last minute when I had a date. I knew he was just doing it to piss me off. He was pissed I was going away to college, and he was going to screw with me until the day I left. I counted the days on my fingers. *You've got five more days*, I thought as I stomped out.

# CHAPTER 75

Susan had been bitterly disappointed. Probably not as much as I was. I thought of her soft lips touching mine. She was the girl of my dreams.

I was conflicted. I wanted to stay in Martinsville and be with Susan forever. On the other hand, I was excited about going to the University of Georgia. I had a plan mapped out. I would be going to school every summer. By doing so, I could finish in three years. Then I would go on to law school or maybe medical school. Would Susan wait that long? I didn't know. But in another year, she was planning to go to Emory University in Atlanta. It was only 60 miles from Athens. We could get together on weekends. We could go to football games and movies and plays in Atlanta.

Who was I kidding? I wouldn't have enough money to buy a hot dog. And I would probably have to work every weekend. But what was that famous Buddy Moore expression. "If there's a will, there's a way." We would just have to find a way. Our love was strong; we would find a way. If I could just survive this first year.

My father returned from bailing T-Bird out of jail around eleven. I had lowered the temperature on the gas cookers in the tobacco barn twice. I thought it was getting a little too hot. He walked in and checked the thermometers.

"How's my tobacco cookin?" he asked.

"It's cookin," I said.

"This damn barn ain't hot enough!" he screamed. "Why the hell did you turn it down so low?"

"I turned it down because I thought it was a little too hot. The tobacco was turning a little dark and it looked like some on the lower tiers were getting wrinkled."

"Bullshit. You don't know nothin about cookin no tobacco. You wuz tryin to sabotage it, weren't cha? Jest 'cause I made you miss your date with ya little honey, you turned that heat down. Now I got to stay up all night out here cookin it to git it right."

"I turned it down so it wouldn't burn up!" I yelled.

"Bullshit. I oughtta kick yo ass."

"Go ahead. You've got five more days to kick me around!"

"Don't you sass me, boy!" he screamed as he picked up a tobacco stick. He drew it back to hit me. I stood my ground, I had been hit with worse.

"You ain't got no business going off to no college. You need to stay here and help me!"

"That's what this is all about, isn't it? You're pissed I'm leaving, so you're gonna make my last days miserable. Well, you can't do anything to make me change my mind. I'll soon be outta here and there ain't a friggin' thing you can do about it. In five more days, you can kiss my ass."

He leaped at me like a lightning bolt, striking me with the tobacco stick across my head. The stick splintered. The blow knocked me to the ground. He grabbed another stick and tried to hit me again, but I blocked it with my boot. He threw the stick to the ground and jumped on top of me. We rolled over on the wooden floor of the barn, and he slapped me in the face so hard my teeth shook. My nose exploded, blood running down my chin and dripping onto my shirt. I tried to get my arms around his neck, but he was too strong. He pinned me to the floor and hit me in the face several times. He elbowed my ribs and kneed me in my left kidney. I flailed my arms at him and hit him in the right ear with my fist. This really pissed him off and he slapped me again in the face. I felt a loose tooth. He then hit me in the eye so hard my head bounced off a wooden rail on the first tier of hanging tobacco. It was the last thing I felt before I passed out.

I don't know how long I lay there. I heard footsteps and someone grabbed my hand and pulled me into a sitting position. I felt my face and eyes. My right eye was swollen shut; my face was numb. Dried blood was caked in my nose. I could taste blood in my mouth. I felt my lips. They were cracked and swollen. I ran my bloodied hand through my hair and felt wooden splinters sticking into my scalp in several places. I rolled onto my knees and grabbed a metal rail on one of the gas cookers and pulled myself to my feet. I stood there a moment, unsteady, trying to find stability. I took a couple of steps. My ribs felt like a hot stake had been driven between them. My left kidney screamed at me. The pain almost made me pass out. I looked to my left. He was sitting by one of the gas burners looking like he was ready to inflict more pain. I took a few steps towards the door.

He stood up and yelled, "Go on, get the hell outta here, go on to the house! I don't want cha around me!"

I was more than glad to leave him to cook his damn tobacco. I stumbled up to the house. It was past midnight. I washed my face and doused some of the cuts with hydrogen peroxide. I sneaked into the kitchen and got some ice to put on my eye and some Tylenol. The swelling went down some after holding the ice pack on my eye. I could open it again. I took a hot shower, letting the water cascade down my bruised body. The water stung but it also felt good, washing away dirt and dried blood. I crawled into bed and tried to read but my eyes wouldn't focus.

I couldn't sleep. I tossed and turned, hurting every way I laid. I finally drifted off around three and was shocked when my alarm sounded.

# CHAPTER 76

Getting out of bed Sunday morning was a Herculean task. I hurt in places I never knew I had. My left eye was swollen shut and was surrounded in a purple mess of bruises. My lips were swollen and blue, and my arms had several cuts and bruises. I had to be in the tobacco field by six, so I drank a glass of milk, made a pork chop sandwich and grabbed a couple of biscuits. I fixed a quart jar of iced tea and escaped the house without anyone seeing me. I ate the two biscuits as I walked to the barn and got on the John Deere tractor. The old man was nowhere to be found. I was glad; I didn't want him to see my eye or let him see me limping.

When I arrived at the tobacco field, he had already dropped off the hands. I hooked my tractor up to a tobacco platform and instructed one of the hands to drive it. None of the hands said anything about my appearance. I was ready to tell them it was none of their damn business, but I was spared any inquiries.

It was a brutal Sunday. The late July sun beat down on us like a giant torch. The stifling heat low among the tobacco plants, where we rode on our little seats, drenched us in sweat. We toiled all morning, and the time passed quickly. My aches and pains almost made me pass out a couple of times as I cropped the damp, sticky tobacco leaves.

As the sun drifted directly overhead, I told the hands to take a lunch break for thirty minutes. All the ice was melted from my quart jar of tea. I ate my pork chop sandwich and sipped the warm tea and sweated in the shade. My hands were sticky from cropping the tobacco and I couldn't clean them. My fingers stuck to the glass jar as I sipped the last swallow of tea. I limped over to the tractor, climbed onto my little cropper's chair and we were off for more fun and games in the tobacco field. It was past six when we finally finished the southwest field.

We took three truck-loads and three trailer-loads of tobacco on sticks over to Mr. Griggs' farm and hung them in his two tobacco barns. My father showed up to supervise the unloading and hanging of the sticks in the barns. He screamed at us if we hung the sticks too close together, exclaiming, "Tobacco's gotta have room to breathe! Don't get 'em too close!"

He didn't say a word to me, and I didn't return the favor. I was hoping he would fire up the barn and stay there to cook the tobacco overnight.

When we finished hanging the tobacco, I drove the tractor home in an exhausted daze. I could barely move I was so tired. I hurt all over from my injuries. I hoped to avoid my mother as I slipped in the back door.

Emma saw me and shouted, "Good Lord, baby boy, what dun happened to yo eye?"

"I fell off the tobacco platform and hit my eye on one of the rails. I'm gonna wash up and go to my room. Can you bring me something to eat?"

"Shore I will. We got us some fried chicken, peas and beans, got mashed potatoes and I dun made some fresh biscuits."

"Sounds good. I'd appreciate it if you could bring a plate to my room. I'm so tired, I just wanna lay down."

Emma came into my room with the food and sat on the foot of my bed while I ate.

"Yo momma and Betty Jane dun gone to church. They went to the evenin service over at Mt. Hebron."

"Yeah, I forgot it's Sunday."

"Baby, old Emma dun been round a long time. Dun seen all kinda bruises and scrapes. Dat don't look like no fall. Dat look like you dun run up into somebody's fist. Who dun beat you up like dat?"

"My business, Emma. I'll handle it. Please don't say anything to my mother. You know how she worries."

"Alright den, baby. It's yo bizness. I'll jest tell yo momma you dun had a little fall, thass all."

"Okay, I'm gonna get a shower and get to bed. I'm so tired."

Emma gently hugged me and told me goodnight.

I had hoped to clean up and go to Susan's for a while. But I was too tired. I called her and told her I had been working all day and I was dead. I fell into my bed without taking a bath.

# CHAPTER 77

I felt as though I had only been asleep for thirty minutes when my mother called me to get up.

"Johnny, your daddy wants you to go pick up the hands. Y'all are loading watermelons today."

I hurt all over and could barely get out of bed. A huge purple bruise covered the left half of my chest. My eye was black and purple and still swollen almost shut. I took a two-minute shower, grabbed a biscuit and a piece of ham from the kitchen and raced out without letting my mother see me.

I picked up a dozen of the hands who knew how to work in melons and headed for our one of our watermelon fields. I drove a tractor pulling a trailer whose floor was covered in wheat straw. As I stopped at stacks of melons, two of the hands would come over and one would jump up in the trailer and another would stay at the stack. He would throw the melons up to the trailer where they would be neatly stacked in the wheat straw. This procedure would go on all day until all the melons were cut and loaded. We could normally get twenty to thirty trailer-loads of melons from this size field. Semi-trucks from supermarkets in Atlanta would arrive the next day, and we would load the melons from the trailers onto their trucks.

It was a grueling day. The July sun burned us through our clothes, and we sweated all the water we drank. Dust clouds covered us most of the day, and I was almost as black as the hands when we loaded the last melons. We finished around six. I was determined I would see Susan that night, and so I rushed to feed the pigs, cows, horses and chickens. My mother came out to the barn to inspect my injured eye. Emma had told her I had a shiner. I told her it was fine, and she shook her head and told me she did not believe my story about a fall. I insisted I had to fight my own battles. She hugged me, and then walked back to the house continuing to shake her head.

I was squirting water into Appaloosa's trough when my father walked into the barn. I didn't speak, and he didn't either for a long time. The silence was palpable.

Finally, he asked, "How many trailers of melons did y'all get?"

"Twenty," I said.

"Damn, I thought we'd git at least twenty-five. Them blacks probably missed some. I caught 'm skipping over ripe melons before. They do that so that's more they don't hav'ta cut, tote and load. They a lazy damn bunch, and you probably didn't watch 'em like ya shoulda."

I didn't answer. I had nothing to say to him and concentrated on finishing my chores. I turned off the spigot, rolled up the water hose and headed for the door. He stepped in front of me blocking my exit.

"One more thing. You know ya momma ain't thrilled about you going off to Athens. Ya gonna worry her to death. It ain't right."

"That's not true; she's very happy about me pursuing my education."

"You ain't learned a damn thang, have ya, boy? You callin' me a liar right to my face? That ass kickin' you got last night ain't taught you nothin', has it?"

"I guess not. But I know the truth. And I know she's happy for me and she supports me getting an education."

"I could kick yo ass again, right here."

"Yes, you could. And I will still get up, and in three days I will drive to Athens and I will get my education. No one is going to stop me. Not you, or anyone else."

He stared at me for a full minute. I could feel the rage in him. I prepared for another beating. But he turned and took a step towards the door. Then he stopped, turned and pointed his finger at me and stabbed the air with it.

"Well, you go on then! You go on, leave here dragging yo tail between yo legs! And don't you ever come back! I want you outta my sight!"

He stormed out, and I left the barn and walked up the hill to the house with my shoulders straight and my head held high. Those were the last words we spoke to each other until more than ten years had passed.

I called Susan Regan and told her I could be there in an hour. I also told her I had an accident and looked rough. I didn't want her parents to see my bruised face and black eye, so I asked her if we could meet at Sloan's Drive-In. She agreed. I took a quick shower, dressed and was out the door in less than thirty minutes.

Susan arrived at Sloan's a few minutes after I did. She parked her car next to mine and hopped into the front seat with me. She leaned over to kiss my cheek and gasped.

"Oh my God, Johnny! What happened to your face?"

"I fell off a trailer and hit my head on the back of the tractor."

"Did you go to the hospital? That cut over your eye needs stitches."

"Naw, I'm fine. Just bruised up a little. My eye hit the trailer hitch on the tractor," I lied.

"Well no offense, but you look awful. Are you sure you wanna go out tonight?"

"Susan, we've only got three more days. I wanna spend as much time with you as I can."

"Don't say that. You're gonna make me cry."

"Well, it's true. Don't be sad. Let's be happy and enjoy these last days. It's not like I'm leaving forever; I'll be back."

"You promise?"

"Sure, I will," I lied again. I had no plans to return to Martinsville for a long time. I would miss Susan, my mother and sister, but I knew I wasn't coming home, not for Thanksgiving or Christmas. I planned to study and work.

Susan and I made love that night. It was sweet and tender. It was the last time I saw her for more than two years. I had decided I was leaving early.

I arrived home a little after midnight. My mother and Emma had washed and ironed all my clothes. I loaded them into the back seat of my car and packed a few other items for my dorm room into the trunk. I was about to get into bed when my mother came into my room.

"Johnny, can we talk for a minute?" she asked.

"Sure, sit on my bed," I said.

"I want to tell you about something that happened before you were born."

There was a pregnant pause before she continued.

"Two years before you were born, I was pregnant and had a miscarriage. I was hospitalized for several days and was very sick. Your father and I agreed we would not have any more children and took steps to make sure.

You never knew him, but we had an interim preacher at Mt. Hebron named Will Tolbert. He was young and very nice. He came to visit me a lot when I was recovering and we would sit on the porch and talk about God."

"Mom, I don't like where this is going," I said.

"It's okay, just hang on," she said.

"One day Reverend Tolbert came to see me and we were sitting inside on the couch talking. Suddenly, he reached over and tried to kiss me. I screamed and jumped up. Your father was just coming up the front steps. He ran in as Reverend Tolbert was running out. I told him what happened and he drove into Martinsville and confronted him. The Reverend decided to return to Atlanta soon after that and we got a new preacher. We learned Reverend Tolbert had tried that with a few other women in the community."

"But Daddy assumed something was going on," I said.

"Yes, he questioned me like it was my fault and accused me of having an affair, which was a lie. Then a couple of months later, I learned I was pregnant with you. Our precautions had failed somehow, which was a wonderful thing, because we had you. But your father was suspicious that you were not his."

"So that is why he has hated me all these years."

"He never hated you, he just wasn't planning on having anymore children, and then you came along."

"And he suspects I belong to the Reverend Tolbert."

"No, he knows there is no way I had an affair, it just surprised him when you came along.""Why did you wait until now to tell me about this?" I asked.

"Because now you are old enough to understand. And you are a wonderful gift and I am so grateful you were born. You are kind and compassionate and maybe now maybe you can understand your father a little better."

"I don't think I'll ever understand him. It's not my fault I just showed up here. Knowing this doesn't change anything. Our life's history is why we fight with each other. I know I was not wanted and was a disappointment to him. He has told me often enough."

"You were wanted. And you are a wonderful human being."

I hugged my mother and held her for a few moments. I was afraid tears would flow, but I was done crying. I kissed her goodnight and got into bed and set the alarm for five. When it buzzed, I popped out of bed and got a quick shower. I heard my father leave the house and tell my mother to make sure I was in the cotton field by sunup.

It was a tearful goodbye with my mother, Betty Jane and Emma. A lot of hugs and kisses were exchanged, along with promises to write. Emma had fixed enough food to last me a week. I waved goodbye as I circled the driveway. I drove by the cotton field where I was supposed to be working and waved goodbye to it also. I would never work in a cotton field again. Waving goodbye to Riverdale was a little sad as I headed to the University of Georgia.

It was a rough Christmas that first year at college. I called my mother and told her I had to work and would not be coming home. I worked one of my three jobs Christmas day and had Christmas dinner at Krystal, a hamburger institution in Georgia. My mother and Betty Jane came up the next day and brought me presents and some good home cooking. They hung out with me until I had to report to work. They left for Riverdale with a promise to come back soon.

I called Susan once during my first year away and learned she was dating some guy I hardly knew. I acted as though I was happy for her, but I wasn't. I ached for her and wanted to be with her. But I wanted to get my education more.

I stayed extremely busy. I went to everything that was free: lectures, poetry readings, impromptu concerts and of course all the sporting events.

My mother wrote at least twice a month and sent me goody packages containing homemade cookies and cakes. She and Betty Jane visited a few times, and I was always thrilled to see them. Emma sent jellies, jams and roasted peanuts she coated in chocolate. I never got a letter, a call or a goody package from my father. I guess he was too busy. It would be more than ten years before I saw him again.

# CHAPTER 78

PRESENT DAY
ATLANTA, GEORGIA

**W**ednesday morning, the day before Dylan Johnson and his team of GBI agents were planning to take Clarence Dawkins down to Riverdale, I called him to get the details. He informed me his team would be heading to Martinsville Thursday afternoon.

Clarence Dawkins was being transported to the county jail where he would spend the night. I called my sister and told her I was coming down Thursday. She was as nervous as a cat in a room full of rocking chairs. She had cried a lot when I told her about Dawkins.

She told me she had run into Susan at the grocery store and had told her what was happening. Susan called me and we talked for a few minutes and I assured her I would see her while I was in town.

Betty Jane and I spent a restless Thursday night talking about Jack, Joe, our parents and Riverdale. We discussed making funeral arrangements if Jack's body was found. Our family burial plot at Mount Hebron Baptist Church had room for six graves. Our parents and Joe occupied three, and we discussed placing Jack's remains there if he was found. I told Betty Jane, she and Kristen could have the other two plots. I joked that if I were buried next to my father, we would be kicking up dirt and disturbing our departed neighbors. She laughed and agreed.

I headed to Riverdale at ten. The GBI had sheriff's deputies posted at a trail leading into the woods about a mile from the Flint River. I parked my car on the roadside and chatted with them. I told them I was the owner of the property and would be standing by to talk with Dylan Johnson when he was available. They advised me I could go no closer, so I sat in my car with the air conditioner running until I got bored. I then walked up and down the dirt road that led down to the river and the border to our property.

I looked at my watch and estimated the GBI had been at work for about four hours when I saw two cruisers drive out of the woods. As the first one turned on to the dirt road, I saw Clarence Dawkins seated in the back seat behind a steel cage. The two cars sped away in a huge cloud of dust. Clarence was headed back to jail. I called Dylan's cell phone.

He answered on the fifth ring and he agreed to allow me to come to the crime scene. A deputy talked with Dylan and told me to get into his cruiser and he would drive me to the scene.

After a hundred yards, the trail turned from a woodland road into an animal trail. Scruffy pine limbs scratched the sides of the cruiser as we ventured into the pine and hardwood forests. After five minutes of twists and turns to avoid limbs and small trees, we arrived at the scene.

"Hey Johnny, good to see you," Dylan said as he shook my hand. "We gotta go over a few things and then I'll fill you in on what we know so far."

"Okay," I said.

"Well, first, you can't go near that blue canopy over there," he said pointing. "Or anywhere inside the yellow crime scene tape. We have a large area taped off and we're gonna go over it with a fine-tooth comb."

"I understand," I said. I looked over at the canopy and saw a dozen agents gathered around. They appeared to be looking into a hole. Several held shovels, and others in white coveralls were holding various implements.

"Now as you know, we brought Dawkins out here early this morning. He's cooperating with us and agreed to tell us about the moonshining and marijuana operation from thirty years ago. He took us up the river about a half mile north of here and showed up where the actual stills were located. Now, over yonder where it's a little more open, that's where he said they had several marijuana fields growing. Now, if you're ready, I'll tell you how he said it went down and he says he witnessed everything."

"Okay, I'm ready."

"Dawkins told us that him, Ray Slocum, Jr., and Brady Lyle came down here on a Friday night to pick up a load of marijuana and moonshine from the still. The three of them came back here to the marijuana fields to cut it down with machetes. He said the still was being run by your daddy and a black man named Isaac. The marijuana was Ray's idea, but your daddy allowed it. They drove a box truck back here to load up the marijuana. They had just finished cutting the marijuana and loading it in the truck when Ray, Jr., told them to be quiet. He saw a set of headlights driving back into the woods about a half mile away. The car stopped and they heard a man and woman laughing and talking. They sneaked up near to where the car was parked. As they got closer, they saw the man and woman had opened the trunk. They watched the man take out a burlap sheet filled with cotton. Then they watched them laying down on the cotton and start making out. Ray, Jr., wanted to get a little closer and watch them. As they watched, one of them stepped on a tree limb and it made a loud snap. The man raised up and said, 'Who's out there?'

"He got up and reached in the back of the car's trunk and came out with a rifle. He grabbed a flashlight and started walking towards them. Ray, Jr., confronted him with his machete.

"The man pointed the rifle at Ray, Jr., and yelled, 'Who the hell are you and what are you doing on our property?'

"Ray threw the machete and it struck the man in the stomach. He dropped the rifle and fell to the ground. He was moaning and bleeding bad and rolled over. The woman lay down with him and was holding him. Ray, Jr., walked up to them and the woman screamed, then jumped and started running away. Brady Lyle chased her down and she fought with him and scratched his face. He hit her with his machete several times and cut her across her neck. Ray, Jr., went over to the man and stabbed him again with the machete. He lay there for a minute and got still."

A cold chill ran up my spine. I wasn't aware of the tears running down my face until Dylan handed me a handkerchief. I wiped my face and held on to it knowing I would need it again.

"You okay, Johnny? You want me to go on?"

"Yes, I want to know all of it."

"So, the three of them rolled Jack and Becky onto the sheet of cotton. They talked about taking the sheet down to the river and dumping them. But Ray, Jr., said they had to bury them. If they just dumped them in the river, the bodies would float up and be found. Then the cops would be swarming around the still.

"They had a shovel in the truck. Dawkins and Lyle took turns digging a hole about four feet deep, then dumped the bodies into it. They packed it down good and spread leaves over the loose dirt. They took the sheet full of cotton with them. It had a lot of blood on it and they dumped it along the roadside on the way back to Atlanta. Ray, Jr., and Lyle drove Jack's car to the dead-end road and pushed it into the river and watched it sink. Lyle's face got scratched up pretty good when he was fighting with the woman."

Raw images of what Dylan was saying filled my mind. I could see Jack trying to protect Becky. And I could see him lying on the cotton sheet with mortal stab wounds in his stomach. I was frozen. I couldn't move. I could see the red blood on white cotton.

Dylan put his arm around me.

"Johnny, I know it hurts. I know you was hoping an accident occurred or something not so brutal. I was too; you know I loved Jack like a brother."

I cried openly now. My tears flowed like the Flint River. I sobbed and wet Dylan's handkerchief completely. He paused for a minute and let me regain control.

"You okay?"

I nodded, but I wasn't okay. I was trembling and continued to sob.

"Well, let me finish. Dawkins remembered where the grave was because of the three big oak trees. We've located the grave site and we found skeletal remains. That's why the canopy is set up over there. We're gonna recover the remains and take them back to the GBI lab in Atlanta. We'll have to make an official identification, and one final thing. The female still had some partial nails on one hand. We might be able to get DNA we can match to Lyle. The techs have bagged that hand to protect any trace evidence. We need it. Otherwise, all we got is Dawkins' testimony. You're a sharp attorney; you understand we need more evidence, right?"

"I understand, and I want to thank you for seeing this thing through. You did a hell of a job and I really appreciate it."

"Hey, it's the least I could do for Jack. I sure hope we can get some justice for him. I'm going after Congressman Brady Lyle with both barrels firing. I hope we can lock his scumbag ass up when we get back to Atlanta. He slapped me on my back. Go tell your sister now, and I'll let you know when we can release Jack's remains to you."

The deputy offered to drive me back to my car. I sat in the front seat of his cruiser feeling numb. I had followed my father's wishes. I had found out who had killed Jack. Before I told Betty Jane about what had occurred, I had a stop to make.

# CHAPTER 79

I drove to Pecan Hill Cemetery down the hill from Hebron Baptist Church. I parked and walked to my parents' grave. I saw a mockingbird fighting with a blue jay as they soared into the azure sky. Were they the same ones I had seen the day of my father's funeral? Were they sending me a sign? Reminding me again of how we had pecked and clawed at each other our entire lives.

I smelled the magnolias in bloom. They reminded me of my sweet mother now lying by his side. She had stood by him her whole life. She was an angelic person. She must have found some good in him to stay with him an entire lifetime. He must have had some good in him. The whole community thought so. He did give to charities and do a lot of good work for the Rotary Club. But he was also a moonshiner and marijuana grower. He had been a criminal, and he had been incredibly cruel to me.

Why had he always hated me? What had I ever done to him? Other than try desperately to love him. I understood I wasn't like Jack, his golden child. He could do anything. He was the first born. I guess he hated me because I was a mistake. I was the last born and I wasn't planned. I was an accident. Is that why he hated me?

I knelt at my father's grave. I read the headstone, "Calvin Lafont Reynolds, a community leader, a gentleman who loved his family." I wondered if it should read "loved most of his family." He said he loved me in his final letter. He left me thousand acres of land. He said he was sorry. He had a lot of reasons to be sorry. Was I ready to forgive?

I had gone for ten years without speaking to him at one point in my life. Then when I finally spoke to him, it was with malicious intent. I wanted him to see what I had done for myself without his help. It was an *in your face* encounter. He had taken it well. He had smiled and shook his head. He had not expected much from me. But I had become a pretty damn good attorney.

He was probably responsible for some of my success. Without him bullying me, I would not have acquired the drive to succeed. If he had paid for my college and law school, would I have tried as hard? I think not. I hated to admit it, but I probably owed my success to him. It was hard to swallow.

I touched his grave. It was cold. I stuttered as I started to talk to him.

With tears coursing down my face, I finally spoke.

"Daddy, I found Jack. The people you were in business with killed him. I know you probably suspected it was them. Was that why you were so mean? Did you hate yourself for what you had done? Did you have to take it out on me? I hated you for most of my life. It would be easy to continue to hate you. But I'm here to forgive you. I can't live with hate in my heart. I'm gonna put Jack here besides you and Mom. Maybe you can finally get some peace. I hope so. I forgive you, and . . . I love you."

I walked back down the hill to my car. I noticed my polo was damp. But I had stopped crying now. I had no more tears. No more tears for Jack. No more tears for my father, mother and Joe. I had lost them all. But life goes on. I had no more time for tears.

I related the gruesome tale told by Clarence Dawkins to Betty Jane. I hugged her and comforted her as she cried her river of tears. I told her

I visited our parents' grave and I told them all that had occurred. I also told her I had forgiven our father. She nodded her approval.

After having spent one of the worst days of my life at Riverdale, I spent one of the best nights at Susan Regan's. I ate a great T-Bone steak, drank a little Old Forrester, listened to hours of Leonard Cohen and loved a beautiful woman.

# EPILOGUE

We buried Jack in Pecan Hill Cemetery, next to my mother, father and brother, Joe. I wasn't sure if anyone remembered Jack, but the whole town attended. They had remembered my parents and were there to console me and Betty Jane. I gave the eulogy for Jack and let the whole town know what a wonderful brother and human being he had been. I talked about his short but active life, his many accomplishments and his dreams of playing football at the University of Georgia. I joked that if Jack had played, maybe we wouldn't have lost so many games during those rough years. No offense Coach Dooley. I held up well and only started to cry as I neared the end of my speech.

At the cemetery, I dropped a handful of red Georgia clay on to Jack's casket. I was rocked by a sense of deja vu. I had been here too much doing the same thing. I had stood in this same spot while four of my family members had been lowered into the earth.

"Goodbye, Jack," I whispered. "You only lived a short time, but everyone loved you and you lived a golden life."

A cool breeze ruffled my hair. I had the feeling Jack was answering me. I looked up because I knew he was in heaven. I wondered if my father was there also. I wondered if he had done enough to atone for his sins. I wouldn't want to place any bets. The only thing that mattered was the fact that I had forgiven him. I was at peace with my decision.

And now for the others.

A microscopic amount of DNA recovered from under a decomposed fingernail of Becky McCord matched the DNA of Brady Lyle. Congressman Lyle was arrested at his regional office in downtown Atlanta and perp-walked to the Fulton County jail. The television cameras went crazy as did the national media in the days that followed. After a two-week trial, Lyle was convicted of the murder of Becky McCord. He was also convicted on five counts of bribery and racketeering from FBI cases brought from information provided by Clarence Dawkins. He was sentenced to life in prison.

After a six-week trial, Ray Slocum, Jr., was convicted of multiple counts of drug trafficking, sale and possession of a controlled substance, racketeering, auto theft, theft by taking and, most importantly, murder in the second degree of Jack William Reynolds. Slocum was sentenced to three life sentences to be served consecutively with no possibility of parole.

Clarence Dawkins pleaded guilty to racketeering and sale and possession of controlled substances. In consideration of his substantial assistance to law enforcement, he received a sentence of ten years in prison and was allowed to serve it at the Eglin Federal Correctional Institute in Pensacola, Florida.

The nine-millimeter Sig Sauer taken from Manny Acevedo was identified as the murder weapon in the death of Lucas McDougal. Acevedo was charged with murder in the first degree. He was sentenced to life in prison.

Tiny Marlowe was convicted of robbery, aggravated assault, violation of parole and attempted murder. He was sentenced to thirty-five years in prison.

Tyrell Knight aka Tyrell Hardeman aka Demetrius Tyrell, real name, Anthony Jackson, failed to appear when subpoenaed to testify against Ray Slocum, Jr. A warrant was issued for his arrest and is still in effect today. He is living in Aruba where he sells beach gear and a little pot on the side. He is now using the name Tyrell Demetrius.

The governor of the state of Georgia appointed Dylan Johnson as the new director of the Georgia Bureau of Investigation. He reluctantly accepted the appointment. He worried it might interfere with his busy travel schedule. He and his wife, JoEllen, just visited Iceland for two weeks, and have a trip to Tahiti planned. We remain close friends and enjoy spending time together in Martinsville hunting and fishing.

My sister Betty Jane sold her nine thousand acres of land, formerly known as Riverdale Plantation. She donated part of her proceeds to the City of Martinsville and the county to build a huge new public library. It is under construction and will bear the name "The Dorothy Jane Reynolds Public Library." She also donated a substantial sum to the Rotary Club in the names of Calvin, Jack and Joe Reynolds. She met and married a nice gentleman who raises and trains racehorses.

My niece Kristin will be entering Yale Law School in the fall after graduating from Stanford with a perfect grade point average. She is working for me this summer to get a taste of the legal arena.

And finally, we get to me. I kept my thousand acres of the land at Riverdale Plantation in accordance with my father's wishes. I sub-divided it from Betty Jane's share in a way that would give me land along the Flint River including my favorite fishing spot. It also includes several hundred acres of hardwood forests for hunting, a beautiful grassland pasture for riding horses and the fifty-acre millpond where I learned to swim and had so many good memories fishing with my brothers.

I married Susan Regan, and we live in Atlanta but maintain Susan's beautiful home in Martinsville for weekend getaways. It's a great escape from the trials and tribulations of living in Atlanta and my continuing battles in the legal trenches. If the weather is nice, Susan and I enjoy hunting, fishing and riding horses at "Little Riverdale," as I now call it. If not, we stay inside and enjoy Leonard Cohen, a splash or two of Old

Forrester and working on making a little John Reynolds, Jr. After all, my father had asked me to keep the Reynolds name going.

# AUTHOR'S NOTE

This novel is a work of fiction. Though I grew up on a farm and many of the antidotes contained within are based on memories from my childhood, all the characters are fictional. My own father, the late Carl L. Long, Sr., was nothing like Calvin Reynolds. He was a wonderful loving father who I admired and miss dearly. My mother, Dorothy Jane Long, was somewhat like Dorothy Reynolds in my book. She was the sweetest, most loving mother one could have. She was also a great cook and a voracious reader. I think she would enjoy this novel. I also miss her dearly.

I would love to hear reader's comments concerning this book, both positive and negative. It was my first attempt and I am striving to improve. You can email me at johnwlongthewriter.com. or connect with me on Facebook.